C000177089

Michelle Douglas h
since 2007, and bel
world. She's a sucke
have a secret stash c
how to laugh. She li
own romantic hero,
an eclectic collection of sixties and seventies vinyl.
She loves to hear from readers and can be contacted
via her website www.michelle-douglas.com

Susan Meier spent most of her twenties thinking
she was a job-hopper – until she began to write and
realised everything that had come before was only
research! One of eleven children, with twenty-four
nieces and nephews and three kids of her own, Susan
lives in Western Pennsylvania with her wonderful
husband, Mike, her children, and two over-fed, well-
cuddled cats, Sophie and Fluffy. You can visit Susan's
website at www.susanmeier.com

Sarah Morgan is a *USA Today* and *Sunday Times*
bestselling author of contemporary romance and
women's fiction. She has sold more than 16 million
copies of her books and her trademark humour and
warmth have gained her fans across the globe. Sarah
lives with her family near London, England, where the
rain frequently keeps her trapped in her office. Visit her
at www.sarahmorgan.com

The Single Dads
COLLECTION

Christmas with the Single Dad

THE NANNY WHO SAVED CHRISTMAS

KISSES ON HER CHRISTMAS LIST

THE DOCTOR'S CHRISTMAS BRIDE

MILLS & BOON

First Published in Great Britain 2019
By Mills & Boon, an imprint of HarperCollins*Publishers*
1 London Bridge Street, London, SE1 9GF

CHRISTMAS WITH THE SINGLE DAD © 2019 Harlequin Books S.A.

The Nanny Who Saved Christmas © 2012 Michelle Douglas
Kisses on Her Christmas List © 2011 Linda Susan Meier
The Doctor's Christmas Bride © 2004 Sarah Morgan

ISBN: 978-0-263-27940-5

MIX
Paper from
responsible sources
FSC® C007454

FSC
www.fsc.org

This book is produced from independently certified FSC™ paper to ensure responsible forest management.

For more information visit: www.harpercollins.co.uk/green

Printed and bound in Spain
by CPI, Barcelona

THE NANNY WHO
SAVED CHRISTMAS

MICHELLE DOUGLAS

For Maggie, who is everything a sister should be.
Thank you!

CHAPTER ONE

NICOLA craned to take in as much of the view as she could from the Cessna's window as they landed on an airstrip that was nothing more than red dirt, bordered here and there with spiky grass and mulga scrub. When the pilot cut the engine the sudden silence engulfed her.

He turned to her. 'Here we are then.'

'Right.' She swallowed and gave a curt nod. *Here* was the Waminda Downs cattle station in the far west of Queensland—the Outback, the Never-Never, beyond the Black Stump—and about as far from civilisation as a body could get. She glanced out of the window again and something in her chest started to lift. This place was the polar opposite to her native Melbourne. The *total* polar opposite.

'May I get out now?'

'Well, as this is your destination, love, I believe that's the plan.'

He let the steps down, she stuck her head outside and the first thing to hit her was the heat—hard, enveloping and intense. The second, when her feet found firm ground again, was the scent—hot, dry earth and sun-baked grasses. The lonely desolation thrust itself upon her consciousness with an insistence that refused to be ignored, greater than the heat that beat down on her uncovered head and greater than the alien sights and scents. A person could get lost out here and never be found.

She surveyed the endless expanse of pale brown grass, interspersed here and there with mulga scrub and salt-bush, and at all the red dirt beneath it, and for the first time in three months she felt like her heart started to beat at the right pace again. Out here she wouldn't encounter acquaintances who would glance at her and then just as quickly glance away again to whisper behind their hands. Or friends who would rush up to grip her hands and ask her how she was doing. Or those people who just plain enjoyed others' misfortunes and would smirk at her.

She closed her eyes and lifted her face to the sky. 'This is perfect.'

'Perfect for what?'

That voice didn't belong to Jerry the pilot.

Her eyes sprang open. She spun around to find a man hauling her suitcase from the plane's cargo hold. He set it on the ground and then straightened. He was tall and broad. He gave off an impression of strength. He gave off an even bigger impression of no-nonsense efficiency.

She blinked. 'Where did you come from?' So much for thinking she and the pilot were alone in this wilderness.

He pointed back behind him and in the harsh glare of the sun she caught the glint from a car's windscreen. 'You're from the station?'

One corner of his mouth hooked up. It wasn't precisely a smile, but she had a feeling it was meant to be friendly. 'I'm Cade Hindmarsh.'

Her boss.

He must be about thirty and he was tanned. Really tanned. He had deep lines fanning out from his eyes. Probably from all the habitual squinting into the sun one must do out here. A habit Nicola found herself mimicking already. He tipped his Akubra back from his head and she found herself staring into the bluest pair of eyes she'd ever seen. The sun might've faded everything else out here, but it hadn't faded them.

His gaze was direct. The longer she looked at him, the lighter she started to feel, a burden of weight slipping free from her shoulders and sinking into the dry earth at her feet. He didn't know her. He'd never met her before in his life. Nobody out here knew her. He wouldn't think her pitiful, stupid or a failure. Unless she did something to give him reason to.

She had absolutely no intention of letting that happen.

'Nicola McGillroy,' she said, recalling her manners and introducing herself. Cool, poised and businesslike, she lectured. That was the impression she wanted to give. And the antithesis of a pitiful doormat.

He strode over and extended his hand. She placed hers inside it and found it so comprehensively grasped it made her eyes widen. He grimaced and loosened his hold. 'Sorry. I'm always being told not to grip so hard.'

She swallowed. 'No need to apologise; you didn't hurt me.'

Cade shook hands the way she'd always thought men should shake hands. The reality, like so many other realities, had disappointed her. Cade didn't disappoint. His grip was firm, dependable. Strong. Men who shook hands like that didn't get pushed around. She wanted to learn to shake hands like that.

From beneath the brim of his Akubra those blue eyes twinkled for a moment. Her lips lifted in response, and then with a start she realised her hand was still held in his. She gently detached it.

Her employer tipped his head back and stared at her for several long, pulse-inducing moments. She lifted her chin and met his gaze square-on. She didn't kid herself that his survey was anything other than what it was—a sizing up…a summing up. For the next two months she would have charge of his two young daughters. She wouldn't respect any man who merely took her at face value, who went only by her résumé and a telephone interview. Even if that telephone interview had been gruelling.

'Will I do?' she finally asked, the suspense sawing on her nerves. She didn't doubt for one moment that if his answer was no he'd put her back on that plane and send her home to Melbourne.

The thought made her throat dry and her heart falter for a couple of beats before it surged against her ribs again with renewed force. She couldn't go back to Melbourne. Not yet!

Melbourne…December…with their joint reminders of the wedding she should've been planning. She didn't think she could stand it.

'Why is this place perfect?'

Perfect? Nicola Ann, you can't be serious!

Her mother's voice sounded in her head. Nicola resolutely ignored it. 'All of this—' she gestured to the landscape '—is so different to what I'm used to, but it's exactly what I imagined.'

'And that's good?'

'I think so.' It was *very* good.

He planted his feet. 'A lot of people who come out here are running away from something.'

She refused to let her chin drop. 'Is that why you're out here?'

Off to one side Jerry snorted, reminding her that she and her employer weren't alone. 'Love, generations of the Hindmarshes have been born and bred out here.'

She raised an eyebrow at Cade Hindmarsh. 'Is that a no, then?'

Those blue eyes twinkled again. 'That's a no.'

'Some people—' she chose her words carefully '—not only want to see what they can of the country, but to experience it as well.'

'And that's why you're here?'

'I know if you were born and bred out here that you're familiar with this kind of life and landscape, but being here is an adventure for me.' It was also a timeout from her real life, a much needed break from Melbourne with all its reminders of her short-sighted stupidity and her cringe-inducing ignorance. She didn't say that out loud though. He might interpret that as running away.

It will all still be here when you get home, you know, Nicola Ann.

And her mother might be right.

Though, in two months' time, hopefully she'd have found the strength to face it all again. She hoped that in two months' time she'd have changed, become a different person—someone stronger, tougher. Someone who didn't get taken advantage of, lied to or cheated on.

Finally Cade smiled. 'Welcome to Waminda Downs, Nicola.'

A pent-up breath whooshed out of her. 'Thank you.' She grinned. She couldn't help it. She wanted to high-five someone for having passed Cade's assessment. Jerry's chuckle told her that her excitement was visible for all to see.

Cade's smile broadened into a grin that made her blink and just like that she could practically feel Diane's elbow in her ribs and her whisper of, *Hot, gorgeous hunk* at her ear. The thought of her best friend pulled Nicola up short.

It made her pull back, compose her features and press her hands together at her waist.

Cade's eyes narrowed and his grin faded too until it had vanished completely. Something inside her protested at that, but she stamped it out. She was here to change. Not to gush. Not to be eager to approve of everything and everyone she met without considered judgement first. And not to be patted on the head and treated like a child.

She strode around him to seize her suitcase. 'I'm really looking forward to meeting Ella and Holly.'

Cade remained silent. Nicola bit her tongue to stop from prompting further. She wasn't here to make friends. She wasn't here to win approval—not from Cade, not from anyone. She was here to do a job…and to get her head screwed on straight again. She'd do both those things to the best of her ability.

'Brought that generator you ordered.'

The men unloaded the generator. Beneath his work shirt Cade's arm muscles bulged. Despite the generator's bulk and weight, he didn't so much as break out into a sweat as he carried it to the car. With a wave to Jerry, she set off after him, admiring the broad sweep of his shoulders and the depth of his chest. The man was a veritable Atlas. He stowed the generator into the tray of his ute with ease and then took her suitcase. She told herself the only reason she let him take it was because he'd know how to load the tray to best effect.

It wasn't because it was too heavy and she had pitiful upper body strength.

Her lip curled. Oh, who was she trying to kid? But getting fit was on her to-do list while she was out here. In two months' time she'd be tossing that suitcase around as if it weighed nothing at all. The way Cade did.

She found her eyes drawn too easily to him so, setting her teeth, she did what he did—shaded her eyes and watched as the Cessna took off. And then, to stop from staring at him again, she completed a slow three hundred and sixty degree turn to survey the landscape. Finally she shrugged. 'Okay, it beats me. The land looks flat for as far as the eye can see. At least until that ridge way over there.' She gestured to her right. 'But I can't see a homestead.'

'The land is deceptive.' He opened the car door for her, and his unwavering scrutiny made her clumsy. She knocked both an elbow and a knee as she climbed into her seat.

Oh, Nicola Ann, you are such a klutz.

He didn't say anything, but she swore those blue eyes of his twinkled before he closed the door.

Without another word he climbed into the driver's seat and they set off along what Nicola could only loosely describe as a track.

'Is it far to the homestead?'

'About five kilometres.'

She waited. He didn't say anything more. On the rough track the car couldn't go much faster than thirty kilometres an hour and the silence pressed in on her. Cade's tall, broad bulk dominated the interior cab and, for reasons she couldn't fathom, that made her nervous.

'Is the land near the homestead unsuitable for an airstrip?'

He flicked a glance in her direction. She doubted much got past those eyes of his. She could imagine them filling with that soul-destroying combination of derision and pity she'd seen in her friends' eyes during the last few months.

Yes, she could imagine it all too clearly and it made bile rise in her throat.

'Fire,' he said.

She blinked. 'I beg your pardon?'

'The reason the airstrip is away from the house is in case there's an accident that could start a bushfire.'

Oh. It made perfect sense when she thought about it.

At that moment they topped a rise and Cade pulled the car to a halt. She stared at the vista spread before her and her 'wow' breathed out of her before she could help it, before she could remind herself about tempering her enthusiasm and keeping things businesslike.

She shook herself and swallowed. 'Very impressive, Mr Hindmarsh.'

'Cade,' he corrected. 'We don't stand on ceremony out here, Nicola.' He gestured out of the front windscreen. 'As you can see, this is the station complex.'

It was much larger than anything she'd imagined. On the side nearest them was a sprawling homestead with two wings that spread out in a V shape from the main structure. The weatherboards were painted a crisp white and the corrugated iron roof a cool deep green. A veranda wrapped around it all, but it wasn't the homestead's size that stole her breath. It was the garden that surrounded it. Even from this distance she could make out the fronds of the two magnificent tree ferns that stood at the end of each wing, as well as the breadth of the date palms that dotted the lawn. 'I can't believe you have a garden. It's like an oasis.'

'Bore water,' he said. 'But I didn't stop here so you could admire the view. I need you to understand some basic facts so you can stay out of trouble while you're here.'

She frowned.

'You might think coming out here for two months is an adventure, but the land is unforgiving. Underestimate it at your own peril.'

She tried to suppress a shiver. 'Okay.' And then she realised how weak and pathetic her voice sounded. She lifted her chin and made her voice stronger. 'What do I need to know?'

'The land is deceptive to the eye. It undulates. You think you know where you are and then you turn around and can't see the homestead or any familiar landmarks. It's that easy—' he clicked his fingers '—to get lost. You're not to go wandering about on your own.'

Her heart sank. There went her plan of jogging her way to fitness and thinness.

Damn it! She'd sworn to return to Melbourne toned and tanned. It would signal to Diane, Brad and all her other friends that she was getting on with her life. It would prove that she had confidence and chutzpah and was no longer an object of pity. She gripped her hands together. And the next time a guy dumped her she wanted to make sure it wasn't because she was half a stone overweight.

'Waminda Downs covers three million acres. That's twelve thousand square kilometres.'

She pulled her mind back.

'That's a lot of ground to cover if someone goes missing.'

She read the subtext. If a person went missing out here they might never be found.

'See that perimeter fence? It's painted white.'

'Yes.'

'That encloses the four acres of the home paddock, including the homestead and outbuildings. You can wander freely within that, but do not cross that boundary unaccompanied.'

Four acres would be plenty! 'Roger.'

'And I'd like you and the girls to stay away from the cattle yards.' He pointed to a series of yards on the side furthest away from them. They were separated from the homestead by a number of outbuildings. He proceeded to name the buildings. 'That's the machinery shed.' It was huge. 'Barn and stables.' He pointed. 'Next to them is the jackaroo and jillaroo quarters. Those smaller cottages at the far end are for the stockmen and their families.'

She blinked. Waminda Downs, it seemed, was its own thriving community.

'Why are the cattle yards out of bounds?' She wanted to understand every hazard in her new environment so she could head off any potential disasters.

'We corralled a herd of brumby in there the week before last and we're going to start breaking them in. It's dangerous work.'

'Okay.' She nodded once, hard. 'Anything else I need to know?'

'If you do go exploring within the home paddock you always take a water bottle with you, and wear a hat and sunscreen. It's only four acres, but it's summer and at the height of the day the sun is merciless.'

'Don't worry, Mr Hindmarsh. I won't be letting the girls outside between eleven a.m. and three p.m.'

'The garden is surprisingly cool.'

She'd make her own judgement about that. Located two hours by plane from the nearest hospital, she had no intention of risking sunstroke in her charges.

'And there's just one final thing.'

Something in his tone made her turn. 'Yes?'

His blue eyes flashed. 'The name's Cade—try it.'

She'd never had a problem calling any of her previous employers by their first name, but it suddenly occurred to her that she didn't want to be on a first name basis with this man. She swallowed. He was too…too confident, too gorgeous…too *everything* that she wasn't. He brought home to her all the things she lacked with a realness that made her want to turn her face away.

Coward.

For heaven's sake, she was his children's nanny. First names could not be avoided. She lifted her chin. She would be cool and poised. She would be competent and clever. She would be respected. She moistened her lips. His eyes followed the action. 'Cade,' she said. His name scraped out of her throat with an appalling huskiness and none of the poised cool she'd tried so hard to carry off.

He cocked an eyebrow. 'See? Wasn't so hard, was it?'

Before she could answer he started the engine again and they set off towards the homestead. This time she curbed any impulse to fill the silence. She focused instead on the homestead and garden, and tried to make out what it was that glittered on the trunks of the date palms and to see what the shapes were that littered the lawn.

And as they drew closer her jaw started to drop. The glitter…it was tinsel. The shapes on the lawn…

Oh. My. God. The shapes were Christmas-themed wooden cut-outs painted in the brightest colours imaginable. On one side of the lawn a Santa sleigh squatted along with four merry reindeer. On the other stood a wooden Santa in all his holiday merriment, a sack of toys at his feet. Gold and silver snowflakes hung from the veranda ceiling, alternating with green and red stars. Tinsel in every colour twined around the veranda posts.

She flinched. *Christmas.* Oh, she'd known she wouldn't be able to avoid it completely—Cade had two young daughters after all—but…

She'd thought that out here in the Never-Never it'd be small-scale, low-key…restrained.

It hit her then that she'd been counting on it. Her chest cramped.

The car stopped at the edge of a path lined with over-sized candy canes that she knew would light up at night.

At the end of the path four broad steps led to the veranda and the front door of the homestead. It was a testament to the door's solidity that it didn't buckle beneath the weight of its enormous wreath. Three wooden angels graced the roof of the veranda, their trumpets raised heavenward as if heralding the arrival of the silly season.

She bit her tongue to stop from blurting out something unpoised and stupid. Her hands fisted and she blinked hard to counter the stinging in her eyes. All this Christmas-ness was a too-vivid reminder of the merriment and festivity she'd known herself incapable of taking part in back home. It reminded her of the wedding she should've been planning. It taunted her with all she'd lost and how nothing—*nothing*—could ever replace it.

It was only the first week of December. She'd taken a month's leave from her job as a teacher and her four weeks of Christmas holidays, because Christmas and wedding preparations had become synonymous in her mind. But Christmas with all its gaudy festivity now stared her in the face. The joke was on her. She swallowed and tried to ignore the ache that spread through her chest.

'Now I'll warrant this isn't what you were expecting.'

Beside her, Cade chuckled. She couldn't open her mouth to either agree or disagree.

'What do you think?'

She hated it! The truth, though, would not endear her to him. Of that she was certain. And while she told herself she didn't give two hoots what her employer thought of her—other than that she did her job well—deliberate rudeness was not in her nature. Nor was it poised, elegant or dignified. She tried to think of something coolly elegant to say…or even something bland and inoffensive.

She turned to Cade, she racked her brain and then realised she needn't have bothered. One glance at his face told her he'd perceived her true feelings on the matter. His eyes narrowed and while there was no denying that he was broad, big and strong, for the first time he looked formidable too.

She swallowed. She couldn't find a smile, but she struggled for light. 'To think I'd left all this behind in the city.'

His lips tightened. 'So that's what you're running from.'

'I'm not running from anything.' Taking a timeout wasn't running.

He leaned back, but his eyes remained flint hard. Blue flint in a landscape of khaki and brown. The pulse in her throat swelled and pounded. 'That generator I just unloaded, it's to run all the coloured fairy lights I'm planning on hanging from the house and around the garden in the next week or two.'

The homestead would look like some tacky fairy tale palace. She sucked in a breath. Or an overdecorated wedding cake.

'We're doing Christmas big out here this year, Ms McGillroy. If that's going to be a problem for you then it's not too late for me to radio Jerry to come back and fly you out of here.'

So she could face all this insubstantial, bubble-popping, fake merriment in Melbourne? No, thank you very much! She could put on a happy face and *do* Christmas. The people at Waminda Downs didn't know her. They wouldn't murmur, *There, there, the holiday season can be tough sometimes, can't it?* She might not be through with gritting her teeth yet, but she was absolutely positively done with pity.

'I thought we'd agreed on first names, Cade.'

Very slowly, the tension eased out of him.

She turned back to stare at all the over-the-top Christmas-ness. 'My mother would find all this the height of tackiness.'

There was no denying that thought cheered her up.

'You repeat that to Ella and Holly and I'll throttle you.'

The words came out on a lazy breath but she didn't doubt their veracity. She stared down her nose at him. 'I'm the nanny, not the evil witch.'

'Just make sure you stay in character.'

She frowned and turned more fully to face him. 'You don't exactly strike me as the Santa Claus type yourself, you know?' And he didn't. Competent, calm in a crisis, perceptive, she'd peg him as all those things, but joyful and jocund? She shook her head.

'Just goes to show what you know, then.'

But he shifted on his seat and she remembered he was a father—a single father—and his first priority was making sure his daughters were looked after and happy. 'I would never ruin the magic of Christmas for any child,' she assured him.

He surveyed her again and then nodded. 'Glad that's settled.'

He still didn't strike her as Father Christmas material, but there was no questioning his devotion to his daughters. It warmed something inside her that she didn't want warmed. It made her draw back inside herself. 'When can I meet Ella and Holly?'

He eyed her thoughtfully, but eventually nodded in the direction of her car window. 'Right about now, I'd say.'

Nicola turned…and fell in love.

Four-year-old Ella and eighteen-month-old Holly wore the biggest smiles and had the most mischievous faces Nicola had ever seen, and they were dancing down the front steps of the homestead and along the path towards her in matching red and green frocks.

Good Lord! She gulped. She hadn't factored this in when she'd plotted to keep her distance and maintain her reserve as she implemented her self-improvement scheme.

She pushed out of the car, a smile spreading through her. Children, she made an amendment to her earlier plan, didn't count. Children didn't lie and cheat. Children didn't pretend to be your friend and then steal your fiancé.

She didn't need to guard her heart around children.

Cade watched Nicola greet Ella and Holly and win them over in two seconds flat.

It wasn't a difficult feat. He refused to give their perplexing nanny any credit for that. Despite all they'd been through, Ella and Holly were remarkably trusting. They'd have shown as much delight if he'd presented Jerry, the pilot, as their nanny.

But as he watched them, especially Ella, delight in Nicola's undeniably female presence, his heart started to burn. It should be their mother here. Not a nanny. And no amount of Christmas cheer could ever make that up to his children.

His hands clenched. It wasn't going to stop him from giving them the best Christmas possible, though.

He pushed out of the car in time to hear Ella ask, 'Can I call you Nikki?'

Nicola shook her head very solemnly. 'No, but you can call me Nic. All of my friends call me Nic.'

Ella clapped her hands, but at the mention of friends a shadow passed across Nicola's face. And just as he had back at the airstrip, Cade found that he wanted to chase that shadow away.

He didn't know why. His children's nanny wasn't particularly winning. She was of ordinary height and weight, perhaps veering a little more on the solid side. When she'd first emerged from the plane and had gazed around with a smile curving her lips, he'd been satisfied. When he'd shaken her hand, he'd been more than satisfied.

And then she'd become stiff and prickly and he hadn't been able to work out why yet. He was pretty sure he hadn't frightened her—given his size and the remoteness of the station he'd have understood her apprehension. He was even more certain that she hadn't wanted to turn around and go back home.

She leant her hands on her knees to talk to his daughters—ordinary hair a nondescript brown and an ordinary face. Ordinary clothes—baggy three-quarter length trousers and an oversized shirt, neither of which did anything much for her. But those eyes—there was nothing ordinary about them. Or their shadows.

Christmas wasn't the time for shadows. And Waminda Downs, this year, was not the place for them.

He hooked a thumb into the pocket of his jeans. Despite what she said, she was running from something. He was certain of it. All the background checks he'd had completed assured him that whatever it was, it wasn't criminal. The way she smiled at his daughters, her easy manner with them, told him she could be trusted with them, that his instincts hadn't let him down there.

But could she be trusted to keep her word and not create a cloud over Christmas? Ella and Holly had suffered enough. They deserved all the fun and festivity he could crowd into their days this Christmas season.

Guilt for last Christmas chafed at him, filling his mouth with bile. They hadn't had a Christmas last year. His lip curled. He should've made an effort, but he hadn't. His hands clenched. Last year he hadn't been able to pull himself out from under the cloud of Fran leaving…of her almost total abandonment of their daughters…of his failure to keep his family together. He'd let his bitterness, his anger and his despair blight last Christmas.

But not this year. This year no effort would be spared.

As he watched, Ella took one of Nicola's hands and Holly the other and they led her across to Santa's sleigh and he thought back to the expression on her face when she'd first surveyed the Christmas decorations—a kind of appalled horror.

Then, unbidden, he recalled a portion of their phone interview last month. 'Mr Hindmarsh, are you widowed, separated or divorced? I know that's a personal question and that it's none of my business, but it can have an impact on the children and I need to know about anything that may affect them.'

He'd told her the truth—that he was divorced. But…

None of the other applicants had asked that question. Nicola had been evidently reluctant to, but she'd screwed up the courage to ask it all the same. His children's best interests were more important to her than her own personal comfort. That was one of the reasons why he'd chosen her.

Nicola threw her head back now and laughed at something Ella said, and Ella laughed and Holly laughed and all three of them fell to the ground in a tangle of limbs. Nicola's face lit up as if from the inside as she gathered his children close to her and the impact slugged him in the gut, making the ground beneath his feet rock.

Blinking, he took a physical step away from the trio.

'The kids have met the new nanny then?'

He glanced down at his housekeeper, Martha Harrison—Harry for short—as she joined him. 'Yep.'

'And they seem to have hit it off.'

Nicola climbed back to her feet, looking perfectly ordinary again as she glanced towards him, her reserve well and truly back in place, and the world righted itself.

He introduced the two women. Harry nodded her approval. It should set his mind at ease. But as Nicola hugged her reserve about her all the more tightly, his unease grew.

He trailed behind as Harry led the way into the house. He waited in the kitchen as Harry and the girls showed Nicola to her quarters. 'What's eating you?' Harry asked, when she returned alone.

'Where are Ella and Holly?'

The older woman chuckled. 'Helping Nicola unpack.'

He huffed out a breath. 'Do you find her a bit…stiff?'

'She appears to be no-nonsense and low maintenance; that's good enough for me.' She shot him a glance as she put the kettle on to boil. 'Don't forget she's a long way from home and this is a lot to adjust to.'

All of those things were true, but…

Cade drew in a breath. He'd let Ella and Holly down enough these last sixteen months. His hands balled to fists. Christmas—bells and whistles…the works—that was what Waminda Downs was getting this year. And he meant to enlist Nicola's help to ensure it all went as smoothly and superbly as he'd planned.

CHAPTER TWO

At ten past six the next morning, dressed in running shorts and an oversized T-shirt, Nicola stepped out of the French windows of her generously proportioned bedroom and onto the veranda. She blinked in the morning sun.

Ten past six? She bit back a whimper. She'd never been a morning person.

Ten past six and it was already getting hellishly warm. It might even be too hot for a run and—

Stop that!

She lifted her chin. She would not sabotage herself before she'd even begun.

Puffing out a breath, she stretched to one side and then the other. She tried to touch her toes. She was here to change. She needed to change. She would change!

She'd exercise if it killed her. She *would* return to Melbourne better and brighter and smarter.

She gritted her teeth and stretched harder. She'd keep getting up at six a.m. if it killed her too. It gave her a good hour before she needed to make sure her young charges were up and at breakfast, and before the heat of the day settled over the place like a suffocating blanket.

At the thought of Ella and Holly, she couldn't help but smile. The two little girls were delightful. While they might've presented her with the biggest flaw in her maintain-a-dignified-distance plan, she didn't regret amending that plan to not include them.

Children didn't pretend to be your friend and then tear the heart out of your chest with treachery and double-dealing.

The bitterness of that thought took her off guard. She brushed a hand across her eyes and straightened. Diane and Brad hadn't meant to fall in love with each other. They hadn't meant to hurt her. For heaven's sake, it had all happened three months ago!

She scraped the hair off her face and pulled it back into a ponytail, concentrating on her breathing until the ache in her chest started to subside.

A lot of people who come out here are running away...

She wasn't running away. It was just...

Seeing Brad and Diane together had become harder, not easier and she didn't know why. She only knew she couldn't spend this Christmas in Melbourne while continuing to maintain her sympathetic, understanding and oh-so-mature façade. She wasn't up to indulging in the usual jolly Christmas with her friends this year. She was out of jolly.

But she'd find it again. Somehow.

She adjusted her cap as Sammy, Ella and Holly's eight-month-old Border collie pup, came skidding around the side of the house to race up to her, full of excitement and delight at the sight of her. Children *and* dogs were the flaw in her plan. He rolled onto his back and she obligingly rubbed his tummy.

'You want to come for a run, Sammy?' She straightened and set off down the back steps. He scurried after her. 'Perhaps you can give me some pointers—' she sighed '—because I don't think I have ever been for a run in my life.'

He cocked his head to one side and watched her when

she halted and planted her hands on her hips. 'Okay, Sammy, here's the plan. We'll jog to the perimeter fence—' she pointed '—and then around to that point there.' She indicated a second spot. Both spots were well away from outbuildings and cattle yards. 'Then we'll make our way back to the homestead.'

Nicola Ann, tell me you are not talking to a dog.

Nicola gritted her teeth and ignored her mother's imaginary voice.

At least you're finally going to exercise.

That almost made her turn back.

Sammy jumped up to rest his front paws against her thighs. She patted him. 'You don't care if I'm fat or frumpy, do you, Sammy?' It was one of the reasons she loved dogs…and children. Sammy wagged his tail and it gave her an absurd kind of comfort. 'Okay, then.' She hauled in a less-than-enthusiastic breath. 'Tally-ho.'

She started to jog. Her brand new sports bra was supportive, but not quite as supportive as she'd hoped. Maybe she needed to adjust the straps again. Though, if she tightened them any further she'd cut off the circulation altogether. The bra started to scratch and irritate the sides of her breasts. It hadn't done that in the fitting room. 'No pain, no gain,' she muttered to Sammy. She'd bought an identical sports bra in a size smaller for Month Two when she'd lost some weight. Both bras had been horrendously expensive. When she'd paid for them she'd told herself the expense would provide her with an added incentive to exercise. She'd thought the expense would translate into comfort too. She'd been wrong about that.

By the time she and Sammy reached the fence she was gasping for air. She sagged against a fence post. It took a concerted effort not to sink to the ground. Oh God! She glanced at her watch.

Three minutes?

No!

She shook the watch. She held it to her ear. It ticked away in perfect working order. She swallowed. 'Okay, Sammy, amended plan,' she panted. 'We jog for three minutes, then walk for three minutes.'

She set off again, fighting doubts and discouragement. She'd known this would take time. It wasn't possible to undo a lifetime of couch-potato-ness in just one day. Besides, she had a lot of chocolate sultanas to shift from her hips and thighs.

To distract herself from bursting lungs and legs that had started to burn, she forced herself to gaze at her surroundings. The quality of the light would've stolen her breath if she'd had any to spare. The clear blue of the sky and the sun low in the sky behind her outlined everything in perfect clarity. It enchanted her, even as half her attention had to remain on the path she took to avoid tussocks of grass and rocks that had definite ankle-turning potential.

She glanced at her watch and sighed. 'Time to jog again, Sammy.'

They set off at a jog, slower this time, and when her lungs started to burn again she reminded herself how much her new trainers had cost—four times what she'd paid for the bras. She *was* going to get her money's worth out of them. She could keep running for another—she glanced at her watch—one and three quarter minutes. She glanced down at her feet to admire the way the red dirt had already tarnished the brand-new perfection of her trainers when Sammy chose that moment to leap in front of her in pursuit of a grasshopper. It happened too quickly for her to avoid contact with him, to dance out of the way, to regain her balance or for anything except a full-frontal plough on her stomach through red dirt. When she came to a halt she blinked and spat out the grit that had found its way into her mouth.

Very elegant, Nicola.

True. But she took a few seconds to savour the sweet stillness of her body until Sammy, distracted from his prey by her fall, chose that moment to plaster wet licks all across her face.

'Sammy, heel!'

Sammy immediately obeyed as a shadow fell across her.

Oh, God! Cade. With a groan she rolled over and sat up. Why did her most undignified and humiliating moments have to occur in full public view?

'Are you hurt?'

'No.'

He turned and waved some signal and that was when she saw another two men—workers of Cade's, she supposed—standing outside the barn. They returned to work. The realisation that so many people had witnessed her pathetic attempt at fitness, not to mention her clumsiness, made her cheeks burn and her hands clench.

'C'mon.' Cade held a hand out to her.

Scowling at him and telling him to go away obviously wasn't an option, so she put her hand in his and let him haul her to her feet. He hitched his head in the direction of the homestead and didn't release her until she nodded her agreement.

Wiping the dirt from her face and the front of her T-shirt…and her shorts and her knees, she managed to avoid his eye. 'You don't need to escort me back.'

'Are you sure about that?'

His voice shook with laughter. She closed her eyes, more heat scorching her cheeks. She wasn't sure what was worse—him being aware of her utter mortification or him thinking her cheeks were this red from such a pitiful amount of exercise.

'I want to make sure you haven't really hurt yourself—twisted an ankle or a knee—but you seem to be walking all right.'

If that was a cue to make her trip up, she had every intention of disappointing him. 'I'm fine.' Except for a bruised ego.

'Good. Then you and I are going to have words.'

Her heart sank. Marvellous.

He made her sit on the back steps while he inspected her knees and elbows for scratches. 'We're a long way from a doctor,' he said when she started to object.

She stared at the sky and tried to ignore the warmth of his fingers on her flesh.

Finally he subsided onto the step beside her. 'So what's with the jogging?'

Heat flared afresh in her face and neck. 'Oh, I…'

She had to look away. There was something about those blue eyes that saw too much. He'd laugh at her. Her lips twisted. Just like her friends in Melbourne would've laughed if they'd seen her earlier this morning. The butt of oh-yet-another joke.

'Nicola?'

What the hell? She lifted her chin. She was through with turning herself inside out to please other people. 'I thought I'd take advantage of all the wide open space and fresh county air to…' she swallowed in readiness for his laughter '…to try and get fit.'

She clenched her hands. Strong in body. Strong in mind. It might not happen overnight, but she *could* work towards it. She *could* change. She gritted her teeth. Losing her fiancé to another woman *did not* make her a loser or a failure.

'Dry dusty air at this time of year more like.'

She didn't say anything.

'You didn't have a water bottle with you.'

That was when it hit her—he hadn't laughed yet. And one look at his face told her he wasn't going to. He didn't think her plan of getting fit was stupid at all. Instead, he was going to tell her off for not taking a water bottle. 'I thought with it being so early and all...'

'If I see you without a water bottle the next time you go jogging, we will have serious words, you understand?'

She swallowed and nodded.

He frowned. 'It's a bit early for New Year resolutions, isn't it?'

'Getting fit and losing weight was this year's resolution,' she sighed. 'I'm trying to get it in under the wire.'

His chuckle held no malice or ridicule. It warmed her blood. 'Getting fit is an admirable goal, but losing weight...' He shook his head. 'Seems to me women get too hooked up on that stuff.'

If she'd been half a stone lighter and had taken more care with her appearance, maybe Brad wouldn't have dumped her for Diane.

Cade sent her a lazy appraisal from beneath heavy-lidded eyes and it did something ludicrous to her insides, made them light and fluttery. She didn't like it.

'Anyway, you look just fine to me,' he said with a shrug.

Her hands clenched. She didn't want to look *just fine*. She wanted to be gorgeous, stunning...confident. She wanted to knock a man's socks off.

She had a horrid sick feeling that even if she did lose half a stone and took more care with her appearance, she would never be able to achieve that anyway.

His eyes suddenly narrowed. 'I don't want you getting

obsessive about your weight while you're out here, dieting and exercising to within an inch of your life.'

She understood where Cade's concern came from. She wasn't a primary school teacher for nothing. 'I have no intention of being obsessive about anything. And I promise I will not send Ella or Holly any negative body image messages.'

He stared at her. It made her self-conscious. She made a show of looking at her watch. 'It's nearly time to get Ella and Holly up for breakfast.'

She stood and made her escape.

When Nicola and the children entered the kitchen a short time later, it was to find Cade seated at the kitchen table too. Nicola's appetite promptly fled.

He glanced up. 'You must be hungry after your morning's exertions.'

His words emerged with a lazy unconcern, but his eyes were keen and sharp. She lifted her chin. 'Absolutely.'

She might have no appetite to speak of, but there was no way she could refuse to eat breakfast. Not after their earlier conversation. The thing was, she had no intention of obsessively dieting. She just meant to avoid cakes and biscuits and chocolate sultanas and all those other yummy things while she was here.

She ate cereal and yogurt. She tried not to focus too keenly on Cade's bacon and eggs and beans on toast. Cereal and yogurt—yum, yum.

Liar.

She might not be able to summon up much enthusiasm for a high fibre, low fat breakfast, but she was well aware that Cade took note of everything that passed her lips. So she ate. It should've irked her that he watched so closely.

For some reason, though, she found it strangely comforting instead.

When they finished, he rose. 'There's something I want to show you, something I think you'll be interested in.'

Wordlessly she followed him through the house. He wore jeans that fitted him to perfection. The material stretched across lean hips and a tight butt and she couldn't drag her gaze away. Her throat hitched. Awareness—sexual awareness—inched through her. Her blood heated up and a pulse started up deep in the centre of her. She moistened her lips, curled her fingers and wondered—

No way!

She slammed to a halt. No way!

He turned back, frowned. 'What's up?'

Her racing pulse slowed as his expression filtered into her panicked brain. The denial in her throat died. She shook herself. This man didn't see her as anything other than an employee. He certainly didn't see her as an attractive, available woman. She might doubt her own strength, but she didn't doubt his.

She'd come here to toughen up, to face reality and get stronger. Lusting after her boss *was not* the answer.

'Nicola?'

She shook herself. 'I just had one of those thoughts, you know? A bolt from the blue, but… Did I leave the oven on?'

He leaned towards her. 'What? In Melbourne?'

She nodded.

'And?'

'No, I'm certain I turned it off.'

He frowned. 'You sure about that? You want to ring someone to check?'

She shook her head. 'I'm positive I turned it off.'

With a shake of his head, he continued down the corridor. He flung open a door near its far end and strode into the darkened room to lift the blinds at the window. She followed him in, glanced around and her jaw dropped. 'You have a home gym?'

There was a treadmill, an exercise bike, a rowing machine and a weight machine. Oh, this would be perfect! She walked about the room, her fingers trailing across the equipment. 'This is amazing,' she breathed. 'Is it okay if I use it?'

'Sure.' Then his face tightened up. 'Someone may as well. I don't think anyone has been in here, except to clean, since Fran left.'

Fran?

'My ex-wife and the girls' mother,' he said, answering her unspoken question.

He didn't smile. His face remained tight and it warned her not to ask questions. He obviously had his demons too. It took an effort of will not to reach out, though, and place her hand on his arm in silent sympathy. When he turned and left, she counted slowly to ten before she closed the door and followed him.

'How was your day?'

Nicola blinked and then lowered her knife and fork when she realised Cade had directed that question at her. It was nearing the end of her second full day at Waminda Downs and they were all seated around the kitchen table eating dinner. She and Cade had barely spoken since he'd shown her the home gym yesterday. 'I…um…good. Thank you,' she added belatedly. 'And…uh…you?'

He ignored that. 'Have the girls given you any trouble?'

'No!'

'So…you're settling in okay?'

'Yes, of course.' She glanced at Ella and Holly and a smile built inside her. The three of them had enjoyed a fabulous day. 'Your daughters are delightful. I can't tell you how much I enjoy their company.'

One side of his mouth hooked up. 'You don't have to. It's written all over your face.'

Was it? She sat back. Maybe that was something she should add to her list of personal-attributes-to-work-on-and-improve. She didn't want to be so easy to read. She didn't want to wear her heart on her sleeve.

She wanted to be coolly poised and self-possessed.

'It wasn't a criticism,' he said quietly.

Definitely something she needed to work on!

She tried to smooth her face out into a polite smile. 'I wanted to thank you for letting me use the home gym.'

He shrugged her gratitude aside, but his eyes started to dance. 'How's the treadmill turning out? Managing to stay on your feet?'

She nearly spluttered her mouthful of iced water across the table, but the grin he sent her made her laugh. 'That was below the belt!'

'I couldn't resist.' He took a long pull on his beer. 'Have you been having any problems with any of the equipment? There must be instruction manuals somewhere around the place.'

'It all seems to be in perfect working order. I might loathe it, but the treadmill is a cinch to operate and I don't hate it as much as that darn rowing machine.'

He stared and then he threw his head back and laughed. Harry chuckled. Ella laughed too, although Nicola suspected she had no idea what she was laughing at. She just wanted to join in. Not to be outdone, Holly let forth with a squeal

Nicola Ann, must you sound so gauche?

Inside, she cringed. She was supposed to be developing polish and self-possession, not blurting out the first thing that came into her head and sounding like an idiot, becoming the butt of the joke.

Frustration built inside her. She clenched her hands so tight her fingernails bit into her palms. Why couldn't she manage one simple thing—to think before she spoke? Was it really that hard?

Failure. Loser. Doormat.

The insults flew at her, thick and fast. Not just in her mother's voice either. Her own was the loudest.

She closed her eyes and drew in a breath. 'I'm sorry, that came out all wrong. I just meant...'

He raised an eyebrow. He'd stopped laughing but he was still grinning. That grin made her heart beat a little harder. It made it difficult for her not to grin back. She swallowed and lectured herself for the umpteenth time about dignity. 'There's absolutely nothing wrong with any of the equipment. It's just that exercise and I have an ambivalent relationship.'

'Love, you ain't the only one,' Harry said with a consoling pat to Nicola's arm. 'Now, how about I bathe the littlies while you stack the dishwasher?'

It was obvious Harry adored Ella and Holly and, if the expression on her face was anything to go by, she enjoyed bath time too. Nicola was happy to divide the chores. 'Deal.' She rose and started to clear the table.

'You promised to read me a bedtime story, Nic!' Ella reminded her. 'Don't forget.'

She planted her hands on her hips and gave an exaggerated roll of her eyes. 'How could I forget something as important as that?'

With a giggle, Ella allowed Harry to lead her away.

A glance back at the table confirmed that Cade watched her. She couldn't decipher the expression in his eyes, but it made her break out in gooseflesh and turned all her fingers to thumbs. She opened her mouth to fill the quiet, but shut it again. That kind of rattling on was neither dignified nor self-possessed. She stacked the dishwasher, and suffered his examination in silence.

'Nicola,' he said, finally breaking the silence, 'you don't strike me as the gym-junkie type.'

No, she was more a curl-up-on-the-sofa-with-a-good-book-and-a-block-of-chocolate type. Admitting that certainly wouldn't be dignified, though. 'I think we've definitely established I'm not the jogging-outside-in-the-fresh-country-air type either,' she managed with a wry, hopefully dignified smile. 'Despite what I said, I do understand the benefits of regular exercise and I am grateful for the use of your home gym.'

She poured detergent into the dishwasher and then switched it on. 'I have every intention of continuing.'

He stood. 'Come with me. There's something I want to show you.'

Last time he'd said that he'd showed her a home gym.

He grinned at her hesitation. 'You'll love it, I promise.'

Nicola smelled like strawberry jam. He'd first noticed it when he'd helped her to her feet yesterday morning. He hadn't been able to get the smell of it out of his head. He'd been craving another hit ever since. Walking beside her now towards the stables, he could drag that scent into his lungs unimpeded and drink in his fill.

Still... He glanced across at her. There was no denying that she was a hell of a puzzle. When she let her guard down her blunt honesty and self-deprecation made him laugh. She was completely unguarded around the children. She was much more reserved around him and Harry. Especially him.

And the shadows in her eyes haunted him. They reminded him of last Christmas, with all of its bleak despair and bitterness. He didn't want reminders of last Christmas. He wanted festivity and merriment and all-out Christmas cheer.

His lips twisted. He had a hunch that plugging away every day on that darn treadmill and rowing machine weren't going to improve Nicola's Christmas cheer. It might just cement those shadows in her eyes for good!

Exercise-wise, he had her pegged as a team player—basketball, cricket, softball, it probably wouldn't matter which. There wasn't a chance he'd be able to organise that out here, though. At least, not until the rest of the family arrived in a week and a half's time.

Which left him with one other option to win her over, and help dispel those shadows.

He ushered her through the door of the barn. She glanced up, spearing him with those amazing eyes. She opened her mouth, and then shut it again. He sensed the effort it took her and wondered why she didn't just ask what she so obviously wanted to.

He took her arm to guide her through the early evening dimness of the barn and through a connecting door to the stables. Her eyes widened as they walked along the line of horse stalls. Her breath quickened and beneath his fingers her skin suddenly seemed to come alive.

He dropped his hand, shook it out, and told himself to stop being stupid. Halting at a stall halfway down the row, he gestured to the horse inside. The mare whickered softly and nuzzled his hand for a treat. He fed her the lump of sugar he'd stolen from the kitchen.

'This here is Scarlett O'Hara.' He glanced down at Nicola, who was staring at the horse as if she'd never seen one before. 'She's yours to ride for the duration of your stay at Waminda Downs.'

She stared at him as if she hadn't understood. The hair at his nape started to prickle. He shoved his hands into his pockets. Did he have her pegged all wrong? It was just…

She liked kids. She liked dogs. It made sense that she'd like horses too.

He hunched his shoulders. 'I mean, if you don't want to ride that's fine. But if you do, I'm happy to teach you.'

Her eyes filled and he backed up a step. Darn it all! She wasn't going to cry, was she? He was trying to instil Christmas spirit, not histrionics.

She clasped her hands beneath her chin. 'Do you really mean that?'

Just for a moment, she reminded him of Ella. He rolled his shoulders and eyed her warily. 'Sure I do.'

She swallowed. Her eyes went back to normal. If amazing could be called normal. 'All my life,' she whispered, reaching out to rest a hand against Scarlett's neck, 'I've wanted to learn to ride.'

Her eyes suddenly shone. Her whole face came alive. She smiled. The same way she smiled at Ella and Holly. A full and open smile. A wholehearted smile. At him.

The impact hit him square in the middle of his chest. The ground beneath his feet tilted. Fire licked along his veins to pool and burn in his groin. Desire stirred inside him for the first time in sixteen months.

He took a step away from her. 'First lesson at six-fifteen sharp in the morning,' he rapped out. Then he turned on his heel and fled. He couldn't even respond to the thank you she called after him.

CHAPTER THREE

CADE had Jack, his head stockman, give Nicola her first riding lesson. He stayed away.

Curiosity, though, defeated him by mid-morning. When he saw Ella and Holly with Nicola on the lawn in the shade of one of the date palms, their tartan blanket a flash of blue and red in the sun, he took a breather from breaking in a promising young colt to make his way over to them.

As he drew nearer he could hear them singing *Waltzing Matilda*, their heads bent over…something. At least, Nicola and Ella were singing, Holly mostly la-laahed. He glanced around the garden at all the Christmas decorations and wondered why they weren't singing Christmas carols.

His gaze returned to Nicola and he chewed the inside of his lip. Without warning, Holly crawled into Nicola's lap. One of Nicola's arms went about her, cradling her easily. With her other hand she pushed the hair back from the child's forehead and dropped an easy kiss there before picking up her…crayon again. She and Ella were colouring in a gigantic picture of a billabong—complete with kangaroos, koalas, wombats, a spindly emu and…a bunyip that Ella was colouring purple and orange.

He surveyed the tableau and something warm and sweet pooled low in his belly. He'd have loved it if they sang *Jingle Bells* and coloured in a festive Santa-themed picture, but it was obvious Nicola had developed an easy relationship with his children in a very short space of time, and for that he was grateful.

'Ella,' Nicola said, halting mid-verse.

It was only when she stopped that he realised what a lovely singing voice she had.

'I have eyes in the back of my head and I do believe your daddy is standing right behind us.'

Ella spun around and with a squeal launched herself at him. He swung her up into his arms. 'Nic's magic,' she told him.

'She must be,' he agreed, wondering what had given him away.

Nicola turned then too and smiled. 'I'm a primary school teacher. Eyes in the back of one's head is a necessary prerequisite.'

Her smile didn't knock his world off its axis, didn't create a fireball of desire. He let out a long, slow breath. Last night's reaction had been nothing more than an overload of hormones—a temporary aberration. Understandable given he'd been celibate for the last eighteen months.

He did notice that her hair looked shiny in the dappled light, though, and that her skin had a healthy glow. 'How did the riding lesson go this morning?'

Her face lit up. 'Oh! It was the best fun!'

Something inside him thumped in response. He planted his legs and tried to quash it. 'I hope you didn't mind that Jack gave the lesson?'

'Not at all. He's a great teacher.'

Something in her voice, if not her face, told him she was glad he'd sent Jack in his stead. It made him want to thrust his jaw out and—

He shook himself.

'He says I'm a natural.'

It was what he'd told Cade too. When Cade had finally shown his face. It was obvious the older man liked her.

'Sore?' It was a malicious question and he didn't know where it came from.

'Not yet.'

He was going to tell her she would be in the morning, but Ella chose that moment to wriggle out of his grasp. 'Come and see our picture, Daddy. Nic brought a whole book of pictures and said we could colour in one a day if we want.'

'Any Christmas pictures?' he couldn't help asking.

The colour heightened in her cheeks, but she merely tossed her head. 'They're all native Australian bush scenes.'

'They're beautiful,' Ella announced.

He stared at Nicola and pursed his lips. 'How about a Christmas carol before I get back to work?'

'Yay!' Ella clapped her hands.

He could've sworn Nicola rolled her eyes.

Ella launched into "Rudolph the Red-Nosed Reindeer". To her credit, Nicola started on the song only a beat later. The sweetness of her voice held him spellbound.

She tossed him a crayon and broke off singing to say, 'Join in or get back to work, those are your options.'

He grinned at the school teacher bossiness of it. He started singing too and coloured a koala blue.

When they finished Ella squirmed in excitement. 'It's only twenty more sleeps till Christmas!'

Nicola didn't say anything.

Cade ruffled Ella's hair. 'That's right, pumpkin.'

'I want lots and lots of presents,' the child announced. 'I want the *Rapunzel* movie and a Barbie camper.'

Cade stifled a grin. He'd ordered the DVD and a whole load of Barbie accessories over six weeks ago. He hadn't wanted to risk the stores running out. They were stowed in the top of his wardrobe at this very moment.

'Nic!' Ella bounced some more. 'What do you want Santa to bring you?'

'I don't expect Santa to bring me anything because I'm a grown-up.'

Cade cleared his throat. 'At Waminda Downs, Santa brings everyone a present.'

Comprehension dawned in those amazing eyes.

'Every year,' Ella confided, 'he brings Harry the biggest box of chocolates and…and…something in a bottle.'

Nicola shot him a quick glance. 'Perfume?'

'Baileys Irish Cream.'

Her lips twitched. 'You know, that sounds exactly what I'd wish for too.'

'Not a Barbie camper van?' Ella said, her mouth turning down.

'I already have one. Santa brought me one when I was six.'

'Oh, okay.' Ella went back to colouring in.

Cade frowned. A box of chocolate-coated ginger and a bottle of Baileys suddenly seemed all wrong for Nicola. He shifted. 'If you could have anything, what would you ask for?'

She shook her head and shrugged. The question obviously didn't interest her and that disturbed him.

'Other than a horse,' he persisted, 'what was the one thing you asked for when you were growing up, but never got?'

She stared up at the sky, lips pursed. 'Romance novels.'

He blinked.

'I loved them when I was a teenager and when I was fourteen I asked for a collection of romance novels. What I received was a leather-bound set of the complete works of

Jane Austen. Which, technically, are romances, and don't get me wrong, I love Jane Austen, but…'

But they hadn't been what she'd asked for.

She frowned. 'I haven't read a romance novel in ages.' She glanced at him and then gave a defiant toss of her head, though he couldn't help noticing how she was careful not to jerk Holly awake. 'And no doubt my life is the poorer for it.'

Romance novels, huh?

He stared at her and his youngest daughter. 'You look like the Madonna and child.'

She snorted. 'There's nothing immaculate about me, take my word for it.'

He choked back a laugh. She stiffened and then did that stupid pulling back thing, as if she wished she hadn't said what she had, even though it was funny and had made him laugh. It ruined his mood completely.

'Time I got back to work,' he said abruptly, climbing to his feet.

'Bye, Daddy.'

He turned away, only to swing back half a second later. 'A soak in a hot bath this evening will help with the sore muscles.' And then he turned on his heel and strode off with long strides because the image that flooded his mind of Nicola stretched out in a steamy bath, her eyes heavy-lidded with pleasure, needed to be booted out again asap before the ground beneath his feet started shifting again.

He bit back a curse. Hormones might be a fact of life, but they could be darn inconvenient.

Ten days later Cade's family arrived—his mother and all her luggage on one plane, his sister and his five-year-old twin nephews on another. His brother-in-law would fly in on Christmas Eve.

This was what Cade had been dreaming of and planning for—a rowdy family Christmas full of fun and laughter and festivity.

He couldn't help noticing the way Nicola kept herself in the background, though. He'd done his best not to notice her this past week. Not that he'd been particularly successful.

He couldn't help noticing the way her gaze kept returning to the bowl of chocolate sultanas that Harry had put out as a treat, along with fruitcake and shortbread, either. She ignored the fruitcake and the shortbread, but she eyed those sultanas as if they held the answer to the universe. It made him smile. He held his breath and waited for her to seize a handful and enter into the Christmas spirit.

She didn't, even though she couldn't seem to stop her gaze from darting back to them again and again. Something in his chest started to burn.

When a bout of family Christmas carols started up, he couldn't help but notice the way her eyes dimmed, even though she kept a smile on her face. Or the way she slipped out of the French windows and onto the veranda.

Ella and Holly didn't notice. They were too entranced with their grandmother, their aunt and their cousins. Nobody else noticed either.

Cade pursed his lips and counted to ten—that was the number of days left till Christmas—and then he pushed out of his chair, had a quick word with Harry and followed Nicola into the night.

Nicola stared out at the darkness and couldn't believe how many stars this Outback night sky held. She had never seen so many stars. Around on this side of the veranda, away from the light spilling from doors and windows and where she could barely hear the Christmas carols, the stars gleamed bigger and brighter.

Away from all that Christmas merriment, the burn surrounding her heart started to ease too.

And then her sixth sense kicked in—Cade—and a different kind of burning started up in her veins. A heat she didn't want. A heat she certainly didn't trust.

She didn't turn from the railing. 'You should be in there with your family and enjoying this time with them.'

'So should you.'

She turned at that. 'They're not my family, Cade. Besides, I think it's nice for Ella and Holly to have a chance to focus on their grandmother, aunt and cousins without me getting in the way. And don't worry, I'm wearing my watch. I'll put them to bed in another half an hour.'

'Three things.' His voice cut the air. 'One, you're not in the way. Two, for as long as you're at Waminda you're part of the family. Three, I asked Harry to put the girls to bed. I saw how much you helped her with dinner.'

His high-handedness irked her. She didn't like his tone much either. Last month the old Nicola would've shrugged it off and tried to ignore it, but not the new improved version of Nicola McGillroy. No, sirree.

'One—' she held up a finger '—I'm here to do a job and I don't need anyone else to do it for me. I can carry my own weight.' She just wasn't prepared to carry anyone else's any more. 'And two, I should be allowed a few moments' quiet time every now and again without you jumping on me with that you're-ruining-Christmas tone in your voice.'

She had no intention of ruining Christmas for Cade and his family. It was why she'd stolen from the living room earlier. All that Christmas gaiety had filled her with such unexpected longing it had stolen her breath and knocked her sideways… For a moment she'd thought she might burst into tears.

She shuddered. How would she have explained that?

'I didn't mean to jump on you.'

The shock in his voice shamed her. All he was trying to do was give his kids and family a nice Christmas. Her hang-ups weren't his fault. She gripped her hands together. She only had to put up with all this Christmas cheer for another week and a half.

Fortitude was never your strong point was it, Nicola Ann?

She gritted her teeth. This wasn't much different from keeping a class entertained at school. She could do that with one hand tied behind her back. This was just a job.

She dragged in a breath. 'Okay then, let's get back to it.' She clapped her hands. 'I've taken the three deep breaths I needed to resist that bowl of chocolate sultanas. My healthy eating plan is still intact. Besides, I don't think we've had a rendition of "Good King Wenceslas" yet and that's one of my favourites.'

'No.'

The single word brought her up short, as did the hand curling about her upper arm and preventing her from going anywhere. 'No?' Why not? She'd just agreed to what he wanted, hadn't she?

'This isn't just a job!'

She begged to differ, but wisely kept her mouth shut. Cade's vehemence ensured that. Parents hated reminders that teaching little Johnny or Jane was actually a job and not the blessing and privilege they considered it.

Besides, if she pointed out to Cade that her title was in fact Nanny and not Friend or Family Member, it would give him the wrong impression. It would make it sound as if she didn't really care for Ella and Holly when she did. She adored them.

It didn't change the fact that this was still a job, though, and that no matter how much Cade and his family welcomed her into their fold, it still didn't make her one of them.

It wasn't anything to be bitter about. It wasn't anything to be hurt about. It was the truth, plain and simple.

Oh, but how she wished she had a family like his!

The warmth of his hand on her arm filtered into her consciousness. The pulse in her throat fluttered to life. 'Unhand me, sir.' Although she struggled for light, the words came out husky.

Cade released her, but he stood so close she could smell the clean scent of soap on his skin. She gulped. Starlit night, a guy and girl alone…

Stop it! She knew her musings were nonsensical and that in all likelihood Cade hadn't even noticed the stars, or the fact that she was a woman. It still took a concerted effort to ease back a step when, by rights, the thought should've had her running for the hills.

Classic rebound reaction, she told herself, her lips twisting in mockery at her own weakness. 'If you don't want me to return inside, what is it you would like me to do?'

'I want you to listen.'

He didn't say anything else. A long moment passed. 'To?' she prompted.

He took her arm again and all that warm maleness flooded her senses. The latent strength of him set her nerves jangling. He led her to a bench, urged her to sit and then released her again.

'I want to tell you why Christmas is so important for me, for Waminda Downs, and for Ella and Holly this year.'

Instinct told her that she didn't want to hear what he

was about to say. She wanted to get up and walk away. She had enough issues of her own to deal with, without adding his to the score. But when she looked up into his face, she found she didn't have the strength to do that. Just for a moment he looked as tired and defeated as she felt each morning when she woke up. Before she'd had a chance to remind herself that she was on a cattle station in the Outback and that she had a riding lesson that very morning to look forward to.

He eased down beside her. She studied him for a moment—the downturned mouth, the slumped shoulders, the way it seemed an effort to draw breath into his lungs, and a lump formed in her throat. It was obvious he needed to share this with someone. Why not the temporary nanny who'd be gone again in six weeks' time?

It's just a job, she reminded herself.

But it felt like so much more and she didn't know when that had happened. She bit back a sigh. So much for keeping her distance.

He was sitting beside her on the bench in the warm night air, their arms and shoulders not quite touching. This time she didn't prompt him. She sat there and stared out at the sky, breathing him in and waiting.

Finally he spoke. 'Last Christmas was our first Christmas without Fran.'

Her heart clenched at the pain in his voice.

'She'd left about four months earlier, but…'

He dipped his head and raked his fingers through his hair. She reached out and laid a hand on his forearm. The muscles tensed beneath her fingertips. 'You really don't have to tell me any of this, you know?'

He laid his other hand over hers and squeezed it, and then he placed her hand back in her lap. It felt like a rejection but she didn't know why. She stared straight out in front of her and focused on her breathing.

'I think it's probably best if you know.'

She didn't say anything, just gave a curt nod.

'Fran left us all here at Waminda in late August and went to Brisbane.' He paused. 'I thought she just needed a break. It can be hard getting used to the isolation of a cattle station, and with two small children—one barely three months old—I could understand her going a bit stir-crazy.'

Nicola frowned. 'You mean…you're saying she left Ella and Holly here?'

Even in the dimness she could see him smile, but it didn't hold any mirth. 'That's what I'm saying.'

She bit her tongue and turned back to stare straight out in front of her. She couldn't imagine anyone wanting to leave Ella and Holly behind, not for any reason. Unless… 'Post-natal depression?'

'That's what she told me. She was seeing a therapist. I even spoke to the damn therapist.'

She understood his frustration, his anger, but… 'She wouldn't have been able to help it, you know.'

The smile he sent her held a world of weariness. 'Depression was something I was fully prepared to deal with, Nicola. I'd have done anything I could've to help her through it. I set her up in an inner city apartment so she could see her therapist as often as she needed, and so she could have the change of scenery she claimed to so badly need. I wired her as much money as she asked for. I took the girls to visit as often as I could, and all the while I made endless excuses for her distance and her erratic behaviour. I mean depression, right? It's out of her control. I might be doing it tough, but she was doing it a whole lot tougher, right?'

With each *right* his voice rose. She swallowed and nodded. 'Right,' but her voice came out on a breath of uncertainty. She gripped the edge of the bench and turned to face him fully. 'But?'

He rested his head back against the wall behind him and closed his eyes. 'But it was all a lie.'

'A lie?'

'A blind, a decoy, a red herring to throw me off the trail of what was really happening.'

Her mouth had gone as dry as the soft red sand of the Outback. 'What was really happening?'

'For three months she let me go on thinking that our marriage had a chance, but all the while she was planning to leave me and Ella and Holly for another man.'

She couldn't stop her jaw from dropping. 'She strung you along for three months?'

His eyes opened. His lips twisted and he pointed to his forehead. 'Can't you see the word Stupid branded here?'

'You weren't stupid! You trusted her, supported her and… You were married, for heaven's sake!' She pressed fingertips to her temples. Thank God Brad had dumped her before they'd married.

'Apparently returning to Waminda was her backup plan if things didn't work out with her Texan millionaire.'

She eyed him for a moment, swallowed. 'I guess they did. Work out, that is.'

'They did.'

'I guess telling you you're better off without her isn't any comfort at all?'

'A little.' This time his smile was genuine. It faded. 'But Ella and Holly aren't better off without a mother.'

She shook her head. 'No.' She couldn't keep the horror out of her voice. 'Whose decision was that?' She understood Cade's anger, his bitterness, but would he prevent his ex-wife from seeing their children?

'Hers,' he replied in a dead voice and she immediately kicked herself for what she'd just thought. She'd seen him with his children. He didn't have that kind of spite in him.

'Quote: "I'm not taking any extra baggage like children from a previous marriage into my new life. Chip wouldn't like it."'

'God!' She didn't try to hide her disgust. 'Where on earth did she pick him up from?'

'The Internet.'

She slouched back. 'Poor Ella and Holly.'

'You said it.'

And poor Cade.

She glanced at him, and roused herself. 'The girls,' she ventured, 'seem to have bounced back okay. Ella is remarkably well adjusted considering all she's been through.' The young girl could be clingy at times, but she understood why now. Holly was still just a baby. Who knew how this would affect her in the years to come?

'I feel we've finally come out the other side.'

His voice told her it had been hell.

'And this Christmas is a…a signal of a new start?'

'It's an attempt to make up to them in some small way for the wretchedness of the last year.' His hands clenched. 'It's my attempt to make amends for all but ignoring Christmas last year.'

If Fran had left him in late August and then strung him along for three months… 'Fran broke up with you in late November?'

'Early December,' he said shortly.

'Oh, Cade, you can't blame yourself for last Christmas. It takes time to adjust to a shock like that.'

'That's no excuse for not giving Ella and Holly one day of brightness amid all that upheaval. My mother and sister tried to talk me into spending the holidays with them in

Brisbane. But Brisbane was the last place I wanted to be, especially knowing that Fran was so close and yet didn't want to see her own daughters.'

He shook his head. He didn't say anything more...not that he needed to.

'I'm sorry for all you've been through. If it helps any, you're giving not only Ella and Holly the kind of Christmas dreams are made of, but your mother, sister and nephews as well.'

He sent her a sidelong glance. 'And yet the one thing I can't seem to give them is a nanny brimming over with the joy of the season.'

The criticism stung. She thought she'd been doing fine and dandy on the Christmas front.

'Considering the way I behaved last year, I realise I'm the last person who should be criticizing someone else's Christmas spirit.'

But it wasn't going to stop him from finding fault with her, right? 'So you're a pot and I'm the kettle?'

He turned to her. 'Why are you spending Christmas at Waminda Downs instead of in the bosom of your family or with your friends—with the people you love?'

It was the sheer gentleness of his voice that was her undoing, an inherent understanding that she was dealing with a hell of her own.

She opened her mouth and he leant forward to press a finger to her lips. 'No nonsense about wanting to experience the majesty of the Outback or searching for adventure or anything else I could get from a travel brochure. At least give me that much respect.'

To her horror, tears filled her eyes. This man had just shared the breakdown of his marriage with her so she could understand why Christmas meant so much to him this year.

The least she could do was explain why Christmas was low on her personal landscape.

She swallowed and nodded. He removed his hand and leant back again.

She didn't speak until she was sure she had her voice back under control. 'I'm not spending this Christmas in the bosom of my family because there's only my mother and my aunt, and my mother's bosom isn't very…um…warm.'

'I'm sorry.'

She shrugged. 'We come from money but the one thing my mother couldn't buy was the daughter she'd always wanted.' She blew out a breath and tried to smile. 'I'm afraid I've been a sore disappointment to her. I was never the blonde, svelte ballerina type she'd have liked to see blossom into a society princess who loved fashion and charity lunches.' Her lips twisted. 'Oh, and the shock and horror of it all when I decided to earn my own living. Why on earth did I have to choose something as unglamorous as teaching? Couldn't I at least have had the consideration to study Law or Medicine? At least she'd have been able to brag about those.'

He rested his elbows on his knees. 'Is she blind?' he demanded.

'No, she just sees the world through her own eyes and can't comprehend anyone else's view of it.' She laughed. 'Nicola Ann, you're twenty-seven and too old to be gallivanting around the countryside as a nanny looking after someone else's children. Think of all that dust and heat… and the flies! What on earth will I tell my friends?'

'She said that?'

'Verbatim.' She glanced down at her hands. 'Christmas lunch with my mother and aunt is an ordeal. They spend at least an hour picking over my myriad flaws and the per-

ceived mistakes I've made for the year. Given my start in
life and all... Yadda yadda yadda. You get the picture.'

'I do.' His voice was grim.

'And this year I just couldn't face it. Normally I only
survive that lunch with my mother because of the promise of a rollicking good party with my friends in the evening—my Christmas highlight.'

'And that's not happening this year?'

Oh, it was happening all right. She just wouldn't be a
part of it.

'Nicola?'

She hadn't meant to reveal her troubles to anyone while
she was here at Waminda Downs. She'd promised herself
that she was through with being an object of pity. And she
was. 'I don't want this going any further. I don't want you
telling your family or Harry or Jack or anyone about this.'

'That always went without saying. But you have my
word of honour.'

Even now she knew she could pull back—plead a head-
ache and retire to her room. Flee to her room. But she suddenly found she didn't want to. She wanted to lance some
of the poison that blackened her thoughts until she could
taste the bitterness in her mouth. She wanted to hurl it into
the darkness where the night could swallow it and hopefully destroy it.

She pulled in a breath that made her whole frame shake.
'Right now I should be in the middle of wedding preparations. *My* wedding preparations.'

His head snapped back. 'You're engaged?'

'Was. Past tense.'

'Hell, I'm sorry. I...'

He trailed off like so many of her friends had when
they'd heard the news.

'He dumped me for another woman and, yes, before you

say it, I agree it's better to have found that out now than after we were married.'

'It's still a tough blow and a lot to deal with, but...'

She glanced up. 'Yes?'

'I'd have thought being with your friends at a time like this would've been the best thing. You could've blown your mother off with some excuse or other.' He rolled his eyes. 'I mean, I can just imagine her comments on a broken engagement, but having the support and understanding of your friends would've been invaluable, wouldn't it?'

She laughed and the bitterness of it cut deep into her. 'I'm sorry I left out one tiny detail. My fiancé dumped me for my best friend.'

CHAPTER FOUR

NICOLA couldn't look at Cade after she'd uttered those words. His shocked intake of breath told her all she needed to know.

Along with the silence.

She hated that kind of silence. She'd dealt with too much of it these past three months. 'We're all still friends. Brad and Diane didn't mean for it to happen. They didn't mean to hurt me.'

'How very adult of you,' he ground out wryly.

She grimaced. He was right. She sounded like a B-grade actor in some corny nineteen-eighties telemovie.

When she glanced at him she recognised the flare of anger in his eyes and she knew it was directed at Brad and Diane, not at her. And God forgive her, but it made her feel good.

The thing was, they hadn't meant to hurt her. She knew that.

But they had.

They'd crushed something vital inside her and she didn't know how to get it back.

'They announced their engagement last month and that's when I realised I couldn't spend Christmas in Melbourne this year. Without meaning to, I'd ruin it for everyone. A lot of our set are angry with them, but are following my lead because I've asked them to. If I'd stayed I wouldn't have been able to keep the brave face up. It would've created a division in the group and I don't want that. It's not fair to force people to take sides.'

'So you applied for a job and came out here.'

Her lips twisted and an apology welled inside her. 'With all my Christmas spirit, I'm afraid.' And that had hardly been fair either, had it? She glanced down at her hands. 'When I arrived you asked me if I was running away from something. I'm not running away. I'm just taking a break and gathering my resources before I have to face it all again.'

He nodded, but didn't say anything.

She bit back a sigh. 'I'm sorry. I can see now that was hardly fair of me. I thought I'd be in the background out here and not of much consequence.' Her actions suddenly seemed horribly selfish and self absorbed.

Cade still didn't say anything.

She winced. 'Do you want me to leave?'

He didn't answer that either. Her heart started to pound. She glanced at him. He glared back at her. 'So what the hell is with the getting fit and losing weight thing?'

Oh.

She swallowed and stared out into the night, unable to look at him. The glory of the stars still awed her. She wanted to reach out and touch one, clasp it in her hand and make a wish.

A childish fantasy, but no more childish than believing she could've built a life with Brad.

'Nicola?'

She bit back a sigh. 'I've come up with a plan to make myself over and improve myself.'

He shifted on his seat. 'You've what?'

She was proud she didn't flinch at his incredulity. She

kept her eyes fixed on the brightest star. 'Strong in body, strong in mind. At least, that's the idea.'

'What are you hoping to achieve?'

He spoke those words much quieter and it took an effort to keep her focus on the starlit sky and not turn to him. 'I want to look better, I want to feel better, and I want people to stop looking at me like I'm a victim. I want to develop some smarts. I didn't see the Brad and Diane thing coming at all. It was a bolt from the blue.' She straightened. 'And I want to develop some…some poise and self-possession. That way everybody will stop feeling sorry for me, they'll respect me, and I'll be able to…move on.'

'Nicola?'

She gave in and looked at him.

'Change is fine, but don't take it too far. Making sure you're not taken for granted doesn't have to translate into being unfriendly.'

Her jaw dropped. 'Is that how I've come across?'

One of those broad shoulders of his lifted. She went back over all their earlier encounters. She considered the way she'd kept everyone here at arm's length and her cheeks started to burn. 'I'm not getting the balance right, am I?'

'It could use some work.'

Changing was proving a whole lot harder than she'd initially envisaged. 'What I need is a fairy godmother to wave a magic wand or a genie to grant me three wishes,' she sighed.

'And what would you wish for?'

'To be fit and healthy.' Which translated to thin, but that seemed far too shallow to say out loud. 'To have the poise and chutzpah to carry myself with confidence,' regardless of how she was actually feeling. 'And…and to stop burying my head in the sand, to realise what's right under my nose and face reality.' And to stop feeling so angry, she added silently.

'That's all very noble,' he drawled. 'Now give me the other wish list.'

She spun to face him. How could he know? And then she remembered all he'd been through with Fran and his marriage breakup. Her mouth dried. 'The less admirable list?'

'That's the one.'

How badly would he think of her if she uttered those things out loud? Then she remembered she was through with caring what people thought of her.

She frowned. She was through with caring *so much* about what people thought of her. She would find the right balance. Eventually.

'Okay, out with it.'

She swallowed. 'I really, really, *really* want to look good at their wedding. I want them to feel bad that their happiness has come at my expense, but at the same time I want them to admire me and…and to miss me. Because, yes, while we're still friends, things have changed and no matter how hard I try I can't make them go back to the way they were before.'

He stared at her. She pushed her hair off her face and tried to shove her self-consciousness to a place where it couldn't plague her. But… He thought her shallow now, didn't he? And weak. She tossed her head. 'What?' she demanded, losing the battle.

'You didn't ask for Brad back.'

'I don't want him back.' If she said it often enough, eventually she'd believe it. And it was partly true. Who wanted a cheating spouse who didn't really love them? But…

Oh, how she ached for the promise of the life they

could've had—the home, the babies, the laughter. The belonging.

Her eyes burned. She blinked hard and forced her chin up. 'I want a hot date for the wedding. That way, no one will feel sorry for me.' Not that she had any idea where to find a hot date, mind.

'You want to look gorgeous. You want to be able to hold your head high, and you want a hunky man at your side.'

She nodded.

'None of those things are ignoble.'

She glanced at him and swallowed. 'I was going to say that the moment Diane saw me again I wanted her to worry that I could steal Brad away from her if I chose to, and that the moment Brad clapped eyes on me again he'd start to wonder if he'd chosen the wrong woman.'

'But?'

'But it's not true. Not really. I just get irrationally angry sometimes.' She glanced down at her hands. 'I do actually hope their marriage is happy and strong. I wish them both well.'

He sat back and stared. 'The anger isn't irrational.'

A part of her agreed, but... 'It comes out of the blue sometimes when I'm not expecting it. It's so...bitter and unforgiving. I hate feeling like that.'

'It'll get easier with time.'

She hoped so.

He was silent for a while, then leant forward to rest his elbows on his knees. 'How about you and I make a deal?'

She raised her eyebrows. 'A deal?'

'I will help you get fit, and I'll do what I can to aid your makeover plans...and I'll also be your date for the wedding.'

Her jaw dropped. He'd be her date? But... An immediate image of her friends' surprise—Diane and Brad's surprise—flooded her.

'And in return…'

She pressed a hand to her chest to counter its sudden and erratic pounding. 'In return?' Her voice had gone hoarse.

'And in return you'll help me make this Christmas and the holidays fabulous for Ella and Holly, and the rest of my family.'

Her heart kept right on pounding. 'Asking you to be my date, Cade, is too much.'

'Do you have someone else in mind for the job?'

'Well, no, but—'

'Call it a Christmas bonus.'

She wanted him as her date for that far-off wedding. His mere presence would fill her with confidence. Somewhere in the past week or so, his confidence and self-possession had become her blueprint for what she was working towards.

She cocked her head. 'Okay, be specific. Exactly how is my Christmas cheer supposed to manifest itself?' She was getting a lot out of this deal. She needed to know she could deliver her side of the bargain.

'Help me and the kids decorate the house. Sing Christmas carols. Help the kids write letters to Santa. Help Ella make gifts for the family. And…and take part in all the revelry, whatever form that takes—charades, telling Christmas stories, whatever. I want you to act like one of the family.'

He would help with her makeover plan, plus he would be her date to the dreaded wedding, and all she had to do was be Christmassy? She imagined the expressions on Brad and Diane's faces when she turned up at the wedding with Cade. She knew Diane so well. She knew exactly what Diane would think—*hot, gorgeous hunk*. Oh, yes, that would be *very* satisfying.

Shallow, yes, but satisfying as well.

To no longer be the object of all those furtive glances, those consoling pats on the arm, those 'poor Nicola' comments! Something inside her lifted.

Was he serious—all she had to do was be Christmassy? She stuck out a hand before he could change his mind. 'You have yourself a deal.'

He closed his hand around hers. His grip was firm and she could feel the way he tempered his strength so as to not crush her fingers. He didn't let go again immediately and her heart started up its silly pounding and erratic fluttering again.

'Nicola…'

Her name was a caress in the warm night air. Brad had never uttered her name like that. Her heart pounded louder, harder. 'Yes?'

'I know your confidence has taken a beating, and I respect the fact that you'd like to get fit, but as for your weight…and everything else, I don't think you need to change a damn thing.'

For a moment she actually believed he was sincere.

Oh, Nicola Ann, the man's a comedian!

She flinched as she imagined her mother's scornful laughter. She pulled her hand from his and leapt up, moving across to the nearest veranda post. She wrapped her hands around it. 'Is that a way of saying you'll help me with my makeover plan, but as you don't think I need to change there's nothing you need to actually do?'

'Damn it, no!'

He shot to his feet and strode across to her, gripping her chin in his hand to force her to meet his gaze. 'You're a hell of an infuriating woman, you know that?'

Infuriating was better than pitiful.

His face softened as he stared down at her. 'Sorry,' he murmured, his touch on her chin becoming gentle. 'I shouldn't have snapped.'

'I...um...' She swallowed. 'I'm probably a touch sensitive,' she allowed.

'A person doesn't bounce back just like that after the kind of blow you've suffered, Nicola. But you don't need to change and eventually you'll see I'm right.'

She doubted that, but she couldn't utter a single sound. Under his fingers her skin had leapt to life. His thumb traced the skin beneath her bottom lip. It made her drag in a breath that made her whole body tremble.

'You have the most amazing eyes I have ever seen,' he murmured.

It wasn't her eyes he was staring at, but her mouth. And he was staring at it as if he was hungry, as if he was starved. That gaze held her spellbound. It promptly cut off her mother's disbelieving comments and hurtful contradictions. She should step away. She should flee. She knew that in some deep, dark recess of her mind, but her hand curled about the veranda post all the more tightly to anchor her into place.

Cade had become the brightest star in the night and she wanted to bask in the glow of his warmth and his...desire. Even if for only ten seconds more.

His free hand travelled down the post until he found her hand. He closed it around hers. He stepped in so close their chests touched. 'You smell like strawberry jam.'

She tried to ask him if that was a good thing, but her throat wouldn't work. All that happened was her lips parted.

And that he saw them part.

And knew what it meant.

His eyes glittered. His mouth took on a wolfish edge of satisfaction. He brushed his thumb over her bottom lip. She gasped and a low rumble of approval emerged from his chest.

'Amazing eyes,' he repeated. 'Hair that shines in the starlight.' His thumb stopped alternately tormenting and pleasing her lips as his hand drifted around the back of her neck to slide into the hair at the base of her skull. He tipped her head back so he could devour her face with his gaze, and she let him.

He was going to kiss her. She knew he was going to kiss her. She hovered between breaths, waiting for it, waiting to welcome it...hungering for it.

And from the glittering satisfaction in his eyes she could tell that he'd read that thought in her eyes—that she wanted it as much as he did, that there would be no argument or resistance.

His mouth descended. The pressure of his hand at her nape partly lifted her to meet him, demanded that she meet him.

And she did, with her lips ready to taste him completely.

The kiss was not tentative on either side—it was assured and demanding. Nicola was twenty-seven years old but she had never had such a blatantly adult kiss in all that time.

Had never enjoyed such a blatantly adult kiss. There was no game playing and no teasing or preliminaries. A question had been asked. An answer given. And then the thorough enjoyment, a wholehearted participation in the slaking of a mutual need.

And the pleasure rocked her to her toes. She clutched his upper arms, not aware of when she'd moved, his heat and strength rippling through the thin cotton of his shirt to her palms and fingers, filling her with a sense of invincibility. His arm snaked around her waist—to pull her more firmly against him or to give her support? She didn't know and she didn't care. She was simply grateful that it gave her the freedom to dance her fingers across his throat, to smooth them over his shoulders and then plunge them into his hair to pull him closer.

The kiss went on and on and it filled her with energy and strength and the yearning for more...so much more!

Eventually Cade lifted his head, but he didn't remove his arm from around her waist. She didn't remove hers from around his neck. She met his gaze head on. With Cade she didn't need to be coy.

His eyes didn't waver from hers. 'If this goes on for much longer we're going to get to the point of no return,' he rasped out.

She nodded.

His chest, pressed to hers, rose and fell. 'I need to think about that.'

So did she.

In unspoken agreement they unclasped each other. Nicola moved back to the bench as reaction set in and her knees started to shake.

Did she want to take this any further? Did she want to go all the way with Cade? Oh, her body was in no doubt but what about her brain...and her heart?

He didn't turn from where she'd left him. 'I'm not ready for anything serious.' He spoke to the night, but she knew the words were meant for her.

After all he'd revealed about his marriage and Fran, she wasn't surprised. 'I'm not either.' It was the truth.

He turned. She could read the question in his eyes.

She'd come out here to focus on getting her life back together. A holiday fling, however brief, would deflect her from that. And her plan for self-improvement was important to her. She didn't want to be the doormat her friends thought her or the failure her mother considered her.

She stood, her knees finally steady. 'No.'

She sensed the relief that flashed through him, along with the frustration. He nodded once. He didn't say anything.

'If I slept with you it'd be partly as revenge on Brad and Diane. You might say you wouldn't care about that.' Men were all hormones and any excuse, right? 'But I'd care.'

'No, Nicola, you're wrong. I'd resent being used like that.'

'The other thing is, I don't want to go falling for you on the rebound. My emotions are all over the place at the moment and I don't trust them. I'm not ready for anything serious and I can say that till I'm blue in the face, but...'

'But sometimes it's impossible to keep things emotion-free and uncomplicated.'

'Neither one of us needs complicated right now.' The blood burned in rebellion in her veins. She swallowed and told herself she was doing the right thing. 'Besides,' she croaked, 'you have the girls to consider.'

'I do.'

'And I don't much trust the whole notion of romantic love any more. I think it's a bubble that eventually gets burst. Down the track, hopefully, I'll meet someone and get married because I want children, but I mean to go into the marriage with wide eyes and a clear head. My head at the moment isn't clear.'

They eyed each other warily. 'I'm sorry,' she offered, because it felt as if she should apologise.

He gave an emphatic shake of his head. 'The first lesson in PD101 is to never apologise for something that isn't your fault. This isn't anyone's fault. Never apologise for being honest.'

'PD?'

'Personal Development.'

That sounded much grander than a makeover plan. 'Personal development,' she murmured. 'I like it.' With that she started to edge away. She might have finally screwed her head on right, but it didn't counter the effect of Cade's continued proximity. Her body clamoured for the feel of him, the touch of his lips and hands—his hardness pressed tight against her softness. And rather than diminishing, it was starting to increase. 'I'll…um…say goodnight then.'

'Nicola?'

She turned at the question, adrift between him and the French windows to her bedroom. She clasped her hands together tightly.

'When you said you wanted to go into marriage with a clear head, what did you mean?'

She didn't move back towards him. That would be foolish. With the moon behind him, and from this distance, she couldn't see his face clearly. 'From what I've seen of relationships, there are those who do the giving and those who do the taking. Until now I've been one of the givers. In the future I'm going to be a taker. I mean to get precisely what I want out of any marriage.'

'Take the poor sod to the cleaners, so to speak?' The air whistled between his teeth. 'Thank God you called a halt to things just then. They could've gotten darn messy.'

And just like that he'd made her laugh. 'Don't worry, Cade. You would never have made it into my sights.' He was a lot of things, but a poor sod wasn't one of them. 'Given all you've been through, I doubt you'd ever want to dip your toe in matrimonial waters again.'

'Damn right.'

'So I wouldn't have made the elementary mistake of thinking you were available.'

He shifted. She still couldn't see his face clearly. 'It seems to me that if your main reason for marrying is to have children, you could dispense with the middleman and use IVF instead. No point in putting yourself in a miserable relationship with a man you would neither respect or trust.'

She stilled. 'You know, you've got a point there.' She could dispense with the mess of romance for good. It was an intriguing idea. 'Goodnight, Cade.' She turned and headed for her room. This time he didn't call her back.

Cade didn't waste any time, he got to work on his side of the bargain the very next day. Nicola's opinion of the human race was at an understandable low and he didn't want to add to it. He wanted to prove to her that some people did keep their promises.

While she was busy outside with all four children playing some game that involved a lot of running, a lot of freezing and a whole lot of laughing, he dragged his mother and Delia into the kitchen, where Harry was preparing lunch.

Verity Hindmarsh glanced out of the window, attracted by the laughter of the children, and smiled. 'Nicola is a gem.'

'That she is,' Harry huffed.

'Awfully quiet, though,' Delia mused. 'But wonderful with Jamie and Simon.'

Jamie and Simon had recently turned five and had the kind of energy that could make Cade dizzy just watching them. Dee was enjoying the advantage of having another person to help out with them. Not that Cade blamed her or begrudged her, but he meant to make sure Nicola didn't get lumped with more than her fair share of the work.

'Nicola is what I want to talk to you about.' As one they turned to survey him. He did his best not to fidget. 'I found out recently that it's not just the Outback she's never experienced, but a big family Christmas. It's just her and her mother who is rather over-critical, from what I can make out.'

Harry stopped chopping salad vegetables to glance out of the window. 'Well, now, that makes sense. Probably why she's got such a bee in her bonnet about exercising and losing weight.'

At the words 'losing weight', Harry instantly had the other two women's attention.

'She tried jogging around the property in the early morning, but...' she flicked a glance at Cade '...but that didn't work out so well. So Cade set her up in Fran's old home gym.'

He didn't know why, when all three women turned to look at him, he wanted to roll his shoulders and back out of the room. 'Someone may as well use it,' he mumbled. 'She's no gym junkie, though.'

Harry sliced through a lettuce with evident satisfaction. 'So when he found out she'd always wanted to learn to ride, he set her up with Jack for lessons each morning.'

'That was a lovely thing to do,' his mother said. While he was no longer a seven-year-old, he found himself momentarily basking in the warmth of her approval. The kind of approval it seemed that Nicola had never received. 'But why aren't you teaching her yourself?'

That wasn't something he was prepared to get into. 'She and Jack have hit it off. He's enjoying it.'

'And Jack's not getting any younger,' Harry observed.

'He's still more than capable of putting in a full day's work.'

'Darling—' his mother laid a hand on his arm, her eyes warm with a mixture of relief and delight '—I thought we'd lost you for ever after everything Fran did, but I can see now that's not the case. I can't tell you how happy I am to see you being your old self again.'

Fran's betrayal had left a mark that would never go away. It had killed something inside him. But for Ella and Holly's sake, he'd had to pull himself together. It occurred to him now just how much he'd put these three women through in the last year or so, but they'd stood beside him through it all. He glanced out of the window. He was lucky.

'I know it's been a bit of a long haul.' He grimaced. 'I'm sorry if I—'

'No apologies necessary,' his mother cut in. 'Just tell me you're over the worst of it.'

He nodded. 'I'm through with looking back and trying to work out where it went wrong. I'm not sure I'll ever understand why Fran did what she did, but it's time to look towards the future. From here on it's onwards and upwards.'

'And does a particular pretty nanny have anything to do with that?' Delia asked archly.

'For God's sake, Dee, not everything is about sex and romance,' he muttered in disgust.

Dee didn't look convinced.

'She's a bit of a lost soul is all and I thought we might be able to…'

She cocked a wicked eyebrow again. 'To?'

He refused to rise to the bait. 'To make her feel at home here. To take her under our wing and…and make her feel better about herself.'

'I think that's a lovely plan,' his mother said.

Cade shrugged and then glared at his sister. 'One thing's for sure, Nicola certainly doesn't think she's pretty, and she thinks she's fat.'

Verity sighed. 'Don't we all.'

Harry snorted. 'And some of us are a bit on the heavy side, but I know my worth.'

Dee had gone to the window. 'She is pretty, but in a quieter way than Fran's flashiness.'

He didn't like the way she spoke about Nicola and Fran in the same sentence. It seemed wrong somehow. He didn't say anything, though. He could just imagine what Dee would make of it if he did.

'A haircut,' she said, suddenly swinging back to face them. 'Something that would make the most of her eyes. Mum?'

Verity hadn't trained as a hairdresser, but she had a knack for it. When she'd lived at Waminda Downs all the station women in a three hundred kilometre radius would come to get their hair done by her.

Dee touched her hair. 'I brought along a couple of bottles of permanent colour and a highlighting kit. I was hoping you'd do my hair for me while we were here, but we can use it on Nicola instead.'

He glanced from one to the other. They wanted to change her hair colour? There was nothing wrong with her hair.

Verity joined Dee at the window. 'I believe I know the exact style that would suit her.'

'Those clothes,' Dee sighed.

'Far too baggy,' her mother agreed.

Harry winked at him. 'Sounds like our Nic's in good hands.'

She wasn't his anything. He wanted that crystal-clear, but...

'I don't want you bullying her into something she doesn't want.'

His mother swung around. 'Of course not, darling. Harry, can you look after the children for a couple of hours this afternoon? Dee and I will help with dinner in return.'

'No probs at all.'

'And I don't want you wrecking her.' He thrust his jaw out. 'She's not a Barbie doll. Don't go making her look all plastic and…and fake.'

Like Fran. The words hung in the air.

The three women exchanged glances but didn't say anything.

'And…and don't make her feel like a charity case either.' She'd hate that and he didn't want to do anything that would make her feel uncomfortable. He hadn't broken her confidence about her two-timing fiancé and back-stabbing girlfriend, but he had verbalised his opinion of her mother and he was pretty sure she wouldn't have appreciated that. He shifted his weight from his heels to the balls of his feet. Now that he had his mother and Dee on board, conversely he wanted to protect Nicola from their ministrations and meddling.

Nicola didn't need doing over or dollying up. As far as he was concerned, she was perfect the way she was. She was brilliant with his kids. She made them laugh but, more importantly, she made them feel secure.

And she kissed like an angel. Like a bad, *bad* angel, and just the memory of their kiss had his blood heating up.

'Darling,' his mother said, 'do give us more credit than that.'

His mother was tact personified. And, despite how much she enjoyed teasing her older brother, so was Dee. They were kind, generous women. They wouldn't do anything to make Nicola feel bad about herself.

He shoved his hands into his pockets. 'Sorry. I didn't mean to suggest… It's just she's been so good for Ella and Holly. I owe her for that.'

His mother nodded her understanding. Dee bit her lip. Harry set her knife down and threw him a challenge. 'You know she still uses that blasted gym each afternoon when she puts the kiddies down for a nap.'

He stiffened. Then he set his shoulders. 'I'll think of something,' he promised. He'd find something else in the exercise line she'd enjoy more.

'In the meantime, we have this afternoon taken care of,' Dee said, rubbing her hands together. 'What fun!'

He glanced around at the three women and a grin full of reluctant admiration tugged at his lips. 'I should've known I could count on you guys.'

CHAPTER FIVE

AT LUNCH, remembering Cade's words from the previous evening, Nicola made an effort to be friendlier. Poised, self-sufficient and self-possessed was the image she wanted to portray, not stiff, standoffish and unapproachable.

'Mum,' Dee said towards the end of the meal, 'I was hoping you'd give me a haircut this afternoon for old time's sake, and I'll set your hair for you.'

'A girls' afternoon, darling? Ooh, what fun.'

Unbidden, pain pierced Nicola's chest, so sharp it almost made her double over. She swallowed back a gasp and lifted Holly out of her high chair to cuddle the child on her lap. The pain shifted and settled in her side like a stitch. She and Diane once had regular girls' nights. They'd slather on face masks and paint each other's nails. Sometimes they'd colour each other's hair. They'd play their music too loud and share their dreams and plans for the future.

They hadn't had one of those sessions in over six months and it was only now Nicola realised how much she'd missed them. She closed her eyes. Diane was still a dear friend. Maybe when Nicola returned home…

Nausea swirled through her. Diane had listened to all of Nicola's dreams for the future with Brad. She'd known how much Nicola had yearned for a home and family.

She'd known all the hopes Nicola had pinned on Brad. And yet she'd still…

Nicola buried her face in Holly's hair. There wouldn't be any more girls' days. She didn't want to hear about Diane's plans for the future with Brad. She wasn't sure she could stand it.

She shook herself, bounced Holly up and down until the child giggled. She would get over this. She would! In the interests of saving an important friendship. First, though, she needed to put a protective barrier around her heart so she would be able to bear it.

She concentrated on her breathing. Eventually she wouldn't mind hearing Diane talk about Brad. One day she wouldn't think twice about seeing them together. One day the sense of betrayal that could still turn her days dark would drain away, leaving nothing more than a faint mark.

She just wished that day would hurry up and arrive.

'Nicola, darling?'

She snapped to and found Verity smiling at her. She made herself smile back. 'Yes?'

'My darling girl, I would just love to get my hands on your hair.'

She would? She touched a self-conscious hand to her hair. These days she just washed it and pulled it back into a ponytail. No fuss. No frills. She suddenly realised she hadn't been near a hairdresser in over four months.

'Mum is magic with hair,' Dee said.

There was no denying that Verity was a very stylish woman. So was Dee, just in a younger, more relaxed way.

'Take it out of its band for a moment,' Verity ordered.

She complied. Holly laughed and reached for it. Nicola distracted her with a napkin. Shredded paper was a whole lot less painful than pulled hair.

Verity studied Nicola for a long moment. 'Hmm…'

Nicola forced herself not to fidget under that gaze, but it occurred to her that she must seem such a frump to these two lovely women. She glanced at Harry for solidarity. Harry's hair and skin glowed with good health, but the housekeeper was totally unconcerned with her appearance.

Harry shook her head. 'There's no denying that Verity has a way with these things. But listen you two...' She pointed a finger at Verity and Dee. 'Our Nic isn't the fussy sort. She won't want to spend half an hour each morning blow-drying and straightening or curling or any of that other nonsense.'

Lord, no!

And then she realised that Harry had called her 'our Nic' and her eyes filled. For a moment she felt as if she belonged.

Verity gave a sudden nod. 'I would take two to three inches off so your hair sat just above your collarbone and I'd layer it to give it some body and movement.' She tapped a finger to her lips. 'And I'd put in a long side fringe. I think it would really make the most of your beautiful eyes.'

'Ooh, yes!' Dee practically danced in her seat. 'It'd be long enough to still pull back because, whatever anyone says, it's hellishly hot out here. Ooh, ooh!' She danced in her seat some more. Her enthusiasm made Nicola laugh. 'You could scrunch dry it with a bit of mousse and I bet it'd go deliciously curly.'

'Or, if you wanted, you could blow-dry it for a more formal look,' Verity said.

'And I think some light streaks through the crown.'

'That would be lovely.'

Dee grinned. 'What do you say, Nicola? A girls' afternoon would be such fun!'

'Count me out,' Harry said promptly.

'Besides,' Dee added, 'you deserve a treat. Since we

arrived you've taken the boys under your wing and I've hardly had to lift a finger. I can't tell you how much I've relished that little holiday.'

Nicola had enjoyed adding Simon and Jamie to her little group. It had been fun. They didn't need to treat her for doing her job. But…

A new haircut?

Another step towards a new her?

Ella suddenly pouted. 'You said we could make Christmas decorations this afternoon.' Simon and Jamie added their protests too.

Nicola pulled her hair back into its ponytail. No matter how alluring the vision of female friendship and a new image promised to be, she was here first and foremost as a nanny. 'So I did. And I never break a promise.'

Dee grinned at her niece. 'I'll make a deal with you, Ella. You get Nicola for the next hour and then…' She glanced at Harry.

'And then I'll drag the paddling pool out and you can all have a splash about,' the older woman announced.

A cheer went up from Ella, Simon and Jamie. Holly bounced, threw her shredded napkin in the air and sent Nicola a toothy grin. Nicola couldn't help but smile back with her whole heart.

Cade promptly pushed away from the opposite side of the table, a dazed expression on his face. She'd been aware of him the entire meal, but had done her very best to ignore him. The memory of last night's kiss was still too vivid… and far too compelling.

'Is that okay with you, Cade?' she asked as something midway between a scowl and a grimace shadowed his face. Maybe he'd wanted to do something with Ella and Holly this afternoon and had needed her assistance, or—

He shook his head. 'I should've left ten minutes ago

when haircuts and stuff came up. Secret women's business,' he muttered. 'I've got work to do.'

'Before you go, darling, we're all dressing up tonight and eating in the dining room.'

'Fine. Whatever.' He rolled his eyes in Nicola's direction. 'My mother loves to dress up for dinner. She'd have us do it every night if she could.'

'But while I'm here I content myself with once or twice a week,' Verity said with a sweet smile. 'You don't mind, do you, Nicola?'

She was to be included? She remembered the deal she'd made with Cade. 'Not at all.'

'I think it's nice for Ella and Holly. I don't want them growing up into barbarian tomboys. I hope they can out-ride, out-muster and out-run every male on the property, but I want them to have nice manners while they're doing it. And while it might be seven hundred kilometres to the nearest shopping mall, that doesn't mean they should be deprived of the delights of nice clothes and dressing up.'

'Don't worry, Mum—' Cade dropped a kiss to the top of Verity's head '—for as long as you're around, you have a more than willing disciple in my avaricious eldest daughter.'

As if she knew he was talking about her, Ella lifted her big blue eyes and said, 'I'm wearing my yellow dress tonight.'

'And you'll look like a princess,' he informed her.

Nicola bit her lip. What on earth was she going to wear?

Cade seized the last sandwich and headed for the back door. He turned as he pushed it open. 'But in return for such a generous display of male tolerance, I want to enlist everyone's help in putting up the Christmas lights tomorrow afternoon.'

'Of course, darling,' his mother said.

'Not getting me up a ladder,' Harry muttered.

'Do we have lots of lights, Daddy?' Ella asked, her face glowing with excitement.

'Trillions,' he assured her, his eyes suddenly twinkling as they met Nicola's for the briefest of moments. And then he was gone.

Nicola, Verity and Dee spent the afternoon primping and preening. Dee set Verity's hair in hot rollers. Verity coloured Dee's hair and while the timer was set for the colour to take, she cut Nicola's hair. Unlike at a hairdressing salon, there was no large mirror for Nicola to watch and marvel as the deed was done. Instead, she sat on a chair on the shady side of the veranda, a towel firmly clasped at her throat, while Verity snipped away.

She was aware of an enormous amount of hair falling to the ground. She swallowed as a particularly long strand caught on her arm. Oh, good Lord, how much was Verity cutting off? She'd be bald!

She was aware of a growing sense of lightness. She didn't know if she liked it or not.

'There, all done.' Verity moved in front of her, lifting Nicola's chin with one finger to survey her with a critical eye. 'Perfect! Now, don't look down to see how much is gone. It'll only make your stomach clench with nerves. It's lovely, trust me.'

Nicola didn't have much choice but to do exactly that. It was far too late to put the hair back. But she couldn't help glancing down at the hair that had collected around her all the same and, as Verity had predicted, her stomach clenched.

The older woman swept the hair off the edge of the veranda and into the garden below. 'It's wonderful for the roses,' she confided.

Nicola didn't bother telling her she was sweeping them into the agapanthus rather than the roses.

Verity and Dee wouldn't let her look in the mirror when they returned to Verity's suite of rooms with its enormous bathroom. Verity put highlights in her hair and Nicola's stomach clenched even tighter. What if they turned out brassy orange or some shade of ghastly? She wanted a new image, she hungered for a new image, but...

What if, after all this work, she still looked like an overweight frump? What if she couldn't change? What if she really was a failure and a doormat and—?

Her stomach swirled. Bile rose in her throat. To take her mind off her doubts, she painted Dee and Verity's nails. Dee chose hot pink. Verity chose scarlet. Nicola painted her own nails gold. It seemed...Christmassy. And she had a deal to keep.

They talked fashion. Nicola confessed to having packed only one nice dress and a pair of black trousers that, at a pinch, she could dress up.

Dee's laptop was promptly brought out and Nicola was introduced to the joys of online shopping. She ordered clothes she'd have never bought except for Dee and Verity's urgings, their pronouncements that this top or that skirt or dress would be perfect for her. They were both so stylish and the clothes were oh-so-pretty that Nicola gulped and decided to trust them. By the time they were finished she was several hundred dollars poorer.

'They'll be here within a week,' Dee said, rubbing her hands together.

Oh, good Lord, what had she done?

With a defiant toss of her head, she unclenched her hands and relaxed her shoulders. She didn't have a wedding to pay for any more and a girl was entitled to the occasional treat, right? Dee and Verity didn't look the least bit guilty and they'd spent as much money as she had. It wouldn't hurt her to emulate them a bit more.

Poised, confident, self-possessed. She repeated the litany silently to herself as her hair was rinsed and blow-dried.

Verity stepped back with a wide smile. 'Okay, darling, time for the grand unveiling.'

Nicola's stomach immediately cramped. She did her best to keep the voice in her head, the voice so like her mother's, which criticized and nagged and told her she'd never measure up, quiet as Verity and Dee led her to a mirror.

She lowered her eyes, dragged in a deep breath and then forced her gaze upwards.

Her jaw dropped.

She lifted a hand to touch her hair.

Her eyes filled with tears. 'You've made me look pretty,' she whispered.

'Darling.' Verity put an arm around her shoulders and squeezed, beaming at her in the mirror. 'You are beautiful. And you were before all of this.'

No, she hadn't been pretty before. But now…

She couldn't believe the transformation. Her chestnut hair was sleek and shiny, the lighter highlights bringing out the colour of her eyes and complementing her skin tone.

When she shook her head, her hair swished about her in a light and flirty perfumed cloud. 'You're a magician!'

'Nonsense, you were just hiding yourself behind all that hair, that's all. It's lovely to see your face.'

You'll never be the kind of woman to turn a man's head, Nicola Ann.

She lifted her chin. *I beg to differ, Mum.*

Would she turn Cade's head?

'In the same way,' Dee added, 'you hide that lovely figure of yours beneath clothes that are much too baggy.'

That snapped her to. 'Lovely figure?' It took a concerted effort not to snort. *Dignified. Friendly and dignified.* 'I am way too curvy.' Fat. 'I need to lose at least ten kilos.'

'Nonsense!' Verity said crisply. 'You're perfect. You have gorgeous curves. I miss my curves.' She ran her hands down her sides from bust to hip. 'I seem to be shrinking as I get older.

'But you look lovely,' Nicola blurted out.

'The secret is good foundation garments.' Verity's eyes twinkled and Nicola couldn't help but laugh. 'Besides, I firmly believe that men who only like stick insects have an innate hatred of women. I, for one, have never been the slightest bit interested in pleasing them. My darling Scott, Cade and Dee's father, liked a full womanly figure. He was a big admirer of Marilyn Monroe and Jane Russell. He'd have hated all of this obsession with being skinny.' Her eyes twinkled again. 'And I'm pleased to say his son takes after him.'

Nicola blinked. Heavens, Verity didn't think there was anything going on between her and Cade, did she? She opened her mouth to disabuse her of any such notion, but Verity swung her back to the mirror. 'Dee has a dress that would look perfect on you. It'd nip you in at the waist and give you the perfect hourglass outline.'

'Ooh, yes, the cherry-red. It'd look fabulous with your hair too. You must wear it tonight. Such a transformation deserves a proper celebration.'

Nicola had to blink back tears as she suddenly realised female solidarity wasn't dead. It was alive and thriving in the world. She turned from the mirror to face the two women. 'Thank you,' she said simply with a smile from the heart.

When Nicola walked into the dining room that evening, Cade's eyes widened. The world tilted to one side and he had to brace his legs to keep his balance. The woman had killer curves!

Femme fatale. The words thumped through him, punching him in the solar plexus and emptying his lungs of air. Femme fatale had been the furthest thought from his head when she'd climbed out of the plane earlier in the month, but now…

He shook himself. He had to stop from lingering on the way her dress hugged her body. He had to get his mind off those curves—well and truly off them or he'd embarrass himself.

Farm business. Think farm business! Calving, branding, mustering…riding in all the wildness of Waminda Downs with nothing but scrub and rock and the line of the hills in the distance…the curvaceous line of those hills and—

He shook his head in an attempt to snap out of the fog he'd descended into. To one side his mother and sister beamed at him and the tie he'd donned for dinner tightened around his throat. Colour flooded Nicola's cheeks and her gaze darted away as if she was embarrassed or afraid of what he might say. She fussed about, placing Holly in her high chair and helping Ella into her seat. A strange tenderness filled him then, helping him to chain his rampant desires back under control. 'Nicola?'

She glanced up and he took his time surveying her new hairstyle. His mother and Dee hadn't ruined her, and they hadn't turned her into a plastic version of herself. They'd somehow managed to reveal the beautiful woman who had been posing as an ordinary girl for far too long.

She stole his breath.

'You look beautiful.'

She smiled then—that smile that could bowl a man over. 'Thank you.'

She bowled him over the next morning too—even though she'd returned to her usual attire of long cotton shorts and a baggy T-shirt as she and the children painted Santa pictures.

But he knew the curves that hid beneath her clothes now. He could picture them in his mind. And if she let him kiss her again—

He snapped that thought off and went to break in a brand new colt—a far more constructive outlet for his energy. He wasn't kissing Nicola again. She might kiss like a temptress. She might look like a temptress. But neither one of them needed the complication.

If he could just get the thought out of his head.

That thought was still there that afternoon, though, when he assembled everyone to help unwind and test the various strings of fairy lights. Her curves were hidden. Her new hairstyle was too because, at some stage during the day, she'd succumbed to the heat and had pulled it up onto the top of her head. But the most beguiling wisps found their way out of the knot to curl about her neck and ears.

Pretty ears.

And a neck a man would love to explore with long, slow kisses and—

Get a grip, damn it, man!

He tried not to look at her too much when he was on

the ladder and she handed him up row upon row of fairy lights to attach to the frame of the homestead.

He kept his eyes averted from her that evening after dinner too when it was time for the grand unveiling. When, at the flick of a switch, the house lit up into a sparkling fairyland.

Fairy lights wound around veranda posts and along the railings. A series of fake icicles hung from the veranda ceiling. Each door and window frame had its own set of lights. So did the shrubs and trees in the garden. Everything winked and twinkled and sparkled. Beside Jamie and Simon, Ella jumped up and down. From her spot in Nicola's arms, Holly's eyes went wide and her mouth formed a perfect O. His heart expanded and his shoulders loosened. This—all of it—was for Ella and Holly. He wasn't going to let anything, not even hormones, get in the way of that.

His smile slipped when he heard Dee murmur to their mother, 'It's a bit over the top, don't you think? I mean, an entire generator to power fairy lights?'

'Oh, I don't know,' Nicola chimed in. 'The kids just love it and it really does look pretty. Ella, Jamie and Simon are gobsmacked and will probably talk about this for years to come.'

'You're probably right,' Dee laughed. 'On his own head be it, though, because I believe he's just started a new family tradition.'

'If so, it's a lovely one,' Verity said. 'Nicola is right. It looks magical.'

'What do you think, kids?' Nicola asked. 'Should there be Christmas lights like this every year at Waminda Downs?'

A resounding cheer went up from all the children, and Cade knew then that Nicola would do everything in her power to keep her side of the bargain—to make this Christmas the best one yet. He meant to keep his word too, but… What excuse could he come up with tomorrow to keep her away from that darn treadmill? He'd run out of fairy lights.

He churned the problem over and slowly a grin spread through him. She might have an angel's own smile but, beneath it, every now and again he'd caught glimpses of a red-hot anger. He didn't condemn her for it. He understood it.

And he knew exactly where to channel it.

'Not a chance, lady.'

The voice whipped out from the shade of the corridor as Nicola reached for the door handle of the home gym. She jumped, spun and then pressed her back to the wall and clutched her chest. 'Cade!'

She tried to catch her breath. Not always easy around Cade and his watchful blue eyes. 'Do you make a habit of sneaking up on a body like that?'

Those eyes twinkled. 'Well, it's got to be said—nice body.' His glance was almost a caress. Her legs went soft and rubbery. 'But I didn't sneak up. I've been waiting here for you.'

She moistened her lips. 'Why?'

'Because a little bird told me that most afternoons when you put the children down for a nap, you head on straight down here.'

'Do you mind?' Maybe he'd had second thoughts about letting her use his ex-wife's equipment. Maybe he wanted to keep the ghosts from his past quiet. Maybe he wanted to simply keep that door closed for good.

'I don't mind at all.'

She scratched her head. 'Did you want me to help put

up more Christmas lights or something?' She brightened at that thought. Climbing ladders would be far more preferable to a stint on a rowing machine.

He leaned against the wall opposite, arms folded, and somehow it only emphasized the breadth of his shoulders. 'Be honest. Do you enjoy using the gym?'

'Enjoy?' She snorted before she could successfully remind herself that *snorting is for pigs, Nicola Ann.* 'Look, I thought we'd established that me and exercise were never going to enjoy each other's company.'

'You enjoy riding.'

'That's not exercise. Well,' she amended, 'it probably is for Scarlett, but not for me. It's fun.'

'It tones and strengthens thigh and calf muscles and it improves balance. Of course it's exercise.'

She tapped the gym door. 'I may not like it, but this is doing me good. I can run for ten straight minutes at six point five kilometres per hour on the treadmill now. I could barely manage three minutes when I started.'

'And the rowing machine?'

Her lip curled. She hated the rowing machine. Oh, who was she trying to kid? She hated that entire gym, but no pain…

'I thought you might like to give something else a try.'

'Like?'

His mouth curled up. 'Don't trust me, huh? I'm the guy that got you hooked on riding, remember?'

He was also the guy who'd kissed her with a thoroughness that still had her waking up in the middle of the night. A whole host of images assaulted her—a whole variety of ways to get some additional exercise.

She backed up a step, pointed down the corridor behind her. 'I'm nearby if one of the children wakes up.'

'I asked Dee to keep an ear out for them over the next

hour.' He frowned suddenly. 'I don't want you becoming Dee's drudge. Those boys are a handful.'

She snorted again. And then winced. She really had to get better at curbing that habit. 'They're great fun and I am in no danger of becoming a drudge. Lord, your mother, sister and housekeeper all help so much with the children that some days I feel I'm hardly pulling my weight.'

He snorted in the exact same fashion. She couldn't help noticing that he didn't sound like a pig. 'Not pulling your weight? You keep everything running like clockwork. It'd all be a shambles if you weren't here.' He sobered. 'It's been a long time since I've seen Ella and Holly so care-free and excited. I'm glad you came to stay.'

At his words, her chin lifted and her shoulders went back. She had to blink hard a couple of times. 'I'm glad I came to stay too.'

'Does that mean you're willing to risk life and limb to try out a new form of exercise?'

She gave in. The siren call of the rowing machine just wasn't loud enough. It couldn't compete with Cade's grin... or her own curiosity.

Without another word, she nodded and followed him.

A few moments later they stood in a cleared space in the barn. When Cade held out a pair of boxing gloves to her, she frowned, blinked and then put her hands behind her back. 'No way.'

'These are boxing gloves, Nicola,' he started patiently.

'I know what they are. And I repeat, no way.'

He stared at her with pursed lips.

'I've seen *Rocky*.' She hitched up her chin. 'I saw what happened to some of those guys in the ring, and they were fit! There's no way on God's green I'm going to let you hit me, regardless of what tripe you give me about how soft those gloves are. So I repeat, no way.'

He grinned so suddenly the impact was nearly physical. She planted her feet in an effort to counter it.

'I won't be hitting you, Nicola. You'll be hitting me.' He smirked. 'Or at least trying to.'

Her eyes narrowed at that. She hauled her hands from behind her back and took the gloves. He smirked again, insufferably superior, as she pulled them on. 'It's just possible that I may grow to enjoy this as much as riding Scarlett,' she warned him.

'I'm counting on it,' he said, sliding his hands into thick square mitts that had even more padding than her gloves.

'Ah, so you won't be wholly unprotected, then?'

'Nope, which is just as well when the woman I'm about to face has such a martial light in her eye.'

That made her laugh. When he squared up to her and ordered her to show him what she had, though, she found it curiously difficult to do as he asked.

He lowered his protective mitts. 'What's wrong?'

'It just seems wrong to hit you. Terribly impolite and… well, violent.'

'Pretend I'm that rowing machine.' He squared up again. 'Hit me in the middle of my left mitt.'

She did.

He lowered his hands and glared. 'Put some oomph into it!'

'I don't want to hurt you.'

'Honey, that'll be the day.'

That patronising 'honey' set her teeth on edge.

'Boxing, when it's done right, is an excellent cardio-vascular workout. And it's a good way of getting rid of pent-up tension.'

'I don't have any pent-up tension,' she managed between gritted teeth.

'Really?' His eyes narrowed. 'What did your mother

say when you told her you were coming out here for Christmas?'

Run away, Nicola Ann, with your tail between your legs, but the mess will still be here when you come back.

She let fly with a punch that thwacked satisfyingly into Cade's left mitt.

He raised an eyebrow. 'And I've been wanting to know…'

'Yes?' she ground out.

'If you've come up with a strategy for the cruel remarks that'll be headed your way at the wedding?'

Thwack! Thwack! 'What comments?'

He assumed a mocking high-pitched voice. 'You're putting on a very brave face, dear, but I can imagine how you're really feeling.'

Thwack! Thwack! Thwack!

'Put some feeling into it,' he ordered. 'Put your whole body behind it.'

Her whole body, huh?

He lifted his chin and assumed that voice again. 'This wedding must be a nightmare for you, I know, but even you have to admit that the bride is glowing. They look so happy together, don't you think?'

Thwack!

'I bet you fifty bucks that Diane throws the bouquet to you.'

She paled at that one. Thwack!

'Don't worry,' he simpered in that high-pitched voice again, 'I expect Brad will two-time her too.'

'Stop it!' she croaked. 'Stop saying such cruel things.'

'It's what people will say.' He lowered his mitts.

'And you think I'm so pathetic that I won't be able to cope with it or defend myself?'

'I think you ought to be prepared, that's all.' His eyes

suddenly flashed and his hands came back up. 'But while we're on the subject, I think your ex is a two-timing, cheating scumbag and your best friend a back-stabbing witch!'

Nicola wasn't even aware that she'd thrown the punch until it connected with Cade's jaw and sent him sprawling to the ground.

CHAPTER SIX

NICOLA stared at Cade, sprawled at her feet and with a little cry she shook off her boxing gloves and knelt in the dirt beside him, wrung her hands before touching his face. 'Oh, my God! Did I hurt you? Cade?'

Those blue eyes, normally so piercing, stared up at her, slightly dazed.

She'd meant to throw that punch, but she'd thought... Well, she'd thought he'd block it!

She swallowed. Who'd have thought she had such lightning reflexes? That punch had been fast...and...um...hard. *Put your whole body behind it.* Oh, she'd done that.

Nausea swirled through her. She'd thought he'd block her punch, but that didn't change the fact that she'd lashed out in anger.

'Cade?'

He didn't speak. Guilt, regret and remorse pounded through her and, before she could think better of it, she pressed her lips to his in an effort to take away the pain, to communicate her remorse and apologise.

He smelled of dust and sweat and horses, which should have turned her off, only it didn't. His lips were an intriguing combination of firmness and softness and they parted slightly as if he meant to deepen the kiss. Then he froze and his hands came up, gripped her arms and pushed her back as he sat up. 'What do you think you're doing? Kissing me better?'

His scorn almost scorched the flesh from her bones. 'I…'

'I'm not a child, Nicola.'

It was too much. His anger… Her guilt and remorse. That final punch had torn the lid off the emotions she'd bottled up for the last three months. She tugged herself out of his grip and stumbled blindly across to a wooden crate and collapsed on top of it, her back to Cade as she tried to tamp down on the pain and numbing sense of loss that cut deep inside her, but now that it was freed it seemed to grow in both volume and intensity.

She'd punched Cade in anger!

And then she'd kissed him. What on earth had she been thinking? The expression on his face…

I think your ex is a two-timing cheating scumbag and your best friend is a back-stabbing witch.

The words ripped off the poorly formed scab she'd tried to place over her heart and, try as she might, she couldn't control the sudden shaking of her shoulders or the silent sobs that clawed free from her chest or the tears that scorched her cheeks as her body tried to find a way to lance the poison that tangled her in knotted torment. Dropping her head to her hands, she could do nothing but give into it.

Somewhere, in a dim place of her consciousness, she was aware of embarrassment and her mother's scornful voice. *Nicola Ann, pull yourself together! You're not a child any more. What a display! You're making a spectacle of yourself.* But none of it had any effect. It didn't stop the shaking and the sobs. It didn't help the pain.

An arm went about her. Her face was pressed against the thick scratchy cotton of a work shirt encasing a warm chest that smelt of dirt and sweat and horse. A hand rubbed her back and a rich voice murmured words that didn't make sense except for their rhythm and depth, and very slowly the pressure in her chest abated. The shaking of her shoulders slowed. The sobs eased and the tears dried.

She remained where she was, drawing as much comfort and strength as she could until the internal voices grew too loud to ignore and she finally drew back, scrubbing her hands across her face in an effort to erase the traces of her tears. She didn't dare glance at Cade. Instinct told her his expression would score her too-vulnerable-at-the-moment heart, and she refused to cry again today. She'd need more deep breaths before she could face that.

'I went too far.' His voice broke the afternoon silence. 'The thing is...' he drew in a shaky breath '...I wanted to insult Brad and Diane. I don't know them and I have no right to say anything, but I am so dirty with them for what they've done to you. Nobody deserves what they did. Especially not someone like you, Nicola.'

She had to look at him and he gave her a rueful half smile and it didn't make her flinch or cringe. It helped her lift her chin and push her shoulders back a fraction.

'I think,' he continued, 'you would be a great friend to have. And I think you were probably a lovely fiancé, and you sure as hell didn't deserve what Brad and Diane did.'

His words put strength back into her spine. 'No more than you deserved what Fran dished out to you.' She moistened her lips and glanced down at her hands. 'I'm sorry I hit you. Did I hurt you?'

He shook his head. 'I wasn't expecting it, that's all. But I deserved it. I was deliberately trying to rile you. You thought I was going to block it.'

'I wasn't thinking at all, that's the problem. I just lashed out.'

They were both silent for a moment. She moistened her lips again. 'Why were you trying to make me angry?'

One of his shoulders lifted. 'I sensed you might need to vent some of your anger. I remember how angry I was in the months after Fran left and…' He shrugged again. 'I thought boxing would be more constructive than a treadmill.' He eyed her for a moment. 'It seems to me you've been bottling a lot of stuff up. It's not healthy.'

'I didn't mean to. I…' She rested her elbows on her knees and dragged her hands back through her hair. 'It's just that my two closest confidants were Diane and Brad, and they weren't exactly available. And there was no way I was going to confide in my mother.'

'What about your other friends?'

'I didn't want to cause a big rift among our set. I didn't want people feeling they had to take sides.' She straightened. 'And the honest truth is, I don't want to lose Diane and Brad as friends. I really don't.'

Behind the blue of his eyes she could see his mind race, but he said nothing.

'Diane and I go all the way back to our first day of school. Her family have been there for me all my life. They were a haven for me when my father died, and whenever my mother became too much, and…and just everything! I can't turn my back on all that history just because she fell in love with Brad.'

'That doesn't mean you can't acknowledge your pain or your anger. If she values your friendship as much as you do, then it will survive that.'

'And if she doesn't?' She spoke her real fear out loud for the first time.

Cade didn't say anything, but she could read the answer in his eyes—if their friendship couldn't survive her honesty, then it wasn't worth saving.

She leapt up and started to pace. Gripping her hands together, she swung back to Cade. 'You know, I could've dealt with all of this so much better if they'd just been honest with me from the get-go. Instead, they kept meeting up behind my back for months before Diane eventually confessed what had happened. Brad didn't even have the courage to show his face that evening.' She flung an arm out and then started to pace again. 'I know they didn't want to hurt me, I truly believe that, but to let it all go on for so long without telling me…'

She folded her arms and paced harder, faster. 'That made me angry. That made me feel like a fool, like an idiot they didn't have any respect for. I…' She gripped her upper arms. 'I kept wondering what on earth I'd done wrong, how had I managed to so spectacularly alienate them. Had I neglected them? Had I not picked up on key signals? I mean, Diane told me that I had always been too needy and that she felt pressured, but…' She swallowed and lifted her chin. 'I didn't do anything wrong, did I?'

Cade shot to his feet. 'Hell, no!' He cupped her face in his hands. 'You didn't do one damn thing wrong.'

His eyes blazed with a ferocity, an intensity that did her soul and her confidence no end of good. 'Oh, hell, Cade.'

His eyes narrowed. 'What?'

'I said I'd be her bridesmaid,' she whispered.

Just for a moment his entire face went slack in shock. Very gently she disengaged herself from his hands. It seemed wiser not to get too close. Or needy. Because there had been a thread of truth in Diane's accusation, and Nicola had no intention of transferring her neediness to Cade.

'And I'm starting to think that maybe that was a crazy thing to agree to.'

He rolled his eyes. 'You think?'

She collapsed back down to the crate, her shoulders sagging. 'The thing is, we always said we'd be each other's bridesmaids—best friends forever and all that jazz, but...' She glanced across at Cade as he sat back down beside her. 'But now I don't think I can do it.' She swallowed. 'I don't want to do it.'

'Why did you say you would?'

'Because I do wish Diane and Brad well. I know I sound contradictory and conflicted, and that I'm angry and hurt.' She stared at her hands. 'But I really do hope they'll be happy. I agreed to be her bridesmaid because I wanted to prove that we could still be friends. And I thought that a show of solidarity like that would help prevent a falling-out among all our other friends.'

'And what's changed?'

She thought long and hard about that. 'I still want them to be happy, but it doesn't seem fair that I should be the one to tie myself into knots to make that happen. Their happiness is up to them, not me.'

She blinked and a weight lifted from her as she said the words—a load of guilt and pressure she hadn't even been aware that she carried.

'Anything else?'

'I can't make our friendship go back to the way it was before all this happened. No matter what I do. No matter how much I want it to.'

She pressed a hand to her chest to ease the sudden burning there, drew in a deep breath and blinked hard. When she was sure her voice was steady, she said, 'Those are the cold, hard facts, I'm afraid, and they need to be faced.' She couldn't hide from the truth any longer.

He reached out and squeezed her hand. 'I'm sorry, Nicola.'

'Me too.'

They sat like that for a moment. The shade that settled throughout the barn soothed her, as did the whickering of the horses in the nearby stable and the stamping of their feet. It reminded her that she had a ride to look forward to in the morning. A ride she could look forward to for every single day that she remained at Waminda. She might be down, but she wasn't out.

'What are you going to do?' Cade eventually asked.

'I have to let Diane know—tell her as soon as I can that I can't be her bridesmaid so she can make other arrangements.' And she couldn't do it by email from her laptop. She would have to speak to her friend. If not face to face, then at least ear to ear. 'Do you mind if I use the satellite phone this evening?'

'You're welcome to use it whenever you want.'

'Thank you.' She rose. 'I…um…I really ought to see to Ella and Holly now. But…Cade, thank you. All of this helped and I want you to know that I appreciate it.'

'You're welcome.'

She started to walk away and then stopped and turned back. 'About that kiss…'

He leaned back on his crate and a slow smile hitched up one side of his mouth. 'I lied. It sure as heck made me feel a whole lot better.' His body angled towards her in open invitation. Her eyes widened. Her mouth went dry. 'Any time you want to repeat it, you can bet that I'll be willing and able.'

She picked up the boxing gloves and hurled them at him. His laughter followed her all the way outside. She found herself grinning as she strode towards the house.

Later that evening, Cade waited for Nicola to emerge from his study. The rest of the family had decided on an early night and the house was quiet and still. Nicola pulled up short when she saw him.

He raked his gaze across her face and his heart clenched. She looked pale and worn out. 'How did it go?'

He spoke softly, using the same tone he used when handling a spirited horse that had been spooked. Nicola's shattered confidence, her self-belief, didn't need another battering, and he'd had no intention of retiring before finding out how her phone call with Diane had gone.

Her face crumpled and he held his arms open. She walked into them and he held her close—felt every breath she took as she fought for composure. He couldn't believe how right it felt to have her there.

Not that he had any intention of getting used to it—he was being a friend, that was all—but as the scent of strawberry jam drifted around him, all he could remember was the warmth of her lips as they'd touched his this afternoon, and the rush of sweetness that had stolen through him.

Long before he was ready to let her go she stepped back, forcing him to drop his arms. 'You didn't have to wait up for me.'

'Thought you could use a friend.' He held up two beers. 'And I thought you could use one of these.'

She eyed the beer hungrily. 'Bad for the diet,' she murmured.

'To hell with the diet.' He grabbed her hand and hauled her through the nearest set of French windows and outside into the almost cool of the night. Not that it was ever properly cool out here in December.

'Sit.' He pointed to the front step and handed her a beer. 'Drink and enjoy.'

A laugh gurgled out of her. 'Aye, aye, Captain.'

He planted himself on the step beside her. They cracked

their beers open at exactly the same moment, touched them in a silent toast and then drank deeply.

With a sigh, Nicola stretched her legs out and stared up at the night sky, her face pensive. He dragged his gaze from her lips and took another pull on his beer. 'So it was a bit rough, huh?'

'She cried. She accused me of wanting to ruin her big day. Once she got over the initial shock she apologised, said she understood, but…'

His beer halted halfway to his mouth. 'But?'

She glanced at him. 'It just cemented that our friendship will never be the same again.'

Her sadness tugged at the sore spaces inside him. 'Maybe not, but it doesn't mean you can't still be good friends, that you can't enjoy each other's company. It'll just be different. And I promise it will get easier with time.'

She stared at her beer. 'I guess you're right.'

From the light that spilled from the house and the light from the stars, he could see her face clearly. The plump full promise of her lips made things inside him clench up. The question that had been burning through him since she'd landed her punch this afternoon burst free from suddenly dry lips. 'What about Brad?'

She turned to him. 'What about him? I didn't speak to him, if that's what you mean.'

But had she wanted to? Had she hoped Brad might answer the phone? Did she secretly yearn that more than her friendship with Diane could be salvaged? Did she want Brad back?

Bile rose in his throat. 'Do you still love him?'

'I…I still care for him as a friend. He was a big part of my life for two years.'

'But if he came to you now and said he'd made a mistake and wanted to get back together with you, would you rush back into his arms?'

'I used to think that's what I wanted.'

'But?'

She turned those glorious eyes of hers on him and everything inside him tightened up. She opened her mouth. She closed it again. And then she blinked as if she'd just realised something stupendous. 'Heavens! It seems the sad fact of the matter is…' she tilted her beer at him in a kind of salute '…is that I miss Diane more than I miss Brad.'

He stared at her.

She stared back.

Then she snorted.

He couldn't help it. Suddenly his shoulders started to shake, and then they were both flat on their backs on the veranda laughing so hard he thought they'd wake the dead, or at the very least the rest of his family—and he knew exactly what his mother and Dee would make of this—but not even that thought could get his mirth back under control. Every time he thought he had it, she'd snigger, or he would, and they'd be off again.

Somewhere along the way her hand had found its way into his, but he didn't know if she had initiated the contact or if he had.

He remembered the way her lips had felt on his this afternoon. His lips ached. His groin ached. Damn it, even his skin ached.

Grinning, Nicola pushed up into a sitting position. All of the reserved hardness that she'd stepped off the plane with gone. He remained where he was, his grip around her hand tightening. He wanted a repeat performance of this afternoon, craved her kiss, her touch. All he'd have to do was tug and she'd fall sprawled across his chest.

He craved to taste the laughter on her lips. He hungered

to sample her sweetness once more. He ached to have the full sweet temptation of her pressed up against him.

She glanced down at him and slowly the sparkle left her eyes, the generous smile faltered and disappeared. She pulled her hand free.

Disappointment flushed through him, and something darker and more insistent. He pushed up into a sitting position too. 'Scared?' he taunted, though he knew that was hardly fair.

She tilted her head back and took another swig of her beer. 'How long is it since you've been with a woman?'

The question took him off guard. He scowled. 'That's none of your damn business.'

'And yet you're inviting me to share your bed and your body.'

'And you're going to refuse and turn me down.' He could read her as well as it seemed she could read him.

'Sleeping with me won't prove you're over Fran.'

He blinked, stiffened. What the hell…?

Her eyes flashed. 'How about you answer your own question? If Fran turned up here tomorrow and wanted to give your marriage another try, what would you do?'

He reared back as if she'd struck him. 'That's not going to happen.'

'That's the exact same answer I could've given you about Brad.'

She rose. His heart pounded. He didn't speak. Couldn't. The desire that had flooded him two seconds ago drained away.

Fran was Ella and Holly's mother. He owed them. If Fran came back, he'd owe it to his two daughters to give the marriage another shot.

But…

His hands clenched.

'Thanks for the beer, Cade. Goodnight.'

Nicola left and he couldn't even manage to croak a goodnight after her.

If Fran came back...

He slashed a hand through the air. Fran was never coming back and he could taste the bitterness of that knowledge on his tongue. Ella and Holly no longer had a mother. He'd failed them.

His hand clenched around his beer. He scowled into the night. He wouldn't fail them again, though.

He downed the rest of his beer and considered his intriguing nanny's strategic retreat. She wasn't immune to him. He'd felt it in her kiss. In both kisses they'd shared so far. He felt it in her gaze when she didn't think he was paying her any heed. It arced between them, unspoken, whenever their eyes locked.

He shook his head. Nicola was wrong. Things didn't have to get complicated between them. Some uncomplicated *adult* Christmas fun could be exactly what the doctor ordered. It'd provide them—him—with a much-needed release, and he'd make damn sure that it restored her confidence. Win-win.

He nodded once, hard. He had every intention of bringing Nicola around to his way of thinking as soon as he could. First, though, he'd give her some space.

Cade didn't offer to give her a boxing lesson the next afternoon. Not that Nicola expected him to. She went back to the treadmill, and to glaring at the rowing machine... and to lecturing herself.

She had to remain strong.

Sleeping with Cade... A betraying thrill shot through her. She increased the speed of the treadmill and gritted her teeth. Sleeping with Cade would undo all she'd accomplished so far. It would make a mockery of her growing sense of self-sufficiency and the realisation that she was responsible for her own happiness.

She loved her friends, she needed them, but she could rely on herself too. If she made love with Cade she would be in danger of transferring all her misplaced need to him instead of learning to stand on her own two feet first.

Developing her self-reliance and inner strength was more important than physical release and temporary pleasure.

She gritted her teeth and increased the speed of the treadmill yet again.

Nicola's eyes narrowed a couple of nights later as she watched Cade give Ella yet another sweet. She caught his eye and shook her head, but he ignored her.

They hadn't long finished a noisy game of charades and the children were buzzing and jumping, primarily due to Cade's influence. It was beyond time that they started to quieten down and get ready for bed.

He gave Ella yet another sweet. Nicola refused to let her gaze stray to the bowl of chocolate sultanas. 'You'll make her sick,' she chided.

'Nonsense! Just because you won't relax and allow yourself a few chocolate sultanas doesn't mean the rest of us have to abstain.'

'Cade!' his mother chided.

Nicola shifted on her chair. How on earth did he know about her battle with those darn sultanas?

With a giggle, Ella climbed up onto her father's lap and requested, and was given, another sweet. She grinned in triumph at Nicola.

Little monkey! But Nicola could hardly remonstrate

with her. Besides, it wasn't the child's fault but Cade's. 'Bedtime soon,' she said instead.

'Nooooo,' Ella wailed. 'Daddy, Daddy, can't we stay up a bit longer?'

She was about to tell Ella that it was already an hour after her bedtime, but Cade merely said, 'Sure, sweetheart. It's Christmastime, of course you can stay up.'

He broke into a rowdy Christmas carol. Ella promptly slid off his lap to dance with Jamie and Simon. Holly, who had started to fall asleep in Cade's other arm, promptly woke up and squealed in excitement and demanded to join in…with two sweets—one for each hand.

Nicola gritted her teeth and subsided into her chair. All of the children would be grumpy and out of sorts tomorrow. When Cade handed out more sweets and chocolates she had to get up and leave the room.

One savage tug had the refrigerator door swinging open. She seized a jug of iced water and helped herself to a glass to cool off. Cade was trying to make this Christmas memorable for his children. He wasn't flouting bedtime and mealtimes just to annoy her.

She scowled and slouched against the counter. Not that he'd be the one to deal with the fallout. He'd leave that to the hired help.

She snorted. Get over yourself, Nicola Ann. She used her mother's moniker for her. You're just grumpy because Cade has avoided you ever since that beer on the front steps.

When what you want him to do is pursue you harder.

She snapped upright. No, she didn't!

'I thought I'd find you sulking in here.'

Cade.

She turned. 'What? Have you had enough of revving the kids up for one night and now you're heading off to bed and leaving Dee, your mother and I to deal with four hyperactive children?'

'Loosen up, Nicola, and give the kids a break. It's Christmas. They're allowed to have some fun and to enjoy the season.'

'Within limits,' she shot back. 'Kids thrive on routine. Too many late nights and too many sweets will—'

'You mean that *you* thrive on routine, that *you* thrive on the safe option.'

That was when she knew they were no longer talking about the children.

'Seems to me you don't have any room in this makeover plan of yours for any spontaneity whatsoever. You stick to the plan and refuse to deviate.'

Cade was talking about what had almost happened between them and would be happening between them right now if she'd said yes instead of no the other night.

'Funny.' Her voice had gone tight and she had to swallow. 'I never picked you for a sore loser.'

The laugh he gave was harsh. 'This is about you, not me. It's about you refusing to let go and loosen up.'

She leaned forward and poked him in the chest. 'No, this is about you equating my loosening up, as you call it, with whether I'll sleep with you or not.'

'I'm not that pathetic.'

'Really?' She folded her arms. 'That night you told me you thought I needed a friend—that's the role you were playing—but you didn't really mean it, did you?' Her voice wobbled and she winced at the vulnerability that stretched through it. 'A real friend wants what's best for their friends. They don't want to see them do something that will hurt them.'

His hands clenched, his muscles stiffened and all she could think of was the way he'd held her when she'd cried, the concern in his eyes when she'd emerged from his study after her phone call to Diane.

'Look at me, Cade,' she insisted. 'I'm a mess! You're letting your frustration and your hormones override your judgement. You know all the reasons why we shouldn't...' She waved a hand to indicate what it was they shouldn't be doing. 'But you're still crazy angry with me. Well, let me plant one seriously scary picture in your mind.'

He'd gone still. She had to pause to drag in a breath. 'I might've come to the conclusion that Brad and I are better off apart, but it doesn't mean I've reconciled myself to the loss of the life I'd planned and dreamed about or to the children I dreamed of having.'

She closed her eyes against a rush of pain. When she opened them again she saw that Cade's shoulders had slumped. She had to swallow before she could continue. 'I want children so bad that some days I can't see straight. My head is not screwed on right at the moment.' She hitched up her chin. 'Say we do start an affair. What if that yearning takes me over? What if we're not as careful as we might be one time and then we're dealing with that? Do you want to be a part of that?' she asked hoarsely.

'No.'

'Me neither.'

Neither of them moved. Neither of them said a word.

'Can I put the children to bed now?' she whispered.

'Please.' He nodded, his voice as hoarse as hers.

She fled before she could do anything stupid like kiss him.

CHAPTER SEVEN

CADE jerked awake from a dead sleep. What the…?

Thump! Somebody whacked his feet. For the second time, he suspected.

'Get up, Cade.'

'Mum? What the hell…?' He struggled upright and tried to blink sleep from his eyes. His room was in complete darkness.

He clicked on the bedside light. The clock showed three a.m. He snapped into instant alertness. 'Who's ill?' He shot out of bed, pulling a T-shirt on over his head. He didn't bother with jeans over his boxers. This far from civilization, every second counted. If someone needed the Flying Doctor…

An icy hand wrapped about his heart. 'Ella? Holly?' he croaked.

Verity Hindmarsh folded her arms and glared at him. 'It's not serious but it's certainly unpleasant and of your making. So you can haul your butt out there and help that poor girl.'

He didn't wait to hear more, but shot towards the children's bedrooms. He stopped short in Ella's doorway and his heart clenched. Nicola sat on Ella's bed holding a bowl for the child as she was monumentally and comprehensively sick. There was evidence that Ella had been sick before Nicola had been able to reach her.

To make Nicola's task all the more difficult, Holly clung to her, grizzling into her neck. He could see that Holly had been sick all over herself and Nicola. Nicola's cotton nightie clung to one breast, the wet material practically transparent.

He turned his gaze away and pushed himself forward into the room. Nicola glanced up and relief lit her eyes. How long had she been struggling with this alone?

Ella lifted her head, her eyes swimming with tears, her face a picture of misery. 'Daddy, I did eat too many lollies and they made me vomit.'

Only she pronounced it 'bomit', which would normally have made him smile, except…

It's not serious, but it's…of your making.

He'd created this mess? He'd made his children sick? Bile rose in his throat as he battled a cold, hard anger with himself. There'd be plenty of time for recriminations later. Recriminations wouldn't help Ella and Holly at the moment. Or Nicola.

He swallowed. 'What can I do?'

'Holly needs to be cleaned up. Ella…'

Her eyes told him that Ella wasn't through with being sick yet.

'Holly, honey, you want to go to Daddy?'

Holly screamed and clung tighter to Nicola's neck. Ella started to cry. 'I want Daddy to stay here.'

No further communication was needed. He took Nicola's spot on the bed. She handed him a damp washcloth and a clean bowl. 'I won't be long.'

'Take the time to have a shower too,' he said softly. She deserved to be as comfortable as she could be given the situation. He predicted that with Holly in her current mood, it'd take them an age to get her back down to sleep.

She glanced down at the front of herself and her cheeks reddened. With a nod she was gone, taking Holly, the dirty bowl and her magnificent breasts with her.

He shook that last thought away and tended his daughter.

Nicola was back wearing a fresh nightie and a terry-towelling robe in less time than he dreamed possible. He frowned. 'Holly?'

'Sleeping like a baby.'

He gaped. 'But how…?'

She shrugged but her eyes danced. 'What can I say? I'm a hell of a woman.'

Her teasing lightened something inside him. She'd returned smelling all the more strongly of strawberry jam and it eased the sour smell of sickness that pervaded the room. He pulled a deep breath of it into his lungs.

'Besides, it's what you pay me for.'

'You deserve a pay rise.'

'Too many nights like this and I'll take you up on that.'

Amid all the vomit and guilt, she'd made him want to smile. He wouldn't have believed that possible. He watched her assess Ella, who was drooping.

'She needs to be bathed and her bed needs to be stripped and remade.' She quickly and deftly removed Ella's pyjamas as she spoke. 'I've run a bath and as you're stronger than me…'

He nodded and took Ella through to the bathroom and bathed her. She cried and protested, but was too tired to put up much of a fight.

When he returned to the bedroom, the bed had been made up with fresh sheets and Nicola quickly helped Ella into a cool cotton nightie. He tucked her into bed, the guilt he'd kept at bay starting to prickle and burn.

Nicola knelt down in front of Ella. 'Sweetie, I need you to take three little sips of water for me.'

'I don't want to!'

'Honey, have I ever lied to you?'

Ella shook her head.

'I promise you'll feel better if you have a little drink.'

Ella finally nodded, but she needed coaxing and cajoling every step of the way. Cade couldn't help but marvel at Nicola's combination of patience, firmness and gentleness.

'Sing me a song,' Ella demanded with a fretful squirm.

Cade wanted to order his daughter to say please, but Nicola forestalled him with a light touch on his arm. 'First Daddy has to dim the light, and then you have to lie still and close your eyes.'

''Kay.'

Cade dimmed the light and then stretched out beside Ella, his back resting against the headboard as he gently wiped her hair back from her forehead. Nicola settled on the end of the bed. She pulled in a breath and then calmly and quietly sang "Silent Night."

The soft strains of the song soothed Ella and helped ease the beast raging in Cade's own breast. He closed his eyes too and drank the song in, her voice so true it lifted the hairs on his arms.

When it was finished they sat in the quiet for a bit. Her touch on his arm had his eyes flying open. With a finger to her lips, she led him out of Ella's bedroom, the child sleeping quietly now.

With a quick smile she swooped down and picked up the soiled bed-linen and walked away with a soft 'Goodnight, Cade.'

He wouldn't sleep. Not yet. He followed her into the

kitchen, but she moved all the way through to the laundry and set a load going.

He put the kettle on and waited. 'Tea?' he offered when she reappeared.

She hesitated, her gaze sweeping across his face. Finally she nodded. 'Something herbal would be nice.'

He made them mugs of peppermint tea, even though he didn't like the stuff. Penance, he told himself.

'I'm sorry about that,' he murmured once they were both seated. 'You tried to warn me that too many sweets would make them sick. I didn't listen.'

She shrugged. 'We live and learn. Don't beat yourself up about it.'

Don't beat himself up? He shot to his feet. 'I made them sick! I'm supposed to protect them and look after them and…'

Her eyes widened.

'I want to make Christmas special for them, but…damn it, I'm making a hash of everything! Those poor kids.' He fell back into his chair. 'They drew the short straw in the parents stakes, no mistake about it, and…' He couldn't go on. His throat had grown too tight.

'Now where did I put that hair shirt?' Nicola said with an efficient crispness so utterly devoid of sympathy it made him sit back in shock.

'Stop being such a martyr.'

Martyr? Him?

'I'm going to tell you a hard truth.' She leaned towards him, her voice still crisp, but her eyes incredibly gentle and soft. 'It doesn't matter how fabulous you make this Christmas, it doesn't matter how many fairy lights you put up or how many sweets and chocolates you stock up on or how many presents you buy them, it will never make up to them for not having their mother. Furthermore,' she added when he opened his mouth, 'you will never be able to make that up to them. Ever. No matter what you do.'

The truth of her words had the fight whooshing out of him. He ached to make it up to Ella and Holly, wanted to so badly—needed to—but…

He closed his eyes.

'Cade?'

He opened them again. The softness, tenderness, in her eyes belied the hard truths she'd uttered.

'Stop fighting a losing game and just focus on ensuring they feel secure in your love. Do what you've been doing—be fully involved in their lives, surround them with their extended family at every opportunity, and create a community here at Waminda Downs that they can rely on.'

'There has to be more that I can do!' He wanted there to be more that he could do.

'There is.'

He glanced up.

'You can stop punishing yourself for what happened between you and Fran. How are you going to help Ella and Holly come to terms with their mother's desertion if you haven't come to terms with it yourself?'

He had no answer to that. He wanted to rant and rail and break things, but Nicola didn't deserve that.

'But I can tell you that having one parent who is completely invested in your life is far better than two parents who are distant and critical. Ella and Holly at least have that.'

Too right! He was a hundred per cent behind his kids, but his heart burned as he gazed into Nicola's eyes and the shadows there. She obviously knew what she was talking about. No wonder she'd made a family from her friends. No wonder Diane and Brad's betrayal had rocked the foundations of her world and all she held dear.

'Ella and Holly are lucky in lots of ways.'

He forced himself to consider her words seriously, and for the first time in a very long time he recognised their truth. 'They're healthy,' he said slowly, and then grimaced. 'At least, as a general rule they're healthy.' He paused. 'They have a grandmother, an aunt and cousins who adore them. And…and Waminda is a great place to live.'

'And they have you,' she said with a warmth that engulfed him. 'You should take a lot of heart from the fact that Ella is so well adjusted. Fran's leaving would have been traumatic for her, but she's a happy, stable little girl. She's not too clingy, isn't waking up in the middle of the night screaming with nightmares, and she doesn't constantly worry where you are.'

'We've been through all that,' he admitted.

'It seems to me she's over the worst of it now.'

Nicola was right. He nodded. 'This single parent gig isn't easy. Half the time I don't seem to know what I'm doing. And the rest of the time I simply feel clueless, but…' He rubbed a hand across his jaw. 'Maybe I should have more faith in Ella and Holly.'

'And yourself.'

He met her gaze. 'Thank you.' He meant it.

Nicola smiled back, but her gaze had dropped to his lips and he could read the hunger that raced across her face. The same hunger surged through him.

She snapped away, and then rose and rinsed her mug. 'I'm off to bed.' She turned in the doorway. 'Would you tell Jack that I won't make my riding lesson in the morning?'

'Sure thing. You deserve a lie-in.'

She shook her head with a low laugh. 'The children are going to be out of sorts and all over the place tomorrow. I'd like to be close by in case they wake early.'

It struck him then that she'd be paying for his evening's folly for the next twenty-four hours. He wanted to apologise again, only he had a feeling she'd make another hair shirt quip or call him a drama queen.

'Goodnight, Cade.'

He settled for a ''Night, Nicola. Sleep well,' instead.

Cade winced at the dark circles under Nicola's eyes when he saw her at lunch the next day.

All the children were whingey and whiny, hard to please, and he marvelled anew at her patience and her ability to distract them and keep them semi-amiable.

'That girl is a saint,' his mother murmured.

He glanced around. 'Where's Dee?'

'Gone for a lie down. She's only had a morning of this and she's exhausted.'

He bit his lip. 'Were the boys ill too?'

'Unlike you, Dee wouldn't let them have any more sweets, so no. They're just out of routine, that's all.'

He grimaced, suitably chastened. 'I've learned my lesson,' he promised and his mother's face softened. He huffed out a breath. 'I feel bad that Nicola has to deal with the fallout when the fault was mine.'

He bit his lip and pondered his afternoon's workload. 'Will they go down for their usual nap this afternoon?'

Verity nodded. 'It'll be a battle to get them there, but once they're down they'll be out for the count. They probably won't surface for a couple of hours.'

Good. 'Would you and Dee be able to hold the fort for an hour or so, then? Nicola skipped her riding lesson this morning. I thought I might take her out this afternoon to get some fresh air into those cheeks of hers.'

'I think that's a lovely idea.'

With a nod, he grabbed a sandwich and made for the cattle yards, intent on getting his afternoon's work done in good time.

Nicola collapsed into an easy chair in the living room. 'They're down.' Finally. What a day.

'Hallelujah,' Dee murmured.

Nicola opened her eyes when she sensed Cade's presence in the room. He carried in a jug of iced water and five glasses. Slices of lemon floated in the jug and the ice chinked against its side in a cooling, welcoming symphony. He poured each of them a glass.

'I'm sorry,' he said, handing the drinks around. 'It's my fault you've all had such a difficult day.'

'It happens,' Harry said philosophically.

'Are you completely fagged?'

She blinked when she realised the question was directed at her. The short answer was yes, but...

She took one look at his face and tossed her head. 'How pathetic do you think I am? I'm fighting fit.' She emphasized the word fit. Then she grinned. 'I'm a lean, mean fighting machine.'

That hooked up one side of his mouth, enhancing a dimple she found oddly fascinating, enhancing lips she found enthralling. Need mushroomed inside her with a speed that made her hands clench.

He inserted a disc into the CD player and the strains of something soft and classical filled the room. Verity, Dee and Harry all puffed out blissful sighs and closed their eyes. He beckoned to her and she rose and followed him out of the room.

He took her now-empty glass and set it on the sink. 'I thought if you wanted...if you'd like it...we could go for a ride.'

All her tiredness fled. 'I'd love that!'

'Good. Go change and then meet me down at the stables.'

She changed into jeans and pulled on the riding boots Jack had dug out for her use, and was down at the stables in double-quick time. Cade already had Scarlett and his steed—a beautiful big bay called Ben Hur—saddled.

'Need a leg up?'

She stuck her nose in the air. 'Most certainly not.' It had taken her a while to master the skill of mounting, but in the two and a bit weeks she'd been here her legs had strengthened and grown more flexible.

When she mounted, not only without mishap but with credible grace, she could only grin down at Cade and thank the powers that be. Falling flat on her face would not have instilled in him much confidence in her riding ability and she didn't want to give him any reason whatsoever to cancel their ride. She gathered the reins in the way Jack had taught her and watched as Cade leapt up into the saddle.

Ooh, nice! She wanted to make it look that smooth and effortless. Of course, he had the advantage of long legs.

And a nice tight butt that—

Scarlett danced as Nicola's hands unconsciously tightened on the reins and she immediately relaxed them and forced her gaze from Cade's drool-inducing physique to stroke her steed's neck and murmur soothing nonsense.

Cade surveyed her and nodded in evident satisfaction. It made her warm all over. Not that she should dwell on that for too long either. 'Where are we going?' She blamed her breathlessness on the exertion of mounting and controlling her steed. Which, she admitted to herself, was too pathetic to believe, but she held tight to it all the same.

'Has Jack taken you to the canyon yet?'

Canyon? She shook her head, intrigued.

'Then that sounds as good a destination as any. C'mon.' With a jerk of his head, he headed towards the gate that led out of the home paddock.

'Let me,' she said. 'I've been practising this.'

Manoeuvring Scarlett into position as Jack had shown her, she opened the latch and swung the gate open without needing to dismount.

'Nice,' Cade remarked, closing it again once they'd passed though. He stared at her. 'Jack's right, you look as if you were born to the saddle.'

'Would you laugh at me if I told you that's how I feel too?'

'No, I'd ask you why it's taken so long for you to learn to ride when it's obviously such a passion and something you've always wanted to do.'

She pursed her lips, shrugged. 'My mother always refused to keep a horse.'

'Why?'

'She said that if I was that clumsy in ballet shoes I'd be an absolute nightmare on a horse.'

His mouth tightened. 'I get the distinct impression I wouldn't like your mother.'

Nicola gave a short laugh. 'She'd love you. You tick all the right boxes—broad shoulders, good-looking...own your own cattle station.'

'Hmph!'

They rode in silence for a while and Nicola revelled in the swaying motion of her horse and the stark beauty of the landscape and the dry dusty air.

'Why didn't you learn to ride later? Once you became an adult?'

'I...' She frowned. 'It didn't seem very practical in the city. I just kept putting it off.'

As soon as the words left her mouth she realised they

were a lie. She recalled all the resolutions she'd come out here with and hitched up her chin. 'Actually, that's not true.' She thought about it. 'I didn't bother to learn because none of my friends were interested in learning with me.' Horses made Diane shudder. 'I was too spineless to learn on my own.'

He didn't say anything for a long moment. He shifted in his saddle. 'And now?'

'Oh, now I'm hooked. And now that I know what an idiot I've been…' She frowned. 'People do keep horses in the city, don't they?'

'Sure they do.'

'I'm going to join a riding club.' There'd be one in Melbourne somewhere. 'I'm going to get my own horse.' Excitement surged through her. 'It's going to be fabulous!'

He grinned at her enthusiasm and life seemed suddenly so full of possibility she wanted to fly. 'Can we canter?' she breathed.

In answer he tossed her a grin that made her heart thud against her ribs, before he urged Ben Hur into a canter. At the touch of Nicola's heels, Scarlett surged after him, and Nicola gave herself up to the feel of the wind in her face and the exhilaration of the ride. Riding like this quietened all the voices in her head that told her she wasn't good enough, that she'd never be good enough. It allowed her to concentrate instead on feeling at one with her horse. It flooded her with strength and peace and harmony.

When Cade brought his horse to a halt, she pulled Scarlett to a halt beside him. 'Magic,' she breathed.

And then her jaw dropped.

Cade's mouth kicked up at the corners. 'This is the canyon.' He shrugged. 'In all honesty, it's more a gorge, but we have delusions of grandeur so we call it the canyon.'

'Wow!'

'It's something, isn't it?'

Something? Majestic, eternal, imposing were the words that came to mind.

The land in front of them dropped away in a series of dramatic rock shelves. The rock was baked red but deep cream and yellow veins striped through it. Water glinted in the base of the canyon. Its other side rose in a sheer cliff. Three-quarters of the way up, it curved inwards as if eroded by thousands of years of wind and sand. It looked like a giant curling wave waiting to break on a stretch of deserted beach.

The blue sky and the red rock formed a contrast that sang to her soul, though she couldn't have said why. On the other side of the canyon, the land was dotted with saltbush and the dry brown grass that the cattle roamed far and wide to graze upon. From beneath the brim of her hat, she couldn't see any cattle, but she did see a mob of kangaroo. There had to be at least twenty of them, most of them sprawled out in whatever shade they could find. A big buck stared across at them for a moment and then went back to grazing.

'It's beautiful.' The words didn't seem enough to capture the eternal grandeur of the landscape, but it was all she had to offer.

He nodded. 'In times of flood the water roars through here. There's a place to ford further downriver, which is handy when we're mustering.'

'Does it flood often?' It'd be hard being stranded out here so far from civilisation in a flood.

'There've been two decent ones in living memory, but the homestead is built on higher ground. We've never had to evacuate.'

Still…it took a special kind of person to live out here, battling drought and flood and bushfire. Cade had a grit that she admired. A grit she was determined to cultivate for herself.

'I owe you an apology.'

She barely heard him. 'Oh!' She pointed. Her mouth opened and closed. 'Emus,' she gasped out.

He chuckled. The sound was almost enough to make her drag her eyes from the five giant birds that streaked away until they were lost in the distance. She'd never seen an emu in the wild before. It shouldn't have astonished her, she supposed, but…

Lord, what a greenhorn she must seem. She turned to Cade to find him staring at her, an odd light in his eyes. Then she recalled his words. She moistened her lips. 'An apology?'

'Yeah.'

Although he wore an Akubra, he squinted in the light. Or was it that he just didn't want to meet her eye?

His gaze speared hers as if she'd asked that out loud. 'I've been acting like a jerk and I want to apologise.'

'Um…' She blinked. 'Okay.'

'The thing is…' He went back to squinting. 'I haven't been with a woman since Fran left. I haven't wanted to be with a woman.'

She swallowed. 'You've had your mind on other things. I mean, Fran's leaving must've been an enormous shock to begin with, and then there was Ella and Holly's welfare to consider. On top of all that, you're running a cattle station. It's not like you've had a lot of spare time on your hands, Cade.'

She thought back to the way he'd kissed her, to the latent power of his body, to his impressive…um…virility. Sure, their clothes had stayed on, but she'd been just about as closely pressed up against him as a body could get. She'd felt the full might of his masculinity. The memory made her mouth dry and an ache start up between her legs.

Actually, when she thought about it, Cade's abstinence was surprising. Very surprising. But it was also understandable.

His lips twisted. 'The thing is…that all changed when you showed up.'

'Liar.' She adjusted her hat. She suspected he was trying to pump up her confidence. 'There wasn't a hint of anything between us when I first climbed out of the Cessna.'

'Maybe not, but then you smiled at me.'

She had?

'I introduced you to Scarlett. You smiled…and I wanted you then and there. No preliminaries. No warning. It knocked me for six.' He scowled. 'I haven't stopped wanting you since. Kissing you only made it worse.'

Her jaw dropped.

'Look, I'm not trying to excuse my behaviour. I shouldn't have taken my frustration out on you yesterday evening. I shouldn't have pressured you to act against your better judgement. I acted like a horny teenager and I'm sorry, but I thought if you knew why I'd lost my head so completely you mightn't look on me with such a harsh eye.'

The embarrassed half-smile, half-grimace reminded her of Ella when she'd been caught out in some minor misdemeanour. It made her want to smile, but she bit the impulse back. She needed to check something before she could give into it. 'So we're back on the same page as far as…as far as sex is concerned?'

'Yep.' He nodded.

The ache between her legs intensified. She forced herself to smile. 'Okay, apology accepted.'

'Nicola?'

He forestalled her before she could turn Scarlett around and head back towards the homestead.

'I'm hoping that we can be friends. Real friends.'

Three weeks ago that word would've induced a shudder. Now?

She leaned across and held out her hand. He shook it with that firm grip that made her want to swoon. 'You have yourself a deal.'

Beneath the brim of his hat, his eyes shone out blue for a moment. 'Thank you.'

CHAPTER EIGHT

'Nic?'

'Yes, honey?'

It was Christmas Eve, dinner was long over and all the children had quietened down after a rowdy game of Trouble. Ella was sitting next to Nicola on one of the sofas, her head resting against Nicola's shoulder. The soft weight of the child and her absolute trust pierced straight into the centre of Nicola, making her wish...

She pulled in a breath and pushed the thought away. She would not allow it to mar the mood of the evening. Contentment stretched through the living room, along with expectation and hope. The atmosphere as unique to Christmas as the scent of cinnamon and mince pies.

She glanced down when Ella didn't continue with her question. 'What do you want to know, pumpkin?'

Ella chewed her lip and then climbed right into Nicola's lap. 'What if Santa doesn't come?'

She suppressed a smile. 'Why wouldn't he come?'

She shared a glance with Cade. He wore a pair of grey cargo shorts and a blue shirt that matched his eyes exactly. Holly had fallen asleep and he cradled her in his arms. The contrast between the big, tanned man—the broad shoulders and the long, strong legs—and the small child with her delicate pink-white skin and fine blonde hair, made her breath hitch and the pulse in her throat quicken. Everything about him ravished her senses. She forced her eyes back to Ella before he could see the desire that flashed in their depths.

'Well…' Ella drew out, 'Waminda is a very, very, *very* long way from Brisbane.' To her childish mind, Brisbane was the centre of the universe. 'Maybe,' she continued, 'Santa doesn't know we're here.'

'But we sent him a letter, remember?'

'Do you think he got it?'

'I'm sure of it.'

The blue eyes, so like her father's, brightened. Ella's questions, her hope, reminded Nicola of the Christmases of her own childhood—the loneliness and inevitable disappointment. She understood Ella's fear. 'And don't forget,' she whispered to the child, 'Santa is magic.'

'So he'll come?'

'Uh-huh.'

'You promise?'

'I promise.'

Her assurances seem to satisfy Ella, who snuggled into Nicola all the more securely. Cade sent Nicola such a warm smile of thanks it curled her toes.

'Nic?'

What this time? She glanced down. 'Yes?'

'Do you think Mummy will come tomorrow?'

Every adult in the room—Cade, Harry, Verity, Dee and her husband, Keith, who'd arrived earlier in the day—all stiffened. Nicola did her best to keep her body relaxed. Ella would unconsciously pick up on any tension she radiated and it would unsettle and upset her.

Was this—seeing her mother—what Ella had pinned all her Christmas hopes on? The greyness of Cade's skin, the haggard expression on his face, made her heart burn. Whatever anyone else in the room thought, she couldn't lie to Ella. If seeing her mother was the child's dearest wish, it would be hard getting her through tomorrow, but it wouldn't be as bad as giving her hope that would go unfulfilled.

She caressed the hair back from Ella's brow. 'Pumpkin, I haven't spoken to your mummy, but I don't think she'll be able to make it tomorrow.'

'The day after?'

Nicola's chest cramped. How could any woman turn her back on such a beautiful, loving child? Fran must have a heart of stone. She tried to keep her breathing steady. 'We can keep our fingers crossed, but I really don't know. I think she'd let us know if she was coming for a visit.'

She watched as Ella digested her words. 'Will you be here?'

'I promise.' She crossed her heart. 'And we're all going to have such fun tomorrow. I mean, you have your daddy and Holly here, and your grandma, Auntie Dee and Uncle Keith, not to mention Simon and Jamie, and Harry and me. That's pretty lucky, don't you think?'

Ella thought about that for a moment and then she smiled. 'Yes,' she pronounced. 'And you really, truly think Santa will come?'

'I really, truly do.'

Will you sing a Christmas carol?' Ella whispered.

Ella's favourite was *Silent Night*, so Nicola started to sing it. One by one, the other adults joined in. Before the first verse was over, Cade rose to put Holly down. By the end of the song, Keith and Dee had taken a twin apiece and Cade returned to carefully lift Ella from Nicola's arms.

'I'll be fine,' he murmured when she made to rise too.

She couldn't read his eyes, but she subsided into her seat, sensing he wanted to be alone with his daughter, to stare down at her while she slept and to give thanks for her.

Harry pushed out of her chair. 'I'm off to bed.'

'Nicola—' Verity rose '—I suspect we've seen the last of Dee and Keith for the night.'

Nicola grinned. The couple's evident delight at seeing each other after ten days apart had been all too plain.

'I also suspect that it will be a big day tomorrow.'

'I expect you're right on both counts.'

'So I'm going to retire early.'

'Sleep well.'

Verity turned in the doorway. 'I'm glad you're spending Christmas with us this year.'

She couldn't mistake the older woman's sincerity, and she had to swallow down an unexpected lump. 'Thank you. I'm glad too.'

When Cade returned, he glanced around and blinked.

She laughed. 'It seems the consensus was for turning in early.'

He collapsed on the sofa beside her. 'Fair enough.'

She stared at him for a moment. 'You okay?'

'Sure, I…'

'Ella's question about her mum was a humdinger. It seemed to hit you all for six.'

He shook his head. 'It took me off guard. God knows why. I should've expected it, I suppose, but she stopped asking about Fran months ago.'

It took an effort of will not to reach out and touch him. Every atom of her being begged her to, her mouth drying at the memory of the lean hard feel of him. Her fingers curled, her blood quickened, her lips parted to drag in a ragged breath.

He turned, his eyes flashing. 'Why the hell couldn't you just lie to her?' His hands clenched. 'Why couldn't you have left her with a tiny shard of hope?'

She flinched at his vehemence…and the direction her

thoughts had taken. Her heart pounded against her rib-cage. She dragged in a breath and tried to gather her wits. 'Do you…do you think there is any hope?' Had she read that wrong? A heavy weight settled in the pit of Nicola's stomach. Would Fran come back and claim her family?

'No!' He stabbed a finger at her. 'But that's not the point. Ella is just a child, a little girl. It was cruel to…'

Maybe it was his own hope Cade was trying to keep alive, not Ella's. A chill travelled up her backbone. Her chest throbbed. She couldn't speak.

His eyes blazed. 'You could have invented something, fibbed a little. She would've forgotten all about it tomorrow in the Christmas excitement.'

Her chin shot up. 'I will not lie to your daughter—not today, not tomorrow, not ever! I know what it's like to ache for something on Christmas Day. It's a day of miracles, right?' Her hands fisted. 'And I remember the crushing disappointment that came at day's end when I realised my wish wasn't going to come true. I will not put Ella through that. *That* would be cruel.'

His mouth opened and closed, and then he sank back against the sofa cushions and he dragged a hand down his face, swore softly. Neither of them spoke for a while. The Christmas tree twinkled benignly in the corner. 'What did you hope for?' he finally asked.

She'd expected him to continue arguing with her. His unexpected question took her back to a time of vulnerability and disappointment. It took her a moment before she could speak. 'Usually I just hoped that the spirit of the day would infect my parents and that they'd unbend enough to…to play with me.'

He stared and she found herself continuing. 'I didn't lack for presents; it was just…I was always told that I was luckier than most little girls and to go play on my own.'

She shrugged. 'One year I wished with all my might for a rowdy Christmas dinner with lots of crackers to pop and the reading out of corny jokes followed by the singing of Christmas carols.'

That hadn't happened either.

She sensed the exact moment the fight left Cade's body. She bit back a sigh. 'Look, I'm not telling you this to make you feel sorry for me. It's just that, as a child, I knew what it was like to hope for the impossible and not get it—to not even realise it was impossible in the first place. Telling Ella that her mother might show up is only setting her up for unnecessary heartbreak because, believe me, come tomorrow she won't have forgotten. She'd spend the day waiting for it to happen, waiting for her mother to walk through the door. Now, hopefully, she can focus on all the other good bits of the day instead. She might get a bit sad about her mum, but there's absolutely nothing you can do about that, Cade. No matter how much you might want to. Besides, Ella is entitled to her sadness on that count.'

He blinked as if he hadn't considered that before. He opened his mouth, closed it, and then dragged a hand down his face. 'I'm still not sure I agree with the way you handled it, but I appreciate you telling me the reason why.'

At least his anger had abated, if not his worry. She pulled in a breath. 'I think if we lie to Ella we're betraying her trust. I think if we fib to her—even with good intentions—it will lessen her faith in us.'

His jaw dropped open.

'I think fibbing to her will do more harm than good. Her faith in you, Cade, is the biggest gift you can give her. I'm pretty sure you wouldn't want to do anything that might damage that.'

'Hell, no!' He swallowed. 'I hadn't considered it from that angle.'

He didn't say anything for several long moments, but she sensed that beneath the silence his mind raced. He suddenly muttered an oath and swung to face her more fully. 'I wanted to protect Ella from more pain, but lying to her would be unforgivable. You're right. My word should be something she can trust and always rely on—not something to doubt and question.'

Nicola let out a breath.

'I'm sorry I rounded on you. You saw it all much clearer than I did.'

Her heart unclenched a fraction, and then it clenched up tighter than before. She gripped her hands together. 'Are you sure it's not your own hope you're trying to keep alive rather than Ella's?'

His head came up. 'Why the hell would I want to do that?'

'Because if Fran did show up, maybe it'd mean you weren't a failure. And that, in turn, would help ease your guilt.'

And maybe because you still love her? But she left that unsaid. She didn't have the heart for it.

'The thing is,' she continued, 'the breakdown of your marriage doesn't make you a failure. You did everything you could to save it. As far as I can see, you have absolutely nothing to be guilty about.'

He stared at her as if he didn't know what to say and it suddenly hit her that it was Christmas Eve and he'd specifically asked her for Christmas spirit and cheer. She made herself smile. 'You're a wonderful father, Cade.' She tapped her watch. 'And look, it's almost Christmas. All you can do is focus on having a lovely day tomorrow and making it special and exciting for Ella and Holly.' She nudged him with her shoulder. 'Christmas spirit, remember?'

Slowly he nodded and his shoulders went back. 'Just concentrate on the stuff I can control, right?'

He smiled then. And she had no hope whatsoever of controlling the way her heart pitter-pattered.

Or the way the breath hitched in her throat.

His gaze lowered to her mouth and his eyes darkened to a deep stormy blue. The air between them crackled with energy and electricity.

He shot off the sofa. 'Goodnight, Nicola.'

Pitter-patter. Pitter-patter. She closed her eyes. 'Goodnight, Cade.'

The next morning Nicola rose at six o'clock. A peek into Ella's room and then the boys' room confirmed they all still slept soundly. Holly would sleep through to her usual seven o'clock, but Nicola had fully expected to find the other children wide awake and bouncing off walls.

She sneaked down to the stables to give Scarlett a Christmas carrot. Jack and several of the other stockmen and jackaroos were holding their own Christmas festivities in the stockmen's quarters, so she left a box of old English toffee, that she'd discovered Jack had a fondness for, on the bench by his front door where he had his morning coffee. He should find it first thing.

She turned to make her way back to the homestead, but paused to drink in the early morning air. At this time of the day the light was clear and crisp. The landscape didn't yet shimmer with its usual heat haze, and the light was easy on the eyes. It allowed her to survey, unhindered, all the natural rugged beauty of the place before the sun blazed down with its hard blinding ferocity.

The khaki-green of the mulga scrub contrasted prettily with the yellow-white of the grass...and beneath it all the red dirt of the Outback. She hadn't expected to find so much beauty out here in the western reaches of Queensland. She hadn't fully appreciated it when she'd first arrived. But this place and its people had helped her heal and she gave thanks that she could now see and appreciate the stark and ancient grandeur of the landscape. And that she had the best part of another month in which to enjoy it.

Christmas at Waminda Downs! An optimism she hadn't allowed herself to feel for this day since she was a child welled in her now. She grinned and then set off at a trot for the homestead.

Entering her room via the French windows, the first thing Nicola saw was Ella sitting in the middle of her double bed. Her heart tripped. Had Ella panicked when she hadn't been able to find her? Had she leapt to the conclusion that, just like her mother, Nicola hadn't kept her promise and had deserted her?

'Hey, chickadee!' She swept her up in her arms for a hug and then plonked them both back down on the bed. 'Merry Christmas.'

'Merry Christmas.' A smile warred with a frown on the child's face.

'I went down to the stables to wish Scarlett a merry Christmas,' she confided.

'I thought you were in the bathroom.'

Okay, Ella hadn't been worried about her whereabouts, so...?

'Excited?' she asked.

'What if Santa didn't come?' the little girl blurted out. 'He forgot last year.'

Ah, the puzzle pieces slotted into place.

'Did you look?' Ella whispered. 'Was there anything in our stockings?'

She understood it wasn't the presents that Ella needed.

It was the magic and the hope. 'I haven't looked yet. Do you want to go and do that now?'

Ella nodded, and while she was too big to be carried much any more, Nicola knew that the child needed the security. So she lifted her up onto her hip and started towards the living room.

Then she halted.

Ella's bottom lip started to quiver, but Nicola winked at her. 'You know, I think we need your daddy for this too.' She detoured to Cade's room and knocked on his door. A muffled sound emerged that she chose to interpret as a 'what?' or a 'yes?' rather than an oath.

'Wake up, sleepy-head, the fun's about to start and you don't want to miss it.'

'Don't you dare start without me!'

There was a thump and a couple of bumps and a muffled curse or two and Ella giggled. 'Daddy's funny.'

'Hilarious,' he growled, flinging the door open and seizing Ella in his arms and swinging her around until she squealed.

His T-shirt was rumpled, his hair dishevelled and Nicola's blood heated up.

'Daddy—' Ella clasped him tight about the neck '—we have to see if Santa's been.'

Nicola shook herself, trying to dispel images that had nothing to do with Christmas and everything to do with Cade and rumpled sheets. 'We…uh…thought you might like to join us.'

'You were right.'

His blue eyes sent her a simple message—thank you. It turned her to mush.

Oh, grow a backbone, Nicola Ann!

She ousted her mother's voice from her head immediately. It was Christmas. She wasn't going to tolerate that voice today.

'Shall I lead the way?' she asked Ella.

Ella nodded and, without further ado, Nicola set off for the living room. She might not need a backbone, but a little steel in her legs wouldn't have gone amiss. The presence of warm male flesh moving so closely behind her leached the strength from her limbs with each step she took.

She hummed "Jingle Bells" under her breath in an effort to ignore and counter her traitorous body's reaction. Her newfound Christmas optimism and excitement—it left her so much more receptive to…to other things it would be wiser not to name.

She paused on the threshold of the living room, caught Ella's eye and smiled, and then with an arm partly around the little girl and partly around the father who carried her, she swept them all into the room.

Ella's eyes widened. They grew as large as frisbees as she stared at each of the stockings tacked to the mantelpiece, all full to bursting.

'See, sweetie? Didn't I tell you Santa would come?'

Ella pressed her face to Cade's neck and promptly burst into tears.

He stared at Nicola over the top of Ella's head, his eyes wide with panic.

Nicola shook her head and gave him a thumbs-up. 'Excitement,' she mouthed silently.

In no time, Ella wriggled from her father's arms and had seized her stocking, squealing in delight as she extracted her bounty.

In less than ten minutes, the rest of the family had joined them, Verity carrying Holly. With nothing to do but to watch and enjoy, Nicola sat back and took it all in, soaked up the joy and awe of the children, the warmth and affection of the adults and the promised magic of the day.

'You okay?' Cade asked, plonking himself beside her on the sofa, one of his hands resting briefly on her knee.

'Yes, of course. I…'

To her horror, she found her eyes prickling with tears. Cade's expression sharpened in a heartbeat. He moved towards her but she shook her head, gave him a thumbs-up and mouthed 'excitement' to him. He grinned then and she was grateful she witnessed it through a sheen of tears or it might well have slayed her where she sat.

When she was sure she could speak without disgracing herself, she said, 'I've never seen anything like this before except on the telly. I've never experienced this much…unadulterated joy.'

His eyes softened, those amazing blue eyes that could look as hard as the sky or as soft as a breeze, depending on their mood. 'Nic—'

'No, no.' She didn't want him feeling sorry for her. 'It's wonderful.' She beamed at him. 'I want to thank you for letting me be a part of it.'

She couldn't explain to him what a privilege she found it…or what a revelation. In Melbourne she'd developed a veneer of cynicism about Christmas to protect herself from disappointment and inevitable letdown. She realised now how self-defeating that had become. She made a vow to dispense with that cynicism for good. Christmas should never be a chore or something to run away from. It should be celebrated and cherished.

Cade tried to keep his attention on the children—on their merriment, their wide-eyed delight and their comical glee with their presents—but the smell of strawberry jam filled his senses and he found his eyes returning to Nicola again and again.

Her eyes shone with as much delight as the children's. A soft smile curved her lips. He found it particularly hard to drag his gaze from those soft, plump, kissable, strawberry-jam-scented curves. If he could have just one Christmas wish, it would be for another taste of those lips. Not a quick brush of his lips against hers, but a thorough and devastating rediscovery of their shape and texture, of their give and take, of their taste and the way her body with its killer curves melted into his when—

'Daddy?' A tug on his shirtsleeve brought him back with a start. A glance at Nicola's pink-tinged cheeks told him his hungry survey hadn't gone unobserved.

Friends! He'd promised they'd be friends. *Nothing more.*

He swiped a forearm across his brow. He had to get these darn hormones back under wraps before they flared out of control and brought him undone. But, damn it, they dodged and weaved and bucked his restraint with greater ferocity than the brumbies he'd been breaking in these last few weeks.

'Daddy?' Another tug.

'What, princess?'

'When can we open the presents under the tree?'

The presents under the tree were from the family members to each other.

Ella hopped from one foot to the other. 'I have five presents under there!'

He understood the lure and excitement of presents—he'd admit to a certain amount of curiosity about the present under there with his name on the gift tag, written in Nicola's neat schoolteacher's hand—but he didn't want his daughter growing up to think that was all Christmas was about.

'Not until after Grandma reads us the Christmas story after breakfast. Then we'll all take turns to say what we're grateful for. That was a tradition from his own childhood.

Ella leaned in close. 'I'm grapeful for lots and lots of things, Daddy.' She climbed up onto his knee and snuggled in close. 'I'm very grapeful that Santa came, that he didn't forget. And I'm grapeful that you're here and Holly and Grandma and Nic and Harry and Auntie Dee and Uncle Keith and Simon and Jamie…and that it's like a big party.' She glanced up at him. 'Aren't you grapeful for that?'

His chest expanded until he thought it might explode. He had to swallow before he could speak, infected by all that darn female emotion that had been flying around no doubt. 'You bet.'

But as Ella slid off his knee with a final squeeze, he knew he couldn't blame anyone else for the prickle of heat that threatened his eyes and his heart. He'd accomplished what he'd set out to—he'd given his daughters the Christmas they deserved. It filled him up and made him breathe easier. He would never neglect Christmas again. Never. It was too important. In a world that could be cold and brutal, it was too…necessary.

He glanced at Nicola. His children's infuriatingly delightful nanny had helped him make this day a reality, just like she'd promised she would. He wondered if she realised that was because of who she innately was, though, rather than some artificial taking part that she'd felt obliged to perform.

He closed his eyes for a moment when he recalled Ella's heartbreaking question about her mother the previous night. He was grateful now—so grateful—that Nicola had answered the way she had. There might be tears over Fran before the day was through, but Nicola was right—he could only control those things that lay in his power. Fran did not come under that particular banner. He could rest safe in the knowledge that he'd done everything he could to give his girls the Christmas they deserved. But rather than Ella or Holly, his gaze returned constantly to Nicola.

Nicola, Dee and Verity laughed in unison when they unwrapped their gifts from each other—they'd bought one another silk scarves, admired together from the same website. The children all momentarily glanced up from the *Amazing Facts* picture books and activity packs that Nicola had bought for them, but they quickly went back to oohing and ahhing over their pictures. Cade shot Harry a surreptitious glance to find she was grinning too, and sporting her Wonder Woman apron—again, one of Nicola's gifts— with pride.

He stretched his legs out, leaned back and savoured the moment. Then he seized two presents from beneath the tree and placed them into Nicola's lap.

She glanced up at him with a shy smile. 'Thank you.'

'You're welcome. Now open them.'

She tore the wrapping paper from the first, grinned and rolled her eyes. 'What are you trying to do to my waistline?' she demanded, holding up the biggest jar of chocolate-coated sultanas he'd been able to find.

'A little indulgence is good for the soul,' he countered, and then had to drag his gaze from her mouth. *That* wasn't the kind of indulgence he'd meant.

He watched as she unwrapped the second gift. Her soft 'Oh!' and wide eyes were the only thanks he needed.

'What did you get?' Dee demanded.

Nicola held up her bounty. 'Novels,' she said, and her eyes shone. 'Romance novels.'

'Ooh, that looks like a good story,' Dee said, 'and I love that author.'

'Let me see,' Verity said. 'Oh, I've read that one. It's fabulous!'

But Nicola wasn't looking at Dee or Verity, who were admiring the cache of books. She was staring straight at him with an expression that made him push his shoulders back.

'You remembered.'

'I did.' It occurred to him that, as far as Nicola went, there'd be very little he'd ever forget. Her eyes and her smile told him he'd given her the perfect present. It hadn't been much, but her true delight in the gift moved him far more than he'd expected. It made him suddenly awkward. It made him wish he could buy her a whole library of romance novels if that would make her happy.

'Open yours,' she urged with a nod towards his present under the tree. 'It's just something little. A joke really,' she said.

Her eyes danced and anticipation fizzed through him. He didn't need a second bidding. He seized the present and tore off the paper. He stared for a moment and then started to laugh. She'd given him the largest box of assorted chocolates and sweets he'd ever seen with a big *Beware* sticker plastered across the front. The accompanying note read: *Please eat in moderation!* Somehow she'd taken a bad memory, a moment of awfulness, and had turned it into something he could laugh about.

As he made a move to kiss her cheek, a second item fell out, wrapped in bubble-wrap. Intrigued, he unrolled it, and then a grin spread across his face. In his hand he held a finely wrought pewter figurine of a boxer.

Nicola grinned back at him. 'I couldn't resist.'

Verity stared from one to the other. 'I sense there's a story there.'

'Perhaps,' Nicola conceded. 'Though maybe it's more of a private joke.'

Her tact touched him, but he had no such qualms. 'Very private,' he declared, 'as I have no intention of ever telling anyone how you managed to flatten me when I gave you a boxing lesson.'

Dee promptly held her hand up and Nicola high-fived her. 'What can I say?' she said mock modestly. 'Horse-riding and boxing—it appears I'm a natural at both.'

When Dee and Verity had turned away, caught up in admiring Keith's gift to Verity—a lovely opal bracelet—Nicola nodded towards the tree again. That was when he saw a second present sporting his name on the gift tag in Nicola's handwriting. 'That one is from Ella and Holly.'

He glanced at his daughters and then ripped off the paper to find a photo frame—obviously decorated by them, no doubt with Nicola's assistance. While he instantly loved the haphazard stars and lopsided flowers painted on the frame, it was the photo that caught his attention, and held it.

Ella and Holly didn't just smile from the frame and they didn't just giggle—their entire faces and bodies glowed and roared with laughter. It spoke of their youth and their innocence, and there was no shadow of the past sixteen months there—it was a moment of straight-down-the-line exhilaration.

And it stole his breath.

He suddenly realised why this Christmas—why making it so perfect for Ella and Holly—had become so important for him. He'd been searching for optimism, for hope for the future, and an assurance that they would all be okay.

He held that assurance in his hand.

He met Nicola's gaze. 'Thank you.'

CHAPTER NINE

NICOLA paused in the doorway to the living room and drank in the stillness and silence of the Christmas night. The children had all gone to bed a couple of hours ago, and it appeared that the rest of the household had retired too.

It had been a big day.

It had been the most amazing Christmas she'd ever had.

It was getting late, but she was still too keyed up to sleep. Perhaps she just wasn't ready to let it all go yet. Sinking into the largest of the sofas, she slid sideways so she half-sat, half-lay across it, her head resting on its arm. So much fun had taken place in this room today. Her lips curved upwards as she remembered it all. And at the centre had been Cade.

Always Cade. The thought of him warmed her blood.

'I thought you'd gone to bed.'

Before she could haul herself upright again, her feet were lifted so that she lay full length on the sofa. She couldn't help groaning her appreciation at the cushioning softness that cradled her or the warmth of Cade's hands at her ankles.

With a small sliding caress, he released them and hunkered down on the floor with his back against the sofa. He smelled of soap and the single malt Scotch that he drank.

It took an effort of will not to reach out and push her fingers through his hair.

'I still feel a little too keyed up to sleep,' she admitted.

He glanced at her, the blue of his eyes a caress against her face. 'You could've settled in with one of those romance novels.'

'Ah, but then I'd be up all night devouring it.'

He opened his mouth, but then his eyes stilled, his gaze seemingly arrested by her lips—arrested and absorbed. It made her blood chug and it chased her tiredness away in the time it took the lights on the Christmas tree to wink on and then off. And the longer he stared, the more she remembered the feel of his lips on hers and the taste of him, and the yearning, the craving, built inside her until she had to cover her mouth with her hand to stop him from looking at her like that.

He jolted away from her, his gaze shooting to the Christmas tree. She closed her eyes and tried to get her breathing back under control. 'I…' She swallowed. 'It's been a great day. You must be over the moon. You gave Ella a Christmas she'll remember for ever, and Holly had a ball. Not to mention the rest of your family.'

'And you?'

When he turned back it was almost as if that earlier moment hadn't happened. Her heart burned in protest even as her common sense told her it was for the best. 'I've had the best Christmas ever.' Her voice emerged on a husky whisper. She couldn't help it. 'What about you? Did you enjoy today or were you too preoccupied with making sure everyone else had a good time?'

He lifted his tumbler, breathed in the fumes, but he didn't drink. 'I had a great day.' He started to lift the tumbler to his lips and then paused and offered her the glass.

She wrinkled her nose and shook her head. 'I'm not a

fan of whisky.' Not even the gorgeous single malt Scotch that had been Verity's gift to Cade. 'I prefer something sweeter.'

He took a sip and his eyes suddenly gleamed. 'Something sweeter, huh?'

'I'm fine, Cade. I don't want anything, honestly.'

'I noticed you didn't stuff yourself senseless at lunch like the rest of us and then spend the afternoon nibbling on all the assorted goodies.'

'I ate my fair share, thank you very much!' She just hadn't gone back for seconds. And she hadn't picked too much between meals—other than a couple of handfuls of cherries. She was still intent on slimming down.

She had slimmed down.

Today had shown her just how much she'd always comfort ate at Christmas…and how much she comfort ate full stop. She didn't want to do that any more.

'Yet you have a sweet tooth.'

'That I'm doing my best to control.' She wasn't given to pats on the back—not for herself—but she couldn't help feeling she deserved a big fat pat on the back for that. There had been moments when that self-control had been sheer torture.

'You have a sweet tooth,' he repeated, 'and it's Christmas.'

She didn't trust that gleam in his eye. 'So?'

He slid across the floor and seized her jar of chocolate sultanas and lifted them in her direction. Her mouth promptly watered. No amount of self-control could prevent that.

She tried to distract herself. 'Harry and your mother wouldn't let me tidy up.' Presents still sat in festive stacks about the room.

'Absolutely not. That's what Boxing Day is for.'

He said it exactly the same way Verity had.

He shook the jar. 'Nicola, these are unopened.'

The sound of chocolate sultanas tinkling against glass sounded like raindrops hitting parched earth and cued more mouth watering. 'I...um...' She stared at the jar. Simon had kindly informed her that its contents looked like kangaroo droppings, but not even that thought could stop her from salivating. She swallowed. 'I'm saving them for when there's not quite so many other nibblies around.'

'You're not bringing these out to share with anyone.'

She wasn't?

'They are all yours.'

Her heart thudded in anticipation...and greed.

He slid back over to the sofa, bringing the jar with him. He broke the seal. 'Oops.'

His utter lack of remorse should've made her laugh, only he waved the jar under her nose and the combined scent of chocolate and sultana hit her. Her stomach clenched. Her resolve faltered.

'They're open now.'

The invitation in his voice could tempt a stronger woman than her. She forced herself to think of Melbourne, of Diane and Brad...and her mother. She sat up. She planted her feet on the floor. 'Then by all means help yourself to as many as you'd like.'

The gleam didn't leave his eyes, but a new determination entered them as he planted himself on the sofa beside her. He tipped a pile of the confectionery into his hand and held it out towards her. Taking one sultana, he lifted it to his lips and ate it slowly. 'Mmm...delicious.'

For a moment she couldn't move. She wanted to yell at him for tempting her resolve so outrageously.

A second sultana followed suit. That hand waved temptingly beneath her nose.

He lifted a third...

She could stand it no longer. She seized a sultana from his cupped hand and popped it straight into her mouth. The chocolate melted on her tongue. When she bit down, the flavour of the sultana exploded through her. She groaned and closed her eyes in ecstasy.

When he took her hand and poured the sultanas into them, she made no protest. She ate them, savoured them.

He watched her devour them. The gleam had left his eyes, replaced with something she couldn't read and was too cowardly to decipher.

'You really do love them.' His voice was low.

'They're my favourite food on earth.'

'Then why deny yourself? Especially today?'

The pile he'd tipped into her hand had gone. She'd eaten them all. And she wanted more. Lots more.

Are you going to be a complete glutton, Nicola Ann?

With a gulp, she seized the lid and tried to put it back on the jar, only Cade wouldn't let her. He captured her hand, his grip tightening until she looked at him. 'Why deny yourself?'

Her pulse throbbed at the contact. She tried to shrug. 'Once I start eating them, I can't stop.'

'And what's wrong with that?'

He couldn't be serious? 'If I keep eating them, I will get fat. Fatter,' she amended. 'How on earth will I lose weight if I keep indulging?'

'So you won't even allow yourself the occasional indulgence?'

'It's dangerous to indulge a weakness.'

His eyes narrowed. He poured more sultanas into his hand and held one out to her. She swallowed. She tried to say no, but his eyes urged her to throw caution to the winds, to live in the moment.

She opened her mouth, helpless to resist either Cade

or the sweet, and savoured every delicious moment of the morsel.

'It's ludicrous to deny yourself such a simple pleasure.'

It wasn't simple, though. She couldn't help but feel this lack of self-control was somehow tied into being treated so badly by Diane and Brad…and all her friends thinking her a doormat. Slimming down, brightening herself up and not allowing herself to be taken for granted would prove to them all that she wasn't a doormat. Or a failure.

He held another sultana up, she opened her mouth and he slipped it between her lips. The inherent sensuality of the gesture was as delicious as the chocolate and sultana combination. 'Would you be happier if you were thin?'

She blinked. 'Well, hello, yes!' Any woman would say yes to that.

He slammed the jar of sultanas onto the coffee table. 'Why the hell is that so? What the hell is wrong with your body? I *love* your body. I can't stand that you hate it.' He ground his teeth together and then poured more sultanas into her hand. 'Your worth is not measured by your weight or your waistline. Eat!'

He loved her body? With tears prickling the backs of her eyes, she ate.

Finally she had to lean back with a groan and shake her head. 'If I have any more I'll be ill.'

Only then did Cade replace the lid on the jar. He turned back to her. 'What do you think losing weight will prove to Diane and Brad…or your mother?'

His perception froze her.

'That you have worth?'

If she said yes, would he yell at her again?

'It's not your weight that's the problem, Nicola, it's your attitude. Until you learn to embrace your body, to love it as you should love it because it's beautiful, then nobody else is going to give you the respect you deserve.'

He reached out and cupped her cheek. His hand smelled of chocolate. She wanted to close her eyes and breathe him in. 'We teach people how to treat us. You don't need to lose weight. You need to learn to walk tall—with pride and confidence.'

She thought about that, and about the way Verity and Dee carried themselves. The way Cade carried himself. They walked with pride and confidence, as if they were sure of who they were and their place in the world.

Growing up with her mother's constant stream of criticism had eroded her confidence and sense of self-worth, but she wasn't a child any longer. She was an adult, able to make her own value judgements, and there were a lot of things she could do well. She was a good teacher and a good friend. She could ride a horse as if it were second nature. When she sang, people stopped to listen. She believed in the values of compassion, kindness and justice.

'Well?'

She stared into his eyes and realised she couldn't believe those values held true for other people and not for herself too. Values didn't work that way.

She blinked, stunned by the revelation. 'I think,' she started slowly, 'that you might be right. I mean, it's such a simple truth but…' She'd never seen it before.

Finally he smiled and it was like Christmas all over again. She leaned forward and kissed his cheek. 'Thank you.'

He stilled. His gaze lowered to her lips and his eyes darkened. Heat threaded through her…and temptation.

'You should go to bed.'

The words growled out of him, but his gaze remained on her lips, the hunger in them identical to her hunger for the chocolate sultanas. It was then she realised there was something she craved more than those—Cade. She wanted him with an elemental savagery that shook her bones.

She should move away and go to bed like he'd ordered, but Cade had set something free in her tonight when he'd tempted her with those sultanas and told her he loved her body. He'd made her face temptation head-on. He'd forced her to indulge it. Now she had no hope of resisting the greater temptation he presented. She had no desire to do so.

She slipped her hands either side of his face and, leaning forward, placed her lips on his. She tasted of chocolate, he tasted of whisky, and the combination of flavours was as heady as anything she had ever experienced.

He held himself still beneath her touch, but he didn't pull away and, emboldened, she moved in closer to deepen the kiss and taste him more fully.

A breath shuddered out of him. Her hands explored the angle of his jaw, the strong line of his neck and shoulders. One of her hands snaked around his head to anchor her more firmly against him while her other splayed across his chest, revelling in the male strength of him.

With that movement it was as if she had released some check or restraint in him. With a groan, he gathered her close and claimed her lips with a potent mastery that had her trembling and reeling both at the same time.

His hand moved to the hem of her shirt, and then under it. The skin on skin contact made her gasp as a delicious new energy and a brand new greed fired through her. He pressed her back against the sofa, angling her beneath him as his lips and tongue teased her lips and tongue, and all she could do was cling to him. One powerful thigh insinuated its way between her legs. She arched against it, wanting to feel him pressed against all of her, gripped by a need bigger than herself.

He'd fed her chocolate sultanas. He'd told her he loved her body. He kissed her exactly how she'd always needed to be kissed but had never been kissed before. The man was perfect!

With a growl, she reached up and tore the buttons from his shirt, raked her fingernails down his bare chest. He hissed in a breath and she revelled in the freedom of touching him. She pressed her palms to his hot skin and breathed him in. He was hard and as smooth as satin.

Perfect!

Slowly, deliciously, she moved her hands down to his stomach. He trembled. Had she done that? She did it again. He trembled again and she revelled in the knowledge that she could affect all of this superb masculinity so easily, with just a touch.

Beneath her shirt, his hand moved to cover one breast. Beneath the thin cotton of her bra her nipple puckered and tautened. He rolled it between thumb and forefinger.

'Oh!' She stiffened and then arched into his touch, her body jerking in reaction, and that slow, lazy smile that she loved so much spread across his face as he continued to torment her fevered flesh.

Boldly, she ran her fingers beneath the waistband of his jeans and the laziness vanished. 'Kiss me,' she groaned. It was half an order and half a plea. He complied and Nicola lost herself in a world of sensation.

Completely. Time held no sway. There was only Cade and her...and magic.

'Daddy?'

A foreign sound filtered into her consciousness and Nicola stilled.

'Nic?'

Cade froze.

It hit her then what the interruption was—Ella!

She and Cade sprang apart. Nicola righted her clothes and pasted on a bright smile for Ella's benefit. 'Hey, pumpkin.'

She glanced at Cade, expecting him to look as discomposed as she felt. He didn't. He'd gone cold and still. He'd withdrawn, utterly and completely. Her stomach dropped and her skin chilled. He'd thrown up a brick wall, complete with razor wire and a watchtower. His body gave off wave after wave of rebuttal and rejection. She wanted to close her eyes so she didn't have to witness it. She wanted to shake him. She wanted…

It didn't matter what she wanted.

'What's up, sweetie?' Her voice came out surprisingly steady, although her insides trembled and her knees felt like jelly. 'What are you doing up?'

Ella raced across to bury her face in Nicola's lap. 'I'm thirsty. I want a drink of water.'

'Oh, I think we can manage that.' She brushed a hand through the child's hair.

She kept her voice deliberately cheerful, even while inside she was dying. Dying of embarrassment and something darker and harder and meaner, although she couldn't put a name to it. But it reared up to stab her every time she glanced at the hard, uncompromising line of Cade's mouth.

'I'll take care of this.'

With an effortless ease that spoke of his strength—and resolve—he lifted Ella into his arms.

'Go to bed, Nicola.'

He turned and walked away. And just like that she was dismissed.

She sat there, stunned, unable to move as her body attempted to process the emotions that tumbled through her in a confusing jumbled rush—the memory of Cade's mouth on hers, with its searing heat, the way her body had come alive in his arms, the way she'd forgotten herself completely…and then the chilled recognition of his withdrawal.

Her hands clenched. She should feel grateful for the interruption, but all she felt was a frustrated sense of disappointment, and it grew and prickled and itched. She would get no sleep tonight.

She rose, Cade's curt and dismissive *Go to bed, Nicola* still ringing in her ears, when a sudden chill dissipated all of her built up heat.

Her arms snaked about her waist. Her mouth dried. What on earth had she been thinking? If they hadn't been interrupted, she and Cade would've gone all the way. They'd have made love. And then what?

She wrung her hands and then gripped them tightly. What was wrong with her? Did she mean to transfer all the dreams she'd had for the future—marriage, babies and a home—to the first man she met? Was she really that weak and needy?

Her chin snapped up. While she suspected Cade wasn't in the right head space to contemplate that kind of commitment, she knew for sure that she wasn't. Her life was complicated enough as it was. She wasn't going to make it even more complicated.

Go to bed, Nicola.

She went to bed.

'What's your New Year resolution, Nicola, darling?'

Nicola started when Verity directed the question at her. It shouldn't have; almost everyone else in the room had taken a turn. Verity wanted to learn Irish dancing. Keith wanted to complete a marathon. Dee wanted to lose weight, which had made everyone laugh with its predictability and droll delivery.

Nicola planned to incorporate a lot of changes into her life when she returned to Melbourne, but what would she choose as her New Year resolution? It had to be something special.

'You don't have to tell us if it's too personal, darling.'

'Oh, it's not that. It's just...' She pushed her shoulders back. 'This year I want to make my resolution matter, and I want to keep it.'

She could feel Cade's eyes on her—their penetrating heat and intelligence. She refused to turn and meet his gaze, afraid of what her face might reveal. They'd carefully skirted around each other this week, kept their dealings short and professional, had never once mentioned their out of control Christmas kiss, but she suspected one look would reveal the desire she tried to keep in check. If an answering desire flared in his eyes she'd be lost. And she didn't want to be lost.

'Okay.' She straightened in her easy chair—she and Cade didn't share a sofa any more. 'This year I will not avoid confrontation if keeping the peace is at my own expense. This last year has shown me that keeping the peace for everyone else's sake is not always good for me.'

'Wow,' Dee breathed. 'That's a tough one.'

Nicola wrinkled her nose. 'Especially as I hate confrontation.'

'You've made me feel shallow.'

'Oh, and I forgot to add that I want to lose five kilos too.'

As she hoped, everyone laughed.

'Cade, darling, what's your resolution?'

She could still feel his gaze on her. She schooled her face and turned her head to meet it.

'Nicola has taught me something this last month.'

She had? He smiled and it was so unexpected she had to smile back. Everyone leaned forward, eager to hear what he had to say.

'I directed all my energies into making Christmas wonderful for the girls—for everyone else too, but primarily for the girls.'

They all nodded.

'I realise now I should be directing my energies into making the rest of the year just as good.'

The breath whooshed out of her. She'd taught him that?

'It's time to look to the future instead of the past. That's what I'll be working on this year.'

'Amen,' Verity said softly. 'Ooh, look, it's nearly time for the countdown to midnight. Keith and Cade, top up everyone's glasses while I turn on the radio.'

They all stood and counted down the final ten seconds to midnight and the brand new year. Nicola prayed that this year she would be able to hold her head high and prove her worth—to herself. It had become less and less important to prove it to anyone else.

'Happy New Year!' all of Cade's family called out, clinking champagne flutes. Then there were hugs and kisses.

'Happy New Year, Nicola.' Cade kissed her cheek and then backed off in super-quick time.

'Happy New Year,' she said, fighting a sense of awkwardness. 'Nice resolution, boss man.'

'Right back at you,' he returned.

He grinned. She smiled. And the awkwardness slipped away and it felt as if their friendship was back on track. And it felt right...even if she had to tamp down on the desire that threaded through her.

'Okay, bedtime for me,' Verity declared. 'Especially if I'm to wake in time for the traditional New Year trek.'

Nicola glanced at Verity. 'Traditional trek?'

They all turned to stare at her. 'Hasn't anybody mentioned Lake Campbell to you, darling?'

Umm…no.

At her blank look, Cade said, 'Every New Year's Day we pack a picnic and head out to the lake. It's a bit of a trek as the lake is two hours away, but…'

'But the children love it,' Dee said, picking up where Cade left off. 'The swimming and the change of scenery.'

'So do the adults.' Verity smiled. 'I know you're used to the coast and the seaside, but the lake is a lovely place to swim, and it's a beautiful spot. I promise you'll enjoy it.'

'I don't doubt that for a moment. It sounds lovely,' Nicola said. It would be wonderful to experience more of this compelling Outback landscape. 'You'll have to excuse me from the swimming, though. I'm afraid I didn't bring a swimming costume.' She hadn't expected to need one.

'The kids won't let you get away with that,' Dee said. 'You've become too firm a favourite. Besides, we play lots of water games and it would be a shame to sit those out. I'll lend you a cossie. We're about the same size.' She suddenly chuckled. 'After all, I did bring four with me.'

Keith shook his head. 'The woman has no concept of packing light.'

Dee slapped him playfully and then her eyes gleamed in a way that reminded Nicola of Cade. 'In fact, I know the exact costume that would suit you best.'

All through this exchange she was aware of Cade's watchful surveillance. The thought of appearing in front of him in a swimsuit… Something inside her trembled. She forced a smile. 'Lovely, thank you.'

As they all drifted away to their separate bedrooms to

retire for the night, it occurred to her that tomorrow Cade would appear before her in nothing but a swimsuit as well.

She couldn't quite stamp out the anticipation that threaded through her.

'What do you think?' Cade asked as she climbed from the ute.

For a moment Nicola couldn't form a coherent sentence. The wild beauty of Cade's lake stole her breath. Never in her wildest dreams had she ever imagined that such a place could exist, or that she'd ever be lucky enough to visit it.

They'd arrived along a long, low, green-brown plain that had extended for mile upon mile and had lulled her with its unending monotony, but that was all at her back. In front of her stretched a large lake, bordered on its far side by a wall of orange and yellow rock that curved at least halfway around towards them. Not even a breeze ruffled the calm surface of the water that reflected back the sky's perfect blue. Paper daisies dotted the shore and a flock of pink cockatoos squalled in a stand of tall skinny gum trees off to her left. 'It's an oasis,' she breathed.

Holly's imperious squeal from her child's seat in the back of the car had her swinging away from the amazing view. 'I'll get her,' Cade said, grinning at whatever he saw in her face.

Ella slipped her hand into Nicola's. 'This is one of my favourite places ever.'

'Mine too,' Nicola found herself agreeing.

It was an almost perfect day. Everyone was in a determined holiday mood and, as Verity explained to her, this really was the last hurrah for their holiday. Tomorrow, she, Dee, Keith and the twins would be returning to Brisbane and 'the real world' as she called it.

The borrowed swimsuit wasn't an exercise in self-conscious agony either. For a start, it wasn't the bikini she'd feared but a one-piece that nipped her in nicely at the waist, even if the bust line plunged much lower than she was used to.

The expression on Cade's face when he first saw her in it made that more than worthwhile. It made her feel beautiful, glamorous even. And then she'd taken in his bare chest and shoulders—the latent power and strength of him on display—and heat had shimmered between them with a dangerous intensity that had held them both in thrall.

Someone's laughter had broken the spell. Cade had turned and plunged into the lake and Nicola had been able to breathe again. After that they were careful to avoid eye contact.

They all swam. They joked and laughed. They played water cricket. They relaxed on the shore and demolished the picnic Harry had packed for them. When offered, Nicola took two whole handfuls of chocolate sultanas and savoured every single one of them. They dozed under makeshift shelters during the worst of the heat and then swam again.

And all the while Nicola was aware of Cade's compelling presence. Of his ease and patience with the children. Of his courtesy to his mother and sister…and to her. And of the undisputed beauty of his body.

In the evening the men built a contained campfire. Not for warmth but to toast marshmallows. It was the perfect end to the perfect day.

Ella planted herself on Nicola's lap, her head resting in the hollow of Nicola's shoulder. Her clean wholesome smell, her soft weight, stirred all of Nicola's not so latent maternal instincts and created an ache deep inside.

She did her best to ignore it. One day maybe she'd be

lucky enough to have a little girl as loving and trusting as Ella. She pulled Ella close for a hug and to plant a kiss on the crown of her head.

'I had the best day in the world, Nic.'

'Me too, sweetie.'

The child was silent for a while and Nicola thought she'd fallen asleep. 'I wish you were my mummy.'

Ella's words were clear in the evening air and rang out around the circle they'd formed about the campfire. Nicola didn't dare look at any of the other adults. Not that she would've seen them for the sudden tears that blinded her. She blinked hard, but nothing could clear the ache that stretched her throat…or the bigger one settling in her chest.

'Honey…' she swallowed '…I think that's just about the nicest thing anyone has ever said to me.'

Ella suddenly straightened. 'Daddy, you could marry Nic. I know you like her because I saw you kissing her.'

CHAPTER TEN

ELLA'S innocently revealing words punched the air from Cade's lungs, robbing him of the ability to speak. It was all he could do to stay upright and not fall face first in the dirt.

To his infinite relief, his mother and Dee tactfully started to pack things away in preparation for the return journey. They didn't raise enquiring or teasing eyebrows in his direction or shoot him sidelong glances. He loved them for the space they gave him, the way they respected his privacy. He'd neglected them this last year and they'd borne it without complaint. He would never be able to thank them enough for their patience.

It didn't mean he could move to help them clean up now, though. It didn't mean he could think of anything to say to ease the situation.

I wish you were my mummy. The words froze him all over again. His temples throbbed. His eyes ached. All he could do was stare at Nicola and pray that...

What? That she could make this right?

I wish you were my mummy. He swallowed the bile that burned acid in his throat.

He had no idea how Nicola managed to maintain her composure, but she did, and while it was true that colour heightened her cheeks, she didn't stumble as she explained to Ella that the kiss the child had witnessed had only been a friendly kiss and that she and Daddy were just good friends. She didn't laugh at Ella, which would've cut the child to the quick. He was seized with a sudden fierce desire to hug her for her easy, confident manner with his daughter. With both his daughters.

'But I don't want you to leave Waminda!' Ella suddenly wailed.

A chill trickled down his spine. He should've seen this coming—the fact that Ella might form an attachment to her temporary nanny. He should've taken it into account, but he'd been too hell-bent on ensuring Christmas went off without a hitch to have considered the possibility.

Perspiration prickled his scalp, his nape, his top lip. After Fran's desertion, it was a possibility he should've considered. He'd left Ella open for rejection, not just by one woman, but by two. His hands clenched. His jaw clenched. He wanted to throw his head back and howl at the mess he'd made of things.

'I love it at Waminda too.' Nicola's voice sounded clear and harmonious in the evening air. It filtered through the furore raging in his mind and somehow helped to soothe it, though he didn't know how.

'But you always knew I had to go back to my home in Melbourne. I have to go back to see my mother and my friends…and I have to go back to my job, remember?'

'As a schoolteacher.' Ella nodded, evidently proud that she'd remembered.

'But it doesn't mean we can't be best friends for ever, though, does it? We can write to each other—letters and emails. That'll be fun, don't you think?'

Ella nodded again. And then she straightened and started to bounce. 'We could Skype!'

His four-year-old had recently discovered the joys of the Internet and particularly Skype. His lips twisted. He could forsee a Skype addiction in the future. But suddenly that didn't seem so bad, because Ella wasn't crying or traumatised by the thought of Nicola's departure from Waminda.

Nicola had managed to quieten Ella's fears and at the same time pump up the little girl's confidence with an ease he couldn't believe. It occurred to him then that she might have foreseen a moment like this, and had come up with a plan that she'd implemented so smoothly nobody's feelings were hurt and all seemed right with the world. Only...

In another three weeks, Nicola *would* leave Waminda, and that suddenly seemed very, very wrong.

He shot to his feet and immediately set about helping with the general clearing up and packing away. They always made an effort to leave the lake and surrounding as untouched as they could.

I wish you were my mummy.

The words burned like a brand. His gaze drifted to Ella and Nicola and his heart clenched at the way Ella rested against Nicola with all the trust in her four-year-old heart. And at the way Nicola held the child as if she were the most precious thing in the world.

Ella deserved a mother—a woman who would love her and provide her with a role model.

Nicola deserved the family, the children her heart craved.

Daddy, you could marry Nic.

The insidious thought slid under his guard and chafed at him. He tried to shake it off. It was a crazy idea.

I saw you kissing her.

His mouth dried. There was no doubt whatsoever that he enjoyed kissing her. No doubt whatsoever that he'd like to do a whole lot more than kiss her.

But marry her?

He shook his head with a muttered curse and set about packing the car.

Cade, Nicola, Ella and Holly—with a little help from Nicola—waved at the plane as it took off into endless and cloudless blue sky.

Ella slipped her hand inside Cade's. 'I'll miss Grandma, Daddy.'

'Me too.' It took him a moment to drag his gaze from the way Nicola kissed Holly's crown and then made her giggle by tickling her. He forced himself to smile down at Ella. 'But she'll visit again soon,' he assured her, ushering them back to the car and helping Ella with her seat belt while Nicola strapped Holly into her car seat.

'She said she'd visit for my birthday.'

He nodded as he started the car and turned it in the direction of the homestead. Dee was going to do her best to bring the boys back for a couple of days then too. He hoped he'd be able to return the favour and take Ella and Holly to visit for the twins' birthdays later in the year.

'Nic, can you come back for my birthday?'

Nicola stiffened. If he hadn't been so finely attuned to her every movement he'd have missed it, it was so fleeting. But he was attuned. And he didn't miss it.

He glanced at her sharply, but she barely met his gaze as she turned to talk to Ella in the back seat. 'When's your birthday, sweetie?'

'Um…Daddy?'

'The eleventh of March.'

Nicola shook her head. 'That's in term time so I won't be able to make it.'

In the rear-vision mirror he watched the joy leach from Ella's face.

'But it doesn't mean I can't come to visit in holiday time…or that I can't send you a present,' she added on a teasing note.

Both assurances made Ella brighten, but they didn't satisfy him. 'What about Easter?' he found himself demanding. 'Could you come then?'

She met his gaze but he couldn't read her expression and he had to drag his attention back to the dusty track before he drove over a mulga bush or fallen log or large rock and ripped a hole in the fuel tank or tore the muffler from the car.

'I'm afraid not.'

'You have plans?' He couldn't let it go.

'I do.'

There was nothing left to say after that.

Something dragged Cade from the depths of sleep. He sat up in bed and tried to shake the fog from his brain so he could identify what had woken him.

Crying… Holly…

He was on his feet in an instant and stumbling in the direction of the nursery.

He paused in the doorway. Nicola was already there. She had Holly in her arms and was walking her up and down singing a low lullaby. He noticed the bottle of baby medicine on the nightstand.

When she turned to walk back towards the doorway and saw him, she shot him a smile that reassured him there was nothing seriously wrong with his youngest daughter. In time and tune to her lullaby, she sang, 'We're teething, Daddy, and it's not very comfortable.'

Holly's cries were starting to ease. Poor little tyke. He wanted to reach out and cradle her head, only he didn't want to disturb her now she was starting to settle again.

Nicola sang that he should go back to bed.

He should. He needed to be up early in the morning—as usual—but he found he didn't want to. He found the sight of Nicola in her nightie, rocking his child to sleep, amazingly comforting...and undeniably erotic. It struck him as unbelievably tantalising when he realised how thin her nightdress was, and how he could almost make out her entire shape beneath it.

His nanny was all woman and pure temptation. When she leant over the cot his breath caught at the free sway of her breasts. He could imagine the weight of them in his hands, he could imagine burying his face in them and the way she would arch against him and—

'Cade, go to bed. Holly is sleeping now. I'm sorry we woke you.'

She'd settled Holly with a minimum of fuss. She was great with her. She was great with both his daughters.

'Can we talk?' The question shot out of him before he realised he'd meant to ask it. But after a moment's thought he didn't regret it. Not one little bit. He pushed his shoulders back.

'Cade, it's one o'clock in the morning.'

'But—'

'This is not a good time for us to talk.' She swallowed. 'It's not a good time for us to be alone.'

When she went to ease past him, he used his body to trap her against the doorframe. His chest touched her chest and he could feel the way her breath caught and her nipples peaked. His groin hardened in instant response. He prayed she'd stay.

With a shuddering breath, she pushed him away. 'In the morning, Cade. We'll talk then,' she choked out, and then she fled down the hallway to her own room.

His hand curled to a fist. He rested his forehead against

the doorframe and bit back a curse. That hadn't been the smartest move he'd ever made. He'd promised he would just be a good friend, but…

But the moment he saw her all good intentions flew out of his head. He'd better get his damn hormones back under control by morning, though, because he and Nicola were going to have a talk. And he meant to keep it completely professional.

He pushed away from the door and headed for his en suite bathroom. He needed a cold shower.

Breakfast the next morning was hell. Every time Nicola's mouth closed about her toast or touched the rim of her mug, his body reacted with the memory of those lips on his flesh and the fire they could send shooting through his veins.

When she reached for the strawberry jam, he shot to his feet. 'When you're done here, could you come to my study?'

She blinked at his abruptness. 'Yes, of course.'

Professional, level-headed, he schooled himself as he strode away. He wanted Nicola to stay at Waminda Downs permanently and he had to outline to her in as attractive a way as possible all the reasons why that was a good idea. Hormones would not help him there.

Less than ten minutes later she appeared in his study doorway. He motioned for her to take the seat across the desk from him. He did his best not to notice the soft plumpness of her lips and to close his mind to the scent of strawberry jam. It wasn't easy, especially as some time during the last few weeks she'd started wearing clothes that accentuated her stunning figure rather than hide it, clothes that highlighted the colour of her hair and eyes and made her skin glow. He gritted his teeth.

'You wanted to talk to me?' she prompted.

He kicked himself into gear. 'Nicola, I want you to consider taking on the role of Ella and Holly's nanny full-time. Both of them adore you and you've fitted in so well at Waminda Downs. Having you here has made me realise that we do, in fact, need a full-time nanny.'

It wasn't fair to ask Harry to take on so much of the child-minding duties on top of all her other chores. Having Nicola here had freed up both him and Harry. He couldn't deny he'd enjoyed the opportunity to work around the station more these last few weeks—had rediscovered his love for a good day's work.

'I believe you're right and you do need a full-time nanny, but, Cade, although I'm touched you asked me first, the answer is no.'

His head snapped back. For a moment he couldn't speak. 'But…but you haven't even taken the time to consider it yet.' His mouth opened and closed. He fought a scowl. 'I thought you liked it here. I thought you loved Holly and Ella.'

'I adore them!' She leaned forward. 'And I have enjoyed it here, but I made it clear from the first that this was a time-out for me and not a permanent venture.'

His hands clenched. 'Why can't you reconsider all that now—?'

'I love my job as a schoolteacher.' She sat back. 'I've worked hard to get where I am. Becoming a nanny would not be making the best use of my skills. It would, in fact, be a demotion.'

'I can afford to pay you your current salary.' Plus more.

'It's not about the money, Cade!' Her eyes suddenly spat fire. 'Look, I have no intention of burying myself out here as if I'm afraid to return home, as if I can't hold my head up and meet anyone's eyes square-on.'

She wouldn't even take a few days to think about his

offer? He slashed a hand through the air. She was perfect for his daughters. And they were perfect for her. If only she'd see it. 'That's just misplaced pride!'

'No, it's not.' Her eyes didn't flash fire any more. She looked cool. Too cool. 'Besides, it's sensible. Down the track, I want to marry and have children of my own. Who am I going to meet out here?'

The thought of another man kissing those luscious lips fired him with an anger he knew he had no right to feel. An unreasonable, unholy anger. He bit back the torrent that clawed at his throat. Think. *Think!* It would be in everyone's best interests if she stayed.

She wanted to be a mother.

He wanted a mother for his children.

He shot to his feet. 'Then marry me, Nicola. That way we can both have what we want.'

Nicola recoiled from Cade and his outrageous suggestion.

He strode around the desk. She shot to her feet but he caught her hand before she could back away.

'Think about it,' he urged in that silky voice that could tempt a saint.

She had thought about it! The life here—her soul craved it. It seemed perfect.

Except…

He didn't love her. And she wasn't sure if she loved him. Lust wasn't love. Nor was a desire for a family. She would not be weak and stupid, as she had been with Brad. She meant to be very sure of her reasons the next time she decided to marry.

If there is a next time, Nicola Ann. At your age there certainly aren't any guarantees.

She swallowed.

'I have a family that would embrace and welcome you.

We'd have more children, of course. We could have as many as you wanted.'

How many more offers of marriage do you expect to receive?

'And you can't deny there's heat between us. It would be very pleasurable creating those babies.'

She couldn't deny that. And she couldn't deny the empty ache that filled her whenever she thought of having children of her own and wondering if that would ever happen, but...

He lifted her chin to meet his gaze, his fingers caressing the skin there. 'I would be faithful to you. I would do whatever I could to make you happy.'

He meant every word; she could see that. She swallowed the lump in her throat. 'You don't love me.'

'I like you. I enjoy spending time with you. I desire you. And you love my daughters. What more could I possibly need?'

'Love.'

He frowned. 'You said the next time you decided to marry, you'd make sure you got exactly what you wanted from the relationship.' He eased back, his eyes serious. 'I am offering you exactly what you want.'

She had to bite her tongue. She had to swallow and then draw in a deep breath. No matter how much this man with his angry wounded eyes and his lips that could transport her to heaven tempted her, she would not make the same mistake she had in the past. 'I was wrong and misguided when I said those things. I was feeling hurt and angry and I wanted to lash out. I wanted to find a way to protect myself, but it was all a lie.'

She pulled herself up to her full height. 'Since I've been here I've come to see how wrong that kind of thinking is. If I treated someone that callously and with that degree of calculation it would make me worse than Brad and Diane. I have no intention of…of being such a bitch.'

His eyes narrowed. 'Love is an overrated emotion and—'

'And it's precisely what I need, and I won't settle for anything less.' She snatched her hand from his. 'I need love *and* friendship.' Her eyes burned and her throat thickened. 'You made me believe in friendship again, but it was a lie. You don't care what's best for me. All you care about is what's best for your daughters and you're more than willing to sacrifice me on that particular altar, aren't you?'

'I—'

'But if you think a loveless marriage is what's best for Ella and Holly then you are truly and utterly mistaken.' She heaved in a breath, taken off guard by the pain that sliced through her. 'There are a lot of nannies out there who would bond with Ella and Holly as well as I have done and whom you wouldn't have to make the supreme sacrifice of marrying.'

He clenched his jaw so hard white lines appeared around his mouth. 'I wouldn't consider marrying you a sacrifice,' he ground out.

For a moment she almost believed him. She gave a harsh laugh and shook her head. 'You are so not ready to get remarried. Are you telling me you're prepared to give another woman the chance to walk out on you and the girls again? Because what makes you so sure I wouldn't, huh?'

His head snapped back. 'I know you. I know you wouldn't do that.'

Really? She folded her arms. 'Let's just play with another scenario for a moment. What if I said I would marry you and Fran heard about it and, as a result, came racing back here to ask you for a second chance? After all, she is

Ella and Holly's mother. Who would you choose? Which of us would you deem as the best choice for your daughters?'

His face, his frame, his fists all tightened. 'That is not going to happen!'

'That's not an answer, Cade.' A terrible tiredness gripped her. Her temples throbbed and her hands shook. Perspiration prickled her nape. 'And until you do know the answer you're in no fit state to marry anyone.'

She recognised the panic that raced across his face then too but she had to harden her heart against it before it led her into doing something she'd regret.

She folded her arms. 'Marrying you would not be the best thing for me.'

Beneath his tan, he paled.

You stupid girl, Nicola Ann!

She lifted her chin. 'I deserve better.'

She turned and left the room. He didn't try to stop her.

The next fifteen days were a new kind of hell, one Nicola had never experienced before. Cade barely spoke to her and yet as each day passed she could hardly bear the thought of leaving Waminda Downs—of leaving Jack and Scarlett and Harry; of leaving Ella and Holly.

Of leaving Cade.

Her heart lurched and ached with each reminder of the hours that passed and the diminishing time that was left to her here. Somehow this place and these people had soaked into her bones.

She hadn't fallen in love with Cade, though. She refused to believe that.

Leaving day finally arrived, and the moment the Cessna left the ground to wing her away on the first leg of her journey home to Melbourne, Nicola burst into tears.

'Sorry,' she mumbled to the pilot—Jerry, who'd brought

her to Waminda Downs seven weeks ago—as he handed her a handkerchief. 'It's just I'm going to miss them all so much.'

He nodded. 'Those little girls are the sweetest things. Kids, huh? They wrap themselves around your heart.'

They were…and they had. But it was Cade's face that rose in her mind. With each mile that took her further away, the more it felt as if her heart was being ripped from her chest.

CHAPTER ELEVEN

Four months later...

NICOLA slipped the orange chiffon dress over her head and smoothed it down across her hips as her mother tied the halter neck into a bow at Nicola's nape, and then adjusted the plunging neckline for a flattering and dramatic effect.

'Nicola Ann, you look lovely. You'll outshine the bride herself.' Angela McGillroy's lips pressed together. 'Not that she doesn't deserve it.'

Nicola suppressed a smile. Her mother's attitude had undergone an amazing transformation ever since a particularly frank and terse discussion they'd had when Nicola had returned from Waminda Downs. She had unequivocally told her mother that if she wanted to maintain a relationship with her, the constant stream of criticism and nit-picking had to stop. She'd told her that the way she chose to live her life was her affair—if it made her happy, why did her mother have such a problem with it?

Her mother hadn't been able to speak for a full thirty seconds. 'But Nicola Ann,' she'd finally said, 'all I want is for you to be happy. I just never thought you were.'

'Maybe because I never am when I'm around you. You always make me feel I'm a disappointment, that I never measure up.'

'Oh, Nicola, why have you never told me this before? I've been pushing the things that make me happy in the hope that they'd help. They weren't supposed to make you unhappier! It's just...that's the way I was raised.'

And for the first time Nicola had recognised her own mistakes in the relationship. She'd bottled up all her resentment and pain and had never told her mother how she'd really felt. But now...

Now they were taking it one day at a time. Relationships like theirs didn't heal overnight, but she had to give her mother credit for trying. Yes, she still occasionally nagged Nicola, but she'd also become incredibly supportive.

Cade had been right—we did teach others how to treat us.

'Are you sure you're happy going to this wretched wedding? Nobody would blame you if you changed your mind, you know?'

'I'm fine, Mum, honestly. The truth is, Diane did me a favour.'

A fact confirmed the first time she'd clapped eyes on the couple when she'd returned to Melbourne. In fact, with Cade so fresh in her mind, Brad had seemed pale and lacking in dynamism...a touch inadequate even. She couldn't believe she'd almost married him.

At the thought of Cade, a cloud drifted across the brightness of the day. Unlike Brad, his influence had not waned with time.

'You know, Nicola Ann, I'm not sure I ever really did like Brad.'

She had to smile at that.

'But I still don't like what Diane did. She was supposed to be your friend.'

'I guess these things happen, Mum.'

She'd accepted that her friendship with Diane had irrevocably changed. There were days she missed their old closeness, but she also enjoyed a new sense of freedom and independence. She'd joined a riding club and she'd started taking singing lessons. She enjoyed her work at the primary school.

But none of it had been able to drive Cade from her mind. None of it had lessened her yearning for him. Without fail, every week she and Ella had a Skype session. But not once had Cade popped his head into view to say hello and ask her how she was doing. And yet, every week she kept her fingers crossed that he would.

She'd tried her best to get over him. She'd had three dates since she'd returned home. Two had ended in a goodnight kiss at the front door. There hadn't been a single spark or flutter or firework. After her last date she'd had to accept what had been staring her in the face for four long months—she'd fallen in love with Cade. She'd fallen in love with him properly, truly and without agenda.

'So why do you look as if the sky is about to fall in?'

She shook herself. She was about to lie and say nothing was the matter, but she knew her mother would see through the lie and be hurt by it. Their newfound understanding was too new to risk damaging with casual deceit. 'That has nothing to do with Diane or Brad.'

'I know,' Angela said softly. 'You only started looking like that once you returned from that cattle station of yours.'

Her mother had noticed? Tears pricked the back of her eyes. 'I'm fine, Mum.'

'I know, but I can't help worrying about you.'

The doorbell rang.

'That'll be your cab. Put on your shoes and powder your nose one last time while I answer the door.'

Nicola did as her mother bid. She stared in the mirror,

pressed the powder puff to her nose…then she put it away and hitched up her chin. Falling in love with Cade was unfortunate, yes, but not insurmountable. At least, she hoped not. Eventually his memory would fade. When it did she would date again. One thing was for sure, though—she didn't regret turning down his offer of marriage. Not for a moment. Not even in a weak moment.

She collected her clutch and wrap and with a deep breath headed for the living room.

'Nicola, this gentleman says he knows you. He claims he's your date for the evening.'

Nicola glanced up as she walked into the living room, to find Cade's bulk framed in the doorway. Wind rushed past her ears, drowning out the rest of her mother's words. She reached out a hand to steady herself on the back of a chair. Cade stood there—*in her living room in Melbourne*—dressed in a tuxedo, and all she could do was stare…and stare…and stare some more. She blinked but he didn't disappear. She gripped the back of the chair more tightly to prevent herself from doing something stupid like racing over to him and hurling herself into his arms.

He shrugged. He didn't smile. 'We had a deal. Did you think I'd forget?'

Cade suspected he might be about to make the biggest fool of himself, but he wasn't sure he cared. Not when it meant seeing Nicola in the flesh and drawing her unique strawberry jam scent into his lungs. He stared at her and something inside him that had stopped and seized the day her plane had taken off from Waminda, started to unfurl, to relax…to tick with anticipation.

He ached to take the three strides that would bring him right up against her, wrap an arm around her waist and pull her hard up against him and kiss her until neither one of them could think.

But she deserved a whole lot more finesse than that. Besides, it might help slake the need pounding through him, but it was her need that counted.

She stared at him with those amazing eyes, but she didn't smile. Her tongue snaked out to moisten her lips. 'I...um...'

She had! She'd thought he'd forgotten their deal. It took an effort of will not to rock back on his heels. He resisted the urge to run a finger around the collar of his shirt as it tightened about his throat. 'Did you organise another date?' His voice scraped out of his throat, but he couldn't help it, couldn't modulate it. He tried to swallow.

Was someone else taking his Cinderella to the ball? His hands clenched about the bunch of flowers he held. He wasn't sure what he'd do if she said yes.

The older woman who'd answered the door nudged Nicola. 'Darling?'

Nicola jumped. Colour flooded her cheeks. 'I really didn't think you'd... I mean, I never really thought that you were serious.'

Of course she hadn't. She thought him a lowlife—the kind of man who'd propose a loveless marriage. He *had* done that and it *did* make him a lowlife. His hands clenched tightly. If he was lucky he might be able to redeem himself a little this evening. The stems of the flowers dug into his hands.

'You...' Her voice trembled. She swallowed. 'You never mentioned it again.'

'I always keep my word.'

'How...' Her tongue moistened her lips and need clenched through him. 'How did you know when it was on?'

'You told Ella. You showed her your dress.' He wondered if he would ever be able to unclench his hand from around the flowers. 'In one of your Skype sessions. I listened in to them all.'

'You never once said hello.'

He could see now what a mistake that had been.

Her hands twisted together. 'I wish you hadn't gone to so much trouble.'

It was all he could do to keep his voice steady. 'No trouble at all.' *She was going to shaft him!* She was going to tell him she had another date, and that he'd wasted his time. She was going to tell him to go home.

With every second that passed the atmosphere grew tenser. The older woman stepped forward to take the flowers. Probably before he could strangle them completely. She had to almost prise them from his hand. She glanced at Nicola and cleared her throat delicately.

Nicola jumped again. 'Mum, this is Cade Hindmarsh, the owner of Waminda Downs station where I was nanny during the Christmas break. Cade, this is my mother, Angela McGillroy.'

Nicola's mother? She was nothing like he'd imagined. He did his best not to stare. 'Pleased to meet you.'

'Charmed,' she returned but her eyes narrowed. 'Do you want to attend the wedding with this man, Nicola, or would you like me to send him packing?'

He might be twice her size but he didn't doubt her ability to dispatch him with ruthless efficiency if she so chose.

He raised an eyebrow. 'Nicola?' If she'd truly prefer to attend the wedding on her own, or if she had another date, he'd leave. He planted his feet and lifted his chin. But he'd be back here first thing tomorrow morning. They had to talk.

His lips twisted. No, correction—he had to beg. His

gut tightened. Hopefully, Nicola would listen. It'd be more than he deserved, he knew that, but he had to give it a go.

Still, scowling and pressing her weren't fair. He made himself smile and for a moment that wasn't hard because it was so damn good to see her. 'It's great to see you, Nicola. You look...fabulous.' He hoped his eyes conveyed just how fabulous he found her. 'And if you don't have another date I would be honoured to attend the wedding with you.'

She smiled back and just like that the ground beneath his feet shifted. 'Thank you, Cade, that would be lovely.'

The tightness in his chest eased when he realised he'd just won round one. As he led her to his hired car he reminded himself that this evening was about her. He meant to make this night special for her, his own impatience be damned. It was the least he could do. Nicola deserved the best and tonight he meant to give that to her. Or die trying.

Only then would he have the right to ask for her hand in marriage. And if he made it that far, this time he had every intention of doing it right.

For Cade, nothing was too much trouble. He anticipated Nicola's every want, he charmed her friends and he made all the right comments about the bride's dress, the bridesmaids, the speeches and the food served at the reception. He even kept his thoughts about the bridegroom to himself. Though, hell... His lip curled. Nicola could do a hundred times better than that colourless prat.

She can do a hundred times better than you too.

Nicola smiled and chatted. She sighed her way through the service before asking if they could give another couple a ride to the reception. She seemed to genuinely enjoy herself and none of that enjoyment seemed forced. The service and the reception didn't appear to give her pain or make her feel awkward. He kept an eagle eye out for either, ready to do whatever he could to help, to boost her confidence, but…

She didn't need it.

Her grace and poise impressed him. It also made him feel at a loss. He knew exactly how to fluster her. All it would take would be a sly caress to her arm and a scorching survey of her lips and—

This is about her, not you!

He refreshed her glass of champagne and, for what felt like the first time that evening, found himself alone with her. 'Is it the ordeal you thought it would be?'

She sipped her champagne and then shook her head. 'No, it's been kind of nice and a lot of fun.'

She hadn't needed him at all. His heart burned at that realisation. 'Would you like to dance?'

Slowly she shook her head. 'I think I'd rather just chat.'

He ached to hold her in his arms, but wasn't sure of his own strength on that score. He gritted his teeth. Chatting would be good. He held her chair out for her. She sat and he planted himself in the seat beside her. 'Your mother isn't anything like I imagined.'

Her eyes lit up and she leaned towards him, swamping him with the sweetness of her scent. 'We had the most amazing discussion when I got home from Waminda.'

'Tell me,' he urged.

They talked for three straight hours. Cade couldn't believe it was time to take her home.

He tucked her into the car and then slid in behind the wheel. 'The night is yet young. Would you like to go to a bar or a club? We could go for a drink or go dancing or—'

'Why?'

The single question pulled him to a halt. He met her gaze. His heart pounded. 'There's quite a long answer to that.'

She stared at him for several long moments and he didn't kid himself that the outcome of those moments would not seal his fate. They would. He held his breath while his chest cramped.

'A walk along the Southbank would be nice. We could grab a coffee, maybe.'

He lifted her hand from her lap and brushed his lips across the backs of her fingers. 'Thank you.'

Nicola's heart thudded against her ribs as she and Cade walked beside the river, the Southbank foreshore bright with lights, Saturday night revelry and Melbourne's bright young things. It was vibrant, zesty and normally she loved it.

Tonight, though, she couldn't focus on it. Tonight, all her attention was on the man who walked beside her with a stern expression on his face and a contrasting warmth in his eyes. He didn't try to take her hand or touch her in any way. She did all she could to combat a growing sense of disappointment.

It was for the best. She knew it was for the best. Her body, however, refused to believe it, found no consolation in common sense.

And, God forgive her, but she couldn't help but lap up every exquisite minute she spent in his company. She closed her eyes and savoured the sound of his voice. She drank in the familiar way he held his head, the breadth of his shoulders and the long masculine stride he adjusted to her shorter ones. The smiles he sent her.

And the warmth in his eyes.

She stowed them all away deep in her heart to take out and cherish later, because she didn't fool herself. Tomorrow he would be gone and in all likelihood she would never see him again. The thought made her heartbeat pound in her ears and pain throb in her chest. She pushed it away. Tomorrow—she'd deal with it tomorrow.

She didn't urge him to talk. The sooner he'd said whatever it was he needed to say, the sooner he'd take her home and this strange, exhilarating, bittersweet night would end. She didn't take his arm and lead him into one of the restaurants or cafés that lined the riverside either. She didn't want to share him with the crowds, the light or the laughter.

Her heart gave a giant surge when he took her hand and led her to a bench that overlooked the river. For a moment she thought he was going to keep a hold of her, but then he let go.

She sat and stared out at the river to hide her disappointment. Those blue eyes of his had always seen too much.

'There's a lot I want to say, Nicola.'

She counted to three and when she was sure of herself, she looked up. She wished her eyes were half as perceptive as his. She'd give anything to know what he was thinking. She remembered the way he'd held her when she'd cried, the way he'd fed her chocolate sultanas and the way they'd laughed and laughed on the veranda that night, and she nodded. 'We have all night, Cade. There's nowhere else I need to be.'

'Good.' He nodded, and then sat. He rested his elbows on his knees, hands lightly clasped in front of him and lips pursed as he stared out at the dark river. Then he straightened again and met her gaze. 'First, I want to apologise to you for that appalling proposal of marriage. I didn't see at the time what an insult it was. I do now and I want you to know I am truly and deeply sorry.'

'That's okay.' It was an automatic response, but she didn't doubt his sincerity.

'It wasn't okay.' He shook his head, but then his lips tilted a fraction. 'That said, I'm still hoping you'll forgive me.' His eyes glittered in the half dark. 'You deserve so much more than that half-baked scheme I offered. You deserve a man who worships the very ground you walk on.'

Her breath caught at the force of his words. And then her heart started to burn. Cade was never going to be that man, was he?

She swallowed back a lump. 'I accept your apology, Cade. All's forgiven. You panicked, that's all.'

She suddenly wanted away from here, away from this man who would never love her the way she wanted him to love her. The sweetness of their meeting could no longer counter its bitterness. She shot to her feet, but then didn't know what to do. She took a couple of steps forward to stare down at the water.

'I've missed you, Nicola.'

She dragged in a breath. She folded her arms and turned back. 'I've missed all of you too.'

His eyes didn't waver as he rose and joined her. 'Yes— Ella, Holly, Harry and Jack all miss you as well. But I'm not talking about them. I'm talking about me. *I* miss you.'

Her mouth went dry. She couldn't speak.

'And yes, I miss seeing you with the girls. I miss watching you tickle Holly until she's laughing uncontrollably, and I miss the way you and Ella have the most serious conversations and then Ella jumps up smiling as if you've given her the secret of the universe. I'd be lying if I said I didn't miss those things. They're not what I miss the most, though.'

They weren't? Her heartbeat drummed out a tattoo she thought anyone within a ten-metre radius must hear.

'I miss the scent of strawberry jam in my days. I miss watching you walk across a room where I can admire the very shape of you.'

Heat flared in her cheeks.

'I miss the shape of your mouth. I miss the taste of you.'

'Oh!' She pressed her hands to her cheeks in an effort to cool them.

He shrugged and sent her a sheepish grin. 'What can I say? I'm a guy. It's how I'm wired.' He took her hands. 'But even those aren't the things I miss the most. I miss...' He stilled. 'I miss talking with you—proper, honest talking with no game playing. I miss laughing with you until my sides hurt. I miss someone noticing the minute I walk into a room.'

His hands tightened around hers. 'I miss someone sensing when something is troubling me. I miss sensing that about you. I miss your laugh. I miss the way you eye chocolate sultanas as if they're the devil's own food and the way you eat them as if they're manna from heaven. I miss the way you lift your face to the sky when you're cantering on Scarlett. I miss the way you stare up at a night sky as if it's the most magical thing you've ever seen. More than anything, I miss your smile. I *really* miss your smile.'

She stared at him. She couldn't say a word as she tried to process his words and what they meant. He missed her, but that didn't mean...

He led her back to the bench. She collapsed onto it, her shaky knees grateful for the respite. Cade didn't sit. He paced up and down in front of her.

'It took me a long time to find an answer to your question.'

'Which one?' she croaked.

'The one about Fran...and what I'd do if she came back and wanted to start over.'

She leaned back although every atom of her being strained towards him. 'And?'

'I'd welcome her back into the girls' lives because she's their mother.'

Nicola nodded. That had always gone without saying.

He frowned and paced harder. 'And then I got all caught up on whether I would choose Fran for the girls—Fran, who has proven herself unreliable—or a woman who I trusted and respected and who I believed wouldn't let the girls down.'

'And?'

'And then I realised that was wrong thinking. I'd welcome Fran back into Ella and Holly's lives.' He stopped pacing. He stopped right in front of her. 'But I wouldn't welcome her back into my life. You were right, Nicola, when you said you deserved better than what I'd offered, that you deserved love and friendship. It hit me then that I deserved those things too. And they're not something I can ever find with Fran.'

Her jaw dropped. Her heart thumped. He looked as if… as if… 'I didn't think you believed in love any more—a fairy tale, isn't that what you called it?'

'It's what I wanted to believe—to protect myself from being hurt again.' He drew her to her feet. 'But then a no-nonsense nanny with killer curves and a smile that practically knocked me off my feet swept into my life and made me feel alive again…made me feel things I never had before and I…'

A smile started up in the depths of her. 'Panicked?' she offered.

He cupped her face. 'Nicola, I have absolutely no right to expect you to believe me, but I love you.'

She wanted to believe him—so much it hurt. The light in his eyes as they rested on her lips left her in no doubt whatsoever that he desired her.

'When Fran left, my life went into a tailspin of shock, panic and pain at the trauma the girls suffered. When you left, it felt as if I'd lost a limb, as if nothing in me worked properly any more.'

Her heart lurched and then thumped hard and fast. What he'd described fitted her own state during these last few months so perfectly that suddenly she knew he spoke the truth. He wasn't after a mother for his children, but a wife to share his life.

He loved her!

He went down on one knee. 'Nicola, I can offer you a family who will adore you, friendship, a horse, life on an Outback station—and if any of those things will sway you I'll use them shamelessly—but mostly I can offer you a heart filled with love for you. I love you, my beautiful girl. I will love you till the day I die. Please say that you'll marry me and let me spend the rest of my life proving to you just how much I do love you.'

Her heart had grown so big she thought she might explode. She knelt down on the ground in front of him and took his face in her hands. She smiled at him with her whole heart. He blinked...and she watched as hope stretched across his face. 'Can we get rid of that awful home gym?'

'Consider it gone.' He grinned that lazy, tempting grin that never failed to bump up her heart rate. 'And I promise to always keep the cupboards stocked with chocolate sultanas.'

Her heart pounded. She leaned forward and pressed her lips to his. For a moment he seemed too stunned to respond but, just as she was about to draw back, his arms flashed around her and he held her so tightly she could barely breathe. He kissed her so thoroughly her head swam and she had to cling to him for support.

He lifted his head. 'I love you, Nicola. I can't even begin to describe how much.'

Her breath hitched. 'I don't know. I think you did a pretty good job.' She reached out to touch his face. 'My days have all been grey these last four months. I missed you so much. I didn't want to believe I'd fallen in love with you—I thought it would prove that I was needy and weak.'

He frowned. 'Do you still believe that?'

She shook her head. 'I know that if you ever walked away from me that I'd survive, but...oh, how much better my life is with you in it!'

Determination blazed in his eyes. 'Are you going to marry me?'

She smiled. She grinned. She threw her head back and laughed. 'Yes!'

He stared at her as if she was the most magnificent thing he had ever seen. 'When can I take you home to Waminda?'

Home. The word stretched through her, full of promise. Wherever this man was, that would be her home. And she would be his.

'Just as soon as we give my mother the wedding she's always dreamed of,' she breathed.

'Whatever will make you happy,' he swore.

And she knew he meant it.

* * * * *

KISSES ON HER CHRISTMAS LIST

SUSAN MEIER

For my friend, Denise.

CHAPTER ONE

SHANNON RALEIGH turned to get a look at herself in the full-length mirror in the bathroom of her executive office suite and gaped in horror. The tall black boots and short red velvet dress she wore exposed most of her legs and the white fur-trimmed *U* at the bodice revealed a sizable strip of cleavage.

"I can't go into a roomful of kids dressed like this!"

Even from behind the closed door, she could hear her assistant Wendy sigh heavily. "Why don't you let me be the judge of that?"

"Because I know you'll say I look fine, when I don't. I can't usher kids to Santa's lap in a skirt so short I can't bend over."

"So don't bend over." Another sigh. "Look, Shannon, it doesn't matter that you're eight inches taller than Carlie. There's nobody else who's even remotely thin enough to fit into that suit. Carlie's car is stuck in a snowdrift. If you don't play Santa's helper there'll be no one to—"

The ring of the phone stopped Wendy midsentence. The next thing Shannon heard was Wendy's happy voice saying, "Raleigh's Department Store. Shannon Raleigh's assistant, Wendy, speaking."

In the lull while Wendy obviously listened to the

caller, Shannon cast another critical eye over her reflection. The little red dress was kind of cute. The color
complemented her long black hair and made her blue
eyes seem bluer. If she were wearing it anywhere else,
she'd actually think she looked pretty.

A long-forgotten ache filled her. It was the first time
in a year she *felt* pretty, sexy. But sexy wasn't exactly
the way a grown woman should dress in a room filled
with babies, toddlers and elementary school kids.

The ache was quickly replaced by fear—which was
the real reason she didn't want to play Santa's helper.
How could she spend four hours in a room full of adorable children? She wanted a baby so badly it hurt, but
she couldn't have kids. And seeing all those sweet faces,
hearing their cute little lists, would crush her.

"Um, Shannon?"

"I'm not coming out."

"Fine. That was Tammy in the shoe department. No
one's come into the store for the past hour and she could
tell the storm was getting worse, so she checked the
forecast on the internet. They have no clue how much
snow we're going to get, but they aren't shy about suggesting we might get another foot."

"Another foot!"

Shannon raced out of her bathroom and pulled back
the curtain behind her huge mahogany desk. Thick
fluffy snowflakes cascaded from the sky, coating the
tinsel and silver bells on the streetlamps of Main Street,
Green Hill, Pennsylvania. It blanketed the Christmas
lights that outlined shop doorways, and sat on the roof
of the park's gazebo like a tall white hat.

"Holy cow!"

Her gaze on the little red Santa's helper outfit, Wendy
also said, "Holy cow."

"Don't make fun. We have a serious problem here."
Or maybe a way out. She turned from the window. "I
think it's time to admit that the storm is keeping shoppers away."

"And most of the staff is scared silly about driving
home. The longer we stay, the worse the roads get."

"Okay, announce that the store is closing in fifteen
and tell the employees they can go home. I'll call the
radio stations so they can add us to their list of closings.
Then I'll lock up."

As the announcement went out over the loudspeaker,
Shannon called all the local radio stations and advised
them to let listeners know Raleigh's would be closed
for the night.

Just as she hung up the phone from the final call,
Wendy peeked in. "Okay. Fifteen minutes are up. Store's
empty."

"Great. Thanks. Be careful going home."

"My boyfriend's coming to pick me up in his truck.
I'll be fine."

Shannon smiled. "See you tomorrow."

"If we can make it."

"We better hope we can make it. The weekend before Christmas is our busiest time."

Wendy shrugged. "If shoppers don't get here tomorrow, they'll just come on Sunday or Monday or Tuesday
or whatever. Nobody's going to go without gifts this
Christmas. I'd say your profits are safe."

Shannon laughed. Wendy waved and headed off.
With a few clicks on her keyboard, she activated the
building locks and the alarm system. Reaching for her
coat, she peered down at her little Santa's helper outfit.
She should change, but knowing the roads were getting

worse with every passing minute, she simply yanked her long white wool coat from the closet and ran out.

At the end of the hall, she pushed on the swinging door that led from executive row to housewares. Striding to the elevator, she passed shelves and tables bulging with merchandise, all under loops of tinsel and oversized ornaments hanging from the low ceiling. On the first floor, she hurried past the candy department, to the back door and the employee parking lot. Putting her SUV into four-wheel drive, she edged onto the street and slowly wound along the twisty road that took her out into the country, to her home five miles outside the small city.

As she stepped out into the eighteen inches of snow in her driveway, a sense of disconnect shivered through her. Though it had been a year, it felt like only yesterday that she had been married and living in sunny, happy Charleston, South Carolina, where people didn't often see snow, let alone need winter coats and boots. Then she'd been diagnosed with stage-four endometriosis and forced to have a hysterectomy, her husband had unceremoniously divorced her and she'd returned home to the comforting arms of her parents.

But just when she'd gotten adjusted to being back in town and working at the store, her parents had retired and moved to Florida. Worse, they now wanted her to sell the store to fund their retirement.

Once again, she was alone—and soon she'd be unemployed.

She trudged up the back steps to the kitchen door, scolding herself for being so negative. She knew what was wrong. The near miss with playing Santa's helper had rattled her. Four hours of ushering kids to Santa's throne and listening to their sweet voices as they gave their Christmas lists to the jolly old elf would have been her undoing—a bittersweet reminder to her that she'd never bring a child into this world.

Inside the cold yellow kitchen, she'd just barely unwound the scarf from her neck when the doorbell rang. Confused, she walked up the hall, dodging the boxes of Christmas decorations she'd brought from the attic the night before. She flipped on the porch light and yanked open the door.

A snow-covered state policeman took off his hat. "Evening, ma'am. I'm Trooper Potter."

She blinked. What the devil would the police want with her? "Good evening."

Then Trooper Potter shifted a bit to his left and she saw Rory Wallace. All six foot one, no more than one hundred and eighty-five gorgeous pounds of him. His black hair and topcoat were sprinkled with snow. His dark eyes were wary, apologetic.

"Rory?"

"Good evening, Shannon."

The policeman angled his thumb behind him. "I see you know Mr. Wallace."

"Yes. I do." How could she forget a dark-haired, dark-eyed sex god? While he had dated her roommate, Natalie, their first year at university, Shannon had had a secret crush on him. With his high cheekbones, well-defined chin, broad shoulders and flat abs, he had the kind of looks that made women swoon and Shannon wasn't blind.

"Mr. Wallace was stranded on the interstate. The hotels filled up quickly with travelers and now his only options are a cot in the high school gym or finding someone to take him in. He tells me that he's in

Pennsylvania because he has business with you on Monday and—"

"I came a few days early to get a look at the store on my own," Rory interrupted, stepping forward. "But I ran into the storm. I was hoping you wouldn't mind me staying the night. Normally, I wouldn't ask such a big favor, but as you can see I'm desperate."

Mind? She almost laughed. She would bet that fifty percent of the women he met fantasized about being stuck in a storm with him.

She opened the door a little wider. Not only would having him stay the night get her out of the doldrums about her life, but this also had all the makings of a perfect fantasy. Cold night. Gorgeous guy. And wine. She had tons of wine.

"Daddy, I'm cold."

Her fantasy came to an abrupt halt as she glanced down and saw a little girl standing beside Rory. She wore a pink ski jacket and carried a matching pink backpack. Little strands of yellow hair peeked from beneath her hood.

Her heart pinched with fear. Her breathing stuttered out. Did Fate think it was funny to let her dodge playing Santa's helper only to drop an adorable child on her doorstep?

"You can see why I don't want to stay in a shelter."

Fear and yearning collided as she glanced down at the sweet little girl with big blue eyes and fine yellow hair. As much as she knew spending time with this child would intensify her longing for her own children, she couldn't leave Rory and his daughter out in the cold or ship them to a crowded gym with hundreds of other noisy travelers and a tiny cot.

She also couldn't be a Scrooge. Her problem wasn't their problem. She would be a good hostess.

She stepped back so they could enter. "Yes. Yes, of course."

Carrying a duffel bag and briefcase as he squeezed into the foyer, Rory brushed against her, setting off a firestorm of sensations inside her. She ignored them. Not just because a man with a child was most likely married, but because she probably wouldn't have made a pass at him even if he'd been alone. In the year since her divorce, she hadn't been able to relate to men as anything other than employees. After her husband's anger over her inability to have kids and the way he'd dropped her like a hot potato—no consideration for their five-year marriage, no consideration for her devastation—the fear of another man rejecting her paralyzed her.

Plus, come Monday, they'd be doing business. His family owned a holding company for various types of stores and Raleigh's would probably fit their collection. That's why she'd thought of Natalie's old boyfriend when her parents had decided they wanted to sell the store. It could be a quick, painless sale. She didn't want to jeopardize that.

But, wow. It had been fun to fantasize about being stranded with him, fun for the ten seconds before reality intruded, reminding her she wasn't normal.

As Rory dropped his duffel bag, she said, "It's a terrible storm."

"Worst in ten years," the trooper agreed, staying behind on the porch. "If you're all settled, I need to get back on the road."

"We're fine," Shannon said, as she began to close the door. As an afterthought, she added, "Thank you."

"Yes, thank you," Rory Wallace called out, too.

Already on his way down her front steps, the trooper
waved goodbye and trudged through the thick snow on
the sidewalk to his car.

Awkward silence reigned as Rory Wallace took in the
foyer of Shannon Raleigh's home. As if it wasn't bad
enough that he'd been forced to humble himself and ask
for shelter from a business associate, it appeared she
was moving. Boxes blocked half the corridor that led
from the foyer to the kitchen behind it. They littered the
living room to the right and the dining room to the left.

Which made him feel even guiltier. "Thank you. I
really appreciate this."

She smiled graciously. "You're welcome." Then she
shivered, even though she wore a long white coat and
the house wasn't that cold, just chilled, as if the heat
had been on low all day while she was at work. "Give
me a minute to turn on the furnace." She walked to a
thermostat on the wall and adjusted it. "You might want
to keep your coats on until it heats up in here."

He unbuttoned his topcoat. "Actually, after spending ten hours in a car, your house is warm to us." He
stooped to help his daughter with her jacket. Realizing
he'd never introduced her, he peeked up at Shannon.
"This is my daughter, Finley."

Crouching beside them, Shannon said, "It's nice to
meet you, Finley."

Finley mumbled, "Nice to meet you, too," then she
looked at him as if wanting to make sure he'd noticed
that she'd been polite.

Sliding her arms out of her little pink jacket, he
gave her a subtle nod of approval. Lately, Finley had
been something of a six-year-old diva. Disciplining her
worked, but not always. And some days he was at his

wits' end with her. So he was lucky she'd been polite to Shannon Raleigh. He didn't know how he'd deal with her if she insulted the woman who'd rescued them.

"This is the perfect night to be stranded with me," Shannon said, taking Finley's jacket to the closet behind her. "My parents will be home from Florida next Saturday and I promised I'd have the house decorated for Christmas. All these boxes are decorations they left behind when they moved to Florida. You can help me."

While Rory breathed a sigh of relief that he hadn't interrupted her moving, Finley's nose wrinkled and her eyes narrowed with distaste. Before he realized what she was about to do, she spat, "I hate Christmas."

Shannon reared back as if someone had slapped her. Her pretty blue eyes widened in disbelief. "Hate Christmas? How can you hate Christmas?"

"How can you believe that a fat guy in a red suit brings you presents?"

Anger pulsed through Rory's veins and he shot Finley a warning look. He wouldn't yell at her in front of Shannon, but he did need to provide a few rules for behavior when imposing on someone they barely knew. He faced Shannon. "Why don't you tell me where we're sleeping and I'll take Finley to our room and help her get settled in."

Shannon winced. "Actually, there's only one bedroom."

"Oh."

"It's no big deal. We'll give the bed to Finley, and you and I will use sleeping bags. You can put yours on the floor beside the bed and I'll sleep on the sofa."

Mortal embarrassment overwhelmed him. He hadn't realized how much he'd be putting her out when he gave her name to the state policeman. "This is such an imposition. You can't give us your room. Finley and I don't mind sleeping in the living room."

Finley stomped her foot. "I don't want to sleep on the floor."

He flashed Finley another warning look. "You won't. You can have the sofa."

"I want a bed!"

Rory's head pounded. He understood that this time of year wasn't easy for Finley. Her mom had left on Christmas day two years before. So every year, she got moody, and every year he indulged her by taking her on vacation from Christmas Eve to New Year's. For a guy who'd also lost his marriage on Christmas day, a vacation from the holiday was good for him, too. But the foot-stomping and the pouting and the demands that everything go her way, those had just started. And he absolutely refused to get on board with them. He had to spend the next week looking at Raleigh's Department Store for his family's holding company. He couldn't have her acting like a brat all week.

He turned to Shannon. "Would you mind showing us to the bedroom so I can get Finley settled?"

"Not at all."

She led them into a small first-floor bedroom that was as neat and clean as the rest of the house...minus boxes. A feminine white ruffled spread sat on a simple double bed. Red pillows on the bed matched the red shag carpet beneath it and the drapes on the double windows.

He dropped his duffel bag to the floor. "Wow."

She faced him with a smile. Her shiny black hair was a wonderland of long, springy curls. In the years since university, her face had shifted just slightly and she'd become a softer, prettier version of the young girl he remembered.

"Wow?"

"I'm just a little surprised by your room."

Her smile grew. "Really? Why?"

"The red." He felt the same color rising on his cheeks. The room was girlie, yet incredibly sexy. But he certainly didn't feel comfortable saying that to the woman giving him and his daughter shelter, especially not after Finley's minitantrum. Still, he never would have guessed this sexy combination of color and style from the sweet Shannon he knew all those years ago at school.

"There's a private bathroom for the bedroom—" she gestured toward a door to the right "—over there."

"Thank you."

"Just come out when you're ready." She smiled. "I'll start supper. I hope you like toasted cheese sandwiches and soup. I'm not much of a cook."

"On a cold day like this, soup is terrific."

She closed the door behind her and Rory crouched down in front of Finley. Smoothing his hand down her shiny yellow hair, he said, "You're killing me."

She blinked innocently "What?"

"Ms. Raleigh is doing us a favor by letting us stay. We should be polite to her."

"I was polite."

"Saying you want the bed while you stomp your foot is not polite."

Her bottom lip puffed out. "Sorry."

And *this* was why he had trouble disciplining her. The second he pointed out something she'd done wrong, she turned on that little-girl charm. Batted her long black lashes over her pretty blue eyes.

Scrubbing his hand over his mouth, he rose. "I'll tell you what. You stay in here for a few minutes, while I spend some time getting acquainted with our hostess." And apologizing and doing damage control. "While I'm gone, you can get your pajamas and toothbrush out of your backpack and think about how you'd want a little girl to behave if she were a guest in our house."

Apparently liking her assignment, she nodded eagerly.

"And don't spend all your time thinking about how you'd spoil your little guest, because you wouldn't. If you had to give up your bed for a stranger, you'd want her to be nice to you."

Finley nodded again and said, "Okay. I get it."

Rory was absolutely positive she didn't, but he had to make amends to Shannon. He left Finley in the bedroom and walked up the hall to the kitchen.

The house was small, but comfortable. The furniture was new and expensive, an indication that Raleigh's Department Store did, indeed, make lots of money. So maybe the trip to Pennsylvania might not have been the mistake he'd thought while sitting in his car for ten hours, not moving, on the interstate?

He found Shannon in the kitchen. Still wearing her coat, she drew bread from a drawer and cheese from the refrigerator.

"Thanks again for taking us in."

"No problem." She set the bread and cheese on the center island of the sunny yellow kitchen with light oak cabinets and pale brown granite countertops. She reached for the top button of her coat. "Furnace has kicked in," she said with a laugh, popping the first button and the second, but when she reached for the third, she paused. "I think I'll just take this out to the hall closet."

She walked past him, to the swinging door. Wanting something to do, he followed her. Just as he said, "Is there anything I can do to help with supper?" her coat fell off her shoulders, revealing a bright red dress.

But when she turned in surprise, he saw the dress wasn't really a dress but some little red velvet thing that dipped low at the bodice, revealing an enticing band of cleavage. Tall black boots showcased her great legs.

She was dressed like Mrs. Santa—if Mrs. Santa were a young, incredibly endowed woman who liked short skirts.

His dormant hormones woke as if from a long winter's nap, and he took a step back. These little bursts of attraction he was having toward her were all wrong. He had an unruly daughter who took priority over everything in his life, including his hormones, and he was a guest in Shannon's house. Plus, tomorrow morning, when the storm was over, they'd go into her department store as adversaries of a sort. She'd be trying to sell her family business to him and he'd be looking for reasons not to buy. He couldn't be attracted to her.

He swallowed back the whole filing cabinet of flirtatious remarks that wanted to come out. "That's an interesting choice of work clothes."

She laughed nervously. "I was going to fill in for our Santa's helper in the toy department."

Ah. Not Mrs. Santa but Santa's helper.

"Well, the dress is very…" He paused. He knew the dress was probably supposed to be Christmassy and cute. And on a shorter woman it probably was. But she was tall, sleek, yet somehow still womanly. He didn't dare tell her that. "Festive."

She brought the coat to her neck, using it to shield herself. "That's the look we're after. Festive and happy. And it actually works for the girl who fits into this costume. I was lucky Mother Nature saved me and I didn't have to fill in for her tonight."

Recognizing her acute nervousness, Rory pulled his gaze away from her long, slim legs. He cleared his throat. "I…um…just followed you to see if I could help you with anything."

She motioned toward his black suit and white shirt. "Are you sure you want to butter bread or stir tomato soup in a suit?"

He took off his jacket, loosened his tie and began rolling up his sleeves.

And Shannon's mouth watered. Damn it. She'd already figured out she couldn't be fantasizing about him. Sure, his shoulders were broad, his arms muscled. And she'd always been a sucker for a man in a white shirt with rolled-up sleeves looking like he was ready to get down to business. But as far as she could tell, he was married. That shut down the possibility of any relationship right then and there. Plus, she wanted him to buy her parents' store. She couldn't be drooling on him.

She hung up her coat, then scurried past him, into the kitchen and directly to the laundry room. Leaning on the closed door, she drew in a deep breath. God, he was gorgeous. But he was also married.

Married. Married. Married.

She forced the litany through her head, hoping it would sink in, as she grabbed a pair of sweats and a T-shirt from the dryer and changed into them.

When she returned to the kitchen he stood at the center island, buttering bread. "While we have a few seconds of privacy, I also wanted to apologize for Finley.

I brought her because she's on Christmas break from school and I hate to leave her with her nanny for an entire week. But I know she can be a handful."

Walking over to join him, she said, "She's just a little girl."

"True, but she's also recently entered a new phase of some sort where she stomps her foot when she doesn't get her own way."

Standing so close to him, she could smell his aftershave. Her breathing stuttered in and out of her lungs. So she laughed, trying to cover it. "A new phase, huh?"

"She was perfectly fine in preschool and kindergarten, but first grade is turning her into a diva."

"Diva?"

"Yeah." Smiling, he caught her gaze, and every nerve ending in her body lit up like the lights on the Christmas tree in Central Park. Spinning away from him, she repeated the litany in her head again.

Married. Married. Married!

"You know, I can easily handle this myself. You can use the den for privacy if you need to call your wife."

He snorted a laugh. "Not hardly."

She set the frying pan for the sandwiches on the stove and faced him again. "I'm sure she's worried."

"And I'm sure she and her new husband aren't even thinking about me and Finley right now."

"Oh." Nerves rolled through her. He was divorced? Not married?

Their gazes caught. Attraction spun through her like snowflakes dancing in the light of a streetlamp. She reminded herself that they were about to do business, but it didn't work to snuff out the snap and crackle of electricity sizzling between them.

She pivoted away from him. Pretending she needed

all her concentration to open two cans of soup, she managed to avoid conversation. But that didn't stop the chatter in her brain. As difficult as it might be to have a little girl around, she was abundantly glad Finley was with him. She might have had that quick fantasy of being stranded with him, but now that sanity had returned, she knew the sale of the store had to take precedence over a night of…she swallowed…passion? Good God, she hadn't even *thought* the word in a year, let alone *experienced* it. She'd probably dissolve into a puddle if he made a pass at her.

Finley came out of the bedroom just as Rory set the sandwiches on the table and Shannon had finished ladling soup into the bright green bowls sitting on the pretty yellow place mats. She crawled onto a chair and spread her paper napkin on her lap.

Longing hit Shannon like an unexpected burst of winter wind. She remembered dreams of buying pretty dresses for her own little girl, her dreams of taking her to the park, gymnastics, dance lessons and soccer—

She stopped her thoughts, cut off the sadness and grief that wanted to engulf her. Surely, she could have a little girl in her house without breaking into a million shattered pieces? She hadn't given up on the idea of becoming a mother altogether. She knew that once she adjusted to not having her own child, she could adopt. So maybe this was a good time to begin adjusting?

Finley sighed. "I don't like red soup."

Sounding very parental, Rory said, "That's okay. Just eat your sandwich."

Finley sighed heavily again, as if it were pure torture not to get her own way. Rory ignored her. Shannon studied her curiously, realizing that with Diva Finley she really would get a solid understanding of what it took to be a parent. She was like a little blond-haired litmus test for whether or not Shannon had what it took to adopt a child and be a mom.

Rory turned to her and said, "This is certainly a lovely old house."

She faced Rory so quickly that their gazes collided. He had the darkest eyes she'd ever seen. And they were bottomless. Mesmerizing...

She gave herself a mental shake. It was pointless to be attracted. He wouldn't make a pass at her with his daughter around, and she wouldn't make a pass at him because they were about to do business. She had to stop noticing these things.

She cleared her throat. "The parts I've restored are great. But the whole heating system needs to be replaced."

"Well, you've done a wonderful job on the renovations you have done."

"Really?" She peeked up at him.

And everything Rory wanted to say fell out of his head. Her big blue eyes reminded him of the sky in summer. The black curls that curved around her face had his hand itching to touch them.

Finley sighed heavily. "I don't want this soup."

Rory faced her. "We already agreed that you didn't have to eat it."

"I don't like that it's here."

"Here?"

"In front of me!"

Before Rory had a chance to react, Shannon rose with a smile. "Let me take it to the sink."

She reached across the table, lifted the bowl and calmly walked it to the sink. Then she returned to the table and sat as if nothing had happened.

Technically nothing *had* happened. She'd diffused the potentially problematic soup episode just by reacting calmly.

Of course, he knew that was what *he* should have done, but after ten grueling hours on the road, he was every bit as tired and cranky as Finley. And this confusing attraction he felt for Shannon wasn't helping things.

"I don't want this sandwich."

Here we go again. "Finley—"

"I'm tired."

Before Rory could remind her he was, too, Shannon rose. "I have just the cure for being tired. A bubble bath."

Finley instantly brightened. "Really?"

"I have all kinds of bubbles in my bathroom. It's right beside the bedroom you're using. Why don't we go get a bath ready for you?"

Finley all but bounced off her chair. "All right!"

They disappeared down the hall to the bedroom, and Rory ran his hand down his face.

He didn't know what would drive him crazy first, his daughter or his hormones.

CHAPTER TWO

SHANNON WALKED OUT of the kitchen with a happy Finley skipping behind her to the bathroom. Her self-pity long forgotten and her new mission in place, she was glad to help tired, frazzled Rory with his daughter. It would give her a chance for some one-on-one time with Finley, a chance to prove to herself that she was strong enough to be around kids. Strong enough to adopt one of her own, if she wanted to.

Unfortunately, the second they were out of Rory's earshot, Finley the Diva returned. "You can go. I'll fill the tub myself."

Having watched her friends in Charleston handle their children, if nothing else, Shannon knew the grown-up in charge had to stay in charge. "I'm sure you could, but I want to do it."

Finley crossed her arms on her chest and huffed out a sigh.

For Rory's sake, Shannon didn't laugh. "I like this scent," she said, picking up her favorite bubble bath. "But you can choose whichever one you want."

Finley chose another scent. Shannon shrugged. It didn't matter to her which scent Finley used. She turned on the tap, poured in the liquid and faced Finley with a smile. "I'm going to leave the room while this fills up so you can undress. Call me when you're ready to step in the tub."

"I don't need help."

And with that comment, Shannon decided she had experimented enough for one night. She didn't have the right to discipline this little girl and she definitely needed a firm hand. So she left this battle for Rory. "Okay. That's great."

She walked out of the bathroom and directly into the kitchen. "Tub is almost full and Finley's stripping. You might want to go in and supervise."

Rory rose. "She can bathe herself but I like to be in the next room just in case." He glanced at the dishes and winced. "Sorry about that."

She waved a hand in dismissal. "I can load a few dishes into the dishwasher. You go on ahead."

Alone in the kitchen for forty minutes, she wasn't sure if Finley had decided to have an Olympic swim in her tub or if Rory was reading her a story...or if they'd found the TV and decided to stay on their own in the bedroom.

Whatever had happened, Shannon was fine with it. She knew they were both tired, weary. And once the dishes were stacked in the dishwasher and the kitchen cleaned, she had decorating to do. But just as she dragged the box of garland over to the sofa, Rory walked into the living room.

"Well, she's down for the night."

"I suspected she was tired."

"Exhausted."

"She'll be happy in the morning."

With a weary sigh, Rory fell to the couch. "How'd you get so smart about kids?"

His praise surprised her. Though she'd spent years

watching her friends' kids, longing for her own, she'd also all but ignored them this past difficult year. "I had some friends in South Carolina who had children. I used to babysit."

He laughed. "You *volunteered* to hang around kids?"

"It's always easier to handle children who aren't yours." She brushed her hands together to rid them of attic dust and stepped away from the box of decorations. Eager to change the subject, she said, "You sound like you could use a glass of wine."

"Or a beer, if you have one."

"I do." She left the living room, got two beers from the refrigerator and gave one to Rory.

He relaxed on the couch, closed his eyes. "Thanks."

"You're welcome." She glanced at the decorations, thinking she really should get started, but also knowing Rory was embarrassed about imposing and at his wits' end. Deciding to be a Good Samaritan and give him someone to talk to, she gingerly sat on the sofa beside him. "Must have been some drive."

"There was a point when I considered turning around because I could see things were getting worse, but the weather reports kept saying the storm would blow out soon." He peered over at her. "It never did."

"This will teach you to listen to weathermen."

He laughed. Relaxed a little more. "So you ended up taking over your family's business?"

"By default. I was perfectly happy to work with the buyers and in advertising for Raleigh's. But my dad wanted to retire and I'm an only child." She paused then smiled at him. "I see you also ended up in your dad's job."

Rory tilted his head, studying her. Her smile was pretty, genuine. Not flirtatious and certainly not enough to get his hormones going, but an odd tingle took up residence in his stomach. "Yeah. I did. Who would have thought ten years ago that we'd be running the two businesses we always talked about while I waited for Natalie for our dates?"

"Well, you were a shoo-in for your job. You're the oldest son of a family that owns a business. I thought I was going to be a lawyer. Turns out law school is really, really dull."

He laughed again, then realized he couldn't remember the last time he'd laughed twice, back-to-back, in the same night. Warmth curled through him. Not like arousal from flirting. Not like happiness, but something else. Something richer. Not only was Shannon Raleigh a knockout and good with kids, but she was also easy to talk to—

Good grief. This strange feeling he was having was attraction. Real attraction. The next step beyond the hormone-driven reaction he had when he saw her in the little red dress.

Damn it. He was here to look at her family's store to see if it was an appropriate investment for his family. He couldn't be attracted to her. Not just that, but he was already a loser at love. He'd given in to the fun of flirting once. He'd let himself become vulnerable. Hell, he'd let himself tumble head over heels for someone, and he knew how that had turned out—with her leaving him on Christmas day two years ago, and all but deserting their daughter.

When he'd finally found her and asked about visitation, she'd told him she didn't want to see Finley. Ever. Hoping that she'd change her mind in the two years that had passed, he'd run out of excuses to give Finley for missed birthdays and holidays. Pretty soon he was going to have to tell a six-year-old girl that her mother didn't want her.

That broke his heart. Shattered it into a million painful pieces. Made him want to shake his ex-wife silly.

Which was why he'd never marry again. At this point in his life he wasn't even sure he'd date again.

He rose from the sofa. "You know what? I'm tired, too. I'm going to have to figure out how to get my car from the interstate in the morning and I'm guessing for that I'm going to need a good night's sleep." He gave her a warm smile. "Thanks again for letting us stay."

With that he turned and all but raced toward the door, but he didn't get three steps before Shannon stopped him. "Rory?"

He turned.

She pointed at the sleeping bag rolled up at by the door. "You might want to take that."

He sucked in a breath. The whole point of coming into the room had been to get his sleeping bag. Two minutes in her company and he'd forgotten that. "Yeah. Thanks."

He scooped the sleeping bag from the floor. He hadn't been this foolish around a woman in years.

He was glad he was leaving in the morning.

Shannon was awakened by the feeling of soft breath puffing in her face. She batted at it only to have her hand meet something solid.

Finley yelled, "Ouch!"

Shannon bolted up on the couch as several things popped into her head at once. First, she was sleeping in her living room. Second, she had company. Third, Finley was not the nicest child in the world. But, the all-important fourth, she would be alone with a child until Rory woke up.

"I'm hungry." Finley's tiny face scrunched. Her nose became a wrinkled button. Her mouth pulled down in an upside-down *U*.

Shannon pressed her lips together to keep from laughing. Which heartened her. Because Finley was forceful and demanding, not a cute little cuddle bug, it was easier for Shannon to deal with being around her.

She rolled out of her sleeping bag. Her friends had complained about being awakened by their children at ungodly hours. But a glance at the wall clock told her it was after eight. She couldn't fault Finley for waking her. It might be Saturday, but she still had to be at the store by ten to open it.

Fortunately, she had enough time to make something to eat. "Well, I enjoy cooking breakfast so it looks like we're both lucky this morning."

That confused Finley so much that her frown wobbled.

Laughing, Shannon ruffled her hair. "Which do you prefer pancakes or waffles?"

"Do you have blueberries?"

"Of course."

"Then I'd like pancakes."

Shannon headed for the kitchen. "You and I are going to get along very well."

As she pulled the ingredients for pancakes from the cupboards, Finley took a seat at the table. Before she started to make the batter, Shannon picked up the remote for her stereo and turned it on. A rousing rendition of "Here Comes Santa Claus" poured into the room.

"Would you like a glass of milk?"

"Yes, please."

Shannon dipped into her refrigerator as Finley slid off her seat. Watching Finley walk to the counter, she grabbed the gallon of milk and pulled it out of the fridge. But before she could reach the counter, Finley had picked up the remote and turned off the music.

She blinked. "I was listening to that."

"It was stupid."

"It was a Christmas song."

"And Christmas is stupid."

Shannon gaped at her. Not just because she had the audacity to turn off the music without asking, but that was the second time she'd mentioned she didn't like Christmas.

The temptation was strong to ask why, as she poured Finley a glass of milk, but she wasn't quite sure how to approach it. Did she say, *Hey, kid, everybody likes Christmas. You get gifts. You get cookies. What's the deal?*

As curious as she was, that seemed a lot like interfering and she was just getting accustomed to being around a child. She wasn't ready for deep, personal interaction yet. Plus, saying she hated Christmas could just be a part of one of Finley the Diva's tantrums. Or a way to manipulate people.

So, she turned to the counter and began preparing pancakes. A happy hum started in her throat and worked its way out, surprising her. Breakfast was one of the few meals she was well versed in. She could make a pancake or a waffle with the best of them. But it was a happy surprise to be able to be in the same room with Finley without worrying that she'd fall apart or dwell on her inability to have kids herself.

"So where do you go to school?"

"Winchester Academy."

"Is that a private school?"

Finley nodded.

"Do you like school?"

"Sometimes. Artie Regan brings frogs and scares me. And Jenny Logan beats me to the swing."

A motherly warmth flowed through her. When she wasn't demanding her own way, Finley was normal. And here she was handling her. Talking to her. No flutters of panic. No feeling sorry for herself.

The kitchen door opened and Rory walked into the room yawning. "Sorry about that."

"About what?" Shannon faced him with a smile, but the smile disappeared as her mouth went dry.

His dark hair was sticking out in all directions. His eyes didn't seem to want to open. A day-old growth of beard sexily shadowed his chin and cheeks. He wore a white undershirt and navy blue sweats that loosely clung to his lean hips.

"About sleeping in. Normally, I'm up—" He paused. "Are you making pancakes?"

"Blueberry."

"Wow. We should get stranded on an interstate more often."

She laughed. *Laughed.* She had a sexy man and a cute little girl in her kitchen and she wasn't stuttering or shattering, she was laughing.

But a little warning tweaked her brain. Not only was she enjoying this way too much, but it also would be over soon. They'd eat breakfast, pack up the few things they'd brought with them and head out.

She had about twenty minutes over breakfast before she'd be alone again.

Rory ambled to the counter, where the coffeemaker

sputtered the last drops of fresh coffee into the pot. "Can I get you a cup?"

"That'd be great, thanks. Mugs are in the cupboard by the sink."

But as he reached into the cupboard to get the mugs, his arm stopped. "Holy cats!"

Shannon paused her spoon in the pancake batter. "What?"

"There's got to be two feet of snow out there."

"That was the eventual predication after we already had eighteen inches."

"Yeah, well, it doesn't look like the snowplow went through."

She dropped the spoon, hustled to the window beside him. "Wow."

He turned and caught her gaze. "Even with that big SUV I saw in the driveway, I'll bet you can't get us out to a main road."

Her heart lodged in her throat. Could they actually be forced to stay another day? Could she handle another day?

The answer came swiftly, without hesitation. She couldn't just handle another day; she *wanted* another day.

"With all that snow, I'm not sure the main roads are even clear."

"I'll check the internet."

"If the roads are still closed, you know you're welcome to stay, right?"

"I think we may have to take you up on that."

Though her heart leaped with anticipation, she pasted a disappointed-for-them look on her face. "I'm sorry."

"I'm the one who's sorry."

"Don't be." She brightened her expression. "I don't mind."

Rory nudged his head toward Finley, who sat quietly at the kitchen table.

Lowering her voice, Shannon said, "She'll be fine."

"You want to be the one to tell her?"

"What do you say we get a pancake into her first?" He tapped her nose. "Excellent idea."

The friendly tap shouldn't have made Shannon's heart race, but it did. She pivoted away from him and returned to her pancake batter. They were staying another day as guests. Friends. Nothing more. But being friends meant no stress. No pressure. They could have a good time.

A good time, instead of a lonely, boring weekend.

Who would have thought the day before, when she'd stood trembling with fear over playing Santa's helper, that today she'd welcome having a little girl spend the day with her?

She ladled batter onto the already warm grill and within minutes the sweet scent of pancakes filled the air.

As she piled pancakes on three plates, Rory found the maple syrup and took the pot of coffee to the table.

Finley eagerly grabbed her plate from Shannon. Without as much as a blink from her dad, she said, "Thank you."

Shannon's heart tweaked again. She glanced from happy Finley to relieved Rory. They had no idea how much their presence meant to her. Worse, they probably didn't realize she was actually glad the snowplow hadn't yet gone through. Their misery changed her incredibly lonely, probably bordering-toward-pathetic weekend into time with other people. Company for dinner the night before. Someone to make pancakes for. People who would eat lunch and maybe dinner with her.

And maybe even someone to bake sugar cookies with? A little girl who'd paint them with her child's hand, giving them strokes and color and even mistakes only a child could make. Turning them into real Christmas cookies.

Rory pointed at his pancake. "These are great."

Finley nodded in agreement. "These are great."

"Thanks."

Rory laughed and caught her gaze. "Thought you said you couldn't cook?"

Her heart stuttered a bit. Not because he was paying attention to her, but because his dark eyes were filled with warmth and happiness. Casual happiness. The kind of happiness real friends shared. "I can't, except for breakfast. But breakfast foods are usually easy."

Turning his attention back to his plate, he said, "Well, these are delicious."

Warmth filled her. Contentment. She gave herself a moment to soak it all in before she reached for her fork and tasted her own pancake.

Picking up his coffee cup, Rory said, "I can't believe how much snow fell."

"It is Pennsylvania."

"How do you deal with it?"

"Well, on days like this, those of us who can stay in."

"You play games maybe?"

Ah, she got what he was doing. He was paving the way to tell Finley they couldn't leave. Probably hoping to show her she'd have a good day if they stayed.

"We do. We play lots of games. But we also bake cookies."

Finley didn't even glance up. Happily involved in her blueberry pancake, she ignored them.

Rory said, "I love cookies."

"These are special cookies. They're sugar cookies that I cut into shapes and then paint."

"Paint?"

"With icing. I put colored icing on houses, churches, bells—"

Finley glanced up sharply. "You mean Christmas bells."

Shannon winced. "Well, yes. I'm baking cookies for my family when we celebrate Christmas next week. But it's still fun—"

"I hate Christmas!"

This was the third time Finley had said she hated Christmas. It wasn't merely part of a tantrum or even a way to manipulate people. This little girl really didn't like Christmas.

"Okay. So instead of baking cookies, how about if we play cards?"

"I thought we were leaving."

Rory set his hand on top of Finley's. "I'd like to leave. But I have to check to see if the roads are open. There's a good possibility that we're stranded here for another few hours, maybe even another day."

Finley sighed heavily, like a billion-dollar heiress who'd just received bad news, and who would, at any second, explode. Shannon found herself holding her breath, waiting for Finley's reply. Which was ridiculous. The kid was six. The weather wasn't anybody's fault. She was stuck and that was that.

Setting her fork on her plate, Shannon rose and said, "While I go to my room to check on the roads and call my staff, you drink your milk and finish your breakfast. Then we'll put the dishes in the dishwasher and we'll play Go Fish."

Finley's eyes narrowed and her mouth formed the upside-down *U* again. But Shannon ignored her. From her peripheral vision she watched Finley glare at her dad.

Without looking at her, Rory said, "I haven't played Go Fish in years. I'm not sure I remember the rules."

"It's an easy game, Daddy."

"Good. Then I should catch on quickly."

Shannon took her plate to the sink. "Or maybe she'll beat you."

That brought a light to Finley's eyes. When Shannon returned from checking the road conditions on the internet, calling her staff to say she wasn't opening the store and calling the radio stations to alert the community that the store would be closed again, she returned to the kitchen. Finley eagerly helped clear the table, stacked dishes in the dishwasher and rifled through a kitchen drawer for a deck of cards.

"I had to close the store."

Rory held up his cell phone. "I figured. I checked the road conditions. Nothing's really open. Customers can't get there anyway."

As Finley approached the table with the cards, Shannon said, "So we'll have some fun."

Pulling a chair away from the round kitchen table, Rory said, "Yes, we will. Right, Finley?"

Finley sighed and shrugged, but also pulled out a chair and sat.

Shannon noticed that Rory more or less let Finley win the first game, so she went along, too. But when Rory handily won the second game, Shannon didn't think it was out of line to play the third game without deference to Finley. But when she won, Finley exploded.

"You cheated!"

Shannon laughed. "No. Cheating takes all the sport out of a game. There's no fun in winning if you haven't really won."

"I don't care!" She swung her arm across the table, sending cards flying. But before her hand could slow down, she also thwacked her milk. The glass went airborne and landed on the floor. Sticky white milk poured everywhere.

Mortally embarrassed by Finley's outburst, Rory bounced from the table. "Finley!"

Finley bounced off her chair and raced to the kitchen door. "I hate you!"

The swinging door slammed closed when she flew through it.

Shannon rose and grabbed the paper towels. "Sorry. I should have let her win again."

Rory rubbed his hand across the back of his neck. "No. We were playing a game. She knows she can't win every time." He rubbed his neck again. He'd only ever told his parents about the trouble in his marriage and he certainly hadn't intended to tell Shannon because, technically, they didn't really know each other. But deep down Finley was a sweet little girl who deserved defending.

He fell to his seat again. "Finley's behavior isn't the fault of a confused six-year-old, but a mom who abandoned her."

Using a paper towel to sop up the milk, Shannon said, "What?"

"Her mom," Rory said, not quite sure how to broach this subject because he hadn't spoken with anyone about his ex. So he had no practice, no frame of reference for what to say.

He lifted his eyes until he could catch Shannon's gaze. "Finley's mom left us two years ago on Christmas day."

Shannon took the wet paper towels to the trash. Confusion laced her voice when she said, "Your ex left you on Christmas day?"

"Yeah, that's why Finley's sensitive about Christmas. But what's worse is that her mom doesn't want to see her at all. She doesn't like kids. Didn't want kids."

Shannon returned to the table and fell to her chair, trying to force all that to sink in but not quite able to comprehend. She'd spent her entire adult life attempting to get pregnant, longing for a child, and Finley's mom had left her without a backward glance?

"My ex never did anything she didn't want to do." He rose from the chair, pushed it out of his way and stooped to pick up the scattered cards.

"That's amazing."

He shrugged, but his pinched expression told her he wasn't so cavalier about it. "She'd said at the outset of our marriage that she didn't want kids." Finished gathering the cards, he rose. "Her getting pregnant was a surprise, but I thought we were ready. Turns out she wasn't."

Shannon sat in stunned silence. Rory's wife had *abandoned* her daughter? Disbelief thundered through her, along with a sense of injustice. While she'd do anything, give anything, to be able to have a child, Finley's mom had simply abandoned one?

How could a woman be so cruel?

CHAPTER THREE

RORY NEATLY STACKED the cards on the table. "I need to check on her."

"Okay. I'll start lunch."

As she had the night before, Shannon made soup and sandwiches. This time, she chose chicken soup—a soup with not even a red vegetable in it—and prepared a plate of cold cuts and some bread.

Finley walked into the kitchen in front of her dad, who had both hands on her little shoulders. Looking at the floor, she mumbled, "I'm sorry."

Shannon's heart ached for her, but she didn't think it was appropriate to say, "Hey, it's not your fault. Your mom's a horrible woman who shouldn't have left you." So, instead, she said, "That's okay. I didn't make red soup today."

Finley peeked at her. "You didn't?"

"No. I made chicken noodle."

"I like chicken noodle."

"So do I."

Rory got bowls from the cupboard and he and Finley set them on the place mats Shannon had already put out. Finley found soup spoons. Shannon set the cold cuts on the table. Everybody did everything without saying a word.

Shannon felt oddly responsible. Should she have tried to lose at the card game? Should she have reacted differently to the cheating accusation? She honestly didn't know. But she did know Finley deserved a bit of happiness and if she could, she intended to provide it.

She sucked in a breath. "You know…I still have a few sleds from when my dad and I used to slide down Parker's Hill when I was a little girl."

Finley's face instantly brightened. "Really?"

"There's a bit of a hill behind this house. I never tried it out for sledding because I just moved here last year, but I'm guessing there might be a place we could sled-ride."

This time Rory said, "Really?"

"Sure. It would be fun. Even if we can't go sledding, getting outside for some fresh air would do us all good."

Rory inclined his head. "Maybe." He faced his daughter. "What do you think?"

"I'd like to sled-ride."

"And we will if we can," Shannon quickly assured her. "As I said, I've never checked out that hill."

"I don't have snow pants."

"You can wear two pair of jeans," Rory suggested.

"And we'll put them in the dryer as soon as we come inside, so they'll be good for tomorrow morning."

The mood clearing the lunch dishes improved significantly from the mood when setting out those same dishes. Finley hurriedly dressed in the multiple jeans and double sweaters. Shannon found a pair of mittens to put over Finley's tiny multicolored striped gloves.

When Finley was ready, Shannon quickly dressed in a pair of jeans and two sweaters. She put her dad's old parka over herself and used insulated gloves for her hands.

They stepped outside onto the back porch and the glare off the snow almost blinded them.

"Wow. It's beautiful."

Shannon glanced around proudly at the snow-covered fir trees that surrounded her little home. "Yes. It is. I loved living in South Carolina—close to the beach," she added, slanting a look at Rory. "But this is home. As annoying as snow is, it is also beautiful."

They trudged from the house to the shed behind the garage and found an old sled and two red saucer sleds. Shannon and Finley took the saucers and Rory hoisted the bigger runner sled off its hook and followed them out, into the bright sunshine again.

Again they trudged through the snow, walking the twenty or thirty feet from the outbuilding to the dip behind the house.

"There are trees."

Shannon glanced at Rory. "I know. That's why I couldn't say for sure we could sled. Without a wide path between the trees, there'd be too much chance we'd hit one and somebody could be hurt."

He walked fifty feet to the left. "Too many trees this way." Then fifty feet to the right. "I found something!" he called, motioning for Shannon and Finley to come over. "There's a perfect space right here."

The "hill" was more of a slope. It eased down nicely for about thirty feet. A wide ledge would stop them before they reached what looked to be a bigger hill. Still, given that Finley was only six, Shannon didn't think they should try to go beyond the ledge.

She tossed her saucer to the snow. "I'm ready."

Finley followed suit. "I'm ready, too."

They plopped onto their saucers, scooted a bit to get them going then careened down the hill. Finley's squealing giggles filled the quiet air. Hearing her, Shannon laughed. They flew down the slope and, as predicted, their saucers ran out of steam on the ledge.

Finley bounced up. "Let's go again!" She grabbed her saucer and started up the hill.

"Walk along the side!" Shannon called. "We don't want to make our slope bumpy from footprints."

To Shannon's complete amazement, Finley said, "Okay!" and moved to the side of the hill.

When they reached the top, Rory said, "Okay, everybody out of my way. I'm taking this puppy for a ride."

He threw the runner sled onto the snow and landed on top of it, sending it racing down the hill. He hit the ledge, but his sled didn't stop. The ledge didn't even slow the sleek runners. Smooth and thin, they whizzed across the ledge as if it were nothing. In seconds Rory and his sled headed down the bigger hill and disappeared.

Finley screamed.

Thinking she was terrified, Shannon spun to face her, but the little girl's face glowed with laughter. Shannon's lips twitched. Then she burst out laughing, too.

"Do you think we'll ever see him again?"

Finley's giggles multiplied. "How far down does the hill go?"

"I don't know. I've never been back that far."

The world around them grew silent. Now that the fun of seeing him disappear was over, Shannon's tummy tugged with concern. As fast as he was going, he could have hit a tree. He could be at the bottom of the hill, unconscious.

"We better go check on him."

"Can we ride our sleds down to the ledge?"

Shannon laughed and patted Finley's head. Kids really had no comprehension of danger. But before she could reply, Rory called, "I'm okay!"

His voice echoed in the silence around them. But knowing he was fine, Shannon tossed her saucer to the ground. "Race you to the ledge."

Finley positioned her sled and jumped on. They squealed with laughter as they sped down the hill. On the ledge, both popped off their sleds, ran to the edge and peered over. At least fifty feet below, Rory dragged his sled up the hill.

He waved.

Finley waved. "Hi, Daddy!" Then she glanced around when her voice echoed around her. "That is so cool."

"It's a cool place." She turned Finley toward the top of the hill again. "I'll bet we can sled down twice before your dad gets to the ledge."

Finley grabbed her sled. "Okay!"

They raced down another two times before Rory finally joined them on the ledge. "That was some ride."

Shannon peered over the edge. A reasonably wide strip wound between the rows of trees, but the hill itself was steep and long. "I'll bet it was."

He offered the runner sled to her. "Wanna try?"

She laughed. "Not a chance."

"Hey, sledding was your idea. I thought you were a pro."

"I haven't really gone sledding in years—"

Before she could finish her sentence Rory tossed the sled to the ground and punched into her like a linebacker. She fell on the sled. He fell on top of her and they took off down the hill. For several seconds she had no breath. When she finally caught a gulp of air, she screamed. Really screamed. But soon her screams of fear became screams of delight. The thrill of the speed whooshed through her. The wind whipping across her face felt glorious.

They hit the bottom with a thump.

Obviously paying attention to the grove of trees ahead of them, Rory banked left, toppling the sled to a stop. She rolled on the ground. He rolled beside her.

She turned her head to face him; he turned to face her and they burst out laughing.

Finley's little voice echoed down the hill. "Me next, Daddy!"

He bounced up and held his hand out to Shannon, helping her up.

"That was amazing."

He picked up the sled. "I know. It was like being a kid again. Fun. Free." Holding the sled with one hand, he looped his other arm across her shoulders. "Now we have to trudge about fifty feet up a hill."

She laughed, but her insides tickled. Even working at the store, she'd been nothing but lonely in the past year. Not because she didn't have friends. She did. Lots of them. Not because she missed her husband. Any man who'd desert a woman the day she had a hysterectomy was an ass. But because she'd missed belonging. With Rory and Finley she felt as if she belonged.

She sucked in a breath, erasing that thought. These two would be with her for one more day—well, one evening and one night. Maybe breakfast in the morning. She couldn't get attached to them.

Still, when they reached the top and found Finley bouncing with delight, happiness filled her again. Finley was a sweet little girl who deserved some fun. Maybe even a break from the reality of her life—that her mom didn't want her.

Rory scooped her off the ground and fell with her onto the sled. The weight of their bodies set the sled in motion and it slid down the little slope. Shannon fell to her own sled and careened behind them so she could jump off when she reached the ledge and watch them as they whipped down the bigger hill.

Finley's squeals of pleasure echoed through the forest. Shannon's chest puffed out with pride. She'd thought of the idea that had turned a potentially dismal afternoon into an afternoon of joy.

She watched Finley and Rory plod back up the hill. When they reached the ledge, she stooped down and hugged Finley. "That was fun, wasn't it?"

Her eyes rounded with joy. "It was great!" She turned to her dad. "Let's go again."

"Hey, I just slogged up that hill three times. I need a break." He headed up the slope again. "But you can ride your saucer down the little hill as much as you want."

Surprisingly, Finley said, "Okay," and followed him up the slope. At the top, she set her butt on the saucer and sent herself lobbing down the hill.

Rory dropped to the snow. "I am seriously tired."

Shannon plopped beside him. "After three little rides?"

He tweaked a curl that had escaped from her knit cap. "Three *little* rides? You try walking up that hill three times in a row with no break."

Finley's final whoop of laughter as she slid to a stop on the ledge reached them. Shannon's heart swelled again, filled with warmth and joy. This was what it would feel like to have a real family. A loving husband. An adorable child.

Watching Finley trudge up the slope with her saucer, Rory said, "This is why I love having a kid. The fun. When Finley's not in a mood, she can be incredibly fun." He peeked at Shannon. "And spontaneous. The things she says sometimes crack me up."

She glanced down the hill at Finley, saw the joy on her face, the snow on her tummy, and she laughed. "Yeah. She's cute."

Shannon's laughter filled Rory with peace. The whole afternoon had been fun, even though he'd told her about his ex-wife. Or maybe because he'd told her about his ex-wife. She seemed to feel enough sympathy for Finley that she'd gone out of her way to make his little girl happy.

"You really love Finley, don't you?"

Her question surprised him so much that he glanced over at her again. The sun sparkled off the snow that clung to her. Her full lips bowed up in a smile of pure pleasure as she watched his child—his pride and joy— pick herself up and head up the hill.

"I adore her. I love being a dad."

Her smile trembled a bit. "I bet you do."

He snorted a laugh. "You've seen the bad side of parenting in the past twenty-four hours. Most of the time Finley makes me laugh, fills in my world." He shrugged. "Actually, she makes my world make sense, gives all the work I do a purpose."

"You're a great dad."

"Yeah, too bad I won't have any more kids."

Her face registered such a weird expression that he felt he needed to explain. "When a spouse leaves the way mine did, no explanation, no trying to work things out, just a plain old 'I don't love you anymore and I certainly don't want to be a mom…'" He shrugged again, forced his gaze away from her, over to the blue, blue sky. "Well, you're left with a little bit more than a bad taste in your mouth for marriage."

"Marriage doesn't have anything to do with having kids."

He laughed. "You're right. Not in this day and age, with adoption and surrogate mothers." He caught her gaze again. "But it's difficult enough to handle Finley— one child—without a mom. I couldn't imagine adding another. So it's just me and Finley for the rest of our lives."

"Even though you love kids, you wouldn't try any of the other options?"

"Nope. But if I had a wife I would. Of course, if I had a wife I could have kids the old-fashioned way." He waggled his eyebrows, but the truth of that settled over him and he stopped being silly. "If I could commit again, I'd love to have more kids. *My* kids. A little boy who'd look like me. Another little girl who might look like her mom."

When he caught her gaze again, her eyes were soft and sad. He could have been confused by her reaction, except he knew his voice had gotten every bit as soft and sad. He'd revealed some personal tidbits that she probably wasn't expecting. Hell, even he hadn't realized he felt all those things about kids until the conversation had turned that way.

Of course, she'd sort of turned it that way.

Now that he thought about it, she owed him some equally personal tidbits. "So what about you? No husband? No kids? Married to your store?"

She brushed her hand along the top of the snow. "This time last year I was married."

"Oh?" Something oddly territorial rattled through

him, surprising him. Sure, he was attracted to her…but jealous? Of a guy from her past? That was just stupid.

She batted a hand. "I got dumped pretty much the same way you did." Avoiding his gaze, she ran her mittened hand along the surface of the snow again. "One day he loved me. The next day he didn't."

"I'm sorry."

"It's certainly not your fault." She caught his gaze, laughed lightly. "And I'm over him."

"Oh, yeah?"

She shrugged. "Only a fool pines for someone who doesn't want her."

"I'll drink to that."

She craned her neck so she could see Finley again, then she faced him. "She's going to sleep like a rock tonight."

Rory said, "Yeah," but his mind was a million miles away. The easy way she'd dismissed her marriage had caused his jealousy to morph into relief that she wasn't just free, she was happy to be free. That somehow mixed and mingled with his suddenly active hormones and he wanted to kiss her so badly he could taste it.

But that was wrong. Not only had he been hurt enough to never want to risk a relationship again, but she'd also been hurt. After less than twenty-four hours in her company he knew she was a sweet, sincere woman, who might take any romantic gesture as much more than he would intend it.

Still, that didn't stop him from wanting to kiss her. With the snow in her hair, on her jacket, covering her jeans. If he slid his hands under her knit hat, to the thicket of springy black curls, and pulled her face to his, he could kiss her softly, easily just because they were having fun.

But would she realize it was a kiss of pure happiness over the fun afternoon? Or would she make more of it?

He pulled back. They were having too much fun— Finley was having too much fun—for him to spoil it over a craving for something he shouldn't take.

He rose, put his hand down to help Shannon stand. "She'll be back any second."

"Do you think she'll want to go down again?"

"Undoubtedly."

"Hope you're rested."

He grinned. "Hope *you're* rested because I'm taking the saucer and you get the runner sled."

With that he grabbed the saucer and joined Finley at the top of the slope. Shannon pretended great interest in the sled he'd left for her, but she didn't even really see it. Her heart pounded in her chest and her insides had all but turned to mush. For a few seconds there, when their conversation had paused, she could have sworn he was going to slide his hand behind her neck and pull her forward so he could kiss her.

Kiss her!

What a crazy thing to think! Ridiculous wishful thinking on her part, that's what it was. They might be having fun with his daughter, but that was no reason for a man to kiss a woman. She was simply too much of a romantic.

But figuring all this out now was actually a good thing. Rory had come right out and said that if he married again, he would want kids. His own kids. A son of his own. Another adorable daughter.

And didn't that sound painfully familiar? The last man she would have expected to leave her over not being able to have kids was her seemingly wonderful ex-husband. He'd loved her. She'd never had any doubt.

Yet, once she couldn't give him a son—a real son, his flesh-and-blood son—he'd bolted. She wasn't sure she could handle that kind of rejection again. So she was glad they'd had this little talk early on. There'd be no more wishful thinking. No more hoping he'd kiss her.

But right here and right now, she was a lonely woman, and she had both Rory and his daughter in her yard, enjoying her company. She'd be crazy to be upset. Crazier still to withdraw just because there couldn't be anything romantic between her and Rory. The smart thing to do would be to simply relax and enjoy their company.

She picked up the sled. Studied it. Could she ride this down the slope and get it stopped on the ledge? Or would she go racing down the hill?

She smiled. Either way she'd probably make Finley laugh. So why not?

When they returned to the house, Shannon realized she hadn't taken anything out of the freezer for dinner. Her only choice was to thaw some hamburgers in the microwave and make use of the frozen French fries her mom always bought in bulk then had to give away because she and her dad couldn't eat them all.

As soon as they stepped into the kitchen, she walked to the refrigerator, removed the meat from the freezer section and tossed it on the counter. Unzipping her dad's big parka, she said, "That was fun."

Rory helped Finley out of sweater number one. "Really fun."

Finley grinned. "Lots of fun." She sat on the floor as her father tugged off her little pink boots, then helped her slide out of the first of her two pair of jeans. "But I'm hungry."

"Me, too! I thought I'd make burgers and fries."

Finley bounced up. "All right."

Rory ruffled her hair. "Go wash your hands while Shannon and I get started on the food."

She nodded and all but skipped out of the room.

Shannon unwrapped the hamburger, set it in a bowl and put it in the microwave on low.

As it hummed behind her, Rory said, "What can I do?"

"I guess we could plug in the fryer to heat the oil for the fries."

She rummaged through a cupboard beside the sink and found the fryer. After pouring in fresh oil, she plugged it in.

Rory laughed. "That still leaves me with nothing to do."

"You could go check on Finley."

"I probably should. She had such a busy afternoon that I may find her asleep on the bed."

While he was gone, Shannon hung her parka in the hall closet and took the breakfast dishes out of the dishwasher.

When he and Finley returned to the kitchen a few minutes later, Finley was carrying a little laptop. Rory joined Shannon at the counter where she was forming the hamburgers. "She can play a game or two while we cook." He pointed at the hamburgers. "How many of these should we make?"

"How many do you want?"

"I'll eat two. Finley will eat one."

"And I'll eat one." She glanced down at the plate. "We already have four. So it looks like we're done."

He nudged her aside. "I'll take it from here. Usually I grill hamburgers, but I can use a frying pan, too."

Shannon retrieved plates and utensils and stacked them on the table. She grabbed a handful of paper napkins and set them beside the plates.

Finley glanced up. "Can I help?"

Surprised, but not about to turn down help, Shannon said, "You can arrange the plates and silver while I start the French fries."

Finley nodded. Shannon walked back to the refrigerator, removed the frozen fries and put them into the fryer.

Dinner conversation was very different from the quiet lunch. Finley chattered about how much fun she'd had sledding and how silly her dad looked on a sled. Rory reminded her that she didn't think him silly the times he rode down the big hill with her and she giggled.

Shannon basked in the ordinariness of it. A happy little girl and her father who clearly adored her. They bantered back and forth as Rory cut her burger in half and poured ketchup for her fries.

Shannon took a bite of her own hamburger. Rory was a nice guy, with a big heart, trying to raise a daughter abandoned by her mother. She supposed that was why he'd pulled away rather than kiss her that afternoon. He was too busy to be looking for a romance. But as quickly as she thought that she reminded herself of her decision not to even ponder a romance with him anyway. She'd seen the expression on his face when he talked about having more kids. A son. No matter what he said or how busy he was, someday he'd want to remarry. He'd want that family. Those kids.

And she couldn't have any.

The aching pain filled her as it always did when confronted by her barrenness. The loss. The unfairness.

For the first time in months she wanted to flirt. Wanted to be pretty to somebody—and she had to pull back.

For both of their sakes.

CHAPTER FOUR

"WELL, SHE'S ASLEEP." Rory plopped down on the sofa beside Shannon, who was pulling strands of tinsel through her fingers to untangle them. Supper had gone well. But after the dishes had been cleared, Finley had begun to nod off, so Rory had taken her for a bath. "She went out like a light the second her head hit the pillow." Rolling his head across the sofa back, he smiled at her. "You're great with her."

Shannon laughed. "Not really. In case you didn't notice my strategy, I simply kept her busy until she dropped from exhaustion."

He laughed.

"I'm serious. She's obviously a smart little girl. She bores easily. The trick to preventing tantrums might be simply keeping her busy."

"I can't always do that. I have a company to run. So it's her nanny, Mrs. Perkins, who gets the brunt of her moods. Though she spends a lot of time entertaining Finley, there are days when Finley only wants me. If she breaks down and calls me and I come home, we feel like we're rewarding Finley for bad behavior."

"You are." She turned her attention to her tangled tinsel again. She didn't like to pry, but he needed help and now that she'd spent a little time with Finley, she realized she'd learned a great deal watching her friends and their children in South Carolina. "There are lots of things you can do to discipline her. The first is to get her accustomed to hearing the word *no*. But you have to be smart about it. If she's tired or hungry, she won't take well to it. If you don't watch her mood, and discipline her when she's not open, it'll make things worse."

He tweaked her hair. "How'd you get so smart?"

She shrugged. "I pay attention?"

He laughed. "Right." He paused, obviously waiting for her to say more, and when she didn't he said, "I'm serious. I've asked you this before, but you always blew me off. And I'm curious. Did you read a book or something? Because if you did, I'd like to get that book."

"No book." She ran some more tinsel through her fingers, once again debating how much to tell him. After a few seconds, she said, "When I lived in South Carolina with my ex, all of our friends had children. We'd be invited to picnics and outings and I'd see how they handled their kids. My husband really wanted children and I wanted to be a good mom. So I'd watch." She laughed slightly at how stupid she probably sounded. "Technically, I spent my entire marriage watching other people raise kids."

The room grew silent. Every pop and snap of the logs in the fireplace echoed in the quiet room.

Rory finally broke the silence. "So what happened?"

She peeked at him. "Happened?"

"To your marriage."

Once again, she thought before answering. There was no way she'd tell him the truth. It was humiliating to be deserted by the man you loved on the day you needed him the most. Humiliating that a man who'd truly loved her couldn't stay. Humiliating that she'd been abandoned for a physical defect.

Plus, Rory was in Green Hill to buy her store. They might be spending some personal time together because of the storm, but at the end of the weekend they would be business associates.

Still, they were stranded together and he'd told her some personal things. So she couldn't totally ignore the question.

She ran the last of the first strand of tinsel through her fingers and began spooling it around her hand so it would be ready to hang the next day when Rory and Finley left.

"I suspect my ex was a little like your ex."

He laughed. "Really?"

"He had very definite ideas of how he wanted his life." She continued spooling so she didn't have to look at him. "He wanted things to be a certain way. When we hit a point where I couldn't make those things happen, he dumped me."

He sat forward, dropped his clasped hands between his knees, then straightened again and caught her gaze. "I'm sorry your ex was a jerk."

"I'm sorry your marriage didn't work out."

Once again silence reigned and unspoken thoughts rippled through her brain. He was a nice guy and, at her core, Finley was a sweet little girl. She'd give anything to have had a good husband and a beautiful child. Anything.

Rory leaned toward her and her heart expanded in her chest. They were only a foot apart. A shift forward by him, a shift forward by her and their lips could touch.

But uncertainty leaped in the dark depths of his deep brown eyes. Though he didn't say a word, she knew the litany undoubtedly rattling through his head right now. They were both wounded. He had a child. And as soon as they got out of his storm, they'd be doing business. They shouldn't get involved.

He pulled back, away from her, confirming her suspicions, and disappointment shuddered through her.

He rose. "I guess I'd better head off to bed myself. I'll see you in the morning."

She smiled. "Sure. See you in the morning."

But something splintered inside her heart. Since Bryce, she'd lived with a feeling of inadequacy. Not being good enough. Never feeling womanly enough. Though Rory had good reasons not to kiss her, those feelings of inadequacy reverberated through her. Whispering like demons, reminding her that for lots of men she wasn't whole, wasn't good enough…couldn't ever be good enough.

The next morning the world was still a winter wonderland. Rory ambled into the kitchen to find Shannon sitting at the table, drinking a cup of coffee.

She smiled at him over the rim. "No Finley?"

"She's still sleeping."

"Good, then I can tell you I watched the local news this morning."

He winced. "Bad?"

She laughed. "Depends on your point of view. Raleigh's employees get another unexpected vacation day. We got another six inches of snow last night and the roads haven't been cleared from the first storm."

Rory didn't care. Finley was well-behaved, happy, for the first time in the two years they'd struggled without her mom. Another day of not looking at the store didn't bother him. Unfortunately, he wasn't the only person in this equation.

"I'm sorry that you're losing revenue."

"Funny thing about running the only department store in a twenty-mile radius. You might think we'd lose a lot of business by being closed for the entire weekend before Christmas, but the truth is we'll just be busier Monday through Friday." She smiled. "We'll be fine."

Rory got a cup of coffee and headed to the table. Sitting across from her, he noticed she wasn't wearing a lick of makeup. Her hair had been combed but not styled and the riot of curls made her look young, care-free. Kissable.

His heart cartwheeled in his chest as longing sprinted through him. But he'd already been through this in his head the night before, so he ignored the yearning in favor of the more important issue. In spite of the fact that he'd almost kissed her the night before, she wasn't upset, angry or even standoffish. She still liked having him and Finley at her home.

He picked up his coffee, drank a long swallow, then said, "How about if I make omelets this morning?"

"Oh, I love omelets!" Her face brightened in a way that shot an arrow of arousal through him. He didn't know what it was about this woman that attracted him so, but he did know that these feelings were inappropri-ate. She'd done so much for them in the past two days that he owed her. He shouldn't be ogling her or fanta-sizing about kissing her.

"I have some ham, some cheese. I'll bet there's even a green pepper or two in the refrigerator."

"Western omelets it is, then."

Yawning, Finley pushed open the swinging door. "Morning."

Rory scooped her off the floor. "Morning to you, too." He kissed her cheek. "I'm making omelets."

Her eyes widened with delight. "Good!" She scooted down. "I'll set the table."

Shannon caught his gaze, her eyebrows rising in question. He shrugged. But he knew why Finley was so helpful, so accommodating. He'd like to take credit, but he couldn't. Shannon was the one who'd so easily guided her into helping with meals and setting the table, keeping her busy so she wouldn't get bored and misbehave.

And the way he thanked her was with inappropriate thoughts of kissing her?

Not good, Rory. Seriously, not good.

Shannon chopped the green peppers and ham, while he gathered eggs, beat them in a bowl. They worked together companionably, happily, as Finley set out plates and silver. But when breakfast was over, Finley slid off her seat. "Are we going now?"

Rory looked at Shannon. Then realized what he'd done. He hadn't just turned to her for help with Finley. He trusted her. He wanted her advice.

That was not good. Not because she couldn't help, but because his reaction had been automatic. Instinctive.

"Are we ever going to get out of here?"

Shannon rose from the table, taking Finley's plate with her. "Aren't you having fun?"

Her lip thrust out. "Yeah. Sort of."

"The roads are still pretty bad," Rory said. He walked over to her and lifted her into his arms. "Unless the snowplow comes through sometime today, we're still stuck here."

Her lower lip jutted out even farther. "Okay."

Shannon understood her cabin fever, but multiplied

by about fifty. Not only was she stuck in her house, but she was also stuck with a man she was really coming to like who wouldn't want her if he knew the truth about her. Even if he was interested and asked her out, she'd never accept a date. Lying awake the night before, she'd realized that if they dated, at some point she'd have to tell him she couldn't have kids. The last man she'd told hadn't taken it so well. Just like Bryce, Rory wanted kids. Was it worth a few weeks or months of *her* happiness to put *him* in a position of having to dump her when she told him?

It wasn't. Which was why the subject of a date or romance or even liking each other would never come up, if she could help it. And why needing to keep Finley busy was such a lucky, lucky thing.

She walked over to the six-year-old. "I have an idea. I have a neighbor who lives over there." She pointed over Finley's shoulder, out the window. "She's a little bit older and her husband died last year. So when we get stranded like this, she's all by herself. Imagine being all by yourself for three days, no company, nobody to talk to."

Finley gasped and pressed her hands over her mouth. "I'll bet she's scared."

"Maybe not scared. But lonely. So, since the weather's not so bad that we can't go out, I was thinking we could bake a cake and take it to her." She glanced at Rory, silently asking for his approval as she detailed her plan. "We'd have to walk, but we could think of it as fun, like we did yesterday when we were sledding."

Rory frowned. "How far away does she live?"

"Not far," she assured him. "Just far enough that we'd get a good walk in the fresh air." She faced Finley. "So, do you want to try to bake a cake?"

"What kind?"

"I have a box mix for a chocolate cake and one for a yellow. We could make peanut-butter icing for the chocolate. Or chocolate icing for the yellow."

Finley slid out of her father's arms and to the floor. "I like peanut butter."

"So do I." She nudged Finley to the door. "Go back to the bedroom and change out of your pj's and we'll get to work."

Finley nodded and raced out of the room. Rory followed her. "I'll help her."

By the time they returned, Shannon had the box cake mix on the center island, along with a mixing bowl, mixer, eggs, butter and water.

"Give me two minutes to put on jeans and a sweatshirt and we'll get this into the oven."

She scooted out of the kitchen and into her bedroom. The bed was neatly made. The bathroom was also neat as a pin. But the Wallace family scent lingered around her. Finley's little-girl smells mixed with Rory's aftershave and created a scent that smelled like home. Family. She didn't even try to resist inhaling deeply. She might not ever become a permanent part of their lives, but she liked these two. This weekend was her chance to be with them. She might not kiss him, but she wouldn't deprive herself of the chance to enjoy them.

Once in jeans and a University of Pittsburgh sweatshirt, she ambled out to the kitchen. Finley climbed onto a stool beside the center island. "What can I do?"

"I don't know? What can you do?" She laughed.

But not getting the joke, Finley frowned.

Rather than explain, Shannon said, "Can you break eggs into a bowl?"

She glanced back at Rory. He shrugged. "There's a first time for everything."

Shannon set the bowl in front of Finley. Pulling an egg from the carton, she said, "You take an egg, like this—" Demonstrating by putting the egg against the bowl's edge, she continued, "And crack it against the edge of the bowl like this." The egg broke in half, its contents spilling into the bowl.

"My turn." Finley grabbed an egg and hit it on the rim. Miraculously, the white and yoke tumbled into the bowl. She tossed the shell beside Shannon's and clapped her hands together with glee. "I did it!"

"Yes, you did." Shannon handed her the open box of cake mix. "Take out the plastic container. We'll open it and dump that into the bowl, too."

With Shannon giving Finley the opportunity to be involved in every step of the process of cake baking, it took a long time to get the cake into the oven. They played two games of Go Fish while it baked. After lunch, they made simple peanut-butter icing, spread it across the two layers and slid the cake into a carrier.

Once again, they dressed Finley in two pair of jeans and two sweaters. When they stepped outside, the snow glowed like a million tiny diamonds. Rory carried Finley across the field that separated the two houses. They stomped the snow off their boots as they walked across Mary O'Grady's back porch to the kitchen door.

Mary answered on the first knock. Short and round, with shaped gray hair, Mary wore a festive Christmas sweater and jeans. "Shannon!" She glanced at Finley and Rory. "And who is this?"

"Mary O'Grady, this is Rory Wallace and his daughter, Finley."

As Shannon made the introduction, Rory hoped

Finley wouldn't say something awful about the sweet-looking woman's sweater.

"Rory was on his way to Green Hill to take a look at the store when they were stranded on the highway and had the state police bring them to my house." She offered the cake. "Since we're all getting a little bored, we brought a cake to share."

"Well, aren't you sweet," Mary said, opening her door to invite them in. She pinched Finley's cheek. "And aren't you adorable!" She smiled at Rory. "It's nice to meet you."

"It's nice to meet you, too," he said, sliding Finley through the door. The kitchen hadn't been remodeled the way Shannon's had. Old-fashioned oak cupboards dominated the room. A rectangular table, with four ladder-back chairs, sat in the center.

Mary fussed over Finley. "Let me help you with your jacket."

Finley glanced at her dad. Rory nodded his head slightly, indicating she should just go with it.

Unzipping Finley's coat, Mary faced Shannon. "Sweetie, why don't you put on a pot of coffee so we can enjoy that cake properly?"

Shannon laughed. "You're a woman after my own heart, Mary."

After removing her coat, she walked to the counter with the ease of someone who'd been there before. Rory watched her root through the cupboards to find the filters and coffee. She got water and measured grounds.

Mary helped Finley onto a chair. "And what can I get you to drink, sweetie?"

Rory held his breath. She hadn't mentioned the sweater, but she'd gotten a little nervous over having a stranger help her with her jacket. They weren't out of the woods yet.

Finley smiled. "Milk."

Rory breathed again, as Shannon retrieved some plates and coffee mugs from the cupboard and joined them at the table. "That'll only take a minute."

Rory faced Mary. "You have a lovely home."

She batted a hand in dismissal. "I had such plans for this, then my Joe died. And I just sort of lost interest."

"But we're hoping to have a contractor out here next summer, aren't we, Mary?"

Mary's face saddened a little more. "I thought you were leaving if you sold the store."

"Probably." She glanced at Rory, then back at Mary. "But we already looked at the books with the cupboard samples. All you need to do is finalize your choices and you can easily have the entire kitchen remodeled before fall. If you want, you can call me every night with an update or tell me your problems and I'll help you figure out how to solve them."

Mary sat beside Shannon and patted her hand. "You're very good to me."

Rory suppressed a smile. It seemed he and Finley weren't the only strays that Shannon cared for. A few times it had popped into his head that her kindness to him and Finley might be an act of sorts to keep herself in his good graces when he looked at her store on Monday. He'd dismissed that thought, but now he could totally put it out of his mind. Shannon Raleigh was a genuinely nice woman.

His heart twisted a bit. She *was* a nice woman. And Finley liked her. If he were in the market for a romance, she'd be at the top of the candidates list.

But he wasn't looking for a romance.

The coffeemaker groaned its final release and Mary jumped from the table. "Cut the cake, sweetie, and I'll get the coffee."

In a few minutes, everyone had a slice of cake and a cup of coffee or glass of milk. They talked some more about Mary's plans to remodel her house, then Mary asked Finley about school and Finley launched into an unusually happy, unusually lengthy discussion of her classes, her classmates and recess.

Mary seemed to soak it all up, but Shannon really listened, really participated in the conversation with Finley.

When the cake was gone and the conversation exhausted, Shannon rose from the table and gathered their plates, which she slid into the dishwasher. "We really have to get going. Not only do we have to make something for dinner, but it will also be dark soon."

Mary rose, too. "That's the bad thing about winter. It gets dark too early. And with all these clouds, you can't count on the light of the moon to get you home."

Finley laughed. "That's funny."

Mary tickled her tummy. "I'm a funny lady." She pulled Finley's jacket from the back of her chair and helped her slide into it. "You can come back anytime you like."

Finley nodded.

"Just always remember to bring cake."

At that, Finley giggled.

After sliding into her parka, Shannon picked up her cake carrier and headed for the door. "I'll call you tomorrow."

"Oh, you don't have to. I'm fine."

"I know, but Mom and Dad are arriving one day this

week for the holiday. So you'll be invited to Christmas Eve dinner. I'll need to give you the time."

"Sounds great."

Shannon gave her a hug, opened the door and stepped out onto the cold porch.

Carrying Finley, Rory followed her. "She's great."

Leading them down the stairs, Shannon said, "She is. But she was even funnier when her husband was alive." She peeked back at Rory. "He had a heart attack two years ago. She's really only now getting back into the swing of things."

"That's hard."

"Yeah." She caught his gaze again. "But lots of life is hard."

He knew she was referring to her divorce, which she'd barely explained. Still he could tell that life—marriage—hadn't treated her any more fairly than it had treated him. It was no wonder they got along so well. Both had been burned. Both knew nothing was certain.

They finished the walk chitchatting about nothing, making conversation to alleviate the boredom. But when they got into the house and Shannon pulled off her knit cap, throwing snow around her kitchen when she freed her hair, a knot formed in Rory's stomach.

He liked her. He wanted to kiss her so much that he'd almost acted on the impulse twice.

He didn't want to get married again. He wasn't even sure he wanted to get in a serious relationship again.

But he *liked* her.

And he wanted to kiss her.

And if he didn't soon get out of this house he was going to act on that impulse.

CHAPTER FIVE

THE SNOW ITSELF might have stopped by Sunday morning, but on Monday morning the air was still cold, the wind wicked.

They set out to get Rory's car from the interstate at seven o'clock, but discovered it had been towed—with all the other stranded cars—to a used car dealership in the next town over, so the roads could be plowed.

By the time they returned to Green Hill, the store was already open for business. When they entered the crowded first-floor sales department, color, scent and sound bombarded them. Throngs of noisy people crowded the sales tables. Red, green and blue Christmas ornaments hung from the ceiling, along with strings of multicolored lights and tinsel. The scent of chocolate from the candy department wafted through the air. "Jingle Bells" spilled from the overhead speakers.

Shannon cast a quick glance at Finley, who was being carried by her dad. Her eyes had grown huge. Her mouth was a little *O*, as if she were totally surprised or totally horrified. When she threw arms around Rory and buried her face against his neck, Shannon guessed she was horrified.

Rory held her tightly. "Finley, honey, we've been over

this already. I told you the store would be decorated for the holiday. I told you there would be Christmas songs."

Finley only snuggled in closer.

After the lovely weekend that had caused her to begin to bond with a man and child she couldn't have, Shannon had promised herself she would keep her distance. No more private conversations with Rory. No more helping to discipline Finley.

But a frightened child had to be an exception to her rule. She grabbed Rory's hand and led him in the direction of the elevators.

"Come on," she said, ignoring the *thump, thump, thump* of her heart from the feeling of Rory's hand tucked inside of hers. "Before you know it we'll be in my office where, I swear, there isn't as much as a poinsettia."

Pushing through the crowd, Shannon got them to the elevator and immediately dropped Rory's hand. She pressed the button for the third floor. The door closed, blocking out most of the sights and scents of Christmas, but "Jingle Bells" still piped into the little box.

Finley huddled against Rory. She wasn't upset or panicky. Just huddled. Once they got into the undecorated administrative offices she would be fine.

Shannon faced Rory. "Even though we lost the weekend, we can get down to work right away. There are four administrative departments. Buyers, human resources, accounting and advertising. If you take one day with each department, that will give you a full day on Friday to walk the store and some time for questions and explanations."

"Sounds good."

The elevator reached the second floor. "Jingle Bells" became "Rudolph the Red Nosed Reindeer." Finley looked to be getting antsy, so Shannon kept talking. "I only have four departments because I combined a lot of things for efficiency."

"That makes sense—if you've combined the right departments."

"MIS with accounting. Public relations with advertising."

He shrugged. "Should work."

The elevator pinged. Shannon sucked in a breath. Though they were entering the housewares department, it was as decorated with shiny red, green and blue ornaments as every other floor in the store. And the Christmas music? Well, that was piped everywhere, except into the administrative offices. So "Rudolph" still echoed around them.

She hurriedly ushered Rory around the tables of sheets and towels, past the shelves of small appliances, past the rows of dishes, glasses and stemware.

When they finally reached the swinging door into the administrative offices, she pushed it open with a sigh of relief. The second it swung closed behind them, "Rudolph" became a soft hum. As they hurried down the hall, even the hum echoed away.

At the end of the long, thin corridor, she opened the door that led to her office suite. Wendy was already seated at her desk.

"Good morning, Ms. Raleigh."

Shannon shrugged out of her coat. "No need to be formal for Mr. Wallace's sake. We spent the weekend together."

Wendy's eyes widened. "The whole weekend?"

Rory slid Finley to the floor and helped her out of her little pink jacket. "Couldn't get to my car until today."

"It was a mess," Wendy agreed, scrambling to take

Finley's coat and Rory's topcoat and hang them on the coat tree. "So what are you planning for today?"

"Since we're late, I'm only introducing Rory to the staff this morning. Then he can pick a department to spend time with this afternoon."

Wendy said, "Sounds good to me," but her gaze fell on Finley.

Rory put his hands on his daughter's shoulders. "She'll just come with us."

Since she'd promised herself she would distance herself from Rory and Finley, Shannon didn't argue that Finley would be bored. Instead, she set her briefcase on her desk then led the Wallaces into the hall again.

"Accounting is in the suite closest to the door. Buyers are in the next suite. Advertising and PR are in the third suite and the human resources department is on the fifth floor. They need extra space for testing and continuing education so they have half the floor. The cafeteria has the other." She met Rory's gaze. "So where to first?"

With a quick glance down at Finley, he said, "Let's just stay behind the door for as long as we can."

Understanding that he didn't want to take Finley out into the decorations and music until he had to, Shannon said, "How about buyers then?"

"Sounds great."

She led Rory and Finley to the first door and opened it onto a narrow office with a row of desks that led to an executive office in the back. Papers were everywhere. Invoices, catalogues, samples.

Shannon faced him. "I'm sure you're not surprised that we're finalizing our spring merchandise."

He laughed. "Not in the least."

She stopped at the first desk. "Lisa, Robbie, Jennifer,

Bill…" All four employees glanced up at her. "This is Rory Wallace. He's our first prospective buyer."

Everyone perked up. Superenthusiastic hellos greeted Rory. He stifled a laugh. Everybody was clearly trying to give a good first impression.

He met Missy McConnell, the head buyer, then Shannon herded him and Finley out of that office and into accounting. Five desks had been crammed into the narrow space and everyone sat staring at a computer screen.

Having already established a drill, Shannon simply introduced people as she walked by their desks. Though this group looked a little more wary than the enthusiastic buyers, Rory nodded and smiled.

In department three, advertising and PR, copy layout littered a big table in the center of a much wider main room. Employees sat at drafting table desks. The department head, John Wilder, was just a tad too happy for Rory's tastes. Finley wasn't thrilled with him, either.

"So are you going to sit on Santa's lap?"

Finley's little mouth tuned down into her perfect *U* frown. "No."

"Ah. Too old for that now, huh?"

"No, I don't believe he exists."

John laughed, but Finley tugged on Rory's hand. "I don't like it here."

Rory covered for her with a little laugh. "We've been meeting people since we arrived. She's probably ready for a break."

Shannon moved them toward the door. "That's a great idea." In the hall, she stooped in front of Finley. "How about if we go up to the cafeteria and have a soda?"

Her little mouth pulled down even farther. "I want to go home."

Shannon shot a glance up at Rory, and he crouched beside Finley. Putting his hands on her shoulders, he said, "I told you this would be boring and you said you didn't care as long as we went to the beach afterward."

Her bottom lip puffed out. "I know."

"So you've got to keep up your end of the bargain."

Her lip quivered. "I don't have anything to do while you talk."

"Things will slow down this afternoon and we'll stay in one department. We'll find you a chair and you can sit and play on your computer."

"It's noisy when you talk."

"It is," Shannon agreed suddenly. "And lots of those offices don't have room for an extra chair."

Rory glanced up at her, mortified that she was agreeing with Finley, ruining his defense.

"So why don't we set you up in my office? Wendy will be right outside the door, if you need anything. And I have a TV in case your computer games get boring."

"If you have Wi-Fi, I can watch TV on my computer."

Shannon laughed. "My screen's bigger."

Finley laughed, too.

Rory peeked over at Shannon again. Her abilities with Finley were amazing. She'd said she'd babysat some of her friends' kids, but she seemed so much smarter than a part-time, fill-in caregiver.

Unless he was just lacking?

Ah, hell. Who was he kidding? Ever since Finley entered this new diva phase, he'd been behind the eight ball, playing catch up rather than proactively parenting. Shannon, an objective person, knew exactly what to do because she saw things more clearly than he did.

They walked Finley back to the office at the end of the hall. Wendy looked up as they entered. "That was fast."

Shannon said, "We took a quick introduction tour and Finley got bored. So, we've decided to let her watch TV in my office while we go up to human resources."

Wendy rose. "That's a great idea. I also think we have some cola in your refrigerator…maybe even some candy."

"No candy before lunch," Rory said.

Shannon smiled. "I should think not. We've got a great cafeteria upstairs." She caught Finley's gaze. "They make the best French fries. Give us an hour to talk with the people in human resources and I'll race you upstairs. Winner gets a milk shake."

Finley gasped with excitement. Wendy laughed and took her hand. "You two go on. Finley and I will channel surf until we find some cartoons."

When they were in the hall, Rory ran his hand along the back of his neck. "Thanks."

Shannon began walking up the hall. "For what?"

He hurried to catch up with her. "For being so good with Finley."

"Finley is a very easy child to love."

That made him laugh, but Shannon didn't join him. "You're serious."

For that she stopped. "Yes. Why are you surprised?"

He pointed at his chest. "I love her because she's mine. But this diva phase has even me backing off sometimes."

"That's because you take everything too personally."

"She is my daughter."

"Right."

"You know, we've got five whole days of entertaining her."

"I know."

"And Finley's not going to settle into your office for an entire week and just play baby angel."

That time she did laugh.

"So what do you say we form an alliance?"

She peeked at him. "An alliance?"

"A partnership. My side of the bargain is that I need help. Your side is to provide that help. It's win-win."

She laughed again.

And something soft and warm floated through Rory. He hadn't exactly forgotten what it felt like to be in the company of a woman, but he had forgotten some things. Like how everything around them always smelled pretty. Or how their laughs were usually musical.

"I love it when you laugh."

Shannon took a step back, and though she'd pulled away before, avoided him before, this morning it gave him an odd feeling in the pit of his stomach. She had a real problem with him complimenting her.

After nearly three days together he should be at least allowed to compliment something neutral like her laugh.

"Why does that make you mad?"

She started walking again. "It doesn't make me mad."

"It makes you something because you stopped laughing. Pulled away." He paused, watching her race away from him. "Now you're all but running away."

"We have work to do."

"And we also spent the weekend together. We can't spend the week behaving like strangers."

"Not strangers, just people working out a business deal."

Catching up to her, he said, "Ah, so this is your business face."

She motioned a circle in front of the bright red jacket of her suit. "This is the whole business demeanor." Then she sighed. "Look, I'm seriously trying to sell you my store. It would help if you'd forget that I love to sledride. And that I can't cook. And I haven't even started decorating for Christmas yet."

He studied her pretty blue eyes, which were shiny with what he could only guess was fear that something personal might cause him to walk away from their negotiations. His voice was soft, careful, when he said, "Why would that help? People who like each other usually make better deals."

She looked away. "Friendships can also backfire."

Ah. "Did you have a friendship backfire?"

"No, I'm just saying—"

"And I'm just saying relax. We like each other—" For once he didn't try to deny it. All weekend long he'd been coming to know her, getting to like her. Being trapped in her little house with a strong desire to kiss her hadn't been good. But in a store filled with people and with a business deal to discuss she had nothing to fear.

Or was that he had nothing to fear?

No matter. They were both safe.

"We got to be friends over the weekend. I've even asked for help with Finley. Surely, I should be allowed to say you have a pretty laugh."

She stiffened. Then, as if realizing she was making too much out of nothing, she drew in a breath. "Yes. Of course, I'm sorry."

"No need to be sorry. Just relax."

She smiled. "Okay."

"Okay."

They spent an hour in human resources and returned to her office to pick up Finley for lunch. In the huge, bustling cafeteria they drank milk shakes and ate French fries. But Finley tossed her head back and covered her ears when "Here Comes Santa Claus" replaced the more sedate Christmas song that had been playing.

"You know what puzzles me?" Shannon said, tugging one of Finley's hands away from her ears. "How can you watch cartoons?"

Finley's eyes narrowed.

Shannon picked up a French fry. "I mean, they're not any more real than Santa. Yet you like cartoons. Wendy told me you did."

Finley's mouth scrunched up.

Shannon dipped her fry in ketchup. "So why don't you start thinking of Santa the same way you do a cartoon character?"

Finley glanced at Rory and he laughed. "It sounds perfectly logical to me."

Finley raised her gaze to the ceiling as if she could see the music.

"Listen to the words and pretend Santa is a cartoon character."

Finley's face contorted with little-girl concentration, then she smiled. "It's funny."

"Of course, it is. That's why people like to listen. It makes them laugh."

As if to prove that, Finley giggled.

Rory laughed, too. But when he realized he was laughing and Finley was laughing because Shannon had turned Finley's hatred of Christmas songs into acceptance, his laughter stopped.

This woman was really special.

Really special.

She wasn't just pretty or sexy or even really smart. She was attuned to life. People. It was as if she saw things other people missed and knew how to use that information to make everybody feel wanted, needed... happy.

He said nothing as they returned to her office and deposited Finley with Wendy. But when they entered the office for the buyers that afternoon, he noticed something that he probably could have noticed that morning if he'd been clued in to look for it. These people loved her.

"So what are you going to do, Shannon, if the store sells?"

That question came from Julie Hughes, a woman in her twenties who gazed at Shannon with stars in her eyes, as if she were the epitome of everything Julie wanted to be when she got a little older.

"I'm not sure." Shannon smiled, casually leaned her hip on the corner of Julie's desk, clearly comfortable with her staff. "This is only Mr. Wallace's first day here. He may look around and decide he doesn't want to buy us."

"He'd be crazy," Fred Cummings said, leaning back in his chair. "We make a ton of money." He pointed at Shannon. "Due in no small part to changes this woman made after her dad let go of the reins."

Shannon laughed. "I did a few things. They've only been up and running a few months."

Fred said, "Right."

But Rory got the message. Fred wouldn't push anymore because he wouldn't insult the last company president, Shannon's dad, in front of Shannon. But it was clear things hadn't always gone so smoothly at Raleigh's Department Store.

Heading back to the administrative officer, he said, "This is some place."

Though she'd downplayed her efforts in front of her staff, in the hall, away from anyone who could see, her face blossomed with pride. "Thank you."

"But I do have one really big question."

"Fire away. There's no question too sacred."

"Why are you selling Raleigh's? It's clear you love this store. You're also very good at what you do. Why would you want to give it up?"

"My parents need the money from the sale to fund their retirement."

"Right. I get that. But you love it." He paused, then asked the question that had been bothering him for the past few hours. "Why don't you buy it?"

She stopped. Faced him. "I tried. I couldn't get financing."

"Oh. Did you try finding a partner?"

"Are you offering?"

He winced. "My family doesn't partner. We either buy outright or nothing at all."

"I didn't think so."

But Rory wasn't so easily put off. "You said I'm the first person you approached. Surely there are others, investors who might consider a partnership—"

She laughed slightly. "Rory. Are you trying to talk me out of selling to you?"

"No. It's just that it's obvious to me that you're going to miss the store." He paused. When she didn't reply, he said, "There's more to this story. I need to hear it."

For a few seconds it looked like she wouldn't reply. Finally she said, "I've actually only been working at the store a year. My husband had unceremoniously dumped me and I was devastated. So I came home. I expected to sleep away the next few months, but my dad wouldn't let me." She smiled, as if remembering. "Anyway, he got me working in the store, and when he retired a few months ago, he made me company president. Nobody expected that I'd blossom the way I did. I like the work enough that I could have stayed here the rest of my life." She shrugged. "But my parents need the money, so I have to move on. But, on the bright side, at least now I know what I want to do with my life."

"Run another store?"

"Maybe. Or maybe just head up the buyers." She smiled. "Or the advertising department, public relations…"

He laughed. "You won't be happy unless you can have your finger in every pot."

But even as he laughed, an uncomfortable lump formed in his stomach. "I feel like I'm taking away your dream."

She shook her head. "Running my parents' store is not my dream. It's just a really great job."

"So what is your dream?"

She started walking again, but he'd seen the sadness that shadowed her face.

If he wasn't taking away her dream by buying the store, something was up with her. He considered that maybe she couldn't handle another change in her life only one year after her divorce. But she was a strong, competent woman. He believed her when she said she was over her ex and the accompanying sadness from her divorce.

So what was it?

Why did he know, deep in his gut, that something serious haunted her and somehow, some way, he contributed to it?

He caught her arm and stopped her.

When he didn't say anything, she said, "Question?"

He stared into her pretty blue eyes. All the physical reactions he'd held at bay all weekend came flooding back. Only now they were combined with emotions. He cared about her. He cared about her a lot. He didn't want to take away her dreams. He *liked* her.

The urge to kiss her itched through him again and he was growing tired of fighting it. Tired of fighting the first good thing that had happened to him in two long years.

When his head lowed toward hers, he didn't try to stop himself. For the first time since his divorce, he wasn't just physically attracted to a woman. He liked her.

Their lips met tentatively, just a quick brush. But response shivered through him. Attraction. Arousal. Wonderful forgotten sensations that he'd avoided, ignored or smothered over the past two years.

He deepened the kiss, pressing his mouth against hers and though he felt her hesitate, she pressed back.

She liked him.

Just when he would have deepen the kiss, made it a real kiss, she pulled away.

Smoothing her hand along her cascade of dark curls, she turned and started up the hall again. "We should get back to Finley."

CHAPTER SIX

AT SIX O'CLOCK that night Rory and Finley stepped into a very comfortable hotel room. A double bed sat in the middle of the room, and, as he'd requested when he made his reservation, a cot for Finley sat beside the bed. As he tossed their suitcases into the closet and slid his briefcase onto the desk, the feelings from the kiss he'd shared with Shannon that afternoon still vibrated through him. Unfortunately, all those wonderful sensations were mitigated by the awkwardness afterward. Worse, he couldn't stop thinking about Shannon herself. Her future. What would she do without the store?

He might not be taking away her "dream" but he was taking away her job. And maybe her home. With only one department store in her small city, there was no other store in town for her to manage. She'd definitely have to move away.

They'd been so busy all afternoon that she'd easily avoided talking abut her life and that kiss. But he had to talk to her again. He couldn't sit here in a hotel all night and wonder. Plus, he'd finally figured out she probably didn't want to talk about her decisions in the hallway of an office where she could be overheard.

Finley shrugged out of her jacket, but he pushed it up her arms again.

"Hey!"

He stooped down in front of her. "I have a favor to ask."

She blinked.

"You know how Shannon took us in this weekend?"

She nodded.

"Well, she did us a favor."

She tilted her head in question. "Uh-huh."

"So now we have to return the favor."

"We do?"

"Yes." He pulled in a breath. It wasn't a fabulous plan, but it was the only plan he could come up with, so he was running with it. "Shannon was supposed to decorate her house for Christmas over the weekend."

Finley's eyes grew round and large. She wasn't a dummy. She knew what was coming.

He sucked it up and just told her straight out. "But because we were in her home, she didn't decorate. She entertained us. So since we owe her for taking us in, I was thinking we should go to her house and help her do the work she would have done had we not needed her help."

He'd couched his request in such a way Finley would see how much they were in Shannon's debt. Still, she frowned. "I don't want to."

"I don't doubt that. But didn't she give you a way to think about Christmas today that made it seem easy for you?"

"Yeah."

"So, she's done us more than one favor and now we're going to repay her. That's the way life works."

Her lower lip jutted out.

He rose anyway. "Suck it up, kid. We owe her. We're doing this. And no hissy fits or diva behavior. You might not like Christmas but Shannon does and I won't spoil this for her. So we're going."

She sighed heavily but didn't argue.

He found a phone book and ordered Chinese food before shepherding Finley back to the car. They stopped for the takeout food, and were on Shannon's front porch within the hour.

She answered their knock quickly, as if she'd been standing right by the door. When she saw them, a smile of pleasure blossomed on her pretty face, making Rory realize he'd made the right choice. "Hey."

He held up the Chinese food. "I brought a peace offering."

She motioned for them to step inside. "Peace offering?"

He handed her the bags of food, and wrestled out of his topcoat. "We wasted your entire weekend. So we decided to help you decorate."

Her gaze flew to Finley. "Really?"

"Yes." He glanced down at his daughter. "Right?"

Finley sighed. "Right."

Shannon led them into the kitchen. "Well, thank you very much. I can use the help." Depositing the food on the center island, she added, "Would you rather eat first and decorate second, or eat as we decorate?"

"How about eat as we decorate?" He slid his gaze to Finley, hoping Shannon would get the message that if Finley was busy eating then she wouldn't actually have to decorate. An easy way to avoid trouble.

She nodded slightly, indicating she'd caught his drift. "I have some paper plates we can use." She walked to the cupboard to get them. "We'll make it like a picnic."

They set everything up on the coffee table between the floral sofa and twin sage-green club chairs. When it came to dealing with Finley, Shannon was fine. But when the room grew quiet and Finley was busy eating rice and sweet-and-sour chicken, shivers of fear sprinkled her skin.

He'd kissed her. Spontaneously. Wonderfully. And everything inside of her had responded. It wasn't a kiss of lust or surprise, as it would have been had he kissed her over the weekend. This kiss had been...emotional.

They liked each other. Two and a half days of forced company coupled with a day of walking through her store, finding out about each other, had taken their physical attraction and turned it into an emotional attachment.

It was wonderful...and scary...and wrong.

She knew the end of this rainbow. If they got involved—dated—at some point she'd have to tell him she couldn't have kids.

And everything between them would change. Even the way he saw her—

Especially the way he saw her.

She pulled in a breath. Told herself to settle down. If he bought the store, she would leave. If he didn't, he would leave. He'd go back to his life and company in Virginia, and she would stay here. Distance alone would keep them from dating. And if they didn't date, she wouldn't have to tell him.

So why not enjoy the evening?

Or use it as a chance to bring Finley along? No child should hate a holiday filled with wonder and magic. Her mom should be ashamed for ruining one of the best times of the year for her daughter. But in the past three days, Finley gone from being horrified about anything even related to the holiday, to actually laughing at the

Christmas songs piped into the cafeteria. Maybe it was time to nudge her a little more?

Catching a piece of chicken in her chopsticks, she said, "You know, I like Christmas music when I decorate. You laughed about the Christmas songs today at lunch. So I'm just going to pop in a CD right now."

Finley glanced at Rory. He shrugged. "Just think of them like cartoons. The way Shannon told you this afternoon."

Finley sighed. Shannon found the Christmas music but kept the volume low. A soft mellow song drifted into the room. Finley turned her attention to her dinner. Wanting to get as much done as she could while Finley was cooprerative, Shannon grabbed the spools of tinsel she'd created the night before.

"I'm going to hang these from the ceiling."

Rory glanced over at her. "Is that code for I need a tall person to help me?"

She laughed. "Yes."

He took the tinsel from her hand. She pointed at a corner. "What my dad used to do at our old house was string the tinsel from one corner to the center, and from the center to the opposite corner, making two loops. Then we'd do that again from the other corners."

He frowned. "Why don't you just direct me?"

"Okay. Walk to the corner, attach the tinsel with a tack, then loop it to the center of the ceiling."

He did as she said. When they met in the center, she tacked the tinsel in place. "Now walk to the opposite corner and tack the tinsel up there."

When the line of tinsel was in place, he smiled. "Not bad. Sort of festive."

"Glad you like it." She handed him another strand

of tinsel. "Because now we've got to do the other two corners."

He happily took the strand of tinsel and repeated the looping process.

When he was done, she offered him the ball of mistletoe her dad always put in the center. "Just hang this where the strands meet."

He looked at the mistletoe, looked at her.

Then it hit her. The mistletoe was pretty, but it was plastic. They'd hung the silly thing in their living room for years and, basically, no one paid any attention to the fact that it was mistletoe or the traditions that surrounded it.

Obviously, Rory wasn't so casual about it.

Embarrassment should have shot through her. Instead, when their gazes met, the warmth of connection flooded her. She really liked this guy.

But she'd already figured out that they weren't right for each other. Plus, once he made a decision about her store, they'd never see each other again. They had no time to form a deep emotional attachment. There'd be no time for a real commitment. They'd spend so little time together there wouldn't even be a brush with one. Was it so wrong to want another kiss?

It might not be wrong, per se, but it did lead them down a slippery slope. A slope she might not recover from if she actually fell for him in this little span of time they had together. If they fell, and he asked her to stay or asked her to come to Virginia with him, or ask for any kind of commitment at all, she'd have to tell him.

And she couldn't do that. Not again.

She caught his gaze. "We don't have to bow to the whims of superstition or tradition."

He bounced the ball of mistletoe on his palm. "But what if we want to?"

Frissions of delight raced through her bloodstream. She couldn't stop the pleasure that blossomed in her chest. But that only made her realize how easily she could fall and how careful she'd have to be spending the next few days with him at the store.

Still, she didn't want to make a big deal out of this. She tapped his arm playfully. "Just hang the darn thing."

They hung more tinsel in her dining room and threaded it around her doorways. With the shiny silver tinsel in place, she handed Rory a box of bright blue Christmas-tree balls. "Hang these on the tinsel…about three feet apart."

"Okay." He glanced at Finley, who had finished her dinner and was sitting, watching them. He offered the box to her. "Want to hand these to me?"

She shrugged. "I suppose." She scrambled up from her seat beside the coffee table and took the box.

Shannon gathered their dishes and carried them to the kitchen. When she returned to the living room, Rory and Finley had a little assembly line going. Finley would hand him a blue ball. He'd hang it on the tinsel. By the time he turned for another ornament, Finley already had one in her hand for him.

"What do you think I should do with the drapes?"

Rory glanced over. "Do?"

"Should I loop some tinsel across the top?" She pulled some plastic fir garland from the big box on the floor. "Or maybe some of this fake fir stuff."

Finley said, "It's too green," surprising both Shannon and Rory.

"Too green?"

"Yeah. The curtains are green."

Understanding what Finley was saying, Shannon said, "Right. Maybe we should loop some tinsel around the garland so it stands out a bit."

"Or just put up lights."

"Lights!" Shannon said, liking that idea. "My parents left me all kinds of lights." She rummaged through the box of ornaments again. She presented two sets. "What do you think? Little twinkle lights or these bigger lights that don't blink?"

"I think you'll see the bigger ones better."

Rory laughed at Finley's answer. "When did you become an expert?"

Finley's nose wrinkled. "What's an expert?"

"Someone who knows what she's doing," Shannon replied. "You're a natural."

Finley shrugged. But Shannon dug out the bigger lights. With her hands full, she kicked a stepstool over to the front window.

But before she could climb up to reach the top rod, Rory was behind her. "Need help looping those?"

She turned so quickly that she nearly bumped into him. Warmth exploded through her. So did ridiculous need. She didn't remember ever being so spontaneously attracted to a man. But she was to him. And she'd already decided it was wrong. Or pointless. Or both.

She stepped back, putting some necessary space between them. "Just loop them across the top."

Finley ran to the step stool. "I'll help."

Rory laughed. "You're certainly enthusiastic suddenly."

She shrugged. "This is kinda fun."

Shannon ruffled her hair. "I told you."

As Rory and Finley strung the brightly colored lights across the top of the drapes, Shannon rummaged for more decorations from the boxes her parents had left behind when they moved to Florida. She pulled out figurines of two kids skiing and figurines of people sledding and set them out on the end tables. She found a gold table runner and set it on the coffee table with red and green candles.

Seeing Rory and Finley were still stringing the lights, she decided this would be a good time for her to make some cocoa and headed for the kitchen. But she'd barely gotten the milk in the pan before Rory walked in.

"After the way you shot me down over the mistletoe, I'm guessing I should apologize for kissing you this afternoon."

His comment surprised her so much that she turned from the stove. The repentant look on his face squeezed her heart. Because she'd been as much of a party to that kiss as he'd been, she'd be a real hypocrite if she let him take the blame. "No apology necessary."

"Really? Because you're kind of standoffish."

She drew in a breath. What could she say? *There's no chance of a relationship between us, so I'm being careful?* She'd look like an idiot. Especially since in this day and age a kiss didn't necessary equate to a relationship. Hell, for some people sex didn't necessarily equate to a relationship.

"I'm tired."

"Yeah, me, too." He took a few more steps into the room, walking to the center island, where she'd set three mugs on a tray. "What's this?"

"Mugs for cocoa."

He glanced up. Smiled. "I love cocoa. I haven't had it since I was about eight."

"Then it's time you did."

He laughed. "That's exactly why I didn't want to apologize for kissing you. I wanted to kiss you."

Pleasure exploded inside her again. Why did he have to be so sweet? "Because I make cocoa?"

"Because you make me laugh. You're a nice person. A good person. I'd be an idiot if I didn't see how you're turning Finley around. She's actually humming a Christmas song in there."

She walked over to the stove, stirred the cocoa mix into the warm milk. "I'm not really doing much of anything. I think Finley's finally ready to be turned. I just have more Christmas things at my disposal than you do."

He shook his head. "No. I think she's ready because you nudge her along."

She walked to the island, brusquely picked up the tray of mugs to take to the counter by the stove. But he caught her hand. "Why won't you let me compliment you?"

"Because I'm not doing anything. It's the season. The time she's spending at the store." She shrugged, wishing he'd let go of her hand so she could scamper away. Wishing he'd hold on to it because it felt so good to have a man touch her again. And not just any man. Someone she liked.

"Well, we're at the store because of you...so we're back to you being responsible."

Humor crinkled the corners of his eyes, pulled his full lips upward. Her heart stuttered a bit, filled with hope. How easy it would be to simply laugh and accept what was happening. Part of her longed to do just that. To relax. To enjoy. No matter what he decided about the store, they'd separate. She didn't have to fear getting involved in something so deep it would force her to tell her big secret.

But the other part knew that she couldn't spend another four days with this man without falling head-over-heels in love. She was so needy, so desperate, that every scrap of attention he threw her drew her in like a kitten to a bowl of fresh milk. She had to keep her distance.

Still, she argued with her wiser self. Couldn't she enjoy this, breathe it in, savor it…so she'd have pleasant memories for the long cold nights ahead?

She didn't know. If in her desperation she fell in love, those wonderful memories she was creating could actually haunt her.

So she simply shrugged. "I see myself more as having fun with Finley than being responsible for her turn-around."

"And we are a team."

She smiled slightly. She'd forgotten they'd formed a team that morning. "You're right."

"Seriously, you're great with kids. You're going to make a wonderful mother."

Tears sprang to her eyes. His comment wasn't out of line. It wasn't even unusual. But she hadn't been prepared for it.

She yanked the tray of empty mugs from the center island, effectively pulling her wrist out from underneath his hand and scurried to the stove to grab a ladle to scoop hot cocoa into the mugs.

"Want to get the marshmallows?" she asked, her voice cracking just a bit.

He pulled away from the center island. "Sure. Where are they?"

She pointed. "Second shelf, second cupboard."

He opened the cabinet door and pulled out the marsh-mallows.

"Grab a bowl from that cupboard over there," she said, pointing at a cabinet across the room. "And put about a cupful in the bowl. That way you and Finley can take as many marshmallows as you want."

He filled the bowl with marshmallows, set it on the tray in the center of the three cups of steaming cocoa. But he didn't move his hand so she could lift the tray.

So she stepped away again. "You know what?" She walked to the refrigerator and opened the door of the small freezer section on top. "I have some Christmas cookies from a batch I made last weekend." She retrieved a plastic bag of fruit horn cookies. "Since Finley's handling the Christmas music, maybe it's time to indoctrinate her into cookies."

He laughed. "They don't look like Christmas cookies."

But when she brought a plateful of the cookies to the microwave to thaw them, he was in her way again.

She edged past him, first to get a plate to lay them out on, then to open the microwave door. When she set the timer and turned away, once again he was right in front of her.

"My little girl had lost Christmas and you're helping her find it again."

"*We're* helping her find it again," she pointed out, reminding him of the team they'd formed.

"It's more you." As he said the words, his hands fell to her shoulders and his head descended. She realized his intention about two seconds before his lips met hers, but by then it was too late to pull away.

Sensation exploded inside her. Sweet, wonderful need. Her arms ached to wrap around his shoulders.

Her body longed to step into his, feel the total length of him pressed up against her. But fear shadowed every thought, every feeling. What would he say if she told him she couldn't have kids? How would he react? Would he be so loving then? Or angry as Bryce had been?

She swallowed. She didn't want to test him.

Still, there was no need. They'd really only just met. In a few days, they'd part. Couldn't she keep the situation so light that there'd be no worry about falling in love?

Maybe.

Hope bubbled up inside her. They also had a built-in chaperone in Finley. He wouldn't go too far in front of his daughter. Since he was so persistent and she couldn't seem to evade him, maybe she should just enjoy this?

It felt incredibly wrong to be wishing a relationship wouldn't last. Even more wrong to bask in the joy of the knowledge that time and distance would ultimately part them. Right at that moment, with his lips brushing hers and sweet sensation teasing her, she didn't care. For once in her life she wanted to think of herself.

That resurrected her wiser self. Even in her head the voice she heard was hard, scolding. *Your life is not as simple, your problems not as easily solved, as other women's. You cannot be flip.*

Just when she knew he would have deepened the kiss, she pulled away. Sadness bumped into anger and created an emotion so strong, so foreign she couldn't even name it.

But she did know she was mad at her wiser self.

You are such a sap. Such a scaredy-cat sap. Surely you can kiss a man, be attracted to a man, enjoy a man without thinking forever?

The answer came back quick, sharp. *No. You can't.*

She made the mistake of catching his gaze as she stepped back. The confusion in his dark orbs made her swallow hard. But she comforted herself with the knowledge that it was better for both of them if she didn't explain.

She picked up the tray. "Let's get this cocoa to Finley before it's cold."

CHAPTER SEVEN

TUESDAY MORNING Shannon walked through the employee entrance of Raleigh's Department Store a nervous wreck. After the kiss debacle, Rory had gone quiet. He'd enjoyed his cocoa and allowed Finley to drink hers, but he hadn't stayed after. He'd just gone.

Absolutely positive she'd blown her opportunity to spend time with Finley—and that she didn't need to have any more internal debates about how to handle their attraction because she'd pretty much killed any feelings he might have been having for her—she was more than annoyed with her subconscious. Especially when she'd fallen asleep and had a wonderful dream about them. The three of them. Not just her and Rory married, but her and Rory raising Finley.

She walked through the dark, silent first floor of Raleigh's. The light coming in from the big front windows reflected off the shiny oversize Christmas ornaments hanging from the ceiling and lit her way to the elevator. Inside, she pressed the button for the third floor and drew in a long, cleansing breath.

Watching herself interact with a child, even in a dream, had intensified her yearning for her own little boy or girl. She'd awakened with a tight chest and a longing so sweet in her tummy that she knew beyond a shadow of a doubt that she needed to adopt a child. Or maybe two children. Or maybe a whole gaggle of kids. In her gut, she knew she was made to be a mom. Since Mother Nature had stolen her normal child-getting avenue away from her, she would simply go an alternative route.

That solid, irrevocable decision was the good effect of the dream. If she wanted to be a mom, she could be.

But…

Now that she was so sure she would become a mom, shouldn't she want to spend as much time as she could with children? Especially one-on-one time like the kind she got with Finley? And shouldn't she also want to spend time with parents, the way she had in South Carolina? Learning the ins and outs of the things they did automatically. Rory might have stumbled a bit dealing with Finley the Diva, but he did so many things automatically, instinctively. Like get her coat. Slide her little arms into sweaters. Make sure she had ketchup.

She'd been watching other people with kids her entire adult life, preparing to become a mom. Now that she had up-close-and-personal time with a daddy and daughter, wasn't she stupid to throw it away?

She licked her lower lip and remembered every second of both kisses Rory had given her. She remembered the flash of heat that accompanied the sweet, romantic caresses. She remembered the yearning to step into his embrace, the longing to wrap her arms around him, and knew it would be risky to her heart to spend any more time with him.

But just as quickly, she reminded herself that she wasn't weak. In the past year, she'd lost a part of herself, then lost her husband because she wasn't whole anymore. She'd come home. Taken over her family's store. Gotten over her pain.

Surely, she could direct a relationship between herself and Rory away from romantic to a place where they could be friends.

Of course she could. She was strong. Her problems had made her strong. Now that she had sorted all this out in her head and had a solid course of action, she was even stronger. More determined. With her mind set, she could spend a lifetime in his company and not waver.

She walked into her dark, quiet office. Turned on the light. She could do this. She *would* do this.

Twenty minutes later, Rory and Finley strolled in. Finley raced over to her desk and gave her a hug. "I had fun last night."

Closing her eyes, she squeezed the little girl affectionately. Without Finley she might have taken years to make her decision to adopt. For as much as Rory thought he owed her with Finley, she knew she owed Finley more.

"I had fun last night, too."

Shannon rose and helped Finley out of her jacket. "Did you bring your laptop?"

Finley nodded.

"I have a surprise." She lifted a new video game off her desk. "I bought you a game."

Finley's face lit up. "What is it?"

She glanced at the CD. "I'm not sure. Something with frogs and dragons. Wendy said her grandkids love it."

Finley eagerly took the game Shannon handed her.

Shannon laughed and faced Rory. "So what do you want to do today?"

Obviously avoiding her gaze, he shrugged out of his

topcoat. "Chat with the people in advertising and public relations."

She pressed her intercom button. "Wendy, we're ready for you to help Finley install her new game. Mr. Wallace and I will be with advertising."

Wendy said, "Great," and within seconds was in the doorway to Shannon's office.

Shannon walked around the desk and headed for the door. "She's all yours." She pointed at Rory. "You come with me."

Rory swung Finley up and gave her a smacking kiss goodbye. "We'll be back in time for lunch."

Finley said, "Okay," then slithered down.

As Rory and Shannon walked out, Finley eagerly raced to Shannon's chair, where Wendy sat booting up her laptop.

In the hall, Rory glanced over at Shannon. The night before, she'd acted very oddly with him, refusing to let him compliment her, getting nervously quiet after he'd kissed her. He didn't need to be hit on the head with a rock. She didn't want him kissing her.

So that morning in the shower, he'd given himself a stern lecture. Kissing her had been wrong. Her reaction to the mistletoe should have clued him in, but he was so damned sure his charm and good looks would smooth things over that he'd made a mistake. A big blunder. But this morning he would fix that by apologizing.

Except, she didn't seem to need an apology. She seemed strong and in control. No moodiness. No nerves.

He could have been insulted by the second, annoyed that she was denying the attraction he knew hummed between them, but he wasn't that much of an idiot. He might be feeling the stirrings of being interested in a relationship, but it was clear she wasn't. His divorce was two years in the past. Hers was one. He was incredibly physically attracted to her. She might not be incredibly attracted to him. He liked her. She… Well, he might not be as charming as he'd always thought.

Plus, they were together because of a business deal. Once the deal was done, she might feel differently. She could be standoffish right now because she wanted to get a fair price for her store. And if she did like him, if she was only pulling back because of their business deal, wouldn't he be an idiot to push her?

Of course, he would.

When she reached the door marked Advertising, he hustled in front of her and grabbed the knob. It certainly wouldn't hurt to start being a gentleman, and show her his charming, likable side, while they were doing business so that once their business was concluded he might be able to ask her out.

Even the thought sent a ripple of excitement through him. He couldn't believe he'd spent two long years on his own. But he had. And that was probably for the best. But now, he was ready.

She smiled at him as he walked through the door and his heart swelled with ridiculous hope. She obviously wasn't holding a grudge against him for kissing her. He had three or four days left for him to mend his reputation, show her he was a nice guy, and then, when the deal was done, he could pounce.

Good God, he liked having a plan!

John Wilder, obviously having been alerted by Wendy, stood in the center of the big room. "What would you like to see first?"

"Actually, I'd like to talk first." He glanced around the room. "With everyone."

John's brows rose. "Individually?"

He laughed. "We have all day. And I'd like to get a good feel for what this division does to justify its existence."

John straightened with affront. "You can't have a department store without ads in the local paper."

Rory laughed. "Relax." He glanced at a red-haired woman who was the only one in the department still working. "I'd like to start with her."

She glanced up, pointed at her chest. "Me?"

"Yes. You are…"

"I'm Rose."

"And you do what?"

"Layout mostly."

"Great. Where can we talk?"

John gestured toward a small conference room and Rory motioned for Rose to join him there.

Unusually comfortable with Shannon, Rory didn't think twice about the fact that she was always with him when he made his visits, until she stepped into the conference room with him and Rose. It was only day two of his tour, but he suddenly realized that he'd never once been alone with anyone from her staff. Worse, he hadn't once questioned the fact that Shannon stuck to him like glue. Normally, he'd ask for time on his own. Time to see the store. Time to get the real scoop from employees. Yet, with Shannon, he'd never even thought of it.

By eleven o'clock they'd interviewed everyone and were back in John's office. At the end of that time he'd also concluded that he'd never questioned Shannon's continuing presence because he liked her and he liked spending time with her. But even friends checked up on each other's facts and figures in a business deal. He'd been so preoccupied with the personal side of their relationship that he'd fallen down on the job. He might not insist she back off from his department visits just yet, but before this week was out, he'd get some private time with everyone. He'd also spend the evening on the internet, checking things out even more. Then, in the morning, before he came to the store, he'd talk with some of her vendors.

"So are you ready to break for lunch?"

Jarred out of his reverie, Rory said, "Yeah. Sure."

John rose from his seat. Papers of various and sundry kinds and sizes littered his desk. "Why don't I come with you? We can continue our discussions over a hot roast beef sandwich?"

Rory was about to decline with an apology, but Shannon beat him to it. "That would be great, but Rory has his daughter with him. She's been stuck in my office all morning. I don't think we should bore her with business."

John easily backed off. "I'll see you after lunch then."

Shannon said, "Great."

But Rory kept himself a step or two behind her as they walked out of the advertising offices, concerned that she'd answered for him. Normally, he wouldn't care, except the night before she'd been so quiet. And today she was all but bursting with confidence.

Of course, she was trying to sell him her company. And from what he'd seen of her dealings with staff, she was a take-charge person.

His libido instantly wondered how that would play out in bed and in his head he cursed himself. It was that kind of thinking that had gotten them to this place. He'd already promised himself that he wouldn't make another move, wouldn't say another inappropriate word until they had this deal done. And he wouldn't.

When they entered Shannon's office, Finley was deep in play. Striding over to the desk, he said, "Hey, aren't you ready for French fries?"

She didn't take her eyes off her computer screen. "Just one more minute."

He glanced over at Shannon and the look of love on her face for his little girl nearly did him in. How could he not fall for the woman who loved his daughter? Especially when her own mom hadn't?

He sucked in a breath, told himself to think about this later and said, "Come on, Finley. I have lots of work to do this afternoon. We need to go now."

She sighed heavily, but got off the chair and scampered over to Shannon, who took her hand and led her out of the office.

A strange sensation invaded his chest. Four days ago, he thought he'd never see his normal daughter again. But a little bit of time with Shannon had changed everything.

And he wondered if that wasn't a big part of why he liked her so much, why he was so ready suddenly to jump into another relationship.

Was he really seeing Shannon romantically or was he only falling for her because he wanted help with his daughter?

They walked through the cafeteria line, choosing their lunches, and when Finley picked whipped-cream-covered cherry gelatin and pie as her main course, Rory simply took those dishes off her plate and told her to choose again.

But Shannon smiled and said, "I'll bet your dad

would let you keep the gelatin as your dessert if you picked a better main course."

Frowning, Finley studied the available food. Finally, she took a salad and an order of fries. But Rory stared at Shannon. He remembered that they'd formed an alliance. He'd been the one to suggest it. But his question about his motives in wanting a relationship with Shannon came back full force. He suddenly felt as if he were using her. And, even worse, that he might be thinking of Shannon romantically just because he wanted a mother for his child.

Nerves skittered down his spine. What if he was? Oh, lord. What if he was?

Then he was scum.

They found a table in the back and once Rory opened Finley's little packet of ranch dressing and poured it on her salad, she started to eat. Her mouth full of lettuce, she said, "I really like the game, Shannon."

Shannon and Rory both said, "Don't talk with your mouth full."

Shannon quickly looked down at her own salad, but those odd feelings floated through Rory again. It was wonderful to have a partner. Wonderful to have backup. With Shannon around, it wasn't just him against Finley. He had an ally.

Finley chewed and swallowed then said, "I also forgot to say thanks."

The guilty sensations bombarding him intensified. That morning he should have prompted Finley to thank Shannon and he'd forgotten. He was proud as hell that Finley had remembered, but it served as yet another reminder that he wasn't as good with Finley as he needed to be. And he was getting comfortable with Shannon picking up the slack.

Shannon said, "You're welcome. It was my pleasure. I appreciate you being so patient while I show your dad my store."

Kicking her feet under the table, Finley grinned.

Rory's heart about burst in his chest. Not from love or even pride. From some hideous emotion he couldn't name. He didn't have to ponder or think this through. Finley liked Shannon. She liked having a woman around. Having a woman around settled her. Was it any wonder he was interested in Shannon? Any wonder he wasn't demanding to see her store on his own? He wanted to stay in her company and in her good graces. He didn't want any friction between them so she'd continue to help him with Finley.

He was double scum.

Once they returned Finley to Shannon's office and Wendy's care, they started up the hall to the advertising department again, but Rory stopped her by placing his hand on her forearm.

"Wait."

She turned, smiled. "What?"

"I want some time alone with the people in advertising."

She didn't hesitate, her smile didn't slip. "Sure. No problem. I understand that you'd want to see what they'd say when the boss isn't around."

"And I think I'd like to be by myself tomorrow when I spend the day with accounting."

Again, her smile didn't slip. No hesitation when she said, "Sure." Her smile actually grew. "I'll be happy to spend this afternoon and tomorrow with Finley."

His heart lurched. She really did love Finley.

"And I also thought it would be a good idea for the

two of you to come to my house for a little more decorating tonight."

She might not have hesitated, but he did. He wasn't at all sure that was a good idea. Except, he was confused about his feelings for Shannon and maybe a little private time would clear everything up for him?

"Are you sure we're not an imposition?"

She laughed her wonderful musical laugh and his heart about kicked its way out of his chest. How could he ever worry that he only wanted to spend time with Shannon because she was a good mom to Finley? He *liked* her. God, if he liked her any more he wouldn't be able to hold off telling her until after he made a decision about the store.

"I love having you around."

He caught her gaze and found himself trapped in her pretty blue eyes. "Thanks."

"You're welcome. And don't bring food. I'll cook."

He chuckled, glad she'd said something that could bring him back to reality. "Thought you couldn't cook?"

"I wasn't thinking anything fancy. Just macaroni and cheese and hot dogs. Things Finley might be missing since you're on the road."

His heart expanded again. She was so good to Finley that it was easy for him to see how he could be confused. But he wasn't confused anymore. She was beautiful. Smart. Fun. He liked her.

Ha! Take that, Fate. He *liked* her.

He frowned. Great. He liked her. But he couldn't tell her or make a move until after their deal was done. And he was about to spend private time in her company. This night might not be the piece of cake that he thought.

* * *

That night when they arrived at Shannon's house, she opened the door and welcomed them inside, proud of the scent of macaroni and cheese and hot dogs that greeted them.

Impatient while her dad helped her out of her jacket, Finley cried, "Hot dogs!"

"Yep. And macaroni."

"All right!"

She turned to take Finley's jacket and saw Rory shrugging out of his coat and she did a double take. He wasn't wearing his usual dress shirt and dress pants. Instead, he wore jeans and a T-shirt. She'd seen him in jeans, of course, but that was over the weekend when everything was awkward. Tonight he looked so relaxed, so casual in her home, that her pulse fluttered.

She sucked in a breath. Reminded herself she could do this. For the opportunity to spend time with Finley, she could be with Rory without giving in to her attraction.

"Right this way."

She led them into the kitchen and walked directly to the stove. Pulling a tray of hot dogs from the broiler, she said, "Everything's ready. Take a seat."

At the table, Rory put a hot dog on a bun for Finley, who eagerly bit into it. "This is good!"

Shannon took a quick swipe over her mouth with her napkin to keep from scolding Finley for talking with her mouth full. Rory had been giving her odd looks all day. It had taken a while but she'd finally figured out that she might be overstepping her boundaries by constantly mothering Finley. Whether he'd asked for help or not, she was just a bit too helpful. So it was best to back off a bit.

She served yellow cake for dessert then accepted

Rory and Finley's help clearing the table. When the kitchen was cleaned, she turned from the sink and said, "Okay, everybody, let's get our coats on."

Rory's eyebrows rose. "Coats?"

"We're going to put up the outside lights."

Finley clapped. Rory frowned. "It's dark."

"I know. But my dad has a big spotlight that we can use." She laughed. "It'll light up the whole yard."

"Setting up seems like it will take more time than the actual decorating."

"I know. But my parents will be home soon. And I was going to do this last Saturday—" She paused. She didn't want them to help because of a guilt trip. "Never mind. I didn't mean that like it sounded. I only meant that I was running out of time."

But it was too late. Rory said, "Of course, you're right. We'll set up the big light and decorate."

After shrugging into his coat and assisting Finley with hers, Rory followed Shannon out to the shed behind her house. Though they'd been there on Saturday to get the sleds, he took a closer look this time around, as Shannon dug through a mountain of junk stored in her shed.

"What is all this?"

She peeked up. "My parents had no use for a lot of their things when they moved to Florida." She pointed at a snowblower. "Especially winter things." She went back to working her way through boxes and containers. "So they left it all with me."

He looked around in awe. "I'm not sure if I envy you or feel sorry."

"Feel sorry. Because if I have to move to a warmer climate when I sell Raleigh's, I'm going to have to have a huge yard sale. If I stay in snow country, I've gotta move all this stuff to whatever city I end up in."

He laughed.

"Ah-ha! Here it is." She struggled to get the big light out of a box and he raced over to help her. Their gloved hands brushed and though Rory felt an instant connection, Shannon didn't even react.

Which was fine. They were wearing gloves. Besides, did he really expect her to have heart-racing, pulse-pounding reactions every time they touched?

Hoisting the light out of the box, he frowned. *He* was having heart-racing, pulse-pounding reactions around her. It only seemed fair that she would have them, too.

After they set the light on the floor, she scrambled away. "I have an extension cord."

He glanced over his shoulder and saw that she held a huge, orange heavy-duty extension cord.

She grabbed the neatly bound electrical cord of the spotlight and connected it to the extension cord. "I'll unwind as you walk out to the yard. When the cord stops, that's where the light sits. Anything that isn't lit by the light doesn't get decorated."

He chuckled. "Sounds like a plan."

He walked out into the snowy front yard. When he ran out of extension cord, he unwound the light's cord and went another ten feet.

"That's it!" he called and Shannon and Finley came out of the shed. Shannon held a huge roll of multicolored lights. Finley skipped behind her.

"I'd like to put these around the porch roof."

He glanced over at it. "We'll need a ladder."

She motioned with her head to the shed behind her. "It's on the wall. I'll turn on the spotlight."

He easily found the ladder and when he carried it

out of the shed, he quickly noticed two things. First, the spotlight could illuminate a small village. Second, she and Finley sat on the porch steps, laughing, waiting for him.

He stopped walking. He loved that she was so affectionate with Finley, but right now, dressed in simple jeans and her dad's big parka, with the flood light making her hair a shiny sable and her big blue eyes sparkling, he liked *her*. He liked everything about her. He even liked that she'd sort of conned him into helping her with the big job of outdoor decorating.

And he was getting a little tired of pretending. A little tired of holding back. He'd waited two long years to find somebody else. He didn't want to wait another ten minutes to enjoy her. He wanted her now.

He headed to the porch again. Since they'd already proven that they could be professional at work even though they had a totally different connection outside the office, he was going for it. He might not seduce her or even kiss her, but tonight by his behavior he would show her that he liked her. And if he was lucky he might even force her to admit she saw him as more than a potential purchaser for her store.

And after that, let the chips fall where they may.

He thumped the ladder against the porch roof. "Okay," he said, huffing just a bit because the ladder was heavy. "I think we need an assembly line. Put the lights on the porch."

Shannon turned and set the big roll of lights on the floor behind her.

"Finley, you stand by the roll and carefully unwind them as Shannon feeds them to me."

He grabbed the ladder, jostled it to be sure it was steady, and said, "I'll be up here."

He paused, faced Shannon. "Once I get up there, is there something to hang the lights on?"

"The previous owner left her hooks. They're about six feet apart."

He started up the ladder. "Perfect."

He looped the string of lights on the first hook on the right side of the porch and strung them on hooks until he couldn't reach the next one. Then he climbed down to reposition the ladder. At the bottom of the ladder, he smiled at Shannon. She quickly looked away.

Deciding he'd simply caught her off guard, he moved the ladder over to the center of the porch, climbed up and hung the rest of the lights. When he came down, Shannon skittered away from the ladder.

Okay. He hadn't imagined that, but she could be eager to get done, not in the mood for tomfoolery.

He brushed his gloved hands together, knocking the roof dust and snow from them. "What now?"

"Now, I have a Santa's sleigh to set up in the front yard."

He peered at her. "Really?"

"Hey, my dad loves Christmas. It would be a disappointment for him if we didn't set up the sleigh."

"Okay."

They walked into the shed and Shannon went directly to a lump covered by a tarp. Flinging it off, she revealed a life-size Santa's sleigh, complete with a plastic life-size Santa.

Finley crept over. "Wow."

Rory laughed, amazed that things Finley used to hate now amused her simply because Shannon got her to relate to Santa the same way she did cartoon characters.

She turned to him with wide eyes. "It's so big."

"Yeah, it is," Shannon agreed. "But my dad loves it."

Rory walked over. He knocked on the sleigh and confirmed his suspicions. "It's plastic."

"Yeah. That's how I know we can lift it." Shannon faced him, so he smiled at her.

She quickly turned away. "Anyway, it's light. Won't be hard to carry out. We just have to anchor it."

Disappointment rose, but he smashed it down. They were working. She was single-minded in her determination to get the house and yard decorated for her dad. She wasn't rebuffing him as much as she was simply focused.

Once they got into the house, he'd be better able to gauge her mood.

They worked like a well-oiled machine. Rory took one side of the sleigh. Shannon took the other. Because Rory was walking backward, Finley directed their steps. When they had the sleigh set up, they brought the reindeer out and lined them up them in front of the sleigh. Shannon arranged small red and green floodlights around the big plastic sleigh and turned off the huge spotlight.

Multicolored lights twinkled around the porch. Santa's sleigh sat in a flood of red and green light. Finley jumped up and down, clapping her hands. Shannon looked extremely pleased that the decorating was done. And he was feeling downright jolly himself. Now that the work was done, they could play. So he reached down, grabbed two handfuls of snow, patted them into a ball and threw it at her.

She turned just in time to see it and ducked. "Hey!"

"Hey, yourself." He reached down again, grabbed more snow and tossed it before she could react. This snowball thumped into her thigh.

Finley screeched with joy and bolted behind Santa's sled for cover.

Shannon brushed idly at the snow on her jeans, glanced over at him and casually said, "You want a war?"

He motioned with his hands for her to bring it. "You think you can beat me?"

Rather than answer, Shannon bent, scooped snow and hurled a snowball at him. He dived behind an available bush. But that only gave Shannon time to scoop up two more handfuls of snow and heave them at him.

She was good. Fast. Having been raised in snow country, she seemed to have a system down pat. And Virginia boy that he was, he didn't quite have the technique she did.

The battle lasted no more than five minutes and ended when he saw Finley shiver.

Walking out from behind the bush, he raised his hands in surrender. "Finley's cold."

Shannon thwacked one final snowball into his chest. "You lose."

"Hey, I'm from the south. Considering that we get about two snows a year, I think I held my own."

She laughed.

And his heart did a small dance. He'd been correct. She'd missed all his smiles and cues because she was focused on decorating. But things would be different now that they were done.

When he reached the porch steps, he caught Finley's hand and slid his other arm across Shannon's shoulders. She immediately slid out from underneath it.

Running up the steps, she said, "I'll make cocoa!"

Finley scrambled after her.

But Rory stayed at the bottom of the steps. What the

heck was going on here? He wasn't so bad at reading signals that he was misinterpreting Shannon's. She felt something for him. He knew she had.

He frowned. *Had.* Maybe *had* was the operative word? Maybe they'd *had* fun over the weekend, but she didn't feel anything more, anything deeper?

CHAPTER EIGHT

WALKING INTO Raleigh's Department Store the next morning, Rory had the unshakable feeling that whatever he and Shannon had been feeling for each other over the weekend, it had slipped away.

Disappointment lived in his gut. But with his gloved hand wrapped around Finley's much smaller hand as they walked through the brightly decorated store, he reminded himself that he had a child who was his first priority and a potential store purchase that was his second. Sure, Shannon was the first woman in two years to catch his eye, but she clearly wasn't interested.

He had to be a man and accept that.

He walked into Shannon's office with Finley in tow and she jumped off her seat. "Finley! I've got a great day planned for us."

He should have been happy that she was so eager to amuse his daughter while he worked, except he had the weird feeling that their roles had flipped. She now liked Finley more than she liked him.

Which was cute and nice, but he felt like last year's handbag. A must-have when it was in style, totally forgotten now that it was old news.

Finley skipped over. "What are we going to do?"

"Well, first I have to get some work done. But that

should only take me a couple of hours. After that I thought we'd go outside and stroll through the park. So you can see a bit of the city." She glanced at Rory. "If that's okay."

If her eyes shone a bit, it was over the prospect of having fun with Finley. Not because she was happy to see him, or tremblingly aware of their chemistry.

"Sure. It's fine." His heart beat hollowly in his chest. There was no more doubt in his mind. If she'd ever felt anything for him, she'd rejected it. He took off his topcoat, hung it on her coat tree, walked over to Finley and stooped down in front of her. "You be good for Shannon."

She nodded. "I will."

Shannon rounded her desk. "I'm sure she will, too."

Rory peeked up at her. Her pretty black hair spilled around her, a tumble of springy curls. Her blue eyes sparkled with happiness. She was, without a doubt, one of the most beautiful women he'd ever seen. And she was sweet. Nice. Smart. Fun.

An ache squeezed his heart. He'd lost her even before he'd had a chance to fully decide if he wanted her.

Realizing that was probably for the best, he gave Finley another reminder to behave then headed for the accounting department. An examination of the books confirmed what he'd suspected from looking at the annual statements she'd sent him. Raleigh's Department Store made a lot of money even when her dad ran it. But profits had leaped when she'd taken the reins.

At noon, he ambled back to Shannon's office suite. Wendy wasn't at her desk, so he walked back to Shannon's office, only to discover Shannon wasn't there, either. With a sigh, he strolled to the window and gazed out. The city below bustled with activity. Silver bells and tinsel on the streetlamps blew in the breeze. The gazebo in the center of the little park looked like it was wearing a white snow hat. The city was small, comfortable. It would be a good place to raise a child. And, if he bought this store, he'd need to spend so much time here for the first three or four years of ownership that it might be a good idea to move here.

"She's happier than I've ever seen her, you know?"

Wendy's unexpected comment caused his heart to jump. He spun from the window. "Excuse me?"

"Shannon. The past few days she's been happier than I've ever seen her. She came back from South Carolina broken. Genuinely broken." Wendy paused for a second, then shook her head. "Whatever her husband did to her, it was devastating. She doesn't talk about it, but she didn't have to. It was easy to see he broke her."

Indignation roared through him. He'd like to find the bastard and give him a good shaking.

"Then you came along. Spent that snowy weekend with her and she came in that Monday different." She smiled. "Happy. Whatever you're doing, keep doing it."

He snorted. "She might have started off enjoying my company, but she's been a bit standoffish lately."

Leaning against the doorjamb, Wendy shrugged. "I told you. Her ex really hurt her. I don't blame her for being cautious." She glanced at the floor then caught his gaze. "I just… Well, she'd be crazy not to like you and I can see from the way you look at her that you're interested and…" She sucked in a breath. "Just don't give up, all right?"

Giving up was the last thing he wanted to do. Especially since he now knew she was cautious. Not standoffish. Not disinterested. But cautious. For heaven's sake. All this time that he'd been jumping to conclusions, he'd missed the obvious one. A bad divorce had made her cautious. He nearly snorted with derision. He of all people should have recognized the signs.

Finley suddenly appeared in the doorway. She pushed past Wendy and ran over to him. He scooped her off the floor. "Hey."

"Hey! They have a candy store. And a toy store."

Rory met Shannon's gaze over Finley's head. "You took her to see the competition?"

She laughed. "They're fun, interesting shops."

"I'll bet."

Unbuttoning her long white coat, Shannon said, "They really are. And because they're unique and interesting they bring shoppers to town. Those same shoppers buy their one unique, interesting Christmas gift for the year at one of the specialty shops, then they come to us for the normal things like Christmas pajamas, tea sets and trucks."

He slid Finley to the floor. "Makes sense." His entire body tingled with something he couldn't define or describe.

It wasn't fear, though there was a bit of fear laced in there. He should be as cautious as Shannon. His heart had been stomped on, too.

It wasn't excitement, though he couldn't deny that every time he saw her his stomach flipped or his heart squeezed or his chest tightened.

It wasn't anticipation, though how could he not feel a bit eager at the fact that Shannon didn't dislike him? She was simply being cautious. Wendy had more or less given him a green light and now that he had it he didn't know what to do with it.

How did a man woo a woman who'd been hurt?

Finley tugged on his hand. "Shannon said that if it

was okay with you we could go shopping with her tonight."

"Shopping?" He laughed lightly, so uncertain about what to do or say. He knew exactly what Shannon was feeling. The hurt of rejection. The sting of not being wanted, not being good enough anymore for the person who took a vow to love you. He knew how shaky she felt. He'd felt it, too. But attraction to her had quickly gotten him beyond it. Unfortunately, that hadn't left him a road map for how to help her. "Why would a person who owns a department store need to go shopping?"

"For a Christmas tree," Finley answered.

The words came out through a giggle and something that felt very much like a fist punched into his heart. Finley, the child he firmly believed would never experience the joy of Christmas had her joy back. Shannon was responsible for that. Her generosity of spirit was part of the reason he'd fallen for her so hard and so fast.

So maybe he should show her he could be generous, too? "Wendy, would you mind taking Finley into your office for a minute?"

Wendy reached down and took Finley's hand. "Sure. No problem." Very astutely, Wendy closed the door as they walked out.

Cautious himself now, Rory caught Shannon's gaze. "I'd love to go tree shopping, too…if you really want us."

She caught his gaze, smiled sheepishly, hopefully. "There's a huge difference between going tree shopping as a single adult and going tree shopping with a little girl who is seeing the holiday for the first time."

Boy, didn't he know that? Technically, this would be *his* first time of seeing the joy on Finley's face when she walked through a forest of evergreens and chose the perfect one to sit in their big front window, so the whole town could see the lights.

He felt his own Christmas spirit stir, remembered the first time he walked into the woods with his dad to get the family's tree, remembered decorating it, remembered seeing it shining with lights on Christmas morning. His heart tugged a bit.

He swallowed. She wasn't just changing Finley. She was changing him. "All right, then. We're happy to go with you."

Shannon insisted they take her big SUV to the Christmas tree farm on the top of the hill outside of town. Without streetlights, the world was incredibly dark. A new storm had moved in. Though it was nothing like the storm that had stranded Rory and Finley at her home the weekend before, it blew shiny white flakes in front of the SUV's headlights.

She pointed at the big illuminated sign that said Wendell's Christmas Trees. "Take the next right."

Rory smoothly maneuvered the SUV onto the slim country road. After a minute, the lights of the farm came into view. A minute after that she directed him to turn down the lane. Snow coated the firs that formed a tunnel to a bright red barn that was surrounded by four white plank outbuildings. Floodlights lit the area. Cars were parked wherever appeared convenient. Some in front of buildings. Some at the side of the lane. Tree shoppers walked the thin lines between the rows of tall, majestic firs.

They stopped in front of the first outbuilding. Rory helped Finley out of the car seat they'd installed in the back of Shannon's SUV for her. She glanced around in awe. "Wow."

Rory stooped down in front of her. "I'm going to let you walk until you get tired. But as soon as you get tired, you need to tell us. It's too cold to be out here too long."

Even as he said that a gust of wind blew away the tiny white flakes of snow that glittered in his hair and fell to the shoulders of his black leather jacket. Shannon watched, mesmerized. He was so gorgeous, yet so normal.

He rose and took Finley's hand. "So how do we do this?"

Shannon took Finley's other hand. "We get a tag from the cashier over there." She pointed at a young girl who stood in front of a table holding a cash register. "Then we walk down the rows until we see a tree that we like and we tag it. One of us goes out to get one of the helpers to cut down our tree while the other two stay with the tree." She looked around at the large crowd of tree shoppers. It might not have been such a wise idea to wait until this close to Christmas to choose her tree. Of course, with last weekend's storm she hadn't had much choice. "Since they're busy, this might take a while."

Finley grinned. "I don't care."

Rory laughed. "Yeah, *you* wouldn't. If you get cold or tired, somebody's going to carry you."

She giggled.

Shannon laughed, too. Not just because of Finley but because Rory was such a good dad. So easygoing with Finley and so accepting of her limitations.

After getting a tag from the cashier, they headed into the first row and Shannon drew in a deep breath of the pine-scented air.

Rory reverently said, "This is amazing."

Shannon glanced around, trying to remember what

the tree farm had felt like to her the first time she'd seen it. Tall pines towered around them. Snow pirouetted in the floodlights illuminating the area. The scent of pine and snow enveloped them.

She smiled. "Yeah. It is amazing."

He glanced over. The smile he gave her was careful, tentative. A wave of guilt washed through her. She'd been so standoffish with him the past two days that he probably thought she hated him.

"Did you come here often as a child?"

"Every year with my dad." She laughed, remembering some of the more memorable years. "He always had a vision of the tree he wanted. Some holidays it was a short, fat tree. Others it was a tree so tall it barely fit into our living room."

He smiled. "Sounds fun."

"It was." She swallowed. After her behavior the past two days, he would be within his rights to be grouchy with her. Actually, he could have refused to take this trip with her. Instead, here he was, with his daughter, ready to help pick out a tree and carry it into her house for her.

With a quick breath for courage, she said, "What about you? Did you have any Christmas traditions as a kid?"

"Not really traditions as much as things we'd pull out of a hat every year to make it special or fun."

"Like what?"

He peeked over at her. "Well, for one, we'd make as big of a deal out of Christmas Eve as we did Christmas. My mom would bake a ham and make a potato salad and set out cookies, cakes, pies and then invite everyone from the neighborhood." He chuckled. "Those were some fun nights. We never knew what to expect.

Sometimes the neighbors would have family visiting and they'd bring them along. Some nights, we'd end up around the piano singing carols. One night, we all put on our coats and went caroling to the people on the street who couldn't make it to our house for some reason."

"Sounds fun."

"It was fun."

He said the words as if he were resurrecting long-forgotten memories and it hit her that he'd been left that Christmas two years ago as much as Finley had been. She wondered how much of his own Christmas joy had been buried in the pain of the past two years.

"Tell me more."

"After the big shindig on Christmas Eve, you'd think Christmas day would be small potatoes, but my mom always found a way to make it special." He laughed. "I remember the year she tried to make apple-and-cinnamon pancakes."

"Sounds yummy."

"Only if you like charcoal. She got it into her head for some reason or another that they'd taste better if she didn't use the grill but fried them in a frying pan the way her mom used to when she was little."

"Uh-oh."

"She couldn't adjust the temperature and most of them burned. At one point the pan itself started burning." He shook his head and laughed. "I've always been glad my dad was quick with a fire extinguisher."

Finley began swinging their arms back and forth. Rory took another deep breath of the pine-scented air. A small shudder worked through Shannon's heart. It was the perfect outing. Just like a mom and dad with their daughter, they walked the long thin rows, looking for the tree that would make their living room complete. And every time they'd start walking after pausing to examine a tree, Finley would swing their hands.

"What about this one?"

Rory had stopped at a towering blue spruce. Shannon studied it critically. "You don't think it's too tall?"

"Better too tall than too short. If it's too tall, we can always shave a few inches from the bottom."

She looked at it again. The needles were soft but bushy. Healthy. The branches were thick. There were no "holes," as her father would say. No places where you could see the wall behind the tree because there was no branch filling in the space.

"I like it."

"Then let's tag it," Rory said, reaching out to grab a branch and attach the tag. His arm brushed against her and Shannon jumped back. When their gazes met, she immediately regretted it.

He was so good to her, so kind and she was nothing but jumpy.

She swallowed. "I'm sorry."

He pulled away. "You're just nervous."

That sounded like as good of an excuse as any. Especially since it was true. He did make her nervous. He made her shaky and antsy and all kinds of things because she liked him. Still, she didn't need to tell him why she was nervous.

"It's cold. It's close to Christmas. I have lots of work to do." She shrugged. "So, yes, I'm nervous."

He cast a quick glance down at Finley, who was pre-occupied with fitting her little pink boot into the foot-print of someone who had walked down the row before them. "You're not nervous because you like me?" He smiled endearingly. "Not even a little bit?"

His question was so unexpected that she pulled her bottom lip between her teeth, stalling, trying to figure out what to say. She didn't want to insult or encourage him.

Finally, confused and out of her element, she said, "I'm not sure."

He laughed. "You like me."

Her breath stuttered into her lungs at his confidence. She was on the verge of denying it, like a third grader confronted by the cute guy in class and too afraid to admit her crush, but he didn't give her time.

He turned and faced Finley. "Want to stay with Shannon or walk back with me so that we can get one of the tree cutters back here to help us out?"

She didn't even hesitate. "I'll stay with Shannon."

He gave Shannon a wink before he turned and headed down the row. Finley said, "I like your tree."

Shannon glanced down with a smile. "I do, too."

"My dad picked out a good one. He's smart."

"Yes, he is smart," Shannon agreed, but her throat was closing and her knees were growing weak. He hadn't confronted her about liking him to give her a chance to argue. He'd made a statement of fact, then walked away, as if giving her time to accept it.

Accept it?

She *knew* she liked him. She fought her feelings for him every day. He hadn't needed to tell her. He hadn't needed to get it out in the open for them to deal with.

She sucked in a breath. Stupid to panic. In another day or two, he'd be done looking at her store. Then he'd leave. And the rest of their dealings would be done through lawyers. Even if they had to meet to sign an agreement, it would be at a lawyer's office.

They wouldn't spend enough time together for her "liking him" to mean anything. Even if he liked her back.

Which he did—

Oh, dear God. That's why he'd said that! He was preparing her to hear him tell her that he liked her.

With a glance down the row, she saw Rory returning with the tree cutter. She moved Finley out of the way as they approached.

As if he hadn't just dropped the bombshell that threatened to destroy the entire evening, Rory said, "You can go down and pay if you want."

She nodded, and, holding Finley's hand, she raced down to the cashier. She paid for the tree and directed Finley to the SUV, where Rory and the farm employee were tying her blue spruce to her vehicle's roof.

As they got inside the vehicle and headed home, Shannon and Rory were quiet. But Finley chatted up a storm.

"So how do we get the tree in the house?"

Rory said, "We'll park as close as we can to the porch, then I'll hoist it on my shoulder and hope for the best."

Finley giggled. Shannon almost laughed, too. She could picture him wobbling a bit with an entire tree on his shoulder.

"And then what do we do with it?"

He looked over at Shannon. "I'm guessing Shannon has a tree stand."

"What's a tree stand?"

Shannon took this one. "That's the thing that holds up the tree. Since it doesn't have roots anymore, it needs help standing."

Finley nodded sagely. "Oh." Then she grinned. "Do we get hot cocoa after that?"

"As much as you want."

Rory peeked over at Shannon. "But not so much that she's too wired to go to sleep tonight."

An unexpected longing shot an arrow straight to her heart. She wanted them to stay the night. She wanted to put the tree up in the living room, make hot cocoa and decorate the tree with them. Not just Finley, but Rory, too. She'd liked his stories of happy Christmas Eves and Christmases. She liked that his mom couldn't cook any better than she could. She liked that he didn't mind telling stories of his past. She liked that he didn't mind leaving her with his child, doing the heavy lifting of the tree… Who was she kidding? She also liked that he was good-looking, funny, smart—and that he liked her.

She turned to look out the window. *He liked her.* Her heart swelled with happiness, even as her stomach plummeted. He could like her until the cows came home, but that didn't change the fact that they wouldn't ever be together.

Pulling into her driveway, Rory said, "I think the easiest way to get the tree off the SUV is for me to stand on one side, while you stand on the other. You untie your side of the ropes first. I'll do mine second. Then I'll ease the tree off on my side."

"Sounds like a plan."

Finley leaned forward. "Yeah. Sounds like a plant."

Rory laughed. "She said plan. It sounds like a plan."

"But a tree is a plant!"

Shannon slanted him a look. "She's got you there."

They got out of the SUV laughing. Rory stood on the driver's side, while Shannon stayed on the passenger's side.

"Okay," he called. "You untie the ropes on your end."

As quickly as she could, Shannon undid the ropes currently holding the tree to her side of the SUV.

"Okay!"

"Okay!" Rory called back. "Now, I'll untie mine."

The branches of the blue spruce shimmied a bit as he dealt with the ropes. Then suddenly it shivered a little harder, then began to downright shake. Before Shannon knew what was happening, it rolled toward her, and then tumbled off the roof.

Finley screamed and raced up the porch. Shannon squealed and jumped out of the way, but the tree brushed her as it plopped into the snow.

Rory came running over. In a move that appeared as instinctive as breathing, he grabbed her and pulled her to him. "Oh, my God! Are you all right?"

Even through his jacket she could feel his heart thundering in his chest. Feel his labored, frightened breathing.

"It just brushed me." She tried to say the words easily, but they came out slow and shaky. It had been so long since a man had cared about her so much that he hugged her without thinking, so long since she'd been pressed up against a man's chest, cocooned in a safe embrace. Loved.

She squeezed her eyes shut. There it was. The thing that scared her about him. He was tumbling head over heels in love with her, as quickly as she was falling for him. She'd spent days denying it. Then another two days avoiding it, thinking it would go away. But it wasn't going away.

They were falling in love.

CHAPTER NINE

RORY PULLED THE TREE UP and hoisted it over his shoulder the way he'd told Finley he would.

Shannon watched him. Her heart in her throat with fear that he might hurt himself, then awe at the sheer power and strength of him. He might work in an office all day, but he was still a man's man. Still strong. Masculine. Handsome.

Oh, Lord, she had it bad.

And the worst part was, he knew.

Thanking God for the built-in chaperone of Finley, she scrambled up the stairs behind him. She could hear Finley's little voice saying, "Okay, turn left, Daddy." She squealed. "Duck down! Duck down! You're going to hit the doorway!"

Shannon quickened her pace.

Rory dropped the tree to the living-room floor with a gentle thump. He grinned at her. "You women. Afraid of a little bit of dirty work."

Shannon glanced down at the pine needles around her feet. "A little bit of dirty work? I'll be vacuuming for days to get these needles up."

Rory laughed. "Where's your tree stand?"

"It's by the window."

He made short order of getting the tree in the stand.

After removing her boots and coat, Finley stood on the club chair nearby giving orders. "It's leaning to the left."

He moved it.

"Now it's leaning to the right."

They were so cute, and it was so wonderful to have them in her house, that her heart filled with love. Real love. She knew beyond a shadow of a doubt that she had fallen in love with them. Especially Rory. Finley would grow up and move on. But she could see herself growing old with Rory.

And that was wrong. Really wrong. So she ducked out of the living room for a minute or two of private time in the kitchen.

Busying herself with making cocoa for Finley, she chided herself. "So you're falling in love. Big deal. He's gorgeous. He's good with his daughter. And—" She sucked in a breath. "He likes you, too. Is it any wonder you're being drawn in?"

The kitchen door swung open. Rory walked in. "Are you talking to yourself?"

Her blood froze in her veins. This was a consequence of living alone for the past few months. She did talk to herself. Out loud.

Hoping he hadn't heard what she'd said, only the mumbling of her talking, she brushed it off. "Old habit." Turning from the stove to face him, she said, "Not a big deal."

Then she looked into his eyes, saw the attraction she'd been denying and avoiding, and her pulse skittered. What she wouldn't give to be able to accept this. To run with it. Step into his arms and look into his eyes and just blatantly flirt with him.

As if reading her mind, he walked over, caught her

elbows and brought her to him. "Thanks for tonight. Finley had a great time and I did, too."

His entire body brushed up against hers, touching, hinting, teasing her with thoughts of how it would feel to be held by him romantically. Her heart tumbled in her chest. Her brain said, *Say you're welcome and step away,* but her feet stood rooted to the spot. She'd longed to be wanted for an entire year, yearned for it. And here he was a whisper away.

"Do you think we should have a little conversation about what I told you at the tree farm?"

Her tongue stayed glued to the roof of her mouth. Little starbursts of possibility exploded inside her. But her brain rebuked her. *Step away. Pretend you don't understand what he's getting at.*

He nudged her a little closer. Her breasts swept against his chest. Their thighs brushed. The starbursts of possibilities became starbursts of real attraction, arousal. He was here. Hers for the taking. All she had to do was say a word. Or two. Or maybe even just smile.

"I know you're attracted to me." He laughed. "I haven't been out of the game so long that I don't recognize the signs." He nudged her closer still. "And I like you."

His head began to descend and she knew he was going to kiss her. She couldn't have told if it had taken ten seconds or ten minutes for their lips to meet. Caught in his gaze, mesmerized by his soft words, she stood frozen, yearning egging her on while fear stopped her.

But when his lips met hers, pure pleasure punched through her objections. Her brain went blank and she simply let herself enjoy the forbidden fruit he offered. His lips nibbled across the sensitive flesh of her mouth. Shivers of delight raced down her spine. He deepened the kiss, parting her lips and sliding his tongue inside her waiting mouth. Yearning ricocheted through her. Not just for physical satisfaction, but for everything connected to it. Love. Commitment. Family.

But she couldn't give him a family. And pretending she could, stringing him along, was wrong.

She reluctantly, painfully stepped away. The jackhammer beat of her pulse reduced to a low thud. The tingles of desire flooding her system mocked her.

Rory's voice softly drifted to her, breaking in on her personal agony. "Why are you fighting this?"

She leaned against the counter. Tears swam in her eyes. The arousal coursing through her blood competed with the anger and frustration battering her brain.

"If you're worried about the distance, about the fact that you may have to leave town if I buy Raleigh's, you could always continue working for me."

She squeezed her eyes shut as pain shot through her. He liked her enough that he was already making compromises.

"I'd have to stay in Virginia, but it's only a four-hour drive. One week you could drive down to me, the next I could drive up to you." He chuckled. "I'd give you every Friday off. It's one of the advantages of dating the boss."

The tears stinging her eyes became a flood. He liked her enough that he was *planning a future*. A real future. One with kids and a dog and a white picket fence and a husband and wife who really would love each other until death parted them.

When she didn't answer, he walked up behind her. Slid his hands around her waist. "Shannon?"

The tears spilled over. Her heart splintered into a million pieces. Her lips trembled.

"Why are you upset, when I've already worked it all out for us?" He chuckled softly. "I can understand that you'd be afraid of starting something because of your ex. But I'm not like your ex. Not only would I never hurt anyone, but I like you. A lot. More than I ever thought I could like—"

She cut him off when she turned in his arms. Blinking back tears she let herself study his face, his fathomless black eyes, his wonderful, perfect mouth, the mouth that kissed so well.

She wanted to remember this. She wanted to remember what it looked like when a man really wanted her. With the pain shredding her heart, shattering her soul, at the knowledge that she was going to have to tell him she couldn't have kids, she knew beyond a shadow of doubt that she would never, ever get close to a man again. So she'd memorize Rory. Never forget him. Never forget what it felt like to be wanted. If only for a little while.

He tried to pull her close but she shrugged out of his hold. She couldn't handle it if he dropped his arms from around her when she told him the truth. Because she had to tell him the truth. Not only did he like her enough that she had to be fair, but she also liked him enough that she could accept nothing less from herself than total honestly.

She stepped away. Cleared the lump filling her throat. Quietly, with the burden of pain it always brought, she said, "I can't have kids."

His face contorted with confusion. "What?"

She drew a harsh breath, caught his gaze. When reality had to be faced, it was best to face it head-on. Bravely. Now that she had her bearings she could do just that.

"My ex left me the day I had a hysterectomy. I had

the kind of endometriosis that compromises vital organs. I had no choice."

His features softened with sympathy for her. "I'm so sorry."

"And you love kids." Swallowing back a waterfall of tears that wanted to erupt, she turned away. "I see how you are with Finley, but we've also discussed this. The day we went sledding you told me how much fun it was to have Finley and that if—" Her voice faltered. "If you ever found someone to love again you would want more kids."

He stepped up behind her. "Those were words—"

"That was *truth*," she shot back harshly. She didn't want him saying things tonight that he'd regret in the morning. She turned, faced him. She refused to let her misery compromise her pride. "You love kids. You wouldn't even have to say the words. Anybody who saw you with Finley would know. But you told me. You told me plainly that if you ever fell in love again, it would be to remarry...to have kids." She paused long enough to draw in some much needed air. "If we acknowledge that honestly, and stop what's happening between us now, there'll be no hard feelings. No one will get hurt because we barely know each other."

He brushed at the tear sitting on the rim of her eyelash. "Shannon..." Her name was a soft question that she didn't know how to answer.

So she shrugged away from him, swallowed and said, "Don't. Really. I'm fine with this."

He didn't pull her to him again, but she still stood close enough that he brushed at the second tear. "Then why are you crying?"

For a million reasons. She wanted to say it. Hell, she wanted to shout it. Life had stolen her ability to have kids and with it slimmed down her pool of potential life partners. Her husband had dumped her. She hadn't really been held by a man in an entire year. She'd gone through the worst situation life had ever handed her and she'd gone through it alone.

She was crying because she was tired. Alone. Afraid to hope. And when she looked at him, she hoped.

Rory drew a sharp breath, her pain was a living, breathing thing in the room, tormenting them both. He wanted to tell her he wasn't going anywhere. That he didn't care about having kids. That he liked her enough to explore what was happening between them, then Finley ran into the room.

"Where is everybody?"

Shannon spun away from the door so Finley couldn't see her crying and Rory's heart broke for her again. He longed to take her into his arms, to let her cry, but he respected her privacy. If he did something like that, Finley would see and ask questions. But they could— *would*—talk about this in the morning.

He walked over and swept Finley up off the floor. "Hey, kiddo. Tree's up. It's time for us to go home."

"But I didn't get cocoa."

"We'll stop somewhere along the way."

"Okay."

But carrying his daughter to the front hall, strange feelings enveloped him. He remembered the day she was born, remembered walking the floor with her after her two-o'clock feedings. The memories tripped something in his psyche...a love so profound and so deep that it could have only come from the inner sanctum of his soul. Shannon would never know this. But, if he stayed with her, pursued what was happening between them, he would never know it again.

He'd never have a son. His flesh and blood. A little miniature of himself, but with complementing gifts from his mother's gene pool. He'd never teach *his* little boy how to play baseball. Never proudly introduce him around on the first tee of the country club golf course.

Selfish, he knew, but when he thought of life without those things, something tore a hole in his lungs. He felt like he couldn't breathe.

It was a lot to be confronted with out of the blue. This time last week, he didn't believe he'd ever consider dating again, let alone having more kids. Now, he felt like he was in the raging pit of hell because he finally liked someone but she couldn't have kids. And he had to make a choice. A huge choice. A life-altering choice.

He found Finley's jacket on the chair in the living room where she'd tossed it while he'd settled the tree into the stand. He found her mittens on the foyer floor. By the time he had her dressed for outside and had shrugged into his leather jacket, Shannon walked out of the kitchen.

Quiet, but composed, she stooped in front of Finley. "Button up. It gets colder at night."

Finley nodded.

Shannon hugged her. And Rory's chest ached. Now he knew why she'd been so happy to spend time with Finley. Now he knew why she hadn't even hesitated when they'd needed a place to stay.

She loved kids.

And she couldn't have any.

CHAPTER TEN

THAT NIGHT RORY lay awake while Finley snored softly in the cot beside his bed. Staring at the dark ceiling, he struggled with the myriad thoughts that battled in his brain. Was she right? Would he reject her, the way her ex-husband had, because she couldn't have kids?

He didn't know. He honestly didn't know. But he did know that if he followed her lead, pulled back from a relationship, as she had, he'd never be put in the position where he'd have to make a choice. Which might be why she'd been so standoffish. She liked him enough that she didn't want to put him in the position where he had to choose. Then, as she'd pointed out, neither one of them would be hurt.

He fell asleep around four and woke at seven, tired but agreeing that the thing to do would be to follow her lead. Pull back. Hold back. Don't give her hope only to snatch it away again later if he just plain wasn't ready to handle a relationship. Or, God help him, if he couldn't come to terms with never having any more of his own children.

As he and Finley walked into Shannon's office, she rose from her desk. Wearing a red dress, with bright gold earrings shaped like Christmas ornaments, she looked festive. But her smile was cautious, wary.

"So, Miss Finley, are you staying with me this morning while your dad spends some time in human resources?"

She bounced up and down. "Yes! Are we going to do something fun?"

"Well, first I have to get my morning paperwork done." She clicked on her big-screen TV. "You can watch cartoons while I do that. Then I thought we'd just take a walk in the park, get some fresh air." She stooped down in front of Finley. "There should be carolers there this morning."

"Carolers?"

"People who sing Christmas songs."

Not enthusiastic, but at least not pouting or throwing a tantrum, Finley shrugged. "Sounds okay."

Shannon rose. "Okay? It's going to be fun." She smiled tentatively at Rory. "So you'll be back around noon?"

He swallowed. She might be cool and collected, but he knew her heart had been broken. Irrevocably. Life couldn't do anything crueler to a woman who wanted children than to deprive her of the privilege of conceiving them.

He tried to smile, but knew the effort was lacking. "Yeah. I'll be back around noon."

When he turned to go, she caught his forearm. He faced her again.

"Don't worry about me."

"I'm not…"

"You are. But I'm fine. Really. In the past year I've adjusted, and in the past week I've made some decisions about what I want to do with the rest of my life. You just do your part. Decide if you want to buy Raleigh's. And I'll take care of everything else."

He left her office with a strange feeling of finality swamping him. *She'd* made the choice. It didn't sit right, still part of him sighed with relief. He'd just come from a bad, bad, bad marriage. Until he'd met Shannon he'd all but decided never to get close to a woman again. It scared him silly to think he even wanted to try. And the first time he tried it was with a woman who couldn't be hurt, someone who needed promises up front. Promises he was too shaky to make.

So maybe Shannon was right? Maybe it was best that there be nothing between them?

He headed for human resources, but halfway to the door to housewares, Wendy called to him. "Wait! Wait!"

He stopped. Thinking she had a message from Shannon or Finley, he said, "What's up?"

"Nothing…" She sighed heavily. "It's just that Shannon came in sad this morning and I…" She winced. "I just wanted to know if something happened last night."

His breath caught, but he refused to give in to the emotion. She'd made the choice and he respected that— if only because his own failed marriage had left him so cautious that he couldn't promise that he'd give her the love she needed. Not after only a few days together.

"Nothing happened last night." Nothing that he'd tell one of Shannon's employees. But as quickly as he thought that, it dawned on him that if Wendy, her trusted secretary, didn't know why Shannon was so heartbroken then Shannon might not have told anyone.

Except him.

He felt burdened and honored both at the same time.

"I've been divorced. I know how difficult the first Christmas alone can be. Give her some space. She'll be fine."

With that he pushed open the swinging door. He spent the morning listening to the human resources director explain Raleigh's hiring policies, its wage structure, its bonus and pension plans. Glad for the distraction, he listened intently, but the second he left the big office and headed downstairs to Shannon's office, the weight of her troubles sat on his shoulders again.

When he arrived at her office, Finley raced into his arms. "We went to the park! Saw the people sing. They were funny."

"Funny?"

Shannon laughed. "One of the singers dressed up as a reindeer when they sang 'Rudolph the Red-Nosed Reindeer.' It was hysterical."

He smiled. He couldn't help it. Finley was really coming around about Christmas. If she kept this up, in a few more days she might actually like the holiday. But, more importantly, Shannon looked better. More peaceful. He knew that was due in part to Finley's company, but he genuinely believed that since they hadn't really "fallen in love" she'd very quickly gotten beyond their near-miss romance.

"So…" He caught her gaze. "Are we ready for lunch?"

She looked away. "You go on without me."

Finley whined, "Awww!!"

Shannon peeked up, smiled at her. "Sorry, but because we played all morning I have a little work I'd like to catch up on."

A combination of fear and guilt clenched in his stomach. She didn't want to be around him anymore. Or maybe she wasn't having as much fun around Finley as she seemed? Maybe having a child around was pure torture? "If Finley's a bother, I can have her sit in a room with me."

Her eyes softened. "Finley's never a bother."

And he nearly cursed. Of all the mistakes he'd made around Shannon that was probably the stupidest. It had been clear from the beginning that she loved being around Finley. He was the one with the problem. He had absolutely no clue how to relate to Shannon anymore. Probably because he knew something about her that wasn't true for most women, and he was barely accustomed to dealing with "most" women. Of course, he was clumsy and awkward around her.

But at lunch he decided that he wasn't going to abandon her. He might stop his romantic advances. He definitely wouldn't kiss her again. Those things only seemed to make her unhappy, but he wouldn't, by God, take Finley away from her in the last two days of their trip.

That evening, after they'd eaten supper in a little Italian restaurant, he loaded Finley back into the car.

"Where're we goin'?"

"Shannon's."

"All right!"

"I have no idea what she's going to be doing tonight, but whatever it is, we're going to help her."

Blissfully clueless, Finley shrugged. "Okay."

"I mean it, Finley. This might be a little hard for you to understand, but Christmas means a lot to Shannon and I don't want any tantrums if she says or does something you don't like."

"Okay."

He bit back a sigh. He couldn't be sure that Finley really got it. But he did know he couldn't let Shannon alone that night.

She answered the door wearing a bright Christmas-print apron over jeans and a red sweater. Her dark hair swirled around her sexily, but the drop of flour on the tip of her nose made her look just plain cute.

"Hey!"

She stepped away to allow them to enter.

Rory guided Finley inside. "We weren't sure what you would be doing tonight but we suspected you might need some help." He caught her gaze, smiled tentatively. "So we're here."

She headed for the kitchen, motioning for them to follow her. "I'm baking cookies."

Finley gasped. "What kind?"

Shannon turned and caught her gaze. "Christmas cookies."

Finley frowned but Shannon laughed. "Don't you think it's about time you learned how to bake them?"

"I'm six."

Shannon headed for the kitchen again. "I know. But next year you'll be seven and the year after that eight and before you know it you'll be twelve or so and you'll want to be the one who bakes the cookies. So, just trust me."

Finley wrinkled her nose and glanced up at her father. Recognizing she might be more opposed to the work than the idea that the cookies were for a holiday she didn't really like, he said, "Well, you don't think I'm going to bake our cookies, do you?"

In the kitchen, the dough had already been prepared. Shannon had it rolled into a thin circle. Cookie cutters sat scattered along the side of the cookie dough bowl.

He ambled to the center island as Finley hoisted herself onto one of the tall stools in front of it.

"You see these?" Shannon displayed a bunch of the

cookie cutters to Finley. "We push these into the dough."
She demonstrated with a Christmas-tree-shaped cutter.
"Then pull it out and like magic we have a cookie that's
going to look like a tree."

Finley grabbed for the tree cutter. "Let me."

Rory tugged her hand back. "What do we say?"

She huffed out a sigh. "Please, can I do one?"

Shannon laughed. "You may do as many as you like."
She laughed again. "As long as there's dough."

And Rory's heart started beating again. He hadn't
realized how worried he was, how guilty he felt, until
Shannon laughed and some of the burden began to lift.

Finley and Shannon cut twelve shapes and Shannon
removed the cookie dough from around them. They
lifted the shapes from the countertop onto a baking
sheet and Shannon rolled another circle of dough.

They worked like that for about twenty minutes.
When Rory also joined in the fun, it took even less
time to cut out all the cookies in a circle of dough. As
they cut shapes and filled cookie sheets, Shannon slid
the trays into the oven. Using a timer, she kept close
track of their baking times and in exactly twelve minutes she removed each pan of cookies.

When they finished the last tray, Shannon walked
over to the cookies cooling on the round kitchen table
and said, "These are ready to be painted."

Finley frowned. "With a brush?"

"With a lot of little brushes." She brought a plate of
cooled cookies over to the counter then headed for the
refrigerator, where she had icing cooling. She filled four
soup bowls with icing.

"Now we put some food coloring in the bowls and
make different colors of icing."

Grabbing two bottles of the coloring, Rory helped her create red, blue, green, yellow and pink icing.

She carefully caught his gaze. "You're good at this."

He laughed, relieved that she finally seemed comfortable with him in the room. "It's not we're like mixing rocket fuel."

She laughed a little, too. Finley snatched a cookie and one of the thin paintbrushes lying beside the icing bowls.

Now that the cookies had baked, they'd fluffed out a bit and didn't exactly look like their intended design. So Rory said, "That's a bell."

Finley sighed as if put upon. "I know."

Hoping to cover for the insult, he said, "So what color are you going to paint it?"

"The song they sang in the park today said bells are silver. But there is no silver icing."

"Silver bells are silver," Shannon agreed. "But cookie bells can be any color you want."

"Then I'll make mine pink."

"A pink bell sounds lovely."

Though Rory had pitched in and helped cut the cookies and even create the colored icing, he had no interest in painting cookies. He glanced around. "Would you mind if I made a pot of coffee?"

Shannon peeked over at him again. This time more confidently. "Or you could make cocoa."

Rory's shoulders relaxed a bit more. If they kept this up, by the time he was ready to take Finley home, he and Shannon might actually be comfortable in each other's company again.

He found the milk and cocoa. While Shannon and Finley happily painted cookies, he made their cocoa and served it to them. They barely paused. Seeing that it would take hours if he didn't help, Rory lifted a brush and began to paint, too.

They worked until nine. When they were through, and the cookies drying on the kitchen table, Rory told Finley to get her coat while he helped Shannon clean the dishes and brushes. In spite of the goodwill that had seemed to grow between them as they made cookies, once Finley left the room Shannon again became quiet.

Rory still didn't quite know what to say. With every minute of silence that passed, a little more distance crept between them. He knew part of that was his fault. He'd only decided he was ready to date. The decisions thrown at him the night before were usually the kinds of things people discovered after months of dating. When they were comfortable and confident in their feelings.

But he understood why Shannon had told him. They were growing close and she didn't want to.

With the dishwasher humming, she dried her hands on the dishtowel and then tossed it on the counter. "I wonder if she's struggling with her boots."

He laughed. "She always struggles with those damn things. But she loves them. So we deal with it."

Heading out of the kitchen, Shannon tried to laugh, but the sound that came out of her throat was a cross between a hum and a sigh. The whole evening had been strained. Rory tried to pretend things weren't different between them, but they were. This time yesterday, he would have flirted with her. He also would have found something to do in her living room rather than watch her and Finley make cookies. He'd clearly been bored. Yet, he stayed in the room. As if he didn't trust her not to break down.

Expecting to see Finley on the foyer floor struggling

with her boots, she paused when she saw the empty space. "Wonder where she is?"

Rory's steps quickened as he ran to the closet. But as he passed the living room entryway, he stopped. "Look."

She peered into the living room and there, on the sofa, sleeping like an angel was Finley. Warmth enveloped her like a soft sigh of contentment. "She's so cute."

"Yeah," Rory agreed, slowly walking toward her. Gazing down at his daughter he said, "You've done so much for her, helping her to get into the spirit of Christmas."

She swallowed. "It was my pleasure."

"I wonder what other things she might like?"

"Might like?"

"About Christmas." He glanced over. "We've decorated, made cookies. You've even gotten her to like carols. But that's just the tip of the holiday iceberg. There are lots of things she's never experienced. Now that she's open, I'd like to introduce her to everything... make her like everything so that this time next year she'll be excited for Christmas, not sad."

Shannon bit her lower lip. She knew exactly what it was like not to look forward to the holiday. She knew what it felt like to wish every day could be normal because the special days only pointed out that you had no one to share them with. "Maybe we could get her to sit on Santa's lap."

Rory laughed as if he didn't think she'd been serious. He caught her gaze again. "That's like asking a guy who's just learned to hike if he wants to try Everest."

"I suppose." But a weird, defensive feeling assaulted her. Up to this point Rory had taken every suggestion she'd given him. Now that he knew she couldn't have kids, it was as if he didn't trust her. That might have even been why he'd stayed in the kitchen with them during cookie making.

Sadness shimmied through her. She turned and headed for the closet. "I'll get her coat and boots."

"Thanks."

When she returned to the living room, Rory sat on the edge of the sofa cushion beside Finley. Shannon handed him Finley's boots. She didn't even stir as he slid them on. But he had to lift her to get her into her coat and hat. Still, though she stirred, she really didn't waken. She put her head on Rory's shoulder when he lifted her into his arms and carried her to the foyer.

Shannon raced to open the door for them. With Finley sound asleep, it was the first time they'd said a private goodbye at the door.

"Thanks for coming over tonight. Even with the extra time to teach Finley, your help cut my cookie-making time in half." She tried to give him a confident happy smile, but it wobbled. It had meant the world to her to have Finley to teach. To have people to share her cookie-making joy with. Just to have people around who cared about her. Deep down, she knew that was why he'd come, why he'd brought Finley. He now knew she was sad. So he'd tried to cheer her.

But that's all it was. The kindness of one human being to another. Not a gesture of love as it might have been the day before—when he didn't know she couldn't have kids.

The injustice of it punched through her, made her want to rail at the universe. But she didn't. She was the one who had made the choice to tell him, and for good reason. She couldn't be angry that she had.

Rory smiled awkwardly. "We were glad to help." He

cleared his throat. "You know, today, when I asked if Finley was a bother—" He cleared his throat again. "I was just worried that she kept you from getting your work done. She likes being with you. I like letting her spend time with you."

Relief rolled through her, stole her breath, thickened her throat. She whispered, "Thanks."

"So tomorrow, while I'm walking around on the sales floor, talking with staff, watching how things are done, you could keep her all day if you like."

"Yes. That would be great."

"Okay."

"Okay."

Silence ensued again. If she hadn't yet told him, she knew he'd probably try to kiss her good-night right now. Her heart stumbled in her chest. She'd hurt both of them, because she was afraid of a bigger hurt to follow.

But it had been the right thing to do.

It had to be.

Because if it wasn't, she was missing out for nothing.

She twisted the doorknob, opened the door. "I'll see you in the morning then."

"Yes."

"Drive carefully."

He nodded, gave her one last look, then walked out to the porch.

She waited until Finley was securely buckled in and Rory had jumped behind the steering wheel, before she turned off the porch light, closed the door and leaned against it. She had another entire day of Finley's company and, if she was lucky, a little time Christmas Eve morning before they returned to Virginia. She should be overjoyed.

Instead sadness softened her soul. She liked Rory. Really liked him. Probably loved him. And she'd chased him away.

CHAPTER ELEVEN

THE NEXT MORNING Rory kissed Finley goodbye before he walked out of Shannon's office to investigate the store. Dressed in jeans and a leather jacket, so the cashiers and shoppers wouldn't guess who he was, he looked so cute that Shannon felt a lightning bolt of longing. But she contented herself with the fact that she had Finley all day again.

"So any thoughts on what you'd like to do today?"

From her seat on the sofa near the big-screen TV, Finley peeked over at her. "Don't you have papers?"

She laughed. "Yes. But I came in early to review them. I'm all yours this morning. So what do you want to do? Go to the candy store again? Maybe the toy store?" she suggested, hoping Finley would say yes so she could buy her a gift. Something special. Something she knew Finley would want. And maybe keep to remember her by.

Finley sucked in a breath. "I'd sorta like to go shopping."

"Great! Where? The toy store?"

She shook her head, sending her fine blond hair swinging. "I wanna buy a present for Daddy."

"Oh." Wow. She'd never thought of that. A little kid like Finley, especially a child with only one parent, probably didn't get a lot of chances to shop for Christmas gifts. But considering Finley's life, a more important question popped into her head. "Have you ever bought your dad a Christmas gift?"

She shook her head again. "No."

Though her heart twisted with a combination of love and sadness for sweet little Finley, she deliberately made her voice light and teasing so Finley's first experience of Christmas shopping would be fun. "Well, then this is your lucky day because we have an excellent men's department here at Raleigh's."

Finley rewarded her with a giggle.

"Let's go!" She caught her hand and led her to the elevator. Inside the little box with "We Wish You a Merry Christmas" spilling from the speakers, she pressed the button for the second floor. Menswear.

As they stepped out, Finley glanced around in awe at the tables of shirts, racks of ties and mannequins dressed in suits. Customers milled about everywhere, examining underwear and pajamas displayed in long tables, studying ties.

"Ohhhh."

Shannon also looked around, trying to see the store as Finley saw it. Because Finley was only a little over three feet tall, she suspected everything looked huge.

"So what do you think? Shirt? Tie? Rodeo belt buckle?"

Finley giggled.

"We also have day planners, pen-and-pencil sets for a daddy's desk and all kinds of computer gadgets in electronics, if you don't see something you like here."

"You sound funny."

"I'm being a salesman."

Finley giggled again, but out of the corner of her eye,

Shannon saw Rory talking to one of the salesclerks. Grasping Finley's shoulders, she raced them behind one of the columns holding a mirror.

Finley said, "What?"

"Your dad is here."

"Oh."

"And if we want to keep your gift for him a surprise, we'll have to be careful where we walk."

Finley nodded her understanding.

They slipped to the far side of the sales floor. Customers, Christmas ornaments, racks of suit jackets, rows of jeans and walls of ties all provided good cover so that Rory wouldn't see them.

As Finley inspected a table full of dress shirts, Shannon sneaked a peek at Rory. With his hands stuffed into the front pockets of his jeans and his shoulders filling out his leather jacket, he could have been any other extremely gorgeous shopper. He chatted happily with a salesclerk, who eagerly showed him suit jackets and ties, probably expecting a nice commission.

She hated to see him disappoint the clerk, but she couldn't stop herself from watching as he took off his jacket and tried on the suit coat suggested by the clerk. His muscles bunched and flexed as he reached around and took the jacket, then shrugged into it.

"I like this one."

Shannon glanced down at Finley. "Huh?"

Finley waved a shirt at her. Folded neatly so that it fit into a rectangular plastic bag, the shirt was a shade of shocking pink so bold that Shannon had to hold back a gasp.

"That one?"

She nodded.

"Um…have you looked at any of the others?"

She nodded. "I like this one."

"It's very nice, but…um…usually men don't like to wear pink shirts."

"Why not?"

"I don't know.…" And she also wasn't sure why she was arguing with a six-year-old. Rory had enough money that he didn't need a new shirt, and the pink one, the one chosen by his daughter with all the enthusiasm in her little pink-loving heart, would be a nice memento. He could keep it forever. Save it to show her when she got her first gift from her own child. Tears sprang to her eyes. It would actually be fun to see that. To remember this day. Share it with Rory. Make him laugh.

She swallowed hard. "You know what? I like that shirt, too."

She glanced up to see which cash register could take their money, and she saw Rory going to the checkout beside the row of suits. The clerk was taking information from him—probably contact information for when the trousers had been hemmed and/or alterations made—and he was pulling out a credit card.

Her heart swelled with love for him. He *wasn't* going to disappoint the clerk who'd spent so much time with him. He was actually buying something. She pressed her hand to her chest. He was such a great guy.

"You know…I don't really hate Christmas anymore."

Stunned back to the real world by Finley's remark, Shannon peeked down at her. "I was beginning to wonder about that."

Finley grinned. "I like presents."

Shannon laughed. "I do, too. I like to give them as much as get them."

Finley nodded eagerly.

"We'll sneak to that register over there—" she pointed at the register in the far corner where Rory wouldn't see them "—and pay for this, then I'm going to buy you ice cream."

"It's morning!"

"I know. But I think you've earned it."

"What's 'earned'?"

"It means that you did something nice, so I'm going to do something nice for you."

Finley grinned.

Shannon paid for the shirt and the clerk handed the bag containing the bright pink shirt to her. She nudged her head so that the clerk would give it to Finley.

With a smile, the clerk shifted the bag over to Finley. "Thank you, ma'am, for shopping at Raleigh's. Come again."

Finley giggled.

Shannon caught her hand. "Want me to carry your bag?"

Finley clutched it tightly, her little hand wrapped around the folded-down end. "I've got it."

She was quiet as they walked out of menswear and to the elevator. When they stepped inside, amazingly, it was empty.

Shannon almost hit the button for the third floor then remembered she'd promised Finley ice cream and pressed the button for the cafeteria floor.

Finley wiggled a little bit. After the doors closed, her tiny voice tiptoed into the elevator. "Some days I miss my mom."

Shannon glanced down, her heart in her throat because she didn't know what to say. It wasn't her place to talk about Finley's mom, but she certainly couldn't ignore her. "I'm sure you do."

"I don't remember her."

Stooping down in front of her, Shannon said, "You were very small, so you probably don't remember. But you should really talk to your dad about this. I'd love to talk with you about it, but you and your dad were both part of your mom leaving." She swallowed. "And you're family. This is the kind of stuff you talk about with your family."

Her blue eyes solemn and sad, Finley nodded. "Okay."

The urge to hug Finley roared through her. Not just because she was sad, but because they were connected. They might not be family, but somewhere along the way they'd bonded. She wished with all her heart she could have talked with Finley about this. Could have eased her pain a bit. But it really was Rory's place.

Still, though she couldn't speak, she could hug, so she wrapped her arms around Finley's tiny shoulders and squeezed.

Finley snuggled against her. "I wish you were my mom."

She closed her eyes. Only with great effort did she stop herself from saying, "I do, too." Instead, she tightened her hold, pressing her lips together to stop their trembling.

The elevator bell dinged. The doors opened. Shannon rose, took Finley's hand and headed to the cafeteria. They could both use some ice cream now.

She managed to avoid having lunch with Finley and Rory. Partially because she hoped Finley would use the private time to ask her dad about her missing mom. She knew a cafeteria wasn't the best place to have the conversation, but recognized that Rory would be smart enough to stall a bit while they were in public. That would give him time to think through what he wanted to say that night when they were alone in the hotel room.

She spent the afternoon with Finley, taking her downstairs to the gift-wrap department to have Rory's new pink shirt properly wrapped in paper covered in elves and candy canes. When Rory arrived at her office around five to take Finley home, she rose from her office chair.

"So, you're ready to go?"

"Yes." He ambled into her office. "The store is fantastic, by the way. Your clerks are very cheerful."

"Hey, some of them work on commission. And the Christmas season puts a lot of money in their pockets."

He laughed. "Ready to go, Finley?"

She scooted off the sofa. "I need my coat."

Shannon walked to the coatrack. "I'll get it."

She slid Finley's arms into the jacket, her heart aching at seeing them leave. Plus, she wanted to talk to Rory about Finley asking about her mom. The need to invite them to her house that evening trembled through her. More time with Finley was a good thing. More time with Rory was tempting fate.

With Finley's coat zipped, Shannon turned her toward her dad. "See you tomorrow."

Rory scooped her up. "Yep. We'll see you tomorrow."

It was wiser to simply let them go. She could leave Finley with Wendy the following morning, track Rory down on the sales floor, and ask for a few private minutes to talk about Finley's question about her mom. That was a much better plan than asking them to her house again that night. Especially since she was decorating the tree. And that would just feel too much like a family thing.

But, oh, she wanted it.

As their feet hit the threshold of her office door, she blurted, "I'm decorating the tree tonight, if you're interested?"

Rory turned, an odd expression on his face. But Finley clapped with glee. "Yes! I want to see the tree when it's all pretty!"

He cast her a puzzled frown. "It's not decorated yet. She wants us to decorate the tree tonight."

Finley grinned. "I know."

He shrugged. "Okay." He faced Shannon. "It looks like we're happy to help. But this time it's my turn to bring food." He caught her gaze. "Anything in particular you like?"

A million sensations twinkled through her. She nearly said, *I want you to stay. I want you to love me.* But she only smiled. "I like chicken."

"You mean fried chicken?"

She nodded.

"Fried chicken it is."

She was ready for them when they arrived a little after six. Paper plates and plastic forks were already on the kitchen table, so they wouldn't have much clean up and could get right to decorating the tree.

She opened the door with a big smile, but from the shell-shocked look on Rory's face, Shannon suspected that Finley had asked him about her mom.

She hustled them inside. "I set up the kitchen table. We can eat first, decorate second."

Not thinking about her own longings, and more concerned about how Rory had handled "the" question, she shooed Finley ahead and stopped Rory short of the door.

"She asked you, didn't she?"

He rubbed his hand down his face. "About her mom?"

She nodded.

"Yeah."

"What did you say?"

"The truth. Or at least as much of it as I could say without hurting her." He sucked in a breath. "She's six. I don't want to tell her that her mom doesn't love her— doesn't even want to see her."

"Of course not."

"She was oddly accepting of the fact that Bonnie left. Almost as if she was just curious about where she was."

Shannon let out the breath she didn't even realize she was holding. "So that's good."

"Yeah. But I have a feeling bigger questions will be coming."

"Maybe."

He chuckled. "Probably."

Finley pushed open the swinging door. "I'm hungry!"

When she spun around and the door swung closed behind her, Shannon started for the kitchen, but Rory stopped her.

"Thanks."

Her eyebrows rose. "For what?"

"For being so good to her. For listening to me when I need somebody to talk about this stuff with."

"Haven't you talked about these things with your friends?"

He cast her a look. "Do you tell your friends about your divorce?"

She felt her face redden. "Not really."

"That's why it's so nice to have someone to talk to. Someone who will listen without judging."

Understanding, she inclined her head. Even though telling him about her inability to have kids had been painful, it had been nice finally to have someone to talk to.

Someone who understood.

A little bit of her burden lessened. He did understand. She might have effectively ended the romantic aspect of their relationship, but maybe she didn't need a romance as much as she needed somebody who truly understood her pain. Somebody who truly understood that sometimes life could be incredibly unfair.

She smiled at him. "I think we better get into the kitchen."

He laughed, slung his arm across her shoulder. "Yep."

The casualness of the gesture seeped into her soul. He liked her. She liked him. They were friends. Real friends, who knew the worst about each other's lives and didn't feel sorry, didn't feel put off, simply accepted and understood. She didn't have to hide things from him. He didn't have to tiptoe around her. More important, she didn't have to worry about him finding out. *He knew.* It was amazing. Suddenly freeing.

They walked into the kitchen to discover that Finley had already opened the bucket of chicken, chosen a leg and was wrestling with the container of coleslaw.

Rory said, "I'll get that."

Shannon opened the mashed potatoes and gravy. "And I'll get this." She offered the potatoes to Finley. "Would you like some of these?"

"Yes, please."

They ate dinner having a surprisingly relaxed conversation, considering that Finley had asked the big question that afternoon.

As soon as she was done eating, Finley slid off her chair and tossed her paper plate and plastic fork into the trash. She skipped to the door. "I'm going to get started."

Rory bounced off his seat. "Not without us!" He headed for the door, then doubled back and tossed his plate and plastic fork into the trash. "If you have any valuable ornaments, I'd eat quickly and get into the living room before she tries to hang them."

With that he raced away and Shannon chuckled, shaking her head. What she wouldn't give to have them as her real family.

But she couldn't. And she did have another night with them. So she rose, tossed her plate and utensils, closed the bucket, put the remaining chicken into the refrigerator and joined them in her living room.

To her relief, she found Rory stringing lights on the tree, as Finley unspooled them.

"That's going to be pretty."

Finley beamed. "Yep."

Heading to the box containing the ornaments her parents had left behind, she said, "I'll unwrap these and we can get started."

They worked in silence for the next five minutes while Rory finished the lights and Shannon carefully removed the white tissue paper from the ornaments.

When the lights had been hung on the branches and the star sat at the top of the tree, she said, "Plug them in. We'll decorate around them."

Rory plugged in the lights and the tree twinkled and sparkled, causing Finley to gasp.

Shannon said, "It's pretty, isn't it?"

She nodded. "Very pretty."

Hanging the ornaments wasn't as simple as stringing the lights. Finley wanted to know the story behind
every ornament and if an ornament didn't have a story,
Shannon had to make one up.

It was ten o'clock before they got all the ornaments
hung. When it was time to leave, after Finley had had
sufficient time to ohhh and ahhh, Rory carried the
cocoa tray to Shannon's kitchen, leaving Finley with
the instruction to put on her boots and coat.

Shannon held the kitchen door open for Rory. As
they walked into the kitchen "White Christmas" was
playing on the stereo.

"Oops. Forgot to turn that off."

She reached for it as Rory set the tray on the center
island, but before she could click it off, he caught her
hand. "I love this song."

"I'll bet! With only two or three snowfalls a year, a
white Christmas is probably pretty high on your wish
list. But here in snow country there's never really a
happy storm."

He laughed, then surprised her by swinging her into
his arms to dance. Holding her close, he said, "It's a
pretty song. A happy song. A song about someone wishing for something he might just get." He laughed again.
"Don't spoil it for me."

She said, "I won't," but inside her chest her heart
pounded like a jackhammer. She told herself that they
were only friends. Reminded herself that having a
friend, a real friend who knew her secrets and understood her, was a blessedly wonderful feeling. But the
sensations rippling through her were every bit as wonderful. She wanted him to like her as more than a friend.

But she'd snuffed out that possibility, headed it off herself. Her choice.

The song ended and they pulled away. Gazing into each other's eyes, they stepped back. Their initial chemistry kicked up again, but she swung away. Carrying the tray to the sink, she laughed shakily. "Somebody who likes snow...sheesh."

"Hey. It's hard to hate something that frequently gets you a day off."

She laughed, then heard the sound of the door as he left the kitchen. Knowing he was gone, she braced herself against the countertop and squeezed her eyes shut, letting herself savor the sensation of being held by him. Danced with. Only when she had memorized every feeling swimming through her, tucked it away to pull out on snowy winter nights without him, did she turn from the sink and go out to the foyer.

Already in her little coat and pink boots, Finley snuggled into her dad's neck, preparing for sleep. Shannon stood on tiptoes and kissed her cheek. "Good night, sweetie."

"G'night."

"I'll see you in the morning?" She made the statement as a question because he'd never really told her a time or day he was leaving. Given that they were spending another night in Green Hill, she suspected he'd stop in the store in the morning.

She peeked at him expectantly.

"Yes. We'll be there in the morning. I want to see Christmas Eve sales. But we do have a four-hour drive, so we'll be leaving around noon."

"Okay."

He smiled. "Okay."

They stared at each other for a few seconds. She

swore she saw longing in his eyes. The same longing
that tightened her tummy and put an ache in her chest.
Then he broke away and headed for the door.

When they were gone she sat in front of the tree for
twenty minutes. Just looking at it. Wishing she could
keep it up forever.

CHAPTER TWELVE

AFTER BUCKLING Finley into her car seat, Rory slid behind the wheel of his car, his heart thumping in his chest. Not with excitement, but with recrimination. He knew she was sad. He knew he was responsible for at least a little bit of that sadness.

But everything between them had happened so fast. Worse, he wasn't even a hundred-percent sure he was capable of trusting someone enough to love them. He wasn't steady enough on his feet to believe he should try a relationship with a normal woman. Someone as special as Shannon was too delicate to be his romantic guinea pig.

The next morning at the store, he wasn't surprised when Shannon again offered to take Finley around the store for a few hours. Needing to see to a few details, Rory shrugged. "I'll be walking around the store, too. You don't have to do this."

She smiled. "I want to."

Then she gave him some kind of head signal that he didn't quite understand. So he laughed. Which amazed him. Even as upset as he knew she was, she still had the ability to make him laugh. And to think of others.

She angled her head toward Finley and nudged twice.

He still didn't have a clue.

So he just went with the program. "Okay. You take Finley and I'll be a secret shopper again."

Finley jumped up and down. "Okay!"

They walked together to the elevator, but when he got off on the second floor, they continued to the main floor. He walked through the menswear department and poked around in the electronics and small appliances, but couldn't seem to focus. Technically, he'd seen enough the day before. He could report back to his dad that Raleigh's had a huge, faithful group of shoppers. At Christmas time, they seemed to sell goods faster than they could restock shelves.

The store had some drawbacks. It only broke even most months of the year and two months of the year it actually lost money. But Christmas made up for that. In spades.

So why did he need to walk around anymore? He didn't.

He took the stairs to the first floor and glanced around, looking for Shannon and Finley. But the store was packed with customers. He barely squeezed through the aisles on his quest to find Shannon and his daughter, but finally he saw them standing by the candy counter.

He edged his way up. "Hey."

"Hey!" Shannon turned, smiled at him. "I thought you were shopping?"

"I think I shopped enough already."

She winced. "Is that good or bad news for me?"

"I shouldn't really tell you anything because I have to report back to my dad, and he and my brothers and I have to make an official decision…but…I can't see any reason we'd shy away from a deal."

Her eyes sparkled. "Really?"

Seeing her so happy put the air back in his lungs, the

life back in his heart. After everything that had happened between them, this was at least one good thing he could do for her.

"So Finley and I can go home now."

Her head snapped around. "What?"

"I'm done. We can go home."

"But I…" She paused, nudging her head toward Finley. "I didn't get to buy someone a gift."

"You did," he said. "Remember? You bought a g-a-m-e."

"I can spell, Daddy."

Rory laughed, but Shannon's face appeared to be frozen. "I just…you know…I thought we'd have the whole morning."

He glanced at his watch, then out the wall of windows fronting the store, at the heavy snowflakes falling. "I thought that, too, but look at the weather."

Shannon turned to look, then swallowed. "I thought you liked snow."

"In its proper place and time."

"Oh."

Her eyes filled with tears and Rory suddenly got it. She wanted this time with Finley. He glanced at the snow again. If anything, it seemed to be coming down harder.

He caught her gaze. "I'm sorry. Really. But if it's any consolation I can bring Finley back when my dad and I come to present our offer."

She swallowed, stepped away. "No. That's okay. I'm fine."

She wasn't fine. She was crying. *He'd made her cry.* Guilt and sorrow rippled through him. "I'm sorry."

Finley stomped her foot. "Daddy! We were supposed to stay."

And Finley the Diva was back. As if it wasn't bad enough that he had to leave Shannon. Now he had to deal with Ms. Diva.

"Finley, it's snowing—"

"I want to see Santa!"

Shannon looked down. "What?"

"I want to see Santa. I want to sit on Santa's lap." She stomped her foot. "Right now!"

Rory had had his fill of giving in to her tantrums, but this one he understood. From the confused look on Shannon's face, he didn't think she had promised to take Finley to see Santa, but he did suspect that Finley had intended to ask her to. She'd been taking steps all along toward acclimating to Christmas and now she was finally here.

Tantrum or not, he wouldn't deny her this.

"Okay."

Shannon glanced at him. "Okay?"

He shrugged. "She's been deprived too long. I think I should do this." He paused, caught her gaze again. "Want to come?"

She smiled. The sheen of tears in her eyes told the whole story even before she said, "Sure."

He directed Finley away from the candy counter. "Let's go then."

They headed for the elevator and the toy department in the mezzanine that overlooked the first floor like a big balcony. Santa's throne was in an area roped off and called Santa's Toy Shop. Shannon led the way as Finley skipped behind her.

Rory didn't know whether to laugh or cry. In spite of the long line, Rory kept his patience as they waited. Finley was not so good. She stepped from foot to foot.

"Don't be nervous."

She glanced at Shannon. "I'm not nervous. I need to get there!"

Finally, their turn came. Finley raced over to Santa as if he were her long-lost best friend.

Rory snorted a laugh. "Look at her. This time last year—this time last week!—she didn't even believe in him. Just a few days ago, she thought of him as a cartoon character. Now look at her!"

Shannon blinked back tears. "I think she's cute."

His heart stuttered a bit. Shannon always behaved like a mom to Finley and when he saw her tears his own perspective changed. He swallowed the basketball-size lump in his throat. "Yeah, she is cute."

"Ho, ho, ho!" Santa said. "And what would you like for Christmas, little girl?"

"Can you really give me what I want?" she demanded.

Rory hung his head in shame. "Oh, no. This could get ugly."

Shannon put her hand on his bicep. "Just be patient. Give her a chance."

He glanced down at her, once again grateful for her support, his heart hurting in his chest. He liked her so much. But it had all happened so fast and the choices he'd have to make were too big, but the most important thing was he didn't want to risk hurting her.

Santa boomed a laugh. Glancing at Rory and Shannon he winked. "Well, I can't make promises, but I do try my best."

"Okay, then I want you to make Shannon happy again."

Santa frowned. "What?"

Finley pointed at Shannon. "That's Shannon. She's my friend. I wish she was my mother. But this morning she got sad. Really sad." Her nose wrinkled. "I even think I saw her cry." She faced Santa. "I don't want her to be sad. Make her happy again."

Santa—aka Rick Bloom, manager of the toy department—cast an awkward look in Shannon's direction. He clearly didn't know what to say.

Shannon's eyes filled with tears. Though it was strange having a child announce her sadness in front of a roomful of kids and parents waiting to see Santa, her heart looked past that and saw the small child who cared about her enough to ask Santa to make her happy again.

Rory slowly walked over to Santa. He stooped in front of Finley. "Santa actually only handles requests for gifts."

Finley's face puckered. "Why? If he can fly around the world in one night, he can do all kinds of things."

"Yeah, but—" Obviously confused, Rory glanced back at her.

Holding back her tears, Shannon went over. She also stooped in front of Finley. "Honey, all of Santa's miracles pretty much involve toys."

"Well, that's a bummer."

Shannon couldn't help it. She laughed. Rory laughed, too. Santa chuckled. The parents waiting in line with their kids laughed and shuffled their feet.

But in spite of her laughter, Shannon's heart squeezed with love. She would miss this little girl terribly. When the tears sprang to her eyes again, she rose and whispered, "Tell Santa what toys you want for Christmas. Okay?"

Finley nodded. She glanced back at Rick and rattled

off a list of toys. Rory stepped over beside her. "I'll have to remember to get all those things."

She nodded, but turned away. Real tears burned in her throat now. He liked her. He understood her. He needed her. And his daughter liked her.

Rory's hand fell to her shoulders. "Hey. Are you okay?"

She sniffed. "Finley's just so sweet."

He laughed. "Only because of you."

Because her back was to him, she squeezed her eyes shut.

"Are you not going to look at me?"

She shook her head. If she turned around he'd see her tears and she was just plain tired of being pathetic.

A few seconds went by without him saying anything. Finally, he turned her around, saw her tears.

He looked at the ceiling then sighed. "I'm so sorry this didn't work out."

She swiped at her tears, aware that at least thirty parents, thirty *customers,* were watching her. Not to mention employees. People who didn't know her secrets. People she didn't *want* to know her secrets.

"It's fine. You want the store. That's why you came. To see the store." She swallowed again. "It's fine."

"Don't you think I wish it could have been different between us? I like you. But I'm more damaged than you are. I won't take the risk that I'll hurt you more."

She sniffed. Nodded. "I get it."

"I don't think you do—"

"Ho, ho, ho!"

Recognizing the voice as her father's, Shannon snapped her head up and spun around. "Daddy?"

Dressed as Santa himself, carrying a sack of gifts,

Dave Raleigh strode toward Santa's throne, gesturing broadly. "I'd like to thank my helper here for taking my place for a while this morning, but I'm here now." He dropped the sack just as her mom strode over.

Dressed in a festive red pantsuit, with her hair perfectly coiffed, Stacy Raleigh said, "Silly old coot. I tried to talk him out of this but you know how he loves Christmas."

Just then Finley scampered over. Her mom smiled. "And who is this?"

"Mom—" she gestured to Rory "—this is Rory Wallace."

Her mom extended her hand to shake his. "Ah, the gentleman who came to see the store."

"Yes." She motioned to Finley. "And this is his daughter, Finley."

Stacy stooped down. "Well, aren't you adorable?"

Finley said, "Yes, ma'am."

And Shannon laughed. But she also saw her way out of this painful and embarrassing situation. She caught Rory's arm and turned him in the direction of the stairway off the Santa-throne platform. "Thank you for a wonderful visit. We'll look forward to hearing from you after the holidays."

She stooped and kissed Finley's cheek. Unable to stop herself she wrapped Finley in a big hug and whispered, "I love you," in her ear.

Finley squeezed back and whispered, "I love you, too."

Then she rose and relinquished Finley into her dad's custody. She watched them walk down the stairs, then raced to the half wall of the mezzanine and watched as they squeezed through the first-floor sales floor, watched as they walked through the door and out into the falling snow.

Her mom caught her forearm. "Shannon?"

The tears welling in her eyes spilled over. "I want to go home."

CHAPTER THIRTEEN

SHANNON'S MOTHER deposited her in the living room, left and returned with a cup of tea. "Drink this."

Her tears now dried up, she took the tiny china cup and saucer from her mother's hands. "Did you remember sugar?"

Her mom smiled. "Yes."

She took a sip, closed her eyes and sighed.

"Are you going to tell me what's wrong?"

Her automatic response was to say, "I'm fine." But remembering the wonderful sense of release she had being around Rory after having confessed the truth, she wouldn't let herself lie, not even to protect her mom.

She cleared her throat. "I…um…told Rory that I couldn't have kids."

Her mom's eyes narrowed. "Why?"

"Because he was starting to like me and I felt he needed to know the truth."

Her mom's face fell in horror. "You scared him off?"

Oh, Lord. She's never thought of it that way. "I didn't want him to get involved in something that wouldn't work for him."

Stacy drew Shannon into her arms and hugged her. "You always were incredibly fair."

She squeezed her eyes shut, grateful that her mom

understood and even more grateful that the feeling that she'd done the wrong thing had disappeared. "He's a good man who wants more kids."

"And you can always adopt—"

She pulled out of her mom's embrace, caught her gaze. "I am going to adopt."

"On your own?"

"Yes."

She hugged her again. "And you always were brave, too." She squeezed her tighter. "I'm glad."

Shannon returned her mother's hug, closed her eyes and contented herself with the fact that being around Finley had given her enough confidence that she could go on with the rest of her life. So what if it was without Rory? So what if she didn't have someone she felt connected to? Someone who made her feel special? Someone who loved her unconditionally?

Her heart broke a bit. Though Rory and Finley had helped her to make the decision to adopt, she couldn't begin looking immediately. She didn't want to associate getting a child to losing Rory and Finley. She wanted her child to come into her life when she was totally over the loss.

And she didn't think she would be for a while.

Two hours later, Rory was battling traffic on I-95, wondering why so many people needed to be out on Christmas Eve. It was two o'clock in the afternoon when people should be at home with their families.

"So, then, I kinda peeked at Santa's ear and I think I saw something holding his beard on."

Rory absently said, "You might have."

"Because it was fake?"

He glanced at her. Now that she was "into" Christmas

a whole new set of problems had arisen. Her beliefs were so precarious and so fragile that he didn't want to spoil the magic. But she was a smart kid, a six-year-old, somebody who probably would have been realizing by now that Santa wasn't real.

He had no idea what to say and reached for his cell phone to call Shannon. She would know.

His hand stopped. His chest tightened. He couldn't call her. He'd hurt her. Walking out of Raleigh's he'd convinced himself that leaving was sad, but justified, because he wasn't sure he loved her and didn't want to hurt her. But that was a rationalization. He had already hurt her. In a few short days, they'd fallen into some romantic place where it didn't matter if they wanted to like each other. It didn't matter if they spent every waking minute together or thirty seconds a day—they still wanted more. They'd clicked, connected.

But he was afraid.

Who was he kidding? He was terrified.

"So was his beard fake?"

He glanced at Finley, all bright eyes and childlike smiles. "Well, you saw the real Santa come in and take over. So the guy whose lap you sat on was like his helper." A thought came to him and he ran with it. "There's a Santa in every shopping mall around the world for the six weeks before Christmas. The real one can't be in all those places. So he trains lots of helpers."

"Oh." She frowned, considering that.

A few miles went by with Rory maneuvering in and out of the traffic. He spent the time alternating between wondering if he'd told Finley the right thing and forcing his mind away from the sure knowledge that Shannon would have known exactly what to say. Then a worse thing happened. Suddenly, he began wishing he could call her tonight and tell her about this conversation.

"So if there are lots of Santas, that explains how he gets everywhere on Christmas Eve to deliver presents."

"Exactly."

"So that means not everybody gets a real Santa. Most of us get a fake!"

Panicked, Rory glanced at her. "No. No. He's a special magic guy who can go around the world all in one night. Because he's special." He floundered, grasping for words. "Magic. It all has to do with magic."

"But you told me magic is just some guy who knows how to do things really fast or by getting you to look away from what he's really doing."

Caught in the web of an explanation he'd given Finley after they'd seen a young man doing magic tricks on the beach a few months before, he wanted to bounce his head off the steering wheel. This is what he got for having a super-intelligent child. "That is true with most magic. But this is Christmas magic."

"What's the difference?"

He peered over at Finley again. Shannon would have handled this so easily. She would have told Finley the truth. And maybe that was what he needed to do. Tell her the truth. Not the big truth that Santa wasn't real. But the other truth. The truth most parents hated admitting.

"I don't know."

"Why not?"

"Because I'm a guy who buys stores and fixes them up so that they make lots of money. I'm not the guy in charge of Santa. So I'm not in on those secrets."

She nodded sagely, leaned back in her car seat. "I miss Shannon."

He struggled with the urge to close his eyes. Not in frustration this time, but because he missed Shannon, too. He swallowed. "So do I."

"She was pretty."

Gorgeous. He couldn't count the times he'd longed to run his fingers through her thick, springy black curls. He couldn't count the times he'd noticed that her eyes changed shades of blue depending upon what she wore. He couldn't count the time he'd itched to touch her, yearned to kiss her, thought about making love to her.

"She was smart, too."

He'd definitely have to agree with that. Not only was there a noticeable difference in Raleigh's income from when her dad ran the store and when she'd taken over, but she also ran that store like a tight ship. And she always knew what to say to him, how to handle Finley.

She'd thought of sled riding and baking a cake on days when he probably would have been stumped for entertainment for himself, let alone himself and a six-year-old.

A pain surrounded his heart like the glow of a firefly. He could still see her laughing as she slid down the hill on her saucer sled, hear her screams of terror that turned into squeals of delight when he forced her down the big hill on the runner sled.

His throat thickened. He could also remember the sorrow in her voice when she told him she couldn't have kids. She believed herself unlovable—

It hurt to even think that, because she was the easiest person to love he'd ever met.

He drove another mile or two before the truth of that

really hit him. Not that she was easy to love, but that he knew that. How could he know she was easy to love, if he didn't love her?

Shannon's dad arrived home around five. The store stayed open until nine for late shoppers, but Santa's throne was deserted at five with a note that told children that he was on his way to the North Pole to begin delivering gifts.

In the kitchen, where Shannon and her mom were making Christmas Eve supper, he shrugged out of his coat. He'd already removed his fake beard and white wig, but his salt-and-pepper hair had been flattened against his head. He still wore the Santa suit but the top two buttons of the jacket were undone. "So what did Wallace have to say? Is he going to buy the store?"

Shannon watched her mom shoot her dad one of those warning looks only a wife can give a husband and she laughed. "It's okay, Mom. We can talk about it."

Her dad headed for the table. "Talk about what?"

"About Rory Wallace breaking our daughter's heart."

His eyes widened, his forehead creased. "What?"

Shannon batted a hand. She didn't mind talking to her mom, but her dad had a tendency to make mountains out of mole hills. "I'm fine. We just sort of began to get close while he was here and I might have taken a few things he said to heart that he didn't mean."

"Scoundrel!"

"No, Dad. It was me. We were attracted, but he sort of laid everything out on the table early on in the week. He had a wife who left him, who doesn't want anything to do with their daughter."

He fell to one of the chairs at the table. "Oh."

"Then he mentioned a time or two that he loved being a dad and wanted more kids."

He glanced up sharply, held her gaze. "You're not out of that game. You can always adopt."

Though she and her father had never come right out and talked about this, she wasn't surprised that he'd thought it through, that he'd already come to this conclusion. She smiled shakily. "I know."

"So what's the deal? Why can't we talk about him?"

"Because in spite of the fact that I knew we weren't a good match I sort of let myself fall." She sucked in a breath. "But I'm okay now. And I can tell you that he's definitely interested in the store. He has to talk to his family first."

"Maybe I don't want to sell it to him."

For the first time in hours, she laughed. "Don't cut off your nose to spite your face. The Wallaces own a big company, with lots of capital. I'm sure they'll make you a very fair offer."

"Everything in life isn't about money."

She laughed again, glowing with the fact that her dad loved her enough not to take a deal. Even though that was idiotic and she planned to talk him out of it, she said, "That's the first time you've ever said that."

"Well, it's true." He scooted his chair closer to the table. "Are we going to eat tonight or what?"

His mom brought him a drink. "It's only a little after five. I invited Mary to dinner at seven. Have a drink, go get a shower, and before you know it Mary will be here."

A sudden knock at the door had her mom turning around. "Maybe she's early?"

"Maybe," Shannon said, heading out of the kitchen.

"But, seriously, Dad, supper's not ready until seven. So you might as well get a shower."

With that she pushed through the swinging door and walked up the hall. She opened the door with a jolly "Merry Christmas," only to have Finley propel herself at her knees.

"Merry Christmas, Shannon!"

Shocked, she looked up at Rory. Their gazes caught. "Merry Christmas, Shannon."

Her heart tumbled in her chest. It was wonderful to see them. Fabulous that they were still in Pennsylvania this late. That probably meant they wanted to share Christmas with her.

But it was also bad because she'd finally, finally stopped crying and finally, finally reminded herself that she could adopt on her own. Create the family she wanted. Seeing them again only brought back her sad sensations of loss.

"Can we come in?"

Shaking herself out of her stunned state, she said, "Yes. Yes, of course."

Her mom pushed open the kitchen door and came into the hall. Obviously expecting to see Mary, she frowned. "Oh, Mr. Wallace? What can we do for you?"

"Actually, I'd like to talk to Shannon."

Her mother's perfectly shaped brows arched in question.

Shannon said, "My dad is here. If you want to talk about the store…"

He caught her gaze again. "I want to talk to you. Privately."

Finley huffed out a sigh, walked to Shannon's mom. "That means he wants us to go." She caught Stacy's hand. "We can make cocoa."

Stacy laughed. "I'll give you five minutes. After that, I won't be responsible for what the kitchen looks like."

When the kitchen door swung closed behind them, Shannon stood staring it at. After a few seconds, Rory put his hands on her shoulders, turned her around.

"First, I'm sorry."

She shrunk back. "That's okay. I get it. You had to go." She smiled sheepishly. "I'm surprised you're here now. Isn't your family going to miss you?"

"My parents are in Arizona with my sister and her family for the holiday."

"Oh. So this will be good for Finley then—"

He tightened his hold on her shoulders. "Stop. I'm trying to tell you something here." He sucked in a breath. "I think I love you. I know it's crazy. We've known each other only a few days. But hear me out. We've both been hurt. So we're both smart about love. We don't give away our hearts frivolously, so for me to have lost mine, I know this has to be right. Now you can argue, but I—"

Catching his cheeks in her hands, Shannon rose to her tiptoes and pressed her mouth to his. She let the joy of following an impulse flow through her as she deepened the kiss, expressed every ounce of crazy feeling inside of her through one hot press of her mouth to his.

Then she pulled away, stared into his eyes and said the words she'd been aching to say for days. "I love you, too."

He grinned. "Really? In a few days? You don't think we're crazy?"

"Oh, we're definitely crazy, but that's okay." She patted her chest with her right hand. "I know here that it's right."

"So you won't think it out of line for me to ask you to marry me?"

"I think it will go easier on us at the adoption agency if we're married."

He sucked in a breath. "So you won't mind adopting kids? Because I really do want to raise more kids."

"We can adopt seven if you want."

He laughed, caught her around the waist and hauled her to him. This time he kissed her. He let his tongue swirl around hers, nudged her so close that their hearts beat against each other. Savored the moment he knew, truly knew, that he loved her.

And that this time love would last.

Then he heard the swinging door open and he broke the kiss. Seeing Finley slinking into the foyer, he smiled down at Shannon and nudged his head in the direction of his daughter, alerting her to Finley's presence.

"So now that all that's settled, Finley would like to know how Santa gets all around the world in one night."

Her eyes widened in horror. "Seriously, you want me to field this?"

"I already tried and failed."

Smiling, Finley blinked at her expectantly.

She glanced up at him and he raised his eyebrows, letting her know he, too, was eager to hear what she said.

She stooped in front of Finley. "Santa's sleigh is powered by love."

Finley squinted. "Love?"

"It's the love of all the parents in the world that gets his sleigh to get to every house in one night."

Finley pondered that, but Rory's heart expanded. Leave it to Shannon to know exactly what to say. Was it any wonder he loved her?

Shannon glanced up at Rory and said, "Without love nothing really works." She looked back at Finley. "But with love, everything works." She hugged her tightly, then rose and wrapped her arms around Rory. "You do realize we have to sleep on the floor."

"Huh?"

"My parents get the bedroom. We get the sleeping bags—"

Finley let out a whoop of joy. "And I get the sofa!" She headed for the living room. "Let's turn on the fireplace. Oh, and the tree lights. We can have the tree lights on all night!"

Rory cast a confused look toward the living room. "Do you think she'll fall asleep long enough for me to grab the gifts I bought Thursday afternoon from the back of my trunk?"

Shannon laughed. "She better."

"Or?"

She nestled against him. "Or we won't get any snuggle time, either."

Rory said, "Ah." Then he bent his head and kissed her.

EPILOGUE

THE FOLLOWING Christmas Eve, Rory stood near the half wall of the mezzanine watching Finley play Santa's helper. Over the course of the year that had passed, she'd finally caught on to the whole Santa thing. Due in no small part to the new friends she'd made in Green Hill when he and Shannon had bought Mary O'Grady's house. She'd thought the place too big and decided she liked Shannon's house better, so they'd swapped. She took the little house that was remodeled. They got the old house and were in the process of redoing it to accommodate at least four kids.

Finley had discovered a little girl her age about a mile up the road and they'd had enough play dates that they behaved more like sisters than friends. Right now Finley and Gwen wore little green-and-red elf suits with red-and-green-striped tights. Each held a clipboard and pen. They were the naughty and nice elves, writing down names. Finley kept track of the nice. Gwen was in charge of naughty. Funny thing was, Santa never put a kid on the naughty list. Only the nice.

Shaking his head, Rory laughed and glanced down at the first-floor sales floor. Hundreds of customers swarmed around tables and racks. The line at the candy department was six deep. Congratulating himself on the money they'd be making, he glanced at the door and straightened suddenly.

Shannon's parents had arrived. Early.

As if they had radar, they headed for the mezzanine steps. Within seconds, they were beside him.

"Hey, Rory!" Stacy hugged him.

"Rory." A bit more standoffish, Shannon's dad reluctantly offered his hand to shake his.

"I'm glad you're here early. You can see Finley in action."

Stacy glanced over. "Oh, she's adorable!"

Even Shannon's dad's expression softened a bit. "She's quite a kid."

"Due in no small part to your daughter," Rory said, desperately trying to make points with this guy, who still wasn't over the fact that Rory had left Christmas Eve the year before. Never mind that he'd come back and proposed marriage to his daughter even though they'd only known each other a week. Nope. Dave still held a grudge. "She's a wonderful mother. I couldn't raise Finley without her."

Stacy looked around. "Speaking of Shannon, where is she?"

He didn't know. She'd been missing in action all morning and he wasn't sure it was wise to tell her parents that. He hadn't lost her. She was a grown woman, allowed to go Christmas shopping on her own if she chose, but somehow he didn't think her dad would like that answer.

Still, he sucked in a breath, ready to say, "I'm not

sure where she is," when he saw Shannon get off the elevator and stride toward him.

The happy expression on her face hit him right in the heart. He couldn't believe he'd almost walked away from her the year before.

She strode over, directly into his open arms. "Can I talk to you?"

He turned her to see that her parents were already there.

"Mom? Dad? You're early."

Her dad scowled. "Why, is that bad?"

"It's not bad, Dad. It's just that I have something to tell Rory."

Her dad harrumphed. "You can tell him in front of us...unless there's something wrong."

"Nothing wrong," Rory assured him, then prayed there wasn't.

Shannon cleared her throat. "Okay, then—" She slid her arm around Rory again. "I've spent the morning with the adoption agency." She turned in Rory's arms. "Melissa Graham had her baby. She chose us as the parents."

Rory's heart stopped. As he grabbed Shannon and hugged her, he noticed Shannon's parents' faces fall in disbelief. "We get a baby?"

Her eyes glowed. "A boy."

His breath stuttered out. "A boy."

She hugged him again. "A baby. Our baby boy."

The speakers above them began to play the hallelujah chorus. Shannon laughed. Rory bit back tears, not wanting Shannon's dad to see him cry.

Pulling out of his embrace, Shannon said, "Who gets to tell Finley that she's about to be a big sister?"

Rory turned her toward Santa's throne. He put his arm around Stacy's shoulders and tugged on Shannon's dad's arm. "Let's tell her together."

* * * * *

THE DOCTOR'S
CHRISTMAS BRIDE

SARAH MORGAN

PROLOGUE

'MUMMY, I've written my letter to Santa.'

Bryony tucked the duvet round her daughter and clicked on the pink bedside light. A warm glow spread across the room, illuminating a small mountain of soft toys and dressing-up clothes. 'Sweetheart, it's only just November. Don't you think it's a little early to be writing to Santa?'

'All the decorations are in the shops. I saw them with Grandma.'

Bryony picked up a fairy outfit that had been abandoned in a heap on the floor. 'Shops are different, Lizzie.' She slipped the dress onto a hanger and put it safely in the wardrobe. 'They always start selling things early. It's still ages until Christmas.'

'But I know what I want, so I thought I might as well write to him now.' Lizzie reached for the stuffed mermaid that she always slept with. 'And anyway, this present is special so he might need some time to find exactly the right one.'

'Special?' Bryony gave a groan and picked up the book they'd been reading all week. 'Go on.' Her tone was indulgent. 'Hit me with it, Lizzie. What is it this time—a horse?' She toed off her shoes and curled up on the end of her daughter's bed with a smile. This was the best time of the day. Just the two of them, and Lizzie all warm and cuddly in her pink pyjamas. She smelt of shampoo and innocence, and when she

5

was tucked up in bed she seemed younger somehow, less like a seven-year-old who was growing up too fast.

'Not a horse.' Lizzie snuggled down, her blonde curls framing her pretty face. 'Bigger.'

'Bigger than a *horse*?' Bryony's eyes twinkled. 'You're scaring me, Lizzie. What if Santa can't find this special present?'

'He will.' Lizzie spoke with the conviction of youth. 'You said that Santa always gives you what you ask for if you're good.'

'Ah—did I say that?' Bryony took a deep breath and made a mental note to concentrate more when she answered her daughter's questions in future. 'Well, it does depend on what you ask for,' she hedged, and Lizzie's face fell.

'You said he *always* gives you what you ask for if you're good.'

'Well, he certainly does his best,' Bryony said finally, compromising slightly and hoping that the request wasn't going to be too outlandish. Her doctor's salary was generous, but she was a single mother and she had to watch her expenditures. 'Do you want to show me this letter?'

'I've sent it already.'

'You've sent it?' Bryony looked at her daughter in surprise. 'Where did you post it?'

'I went into the post office with Grandma and they said that if I posted it there it would go all the way to Santa in Lapland.'

'Oh.' Bryony smiled weakly, her heart sinking. 'So it's gone, then.'

Which meant that there would be no chance to talk

Lizzie out of whatever it was that she'd chosen that was obviously going to cost a fortune and be impossible to find in the wilds of the Lake District.

Bryony sensed a trip to London coming on. Unless the internet could oblige.

'Uh-huh.' Lizzie nodded. 'And he's got until Christmas to sort it out.'

'Right. Are you going to give me a clue?'

'You'll like it, I know you will.'

'Is it something messy?'

'Nope.'

'Something pink?' Everything in her daughter's life was pink so it was a fairly safe bet that whatever was top of her Christmas list would be pink.

Lizzie shook her head and her eyes shone. 'Not pink.'

Not pink?

Feeling distinctly uneasy, Bryony hoped that her mother had managed to sneak a look at the letter before it was 'posted' otherwise none of them were going to have the first clue what Lizzie wanted for Christmas.

'I'd really like to know, sweetheart,' she said casually, flipping through the pages of the book until she found where they'd left off the night before. She wondered whether the post office had binned the letter. At this rate she was going to have to go and ask for it back.

'OK. I'll tell you, because it's sort of for you, too.'

Bryony held her breath, hoping desperately that it wasn't a pet. Her life was so frantic she absolutely didn't have time to care for an animal on top of everything else. A full-time job and single parenthood was the most she could manage and sometimes she struggled with that.

A pet would be the final straw.

But then she looked at Lizzie's sweet face and felt totally overwhelmed by love. More than anything she wanted her daughter to be happy and if that meant cleaning out a rabbit…

'Whatever it is you want,' Bryony said softly, reaching out and stroking her daughter's silken curls with a gentle hand, 'I'm sure Santa will get it for you. You're such a good girl and I love you.'

'I love you, too, Mummy.' Lizzie reached up and hugged her and Bryony felt a lump building in her throat.

'OK.' She extracted herself and gave her daughter a bright smile. 'So, what is it you want for Christmas?'

Lizzie lay back on the pillow, a contented smile spreading across her face. 'A daddy,' she breathed happily. 'For Christmas this year, I really, *really* want a daddy. And I *know* that Santa is going to bring me one.'

CHAPTER ONE

'Six-month-old baby coming in with breathing difficulties.' Bryony replaced the phone that connected the accident and emergency department direct to Ambulance Control and turned to the A and E sister. 'That's the third one today, Nicky.'

'Welcome to A and E in November.' The other woman pulled a face and slipped her pen back in her pocket. 'One respiratory virus after another. Wait until the weather gets really cold. Then everyone falls over on the ice. Last year we had forty-two wrist fractures in one day.'

Bryony laughed. 'Truly?'

'Truly. And you wouldn't laugh if you'd been working here then,' Nicky said dryly as they walked towards the ambulance bay together. 'It was unbelievable. I wanted to go out with a loudhailer and tell everyone to stay at home.'

As she finished speaking they heard the shriek of an ambulance siren, and seconds later the doors to the department crashed open and the paramedics hurried in with the baby.

'Take her straight into Resus,' Bryony ordered, taking one look at the baby and deciding that she was going to need help on this one. 'What's the story?'

'She's had a cold and a runny nose for a couple of days,' the paramedic told her. 'Temperature going up and down, and then all of a sudden she stopped taking

9

any fluids and tonight the mother said she stopped breathing. Mother came with us in the ambulance—she's giving the baby's details to Reception.'

'Did she call the GP?'

'Yes, but he advised her to call 999.'

'Right.' Bryony glanced at Nicky. 'Let's get her undressed so that I can examine her properly. I want her on a cardiac monitor and a pulse oximeter—I need to check her oxygen saturation.'

'She's breathing very fast,' Nicky murmured as she undid the poppers on the baby's sleepsuit. 'Poor little mite, she's really struggling. I suppose we ought to call Jack—even though calling him will massage his ego.'

Bryony looked at the baby, saw the bluish tinge around her lips and heard the faint grunting sound as she breathed.

'Call him,' she said firmly. 'This baby is sick.'

Very sick.

She didn't care if they massaged Jack's ego. She trusted his opinion more than anyone else's and not just because he was the consultant and she was a casualty officer with only four months' A and E experience behind her. Jack Rothwell was an incredibly talented doctor.

Nicky finished undressing the baby and then picked up the phone on the wall and dialled, leaving Bryony to carry out her examination. She watched the baby breathing for a moment and then placed her stethoscope in her ears, strands of blonde hair falling forward as she bent and listened to the child's chest.

When she finally unhooked the stethoscope from her ears, Jack was standing opposite, looking at her with that lazy, half-bored expression in his blue eyes that always drove women crazy.

And she was no exception.

She'd known him for twenty-two years and still her knees went weak when he walked into a room. She'd often tried to work out why. Was it the sexy smile? The wicked blue eyes that crinkled at the corners when he smiled? The glossy dark hair? The broad shoulders? Or was it his sense of humour, which had her smiling almost all the time? Eventually she'd come to the conclusion that it was everything. The whole drop-dead-gorgeous, confident masculine package that was Jack Rothwell.

When she'd started working in A and E in the summer, she'd been worried about how it would feel to work with a man she'd known all her life. She was worried that finally working together would feel odd. But it didn't.

She'd fast discovered that Jack at work was the same as Jack not at work. Clever, confident and wickedly sexy.

'So, Blondie,' his deep masculine tones were loaded with humour. 'You need some help?'

Blondie...

Bryony grinned. He'd called her 'Blondie' when she'd been five years old, and now she was twenty-seven he was still calling her 'Blondie'. She'd even had a brush with being brunette at one point in her teens but it had made no difference. He'd still called her 'Blondie'. It was one of the things she loved about their friendship. The way he teased her. It made her feel special. And, anyway, it meant that she could tease him back.

'This baby's sick.'

'Which is presumably why she's in hospital,' Jack drawled, leaning across and reaching for her stethoscope, the fabric of his shirt moulding lovingly to the hard muscle of his shoulders. Despite his teasing words his eyes were on the baby, looking, assessing, mentally cataloguing his findings.

Bryony watched him with admiration and more than a touch of envy. His instincts were so good. If anyone she loved ever ended up in A and E, the doctor she'd want them to see would be Jack. He had a brilliant brain and an amazing ability to identify medical problems based on seemingly scanty information. And she'd learned more from him in her four months in A and E than she had from any other doctor in her career so far.

'So what did you notice, Blondie? Apart from the fact that there's a little patient on the trolley?'

He stood back while Nicky attached leads to the baby's chest and connected them to the monitor.

'She's cyanosed, has intercostal recession and she's grunting,' Bryony said immediately, her eyes on the baby. 'Her resps are 60 per minute and she's becoming exhausted.'

Jack nodded, his eyes flickering to the monitor, which was now operational and giving them further clues to the baby's condition.

'She has acute bronchiolitis. We need to get a line in this baby fast,' he ordered softly, holding out a hand to Nicky who immediately proffered the necessary equipment. He handed it to Bryony. 'Go on. Impress me.'

'You want me to do it?' Bryony looked at those

tiny arms and legs and shook her head. 'I'd rather you did it.'

She could see how ill the baby was and she didn't have the confidence that she'd get the line in first time. She knew Jack could. And with the baby that sick, his skill was more important than her need to practise.

His eyes narrowed and his gaze was suddenly serious. 'Don't doubt yourself,' he said softly, his blue eyes searching as he read her mind. 'Do it.'

He was still holding out the equipment and Bryony sucked in a breath. 'Jack, I—'

'Can do it,' he said calmly, those wicked blue eyes locking on hers. 'In three months' time you're going to be working on the paediatric ward and you're going to be taking blood all the time. You need the practise. Go for it.'

Bryony hesitated and Jack lifted an eyebrow, his blue eyes mocking.

'You want me to hold your hand?' His voice was a lazy drawl and Bryony blushed. How could he be so relaxed? But she knew the answer to that, of course. During her time in the A and E department she'd learned that panic did nothing to improve a tense situation and she'd also learned that Jack's totally laid-back attitude to everything rubbed off on the rest of the staff. As a result, they operated as a smooth, efficient team.

Looking at the baby, Bryony bit her lip and lifted the child's tiny wrist.

'Relax. Take your time.' Jack closed long, strong fingers around the baby's wrist and squeezed. 'OK.

Here's one for you. What do you call a blonde with half a brain?'

Bryony was concentrating on the baby's wrist. She found a tiny, thready vein and wondered how she was ever going to hit such a tiny target. It seemed almost impossible.

'Gifted,' Jack said cheerfully, squinting down at the baby's hand. 'You'll be fine. She's got good veins. Stop dithering and just do it.'

So she did and the needle slid smoothly into the tiny vein on her first attempt.

Relief and delight flooded through her.

'I did it.' She looked up, unable to hide her pride, and Jack smiled, his eyes creasing at the corners.

'As I said. Gifted. Now you just need the confidence to go with it. You're a good doctor. Believe in yourself.' His eyes held hers for a moment and then he looked at Nicky. 'OK, we need a full blood count, U and Es, BMG, blood culture and viral titres. And Nicky, let's give the child some humidified oxygen.'

Believe in yourself.

Well, she did believe in herself. Sort of. It was just that she was afraid of making a mistake and Jack Rothwell never seemed to be afraid of anything. He just did it. And it turned out right every time.

Bryony busied herself taking the necessary samples. 'Should I do arterial blood gases?'

'They can do them on the ward,' Jack said immediately. 'Nicky, can you call Paeds and get them up here? This little one is going to need admitting. She's a poorly baby.'

Bryony looked at him. 'You think it's bronchiolitis?'

'Without a doubt.' He smothered a yawn and looked at her apologetically. 'Sorry. I was up half the night.'

It was Bryony's turn to look mocking. 'Was she nice?'

'She was gorgeous.' He grinned, that wonderful slightly lopsided grin that affected her knees so acutely. 'She was also eighty-four and had a fractured hip.'

'You love older women.'

'True.' He checked the monitor again. 'But generally I like them mobile. OK, Blondie. What's the likely causative organism here? Exercise your brain cell and impress me twice in one evening.'

'RSV,' Bryony said immediately. 'Respiratory syncytial virus causes 75 per cent of cases of bronchiolitis.'

He inclined his head, his expression mocking. 'All right, you've impressed me. And you've obviously been studying your textbook again. Now we'll do some maths. What's two plus two?' His eyes were dancing. 'No need to answer immediately and you can use your fingers if you need to. Take your time— I know it's tricky.'

'No idea,' Bryony returned blithely, batting her eyelashes in a parody of a dumb blonde and handing the bottles to Nicky for labelling. 'Jack, should we pass a nasogastric tube?'

'No. Not yet.' He shook his head, his gaze flickering over the baby. 'When you've finished taking the samples we'll set up an IV and get her to the ward. I've got a bad feeling about this little one. She's going to end up being ventilated.'

'I hope not,' Bryony murmured, but she knew that Jack was always right in his predictions. If he thought the baby was going to need ventilating, then it was almost certain that she would.

He looked at her quizzically. 'Is the mother around?'

As he asked the question the doors to Resus opened and the paramedics came back in, escorting a tall woman wrapped in a wool coat. Her face was pale and her hair was uncombed.

'Ella?' She hurried over to the trolley, her face lined with anxiety, and then she looked at Jack.

Bryony didn't mind that. She was used to it. Women always looked at Jack.

Even before they knew he was the consultant, they looked at him.

And it wasn't just because he was staggeringly, movie-star handsome. It was because he was charming and had an air of casual self-assurance that attracted women like magnets. You just knew that Jack would know what to do in any situation.

'I'm Dr Rothwell.' He extended a hand and gave her that reassuring smile that always seemed to calm the most frantic relative. 'I've been caring for Ella, along with Dr Hunter here.'

The woman didn't even glance at Bryony. Her gaze stayed firmly fixed on Jack. 'She's been ill for days but I thought it was just a cold and then suddenly today she seemed to go downhill.' She lifted a shaking hand to her throat. 'She wouldn't take her bottle and she was *so* hot and then tonight she stopped breathing properly and I was *terrified*.'

Jack nodded, his blue eyes warm and understanding. 'It's always frightening when a baby of this size is ill because their airways are so small,' he explained calmly. 'Ella has picked up a nasty virus and it is affecting her breathing.'

The woman blanched and stared at the tiny figure on the trolley. 'But she's going to be OK?'

'We need to admit her to hospital,' Jack said, glancing up as the paediatrician walked into the room. 'This is Dr Armstrong, the paediatric registrar. He's going to take a look at her now and then we'll take her along to the ward.'

'Will I be able to stay with her?'

'Absolutely.' Jack nodded, his gaze reassuring. 'You can have a bed next to her cot.'

Deciding that Jack was never going to be able to extricate himself from the mother, Bryony briefed Dr Armstrong on the baby's condition.

She liked David Armstrong. He was warm and kind and he'd asked her out on several occasions.

And she'd refused of course. Because she always refused.

She *never* went on dates.

Bryony bit her lip, remembering Lizzie's letter to Santa. She wanted a daddy for Christmas. A pretty tall order for a woman who didn't date men, she thought dryly, picking up the baby's charts and handing them to David.

Dragging her mind back, she finished handing over and watched while David examined the baby himself.

A thoroughly nice man, she decided wistfully. So why couldn't she just accept his invitation to take their friendship a step further?

And then Jack strolled back to the trolley, tall,

broad-shouldered, confident and so shockingly handsome that it made her gasp, and she remembered the
reason why she didn't date men.

She didn't date men because she'd been in love
with Jack since she'd been five years old. And apart
from her one disastrous attempt to forget about him,
which had resulted in Lizzie, she hadn't even *noticed*
another man for her entire adult life.

Which just went to show how stupid she was, she
reflected crossly, infuriated by her own stupidity.

Jack might be a brilliant doctor but he was also the
most totally unsuitable man any woman could fall for.
Women had affairs with Jack. They didn't fall in love
with him. Not if they had any sense, because Jack
had no intention of ever falling in love or settling
down.

But, of course, she didn't have any sense.

It was fortunate that she'd got used to hiding the
way she felt about him. He didn't have a clue that
he'd featured in every daydream she'd had since
she'd been a child. When other little girls had
dreamed about faceless princes in fairy-tales, she'd
dreamed about Jack. When her teenage friends had
developed crushes on the boys at school, she'd still
dreamed about Jack. And when she'd finally matured
into a woman, she'd carried on dreaming about Jack.

Finally the baby was stable enough to be transferred to the ward and Nicky pushed the trolley, accompanied by the paediatric SHO, who had arrived
to help, and the baby's mother.

Bryony started to tidy up Resus, ready for the next
arrival, her mind elsewhere.

'Are you all right?' David Armstrong gave her a curious look. 'You're miles away.'

'Sorry.' She smiled. 'Just thinking.'

'Hard work, that, for a blonde,' Jack said mildly, and Bryony gave him a sunny smile, relaxed now that the baby was no longer her responsibility.

'Why are men like bank accounts?' she asked sweetly, ditching some papers in the bin. 'Because without a lot of money they don't generate much interest.'

David looked startled but Jack threw back his head and laughed.

'Then it's fortunate for me that I have a lot of money,' he said strolling across the room to her and looping her stethoscope back round her neck.

For a moment he stood there, looking down at her, his eyes laughing into hers as he kept hold of the ends of the stethoscope. Bryony looked back at him, hypnotised by the dark shadow visible on his hard jaw and the tiny muscle that worked in his cheek. He was so close she could almost touch him, but she'd never been allowed to do that.

Not properly.

He was her best friend.

They talked, they laughed and they spent huge amounts of time together. But they never crossed that line of friendship.

Jack's pager sounded and he let go of the stethoscope and reached into his pocket. 'Duty calls. If you're sure you can cope without me, I'll be off.'

'I'll struggle on,' Bryony said sarcastically, and he gave her that lazy wink that always reduced her legs to jelly.

'You do that. I'll see you later, then. Are you joining the team at the Drunken Fox tonight?'

'Yes. Mum's babysitting.'

The whole of the local mountain rescue team were meeting for a drink to celebrate her brother's birthday.

'Good.' He gave a nod. 'See you there, then.'

And with that he strolled out of the room with his usual easy confidence, letting the door swing closed behind him.

David stared after him. 'Don't you mind the blonde jokes and the fact that he calls you Blondie?'

Bryony shot him an amused look. 'He's called me that for twenty-two years.' She fiddled with the stethoscope that Jack had looped round her neck. 'He's just teasing.'

'You've known him for *twenty-two years*?'

'Amazing that I'm still sane, isn't it?' Bryony said lightly. 'Jack was at school with my two brothers but he spent more time in our house than his own.' *Mainly because his parents had been going through a particularly acrimonious divorce.*

'He's practically family. He and my brothers were at medical school together.'

Nicky entered the room in time to hear that last remark. 'I bet the three of them were lethal.'

'They certainly were.'

David looked at her in surprise. 'Of course—why didn't I realise before? Tom Hunter, the consultant obstetrician—he's your brother?'

Bryony smiled. 'That's right. And my other brother, Oliver, is a GP. When I've finished my rotation I'm going to join him in his practice. He's the reason for the trip to the pub—it's his birthday today.'

Not that they needed an excuse for a trip to the pub. Most of the mountain rescue team members lived in the pub when they weren't working, training or on a callout.

David looked at her. 'I can't believe that I didn't click sooner that Tom Hunter is your brother.'

Bryony shrugged. 'Well, we don't know each other that well.'

'And whose fault is that?' David said in an undertone. 'I keep asking you out.'

And she kept refusing.

Conscious that Nicky was within earshot, Bryony handed David the last of the charts. 'Here you go. Everything you need on baby Ella. I hope she does OK.'

'Thanks.' He hesitated and then gave her a smile as he walked out of Resus.

'That man fancies you,' Nicky said dryly, and Bryony sighed.

'Yes, I know.'

'Don't tell me, you're in love with Jack, the same as every other woman on the planet.'

Bryony looked at her, carefully keeping her expression casual. She'd never admitted to *anyone* how she felt about Jack, and she wasn't going to start now. 'Jack's my best friend. I know him far too well to ever fall in love with him.'

'Then you're more sensible than the rest of the female population,' Nicky said happily. 'Every woman I know is in love with Jack Rothwell. He's rich, single and sexy as sin. And most of us could scratch your eyes out for being so close to him. According to rumour, he spends half his life hanging around your kitchen.'

Bryony smiled. When she'd lived at home Jack had always been there, and when she'd moved into her own cottage he'd taken to dropping round so often that he was almost part of the furniture. 'Don't get the wrong idea. Usually he's telling me about his latest girlfriend. He's my brothers' closest friend, he's my daughter's godfather and we've been in the mountain rescue team together for years. I can assure you there's nothing romantic about our relationship.'

Unfortunately.

Nicky sighed. 'Well, it sounds pretty good to me. I'd love to have him in my kitchen, if only for his decorative qualities. The guy is sublime.'

'Nicky, you're married.'

Nicky grinned. 'I know. But my hormones are still alive and kicking.'

Bryony busied herself restocking one of the equipment trays. Strictly speaking it wasn't her job but she didn't want to look at Nicky in case she gave herself away.

Her relationship with Jack was good.

They had a fantastic friendship.

But even the most fantastic friendship didn't soothe the ache in her heart.

She was about to say something else to Nicky when the doors to Resus opened again and one of the paramedics stuck his head round.

'Has the baby been transferred to the ward? Only I've got her father here.'

'I'll speak to him,' Bryony said immediately, glad

to be given an excuse to get away from the subject of Jack. She followed the paramedic out of the room.

A tall man in a suit was hovering anxiously in the corridor, his face white with strain.

'I'm Dr Hunter,' Bryony said, holding out her hand. 'I've been looking after Ella.'

'Oh, God...' he breathed out slowly, obviously trying to calm himself down. 'I came as soon as Pam called me but I was at a meeting in Penrith and the traffic was awful.'

Bryony gave an understanding smile and slowly outlined Ella's condition, careful to be realistic without painting too grim a picture.

'So she's on the ward?' He ran a hand over the back of his neck and gave a shuddering sigh. 'Sorry. I know I'm panicking like mad but she's my baby and—'

'It's OK,' Bryony said gently, putting a hand on his arm. 'You're her father and you're entitled to be worried.'

His shoulders sagged and he looked exhausted. 'You don't know what worry is until you have kids, do you?'

Bryony thought of Lizzie and shook her head. 'No,' she agreed softly, 'you certainly don't.'

'Do you have children yourself, Doctor?'

'I have a little girl.'

They shared a smile of mutual understanding. 'And the bond between a little girl and her daddy is so special, isn't it?'

Bryony tensed and then she smiled. 'It certainly is,' she croaked, feeling as though she'd been showered with cold water. 'Very special.'

She directed the man to the children's ward and stared after him, feeling sick inside.

She loved Lizzie so fiercely that she rarely thought about the fact that her little girl didn't have a father. She had plenty of father figures—her two brothers and Jack, and she'd always consoled herself that they were enough. But Lizzie obviously didn't think so or why would she have asked for a father for Christmas?

Lizzie wanted the real thing. She wanted a father to tuck her up at night. A father who would read to her and play with her. *A father who would panic and leave a meeting because she was sick.*

Bryony gave a groan and covered her face with her hands. How was she ever going to satisfy Lizzie's Christmas wish this year?

How was she going to produce a father when she didn't even date men and hadn't since Lizzie had been conceived? And not even then, really.

Bryony let her hands drop to her sides, torn with guilt at how selfish she'd been. Because of the way she felt about Jack, she'd shut men out of her life, never thinking about the long-term effect that would have on Lizzie.

It was true that she didn't want a man in her life, but it was also true that Lizzie needed and wanted a father.

And suddenly Bryony made a decision.

She was going to stop dreaming about Jack Rothwell. She was going to stop noticing his broad shoulders. She was going to stop noticing the way his cheeks creased when he smiled. She was going to stop thinking about what he looked like with his shirt off.

In fact, she was going to stop thinking about him altogether and start dating other men.

Finally she was going to get a life.

And Lizzie was going to get a daddy.

CHAPTER TWO

BRYONY paused outside the entrance to the pub, her breath clouding the freezing air. She could hear the muffled sounds of laughter and music coming from inside, and she lifted her chin and pushed open the door.

They were all there. The whole of the mountain rescue team, most of whom she'd known for years, crowding the bar and laughing together. In one corner of the bar a log fire crackled and the room was warm and welcoming.

'It's Blondie!'

There were good-natured catcalls from the moment they spotted her and Toby, the equipment officer, slipped off his stool and offered it to her with a flourish.

'Hi, guys.' She settled herself on the stool and smiled at the barman. 'Hi, Geoff. The usual, please.'

He reached for a bottle of grapefruit juice. 'On the hard stuff, Bryony?'

'That's me.' Bryony nodded her thanks and lifted the glass in a salute. 'Cheers, everyone. And happy birthday, Oliver.'

Her brother grinned. 'Thanks, babe. You OK?'

'I'm fine.' In fact, she was better than fine. She was brilliant. And she was finally going to restart her life.

As if to test that resolve, Jack strolled over to her and dropped a kiss on her cheek.

'What did the blonde say when she walked into the bar?'

'Ouch,' Bryony answered wearily, rolling her eyes in exasperation. 'And, Jack, you really need some new jokes. You're recycling them.'

He yawned. 'Well, I've been telling them for twenty-two years—what do you expect?'

'A bit of originality would be nice,' she said mildly, taking another sip of her drink and making a point of not looking at him. She wasn't going to notice Jack any more. There were plenty of men out there with good bodies. He wasn't the only one. 'Maybe I should dye my hair brown to help you out.'

'Brown? Don't you dare.' Jack's voice was husky and enticingly male. 'If you dyed your hair brown, you'd ruin all my jokes. We love you the way you are.'

Bryony took a gulp of her drink. He didn't love her. And he never would love her. Or, at least, not in the way she wanted him to love her.

'Bry, are you free on Thursday or Friday?' Oliver leaned across the bar and grabbed a handful of nuts. 'Mum wants to cook me a birthday dinner, whole family and Jack in attendance.'

Bryony put her glass down on the bar. 'Can't do Thursday.'

Jack frowned. 'You're on an early shift. Why can't you do it?'

Bryony hesitated. 'Because I have a date,' she said finally, and Oliver lifted his eyebrows.

'A date? You have *a date*?'

Jack's smile vanished like the sun behind a cloud. 'What do you mean, you have a date?' His voice was surprisingly frosty. 'Since when did you go on dates?'

Bryony took a deep breath and decided she may as well tell all. 'Since I saw Lizzie's Christmas list.'

At the mention of Lizzie, Jack's expression regained some of its warmth. 'She's made her list already?'

'She has indeed.'

'Don't tell me.' His voice was indulgent. 'She wants something pink. A new pair of pink wings for her fairy costume?'

'Nope.'

Oliver looked at her searchingly. 'Well? We're all dying to hear what she asked for. And what's it got to do with you going on a date?'

Bryony sat still for a moment, studying her empty glass. 'I'm going on a date,' she said slowly, 'because Lizzie wants a daddy.' She looked up and gave them a bland smile. 'Lizzie has asked for a daddy for Christmas.'

There was a long silence around the bar and the men exchanged looks.

It was Jack who eventually spoke first. 'Does she realise that they're not all they're cracked up to be?'

There was bitterness in his tone and Bryony frowned slightly. She knew that his parents had divorced when he'd been eight and she also knew that it had been a hideously painful experience for Jack.

But it was unlike him to ever mention it.

Like most men, Jack Rothwell didn't talk about his feelings.

'A *daddy*?' Oliver cleared his throat and exchanged looks with Tom. 'Does she have anyone in particular in mind?'

Bryony shook her head. 'No. She's leaving the choice up to Santa, but Mum gave me the letter and she's listed the qualities she's looking for.'

'She has?' Oliver gave an amazed laugh and glanced round at the others. 'And what are they?'

Bryony delved into her pocket and pulled out a rumpled piece of paper. She cleared her throat and started to read. 'I want a daddy who is strong so that he can swing me in the garden. I want a daddy who is funny and makes jokes. I want a daddy who lets me watch television before school and who won't make me eat sprouts because I hate them and I want a daddy who will meet me at the school gate and give me a hug like the other daddies sometimes do.' Bryony broke off at that point and swallowed hard, aware of the stunned silence around her. 'But most of all I want a daddy who will hug my mummy and stay with us for ever.'

No one spoke and Bryony gave a small shrug. 'That's it.'

She folded the paper carefully and put it back in her pocket, and Jack frowned.

'I never knew she wanted someone to pick her up from school,' he said gruffly, glancing between Oliver and Tom. 'We could do something about that, guys.'

'Sure.' Tom nodded agreement immediately and Bryony lifted a hand.

'Thank you, but no. That isn't what she wants. In fact, that would probably make it worse because the person who is picking her up isn't her daddy.'

Oliver frowned and rubbed a hand over the back of his neck. 'So where did it come from, this daddy business?'

'I don't know.' Bryony shrugged. 'I suppose she's just getting to that age where children notice differences between themselves and others. Most of the kids in her class are in traditional families.'

'You've been reading her too many fairy stories,' Jack said darkly, and she shrugged.

'She's a little girl, Jack. Little girls dream of weddings.'

Oliver grinned at Tom. 'Some big girls dream of weddings, too. I find it terrifying.'

'Stop it.' Bryony frowned in mock disapproval. 'How my daughter has ever grown up to be remotely normal with you three around her is a mystery to me. She's always asking me why none of you are married.'

'Did you tell her that we're too busy having fun?' Tom drawled, and Bryony rolled her eyes.

'Actually, I tell her that none of you have met the right woman yet, but that it's bound to happen soon.'

'Is it?' Oliver gave a shudder, his expression comical. 'I hope not.'

'You're awful. All three of you.'

Tom lifted an eyebrow in her direction. 'Well, you're not exactly an advert for relationships yourself, little sister. You haven't been on a date since Lizzie was born.'

'I know that. But that's all going to change.' Bryony lifted her chin. 'I've decided that Lizzie needs a daddy.'

'So what are you saying?' Jack was staring at her, all traces of humour gone from his handsome face. 'You're going to go out there and marry the first guy you meet just so that she can have a daddy?'

'Don't be ridiculous. Of course not.' Bryony lifted her chin and looked around her, her voice quiet but firm. 'I'm just saying that I'm going to start dating again.'

Oliver glanced at Tom and shrugged. 'Well, good for you.'

'Yeah.' Tom nodded and smiled at his sister. 'I think it's great. You've locked yourself up in a cupboard long enough. Get yourself out there, I say. Paint the town red. Or pink, if you're using Lizzie's colour scheme.'

Some of the other men in the team clapped her on the back and one or two made jokes about joining the queue to take her out.

Only Jack was silent, studying her with a brooding expression on his handsome face, his usual teasing smile notably absent. 'You really think you can find her a *daddy*?'

'I don't know.' Bryony gave a little shrug. 'Maybe not. But if I don't at least go on dates, it definitely won't happen.'

When he finally spoke his tone was chilly. 'So who's your date with on Thursday?'

Bryony looked at him in confusion, thinking that she'd never heard Jack use that tone before. He sounded...*angry*. But why would he be angry? The others actually seemed pleased for her. But not Jack.

'I'm not sure it's any of your business,' she teased him gently, trying to nudge their relationship back onto its usual platform, but on this occasion there was no answering smile.

'I'm Lizzie's godfather,' he reminded her, his blue eyes glittering in the firelight and a muscle working in his jaw. 'Who you choose as a *daddy* is very much my business.'

'You want to interview the guys I date, Jack?' She was still smiling, trying to keep it light, but he was glaring at her.

'Maybe.'

Bryony gave a disbelieving laugh, her own smile fading rapidly. 'You can't be serious.'

'You know absolutely nothing about the opposite sex, Blondie,' he said coldly. 'You've always refused to tell us who Lizzie's father was but he isn't around now which says quite a lot about your choice of men.'

Bryony gasped in shock. Lizzie's father wasn't a topic she discussed with anyone and Jack had never spoken to her like that before. He'd always been totally supportive of her status as a single mother.

'I don't know why you're looking so disapproving,' she said softly, aware that all the others had long since returned to their conversations and were no longer listening. Suddenly it was just the two of them and the tension in the atmosphere was increasing by the minute. 'You date all the time.'

His mouth tightened. 'I don't have a seven-year-old daughter.'

'But it's because of her that I'm doing this!'

Jack picked up his glass from the bar, a muscle flickering in his darkened jaw. 'That's ridiculous. You think you can just get out there and produce a happy family like magic?'

She sighed, knowing what was behind his words. 'No, I don't think that, Jack. But I think that it's time to see if I could maybe meet someone who seemed right for Lizzie and me.'

'Your life runs very smoothly,' he pointed out. 'Why complicate things?'

'Because Lizzie needs something more…' She hesitated. 'And I need something more, too, Jack. I've been on my own long enough.'

His mouth tightened. 'So basically you've suddenly decided to get out there and have fun.'

'And so what if I have?' Bryony looked at him, confused and exasperated. 'I just don't understand your attitude! You and my brothers have practically worked your way through most of the females in Cumbria.'

Streaks of colour touched his incredible cheekbones. 'That's different.'

Suddenly Bryony decided she'd had enough. 'Because you're a man and I'm a woman?'

'No.' His fingers tightened on his glass. 'Because I don't have any responsibilities.'

'No. You've made sure of that. And there's no need to remind me of my responsibilities to Lizzie. That's what started this, remember?' She glared at him, suddenly angry with him for being so judgmental. 'Lizzie wants a daddy and it's my job to find her one. And

I'm more than happy to try and find someone I can live with because frankly I'm sick and tired of being on my own, too.'

How could she have been so stupid as to put herself on ice for so long? She should have realised just how deep-rooted his fear of commitment was. Should have realised that Jack Rothwell would never settle down with anyone, let alone her.

It was definitely time to move on.

'I'm going home,' she said coldly, slipping off the barstool and avoiding his gaze. 'I'll see you at work tomorrow.'

She heard his sharp intake of breath and knew that he was going to try and stop her, but she virtually ran to the door, giving him no opportunity to intercept her.

She didn't want to talk to him. Didn't want to hear all the reasons why she shouldn't have a boyfriend when he dated a non-stop string of beautiful women.

She'd call Oliver later and apologise for ducking out without saying goodbye, but she knew he wouldn't mind. They were a close family and she adored her brothers. At least they'd been encouraging.

Which was more than could be said for Jack.

Why had he acted like that? All right, he was absolutely against marriage, but it wasn't *his* marriage they were talking about. It was *hers*, and Jack was usually warm and supportive of everything she did. They *never* argued. They were best friends.

She unlocked her car quickly, feeling tears prick her eyes.

Well, if dating other men meant losing Jack as a

friend, then so be it. She'd wasted enough time on him. He didn't even notice her, for goodness' sake!

And if she'd needed confirmation that it was time to move on, she had it now.

Jack banged his empty glass down on the bar and cursed under his breath.

'Nice one, Jack,' Oliver said mildly, clapping him on the shoulder and glancing towards the door. 'I thought the three of us agreed that we weren't going to bring up the thorny subject of Lizzie's father.'

Jack groaned and ran a hand over his face. 'I know, I know.' He let out a long breath. 'It's just that she knows *nothing* about men—'

'She's twenty-seven.'

'So?' Jack glared at Oliver. 'And we know that she hasn't been out with a man since Lizzie was conceived. That guy broke her heart! I don't want her making the same mistake again. She's obviously never got over him. What if she picks someone on the rebound?'

Tom joined them. 'I'm not sure you can rebound after seven years,' he said mildly, and Jack's mouth tightened.

'So why does Lizzie never date, then?'

Tom looked at him steadily. 'I don't know…'

'Yes you do.' Jack's eyes narrowed as he studied his friend. 'You think you know. I can tell.'

Tom shook his head and drained his glass. 'No. I don't know.' He studied his empty glass. 'But I can guess.'

Jack frowned. 'So what's your guess?'

Tom gave a funny smile and looked at Oliver. 'My guess is that she has a particular guy on her mind,' he drawled casually, 'and until she gets over him, she can't move on.'

'Precisely what I said,' Jack said smugly. 'She needs to get over Lizzie's father.'

And with that he grabbed his jacket and strode out of the pub after her.

Oliver looked at Tom. 'I always thought he was a bright guy. How did he ever come top in all those exams?'

Tom gave a faint smile. 'He'll get there in the end.'

'Unless Bry meets someone else.'

'Bryony has been in love with Jack for twenty-two years,' Tom said calmly, glancing at the barman and waggling his glass. 'She's never going to fall in love with anyone else.'

'So what happens now?'

Tom reached for his wallet. 'I think we're in for a very interesting few weeks. Happy birthday, bro. This one's on me.'

Damn.

Jack strode out to the car park, cursing himself for being so tactless. He couldn't believe he'd argued with Bryony. He *never* argued with Bryony. Or, at least, not seriously. Bryony was the nearest he had to family and their relationship was all banter and teasing and a great deal of confiding. Well, on his part at least. He told her everything about his relationships and she was always giving him little suggestions. And that was one of the things he loved about their friendship. Unlike the women he dated, Bryony never tried to change him or lecture him. She just accepted him as he was. He was more comfortable in her kitchen than any other place in the world. And now he'd upset her.

What the hell had come over him?

He looked round the car park, part of him hoping that she was still there, but of course she was long gone. He just hoped she wasn't driving too quickly. The air was freezing and the roads would be icy.

He gritted his teeth and swore under his breath. She'd been really upset by his comments and there was a very strong chance that he'd made her cry. Despite the fact that she rarely let him see it, he knew she was soft-hearted. He'd known her since she was five, for goodness' sake, and he knew her better than anyone.

Realising that he had a big apology to make, he ran a hand over his face and strolled to his car, pressing the remote control on his keyring.

He could drive over to her cottage now, of course, but she'd still be mad with him and anyway her mother would be there so they wouldn't be able to talk properly.

No. The apology was best left until they could be alone.

If he'd been dating her he would have sent her flowers, but he'd never sent Bryony flowers in his life, and if he did she'd think he'd gone mad.

He slid into his sports car and dropped his head back against the seat.

No doubt, now that word was out that she was going to start dating, flowers would be arriving for her thick and fast.

He growled low in his throat, tension rising in him as he contemplated the impact that her announcement had made.

Why had she chosen to tell the whole pub? Didn't she know that all the guys lusted after her? That with her long silken blonde hair and her fabulous curvy body, she couldn't walk across a room without stopping conversations? And he felt every bit as protective towards her as he knew her brothers did.

And now some sleazy guy would come along and take advantage of her, and she was so trusting and inexperienced with men she wouldn't even notice until it was too late.

Jack reversed the car out of its space, crunching the gears viciously. Well, *not* while he was available to prevent it happening.

She'd become pregnant in her second year at medical school and neither he nor her brothers had been around to sort the guy out. Damn it, she hadn't even told them who he was. Just mumbled something about the whole thing being a mistake and refused to even discuss it even though Tom and Oliver had pumped her for hours.

Well, there wasn't going to be another mistake, Jack thought grimly, his strong hands tightening on the wheel. Because now there was Lizzie's happiness to think of, too. No one was going to hurt either one of his girls.

From now on, if any guy so much as *looked* at

Bryony the wrong way, if there was even a *scent* of someone messing her around, he'd step in and floor them.

Satisfied that he was back in control of the situation, he stopped trying to pulverise his precious car and slowed his pace.

All he needed to do now was plan. He needed to know exactly whom she was dating so that he could issue a warning.

Bryony let herself into the house and found her mother in the kitchen. 'Is she asleep?'

'Fast asleep.' Her mother dried her hands on a towel. 'You're back early, darling. Is something wrong?'

'No.' Bryony unwrapped the scarf from around her neck and tossed it onto the chair. Her coat followed.

'Bryony, I'm your mother. I can tell when something is wrong.'

Bryony glared at her, her eyes sparkling with unshed tears. 'Jack Rothwell, that's what's wrong!'

'Ah.' Her mother gave a smile and turned to put the kettle on. 'Tea?'

'I suppose so.' Bryony slumped into the nearest chair and sighed. 'He is the most infuriating man.'

'Is he?'

'You know he is.'

Her mother reached for the tea bags. 'I know that you two have been very close for almost the whole of your lives,' she said mildly. 'I'm sure that whatever it is you've quarrelled about will go away.'

'The man dates every woman on the planet,' Bryony said, still outraged by his attitude, 'but when

I announce that I'm going to start going out with men, he's suddenly disapproving. And he had the nerve to lecture me on my responsibilities to Lizzie!'

'Did he?' Her mother looked thoughtful. 'That's very interesting.'

'Interesting?' Bryony shot her mother an incredulous look. 'Irritating, you mean. And hypocritical. How many girlfriends has Jack Rothwell had since I first met him?'

Her mother poured the tea. 'Quite a few, I should think.'

'Half the planet,' Bryony said flatly. 'He certainly isn't in a position to lecture me about morals.'

'I imagine he thought he was protecting Lizzie.'

Bryony stared at her. 'From what?'

Her mother put two mugs on the table and sat down opposite her. 'Jack hasn't had a very positive experience of marriage, sweetheart.'

'You mean because of his parents?'

Her mother's mouth tightened with disapproval. 'Well, you know my opinion on that. They were grown-ups. He was a child. They should have sorted out their differences amicably. After his father walked out, Jack spent most of his childhood at our house and I don't think his mother even noticed he wasn't at home. She was too busy enjoying herself to remember that she had a child.'

Bryony bit her lip, suddenly realising why Jack might have been so sensitive about her dating. 'But I wouldn't do that. That isn't what this is about.'

'I know. But you understand Jack better than anyone,' her mother said calmly. 'He wasn't thinking about you, darling. He was thinking about his own experiences.'

Bryony bit her lip. 'Do you think I should start dating, Mum?'

'Certainly I think you should date,' her mother replied calmly. 'I've always thought you should date, but you've always been too crazy about Jack to notice anyone else.'

Bryony stared at her, opened her mouth to deny it and then caught the look in her mother's eye and closed it again. 'You know that?'

'I'm your mother. Of course I know that.'

'He doesn't notice me.'

'You're a huge part of Jack's life,' her mother said mildly. 'He virtually lives here. But that's going to have to change if you really are going to date other men.'

Bryony curled her hands round her mug. 'But I don't want it to change my friendship with Jack.'

'One day you'll get married again,' her mother said quietly, 'and I can't see any man wanting to see Jack lounging in your kitchen every time he comes home from work. Of course your friendship is going to change.'

Bryony stared into her mug, a hollow feeling inside her. She didn't want things to change. Despite their row, she couldn't imagine not having Jack in her life.

But she couldn't carry on the way she was now, for Lizzie's sake.

'Then I suppose I'll just have to get used to that,' she said, raising her mug in the air. 'Cheers. To my future.'

Her mother lifted her mug in response. 'May it turn out the way you want it to,' she said cryptically, and Bryony let out a long breath.

She wasn't really sure what *she* wanted.

But she knew Lizzie needed a daddy.

The next morning she was woken by her pager.

'Is that a callout?' Lizzie was by her bed in a flash, her eyes huge. 'Is someone in trouble on the mountain?'

Bryony picked up her pager and was reading the message when the phone rang. Lizzie grabbed it immediately.

'Hunter household, Elizabeth Hunter speaking,' she said formally, the angle of her chin suggesting that she was very proud of herself. She listened for a moment and then a smile spread across her face. 'Hello, Jack! Yes, Mummy's right here… I'll tell her. Will I see you later?'

Bryony pulled on her clothes and sprinted to the bathroom to clean her teeth. By the time she'd finished, Lizzie was off the phone.

'There's a party of Duke of Edinburgh Award boys overdue,' she said importantly. 'They're sending out the whole team but Sean wants you and Jack to be an advance party. Jack is picking you up in five minutes.'

'Five minutes.' Bryony hurried through to the kitchen, grabbed an apple from the fruit bowl and dropped some bread in the toaster. 'Get your school things, sweetheart. Jack and I will drop you at

Grandma's on the way past and she can take you to school.'

Lizzie sprinted off and Bryony sent up a silent prayer of thanks that she had her mother close by. How did single parents manage without mothers?

By the time Jack hammered on the door, Lizzie was dressed and was standing by the door with her school-bag, munching toast.

She stood on tiptoe and opened the door.

'Hi, there.' Jack stooped and swung her into his arms, squeezing her tightly. 'Are we dropping you with Grandma?'

'We certainly are.' Bryony walked into the hall and picked up her rucksack and the other bits and pieces that she'd piled by the door, avoiding Jack's gaze. She was grateful that Lizzie was there. At least it prevented her from having to continue the conversation from the night before.

She was still hurt and angry by Jack's response to her announcement that she was going to start dating.

They piled into the mountain rescue vehicle and Jack drove down the lane that led to Bryony's cottage and turned onto the main road.

'So what's the story?' Bryony twisted her blonde hair into a ponytail and pushed it under a woolly hat. Then she rummaged in her bag for her gloves.

Jack kept his eyes on the road. 'Two boys have been reported overdue. They should have been back down last night but they didn't appear.'

Bryony frowned. 'So why did no one call the team last night?'

'They were camping and didn't leave their plans

with anyone so no one noticed until their friends stumbled into camp this morning and raised the alarm. The weather was foul last night, which is doubtless why Sean is worried.'

Lizzie stared at him, her eyes huge. 'Have they called the helicopter?'

'Yes, sweetheart.' Jack glanced at her with a smile. 'But the weather is pretty awful so Sean, the MRT leader, wants your mum and me to get going up that mountain in case we can help.'

'Why do you and Mummy always go together?'

Jack turned his attention back to the road and pulled the vehicle up outside Bryony's mother's house. 'Because your mum and I have always worked together in the mountain rescue team,' he said lightly. 'When your mum trained, I was her buddy. I looked after her.'

'And you still look after her,' Lizzie said happily, jumping down from the vehicle and grabbing her school-bag.

'I don't need looking after,' Bryony said crossly, glaring at Jack and calling after Lizzie, 'Sweetheart, ask Grandma to give you some more breakfast. I'll see you later.'

They waited until Bryony's mother opened the door and then Jack gave a wave and hit the accelerator.

Suddenly Bryony was very aware that it was just the two of them and she stared out of the window, for the first time in her life not knowing what to say.

'We think we know where they are,' Jack told her, flicking the indicator and turning down a narrow road.

'It's just a question of what state they'll be in when we get there.'

Which was why Sean had sent them as the advance party, Bryony thought. He wanted doctors. Which meant that he was anticipating trouble.

She picked up the map. 'What's the grid reference?'

He told her and she traced it with her finger. 'They're in the ghyll?'

'Sounds like it.'

Bryony looked at him in concern. 'But the water level is terribly high after all that rain we've had…'

'That's right.' Jack's voice was even and he brought the vehicle to a halt. 'Which is why we need to get a move on. Personally I doubt they'll be able to fly a helicopter in this. Sean has called the whole team out, but we're going on ahead.'

He sprang out of the vehicle and reached for the equipment that they'd need. They worked quickly and quietly, each knowing what the other was doing.

'You ready?' Jack lifted an eyebrow in her direction and she nodded.

'Let's go.'

Jack set off at a fast pace and Bryony followed, knowing that speed was important. After a night out in the open in the wet and temperatures below freezing, the boys would be in serious trouble.

They had to reach them fast.

The path grew steeper, the mist came down and Jack shook his head. 'It's November, it's freezing cold and the visibility is zero.' He hitched his rucksack more comfortably on his broad shoulders and squinted into the mist. 'Who the hell chooses to climb mountains at this time of year?'

'You do it all the time,' Bryony pointed out, checking her compass again. 'One of these days we're going to be out here rescuing you.'

'Never.' He winked and gave her a sexy grin. 'I am invincible.'

Bryony rolled her eyes. 'And arrogant.' She stopped dead and he looked at her questioningly.

'Why have you stopped?'

'Because your ego is blocking my path.'

Jack laughed and then the laughter faded. 'Listen, Blondie, about last night—'

'Not now,' Bryony said hastily. She really didn't want to tackle the subject again so soon, especially not halfway up a mountain.

'I just wanted to apologise,' he said softly. 'I was out of line. You're a brilliant mother and I know you'll do what's right for Lizzie.'

Stunned by his apology, Bryony lost her ability to speak. She'd never heard Jack apologise for anything before.

'Let's forget it,' she mumbled, and Jack nodded, his blue eyes studying her closely.

'All right. We'll talk about it later.' He glanced up the path and frowned. 'There is no way that helicopter is going to fly in this.'

'So we evacuate them down the mountain.'

He nodded and then turned to her, his eyes twinkling wickedly. 'Why did the blonde stare at the can of frozen orange juice?' He leaned forward and tucked a strand of hair back under her hat. 'Because it said ''concentrate''.'

Bryony tipped her head on one side and stared back at him. 'Why are men like government bonds?' He lifted an eyebrow, his eyes dancing, and she smiled sweetly. 'Because they take for ever to mature. Now, can we get on with this rescue?'

They stuck to the path and the mist grew thicker. Jack's radio crackled to life and he paused and had a quick conversation with Sean back at base.

'They're sending out the whole team,' he told her when he came off the radio, 'but I reckon we must be nearly at the place where they were last seen.'

Bryony stood still, listening, but all she could hear was the rush of water. The freezing air snaked through her clothing and she shivered.

'If they didn't have any protection last night, they won't have stood a chance,' she muttered, and Jack nodded, his handsome face serious.

'Better find them, fast.'

He started up the track again and then stopped, squinting down into the ghyll. 'Do you see something?'

'What?' Bryony stepped towards the edge but Jack reached out a strong arm and clamped her against him.

'If it's all the same to you, I'd rather you didn't go over the edge, too,' he said dryly, keeping his arm round her as he peered through the mist into the ghyll again.

Bryony held her breath, painfully conscious of his hard body pressed against hers.

'I don't see anything.' She wondered when he was going to let her go and was about to ask when she spotted a flash of red below them. 'OK, I see something.'

'Me, too.' Jack released her. 'There's a path here but it's narrow and slippery. Think you can manage, Blondie? You have to put one leg in front of the other and not fall over.'

'It'll be a struggle, but I'll do my best,' Bryony assured him earnestly, relieved that their relationship seemed to have restored itself to its usual level. 'What about you? Think you can find your way without asking for directions?'

They kept up the banter as they picked their way down the path, and finally they reached the bottom and immediately saw the boys huddled together by a boulder.

Jack closed the distance in seconds and dropped to his haunches, his expression concerned. 'Hi, there— nice day for a stroll in the mountains.'

'We thought no one was ever coming,' the boy whispered, his teeth chattering as he spoke. 'Martyn keeps falling asleep and leaving me on my own.'

'Right. Put a bivouac tent over them.' Jerking his head to indicate that Bryony should deal with the conscious child, Jack shifted his position so that he could examine the other boy.

He was lying still, moaning quietly, his cheeks pale and his lips blue.

Jack spoke to him quietly and checked his pulse while Bryony checked the other boy for injuries. Once she was satisfied that he was just cold and shaken, she erected the tent and helped him to scramble inside a casualty bag.

'What's your name?'

'Sam.'

'Well, Sam, that will keep you warm until we can get you off this mountain,' she assured him, and he gave a little sob.

'Martyn fell. His leg is awful. I saw bone.'

Bryony slipped an arm round him and gave him a hug. 'Don't you worry about that now,' she said softly. 'We'll sort him out and get you both home. I'm going to pour you a hot drink and that will warm you up.'

She grabbed the flask that she'd packed and poured thick creamy chocolate into a mug.

'Here—drink this. I'll be back in a sec.' Aware that Jack was going to need her help, she slid out of the tent and moved over to him.

'Sam says that his friend fell.'

Jack nodded, still checking the child over. 'He's got a compound fracture of his tib and fib and he's bleeding a lot. We need to get a line in, Blondie, and then splint that leg.'

Bryony reached for the rucksack and found what they needed, aware that Jack was on the radio again, updating Sean on their position and the condition of the boys.

By the time he'd finished on the radio Bryony had a line in. 'Do you want to give him fluid?'

Jack nodded. 'And then we need to splint that leg. It will help the pain and reduce blood loss.' He leaned over the boy, talking quietly, explaining what they were doing, and Bryony gave a sigh. He was so good when anyone was in trouble. A rock. And he always knew what to do. Her confidence came from being with him.

She covered the wound on the leg with a sterile saline-soaked dressing while Jack carefully removed the boy's boot.

He placed his fingers on Martyn's foot, feeling for a pulse. 'That's fine—let's splint this leg. We're just going to give you something for the pain, Martyn, and then we're going to put your leg in a splint. Then we're going to warm you up and get you off this mountain.'

Bryony gave a shiver. The temperature was dropping fast and even in her top-quality gear she could feel the cold.

By the time they'd splinted the boy's leg, Sean had arrived with the rest of the mountain rescue team.

'Nice day for a walk,' he drawled, glancing around him at the thick mist. 'The views are fantastic.'

Bryony smiled. 'Absolutely fantastic,' she said sarcastically. 'Enjoy your stroll, did you?'

Sean grinned in appreciation. 'Didn't want to rush things,' he said, lifting an eyebrow in Jack's direction. 'Well?'

'We need a helicopter but I don't suppose there's any chance of that.'

'You suppose correctly.'

Jack sighed and checked the pulses on the boy's foot again. 'So we'd better carry them off, then. Good. I needed a workout.'

It seemed to take ages to organise both boys onto

stretchers but eventually they managed to carry them out of the ghyll and started down the mountain.

By the time they reached the valley floor the mist had cleared and it was a sunny day.

'I don't believe this,' Bryony muttered, tugging off her hat and shaking her hair loose. 'What is it with our weather?'

Both boys were loaded into the mountain rescue team ambulance and then transferred to hospital under Sean's supervision while Jack and Bryony followed behind.

'Are you working today?' Jack glanced across at her and she nodded.

'Yes. I'm on a late. Why?'

He returned his attention to the road. 'I thought you had a date.'

Bryony looked at him warily. 'That's tomorrow, but I don't know if I'm going because Mum has to go and visit someone in Kendal so I don't think she can babysit.'

'I'll babysit for you.'

Bryony stared at him. 'You?'

'Why not?' His eyes were fixed on the road. 'I often babysit for you. It gives me a chance to talk to my godchild. I like it.'

Bryony looked at him suspiciously. 'But last night…' She broke off and bit her lip, not really wanting to bring the subject up in case it rocked the peace that had resumed between them. 'Last night you said that you didn't think I should be dating.'

'And I've already apologised for that,' he said, flicking the indicator and turning into the road that led to the hospital. 'And to make up for it, I'll babysit for you. What time do you want me?'

Still feeling uneasy about the whole thing but not knowing why, Bryony gave a shrug. 'Seven-thirty?'

'Seven-thirty is perfect. There's just one thing…' He pulled up in the ambulance bay and yanked on the handbrake. 'You haven't told me who you're going out with.'

There was something in his smooth tones that made her glance at him warily but his handsome face was impassive.

She paused with her hand on the door. 'David.'

'David Armstrong? The paediatrician?' Jack's expression didn't change but she sensed something that made her uneasy.

'Look, Jack—'

'I'll be there at seven-thirty. Now, let's get on. I need to get antibiotics into Martyn and call the surgeons. That wound is going to need some attention.'

And with that he sprang out of the vehicle, leaving her staring after him.

Jack was going to babysit while she went on a date?

It seemed harmless enough, generous even, so why did she have such a strong feeling that something wasn't quite right?

CHAPTER THREE

'MUMMY, you look pretty.'

'Do you think so?' Bryony surveyed her reflection in the mirror, wondering whether the dress was right for the evening that David had in mind. He'd said dinner in a smart restaurant, but she never went to smart restaurants so she wasn't that sure what to wear.

In the end she'd settled for the little black dress that her mother had given her three Christmases ago and which she'd never worn.

She'd fastened her hair on top of her head, found a pair of pretty, dangly earrings and dabbed perfume over her body.

And she had to admit that she was looking forward to going out with a man.

So much so that when the doorbell rang she opened the door with a wide smile.

'Hi, Jack.' Her face glowed and she stood to one side to let him in. 'There's a casserole in the oven. I assumed you wouldn't have eaten—'

'I haven't eaten.' His eyes slid down her body and he frowned, his expression suddenly hostile.

Bryony felt the confidence ooze out of her. She'd thought that she looked good but, judging from the look on Jack's face, she obviously didn't.

'Come through to the kitchen,' she said quickly, suddenly wishing that she'd worn something different. Obviously the black dress didn't suit her. 'We've got time for a quick drink before David gets here. He was held up in clinic.'

Jack's mouth tightened with disapproval. 'So he's going to be late, then.'

'Well, only because a child with asthma was admitted at the last minute,' Bryony said mildly, tugging open the fridge and reaching for a bottle of wine. 'You know how it is.'

'Do I?'

Instead of settling himself at her kitchen table as he usually did, he prowled round the room, his eyes constantly flickering back to her dress.

Trying to ignore his intense scrutiny, Bryony poured two glasses of wine and handed him one. 'Here you are. Cheers.'

He took the wine and put it on the table, his eyes fixed on her legs.

Bryony felt her whole body warm with embarrassment. She hardly ever showed her legs. She usually wore trousers for work because they were more practical, and when she went to the pub with the rest of the mountain rescue team she wore trousers, too.

But tonight, for the first time in ages, she'd put on a pair of sheer, black stockings and she was beginning to wish she hadn't.

'You hate it, don't you?' she croaked, and his eyes lifted and welded to hers.

'Hate what?'

She swallowed. 'The way I look. My dress. Me. You're staring and staring.'

Jack let out a breath. 'That's because I don't think you should be going out with a man dressed like that,' he said tightly. 'It sends out all the wrong messages.'

She frowned at him, totally confused. 'What messages?'

He tensed. 'Well—that you're available.'

'Jack,' she said patiently, 'I *am* available. That is the message I want to send out.'

'So you wear a skirt that's up to your bottom?' He glared at her and she stared back helplessly, totally confused by his attitude.

She'd met some of the girls that he'd dated and they were almost all blondes with skirts up round their bottoms.

'Jack, my skirt is just above the knee,' she pointed out, glancing down at herself to check that half her dress hadn't fallen off without her knowledge. 'It is nowhere near my bottom.'

'Well, it's definitely too low in the front,' he said hoarsely, reaching across the kitchen table, yanking a flower out of a vase and snapping it halfway up the stem. 'Try this.'

He walked up to her and slipped the flower down the neckline of her dress and stood back with a frown.

'That's a bit better.'

'Jack—'

Before she could say anything, Lizzie came running into the room wearing a pink gauze fairy dress and wearing wings. 'Jack, Jack!' She flung herself into his arms and he picked her up and gave her a kiss on the cheek.

'Hello, beautiful. Shouldn't you be in bed?'

'I was waiting for you.' Lizzie curled her legs round his waist and waggled her finger at him. 'Look. I'm wearing three rings. They're sweets really, but aren't they great?'

Jack dutifully studied her finger. 'Really great. And if you get hungry in the night you can eat them.'

Lizzie beamed. 'Can we play a game, Jack?'

'Sure.' Jack put her down gently and smiled indulgently. 'Any game you like. Just name it.'

'Weddings.'

Jack's smile vanished. *'Weddings?'*

Lizzie nodded happily. 'Yes, you know. You're the boy and I'm the girl and we get married.'

Jack gave a shudder. 'I don't know the rules, sweetheart.'

Bryony covered her hand with her mouth to hide her smile. Jack was brilliant at playing with her daughter but 'Weddings' was the one game guaranteed to bring him out in a rash.

'It's easy,' Lizzie assured him happily. 'We hold hands and then we get married.'

Jack ran a hand over the back of his neck and looked at Bryony for help, but she simply smiled.

'Weddings, Jack,' she said softly, her eyes dancing as she looked at him. 'That well-known game enjoyed by men and women the world over.'

His eyes shot daggers at her but he turned to Lizzie with a resigned sigh. 'All right, peanut, tell me what I have to do.'

'Well, first I have to go and dress up.' Lizzie shot out of the room and Jack turned on Bryony.

'She's playing *weddings*?'

'She's a girl, Jack,' Bryony said mildly. 'Girls play weddings.'

'I'm breaking out in a sweat here,' he muttered dryly, and she grinned unsympathetically.

'She's seven years old. I think you can cope. Great practice for when you do the real thing.'

His gaze locked on hers, his blue eyes mocking. 'You know I'm never doing the real thing.'

'Well, don't tell my daughter that. I don't want her saddled with your prejudices about relationships.'

'I should be teaching her about reality.'

Before Bryony could answer, Lizzie danced back into the room, this time wearing a full-length sparkly dress complete with glittering tiara.

Jack blinked. 'Wow…' He cleared his throat. 'I didn't know you had a tiara.'

'I've got seven,' Lizzie said proudly, and Bryony smiled cheerfully.

'A girl can never have too many tiaras, can she, Lizzie?'

'Come on, Jack.' Lizzie grabbed his hand. 'First we have to hold hands and walk across the carpet. Mummy can video us.'

Jack glanced at Bryony who could barely stand up she was laughing so much. 'Great idea, Lizzie,' she choked. 'It would make great viewing at the MRT Christmas party. Jack finally getting married.'

Jack scowled, but his eyes were dancing. 'Revenge is going to be sweet, Blondie,' he warned softly, but he was laughing too and shaking his head as Lizzie dragged him into the sitting room and Bryony reached for the video camera.

To give him his due, Jack treated the whole occasion with the appropriate amount of solemnity, sweeping Lizzie's hand to his lips as if she were a princess.

At first Bryony was laughing so much that she

could hardly keep the camera steady, but as she watched Jack playing his role to perfection and saw the delight on her little girl's face, her smile faded and she felt an ache growing inside her. Jack was so brilliant with Lizzie. And although he couldn't see it himself, he'd make a wonderful father.

She was reminding herself firmly that she wasn't going to think that way any more when the doorbell rang and she realised that her date had arrived.

She answered the door and David stood on the doorstep, flourishing a bunch of flowers.

'Are they for me? They're beautiful, thank you.' She smiled at him and was wondering whether she ought to kiss him when she heard Jack clear his throat behind her.

'You'll need a coat, Blondie,' he said coolly, the humour gone from his eyes as he held out the long woollen coat that she always wore to work and which covered her from her neck to her ankles.

'I was going to take my pashmina,' Bryony began, but Jack walked up behind her and draped the coat over her shoulders, pulling it closed at the front so that not one single inch of her was visible.

'It's too cold for a pashmina,' he grated. 'You don't want to get hypothermia over dinner.' He stood back and gave David a nod. 'She needs to be home at eleven.'

'What?' Bryony gaped at him and then gave an embarrassed laugh. They hadn't even discussed what time he wanted her home but she'd assumed that she could be as late as she liked. She knew Jack well enough to know that he didn't go to bed early himself.

And invariably he slept in her spare room. So why was he saying that she needed to be in by eleven?

David gave an awkward smile. 'Eleven is fine.'

Bryony scowled, less than impressed that he hadn't stood up to Jack. Surely he should have said that he'd bring her home when he was ready, or some such thing. She knew for sure that if someone had told Jack that he should bring a girl home by eleven he would have kept her out for the whole night just to prove a point.

But she'd promised herself that she wasn't going to think about Jack, she reminded herself hastily, taking the flowers through to the kitchen and putting them in water.

When she arrived back at the door the two men were staring at each other. David looked mildly embarrassed and Jack was standing, feet planted firmly apart, very much the dominant male and not in the slightest bit embarrassed.

Deciding that Jack had definitely gone mad, Bryony held out a hand to David and smiled. 'Shall we go?'

'Jack.' Lizzie tugged his arm and frowned at him. 'You're skipping bits.'

Jack shook himself and stared down at the book he was supposed to be reading. 'Am I?'

'Yes.' Lizzie grabbed the book from him and went back two pages. 'You didn't read this page at all. And you've got a funny look on your face.'

'Have I?'

Jack tried to concentrate on the pink fairy flying across the page of the book but all he could see was

Bryony in that dress. He hadn't seen her legs since she'd been in the netball team at school and he and her brothers had gone to matches to cheer her on, but he now realised that his best friend had sensational legs.

And if she was going to start showing them, how the hell was he going to protect her?

And it wasn't just her legs, of course...

He closed his eyes, trying to forget the shadowy dip between her full breasts revealed by the cut of her dress.

Right now they were in the restaurant and David was probably sitting opposite her, staring into paradise.

With a soft curse he stood up and the book fell to the floor.

'You said a rude word, Jack,' Lizzie said mildly, leaning over and retrieving the book.

'Sorry.' Suddenly seized by inspiration, he gave Lizzie a smile. 'How would you like to call your mother and say goodnight?'

'Now?'

'Sure, why not?' Before Dr Armstrong had time to get too hot and over-eager. Suddenly driven by an urgency that he couldn't explain, Jack grabbed Lizzie's hand and dragged her into the kitchen. 'We'll ring her mobile.'

Lizzie looked at him uncertainly. 'Grandma says we only ring if there's an emergency.'

Jack was already pressing the keys. 'Trust me, this is an emergency,' he assured her, his mind still mentally on Bryony's creamy breasts. His mouth tightened. 'A big emergency. Her baby girl wants to say goodnight.'

Trying to ignore the fact that Lizzie was looking at him as though he was slightly mad, Jack held the receiver and waited for Bryony to answer.

As the phone rang and rang, his heart started to thud in his chest.

Why the hell wasn't she answering?

Unless she wasn't at dinner after all. What if the rat had taken one look at that dress and whisked Bryony back to his flat?

'Uncle Jack, you're breathing really fast,' Lizzie said, climbing onto a kitchen stool, her fairy wings still attached to her back. 'And you look weird.'

He felt weird.

Why wasn't she answering?

David sat back in his chair. 'Is that your phone?'

Bryony looked at him, startled, and then picked up her bag. 'Oh, my goodness, yes.' She fumbled in her handbag, her stomach turning over. 'I hope nothing is wrong with Lizzie. I don't usually get phoned…'

She delved amongst tissues, make-up, notebooks and various pink hairbands that belonged to her daughter and eventually found the phone.

Feeling distinctly nervous, she answered it. 'Jack?' She cast an apologetic look at David. 'Is something wrong?'

She listened for a moment and then frowned. 'I'm in the restaurant, Jack. Where did you think I was? Well, I couldn't find my phone.'

At that moment the waiter delivered their starter and Bryony smiled her thanks, trying to ignore his look of disapproval. She knew that mobile phones were banned from lots of restaurants but she refused to turn hers off in case Lizzie needed her.

But it seemed that all Lizzie wanted was to say goodnight. Strange, Bryony thought as she spoke to her daughter and then ended the call. Lizzie was normally fine. Especially when she was with Jack. She loved being with Jack.

'Everything OK?' David looked at her quizzically and she smiled.

'Fine. Sorry about that.'

She picked up her fork and tucked into her starter, determined to relax. Part of her mind was still dwelling on the fact that Jack had hated her dress, but she ignored it. David seemed to think she looked nice and that was all that mattered.

They chattered about work and the mountain rescue team and they were just tucking into their main course when her phone rang again.

This time Bryony heard it immediately and stopped the ringing before the waiter had time to glare at her.

It was Jack again, this time telling her that Lizzie was refusing to take her fairy wings off.

Bryony frowned. This was a guy who could save a life halfway up a mountain in a howling gale with nothing more than a penknife and a piece of string.

And he was calling her about *fairy wings*?

'Just take them off when she's asleep, Jack,' she muttered, smiling apologetically at David as she slipped the phone back into her bag.

She tried valiantly to resume the conversation but when Jack called for the third time, David raised his hand and gestured to the waiter.

'I think I'll take you home,' he said dryly. 'Then you can answer Jack's questions in person and he won't have to keep calling you.'

'Sorry.' Bryony blushed slightly. As a first date it had been less than perfect. 'I honestly don't know what's the matter with him. He and Lizzie are normally fine together.'

David drove her home and then walked her up the path to her cottage. At the front door he paused, his expression thoughtful as he looked down at her.

Bryony stared back, feeling slightly awkward. Was he going to kiss her?

Suddenly she felt a flash of panic. She wasn't actually sure that she wanted him to kiss her.

His head was bending towards hers when the front door was jerked open and Jack stood there, broad-shouldered and imposing.

'You're home. Great.'

Bryony looked at David. 'Would you like to come in for coffee?'

'He needs to get going,' Jack said coldly, his face unsmiling. 'The roads are icy tonight and they're forecasting snow.'

David was silent for a moment, his eyes on Jack. 'Right. In that case I'd better make a move.'

'OK, then.' Secretly relieved by the decision, Bryony stood on tiptoe and kissed his cheek. 'Thanks for tonight. I enjoyed it.'

'Me, too.' David was still looking at Jack and then he gave a funny smile and turned to Bryony. 'I'll see you at work.'

With that he turned the collar of his coat up and strolled back down her path towards his car.

Bryony followed Jack into the cottage and slipped her coat off.

'I'm sorry Lizzie was such hard work tonight, Jack.' She strolled into the kitchen and flipped the kettle on. 'She never normally wants to call me. And she doesn't normally care if she's lost the book she was reading—she'll just pick another one. It doesn't sound as though you managed to relax at all.'

'I managed.' Jack sank onto one of the kitchen chairs and put his feet on the table in his usual pose. 'I expect she was just a bit unsettled by the thought of you going out with a strange man.'

Bryony frowned slightly. It was Lizzie who had suggested this whole daddy business, so why would she be unsettled? On the other hand, perhaps she hadn't really thought the whole thing through. It was certainly true that Lizzie wasn't used to seeing strange men in her life. She saw Jack and her two uncles and that was about it.

'She'll get used to it.'

'Maybe.' Jack sounded noncommittal. 'So—did you have a good evening?'

There was something in his tone that she couldn't interpret and Bryony lifted two mugs out of the cupboard, not sure how to answer. Had she had a good evening? If she was honest, she didn't really feel she'd had a chance to talk to David. Every time they'd begun a conversation the phone had rung.

Poor Lizzie.

She'd talk to her tomorrow and see how she felt about the whole thing. She certainly didn't want to go on dates if it was going to upset her daughter.

'I had a nice evening,' she said finally, not wanting

to admit to Jack that it had been anything less than perfect. 'It's a shame David wouldn't come in for coffee.'

'It's not a shame. It was a lucky escape.' Jack swung his legs off the table and glared at her. '*Never* invite a man in for coffee.'

Bryony looked at him in astonishment. 'I was being polite.'

He lifted an eyebrow. 'Offering to have sex with a man is being polite?'

Bryony gaped at him, stunned. 'I did not offer to have sex with him, I offered him *coffee.*'

'It's the same thing.' A muscle flickered in his jaw, rough with stubble so late in the evening. He looked dark and dangerous and Bryony felt her stomach flip.

Why couldn't she find David even *half* as attractive? She'd been less than enthusiastic at the possibility of him kissing her, but if it had been Jack who'd been on the doorstep with her…

Reminding herself that she wasn't supposed to be noticing Jack, Bryony picked up the coffee-jar.

'Coffee is the same as sex?' She twisted the jar in her hand, looking at it with a mocking expression. 'Full of caffeine and sold in supermarkets. I don't think so.'

Jack glared at her. 'You can joke about it, but do you really think a man wants to sit around, drinking your coffee?'

'You're sitting around, drinking my coffee,' Bryony pointed out logically, and his mouth hardened.

'That's different. I'm not trying to get you into my bed.'

More's the pity, Bryony thought wistfully, putting the coffee down on the side. If Jack ever tried to get her into his bed she'd be there like a flash.

'Jack, I'm sure David didn't have anything immoral on his mind.'

'Which just shows how little you know about men,' Jack said tightly. 'Do you know the average man thinks about sex every six seconds?'

'So presumably that's why they say men are like photocopiers,' Bryony said dryly. 'Good for reproduction but not much else.'

For once Jack didn't laugh and she sighed inwardly. There was obviously something about the idea of her dating that short-circuited his sense of humour.

Suddenly she wanted the old Jack back. The Jack that called her Blondie and teased her unmercifully. The Jack with the wicked smile and the sexiest wink known to woman.

'Jack.' Her tone was patient. 'I invited David in for coffee because I was being polite. I had no intention of having sex with him.'

'And what if he'd decided to have sex with you?'

She looked at him in exasperation. 'Well, despite the colour of my hair I do have a brain and a mouth,' she said tartly. 'I can think no and say no. At the same time. Amazing really. If I concentrate really hard I can add two and two. Jack, *what is the matter with you?*'

'I just think you're being naïve.'

'Inviting a guy in for coffee?' Bryony gritted her teeth and shook her head. 'You've gone crazy, do you know that?'

There was a long silence and streaks of colour touched his hard cheekbones. 'Maybe I have,' he said shortly, putting his half-full mug on the table and rising to his feet in a fluid movement. 'I'd better get home.'

'Fine. Thank you for babysitting.'

'You're welcome.'

As a farewell it had none of its usual warmth and Bryony turned away and poured the rest of her coffee down the sink, boiling with frustration and feeling confused and upset.

She heard Jack stride to her front door, heard him pick up his jacket and car keys and then the front door slammed behind him.

Bryony winced and let out a long breath.

Just what was going on with Jack?

Bryony was nervous about working with Jack the next day but he seemed back to his usual self, relaxed and good-humoured as they sat in the staffroom and discussed the shifts for Bonfire Night.

'It's my turn.' Sean Nicholson, one of the other consultants, looked at Jack with a resigned expression on his face. 'You deserve a year off from Bonfire Night. You've had a bad few years.'

Jack rolled his eyes. 'I won't know what to do with myself,' he drawled, and Bryony gave him a sympathetic smile.

'You hate this time of year, don't you?'

'I've just seen too many kids with burns after handling fireworks,' he said grimly, scribbling something on his pad. 'OK, so Blondie and I are officially off that night, but if you need us you can call us.' He looked at Bryony. 'Would you be able to come in that night if we needed you?'

Bryony nodded. 'After eight. I'm taking Lizzie to her bonfire party.'

Jack stared at her, his body suddenly unnaturally still. 'What bonfire party?'

'Her friend is having a few sparklers in the garden. Nothing dramatic,' Bryony assured him, but he shook his head.

'No way.' His jaw was tense. 'She shouldn't be going.'

Bryony sighed. 'She's seven, Jack. She wants to be with her friends.'

'So? Invite them all out for a hamburger.'

'It's just a few fireworks and drinks for the parents. It will be over by eight.'

He let out a breath. 'All right. But I'm coming with you.'

'Jack—'

'I'm off and I'm bored.' His blue eyes glittered dangerously. 'It's that or she doesn't go.'

'You're not her father, Jack!' Suddenly remembering that Sean was still in the room, Bryony coloured with embarrassment and shot them an apologetic look. 'Sorry, you guys.'

'No problem,' Sean said easily, 'and I'm sure we won't need you here so just go and have a good time.'

'Great. That's what we'll do, then.'

Jack ran through the rest of the rota and Sean left the room.

Bryony looked at him. 'So what are you planning to do? Bring the fire brigade?'

'When you've spent as long working in A and E

as I have, you won't let your daughter go to domestic firework parties,' he said tightly. 'It's fine. I'll come, too. And you can tell Lizzie's friend's mother that I want a bucket of sand and another bucket of water handy.'

'Why don't we just have an ambulance on standby, just in case?' Bryony suggested tartly. 'Anne's mother will think I've gone barmy.'

'Better barmy than burned.' Jack strode to the door. 'What time does it start?'

'We're getting there at five-thirty for tea and then fireworks,' Bryony said wearily, and Jack nodded.

'Right. I'll pick you both up at five-fifteen. And I want Lizzie in gloves. She's not touching a sparkler with her bare hands.'

Bryony stood up and followed him out of the staff-room, wanting to argue but knowing that he was only being cautious.

He had dealt with a huge number of burns on Bonfire Night, all of which could have been avoided.

And he did adore Lizzie.

Deciding that she should be grateful that he was so protective of her daughter, she picked up a set of notes and called the next patient from the waiting room.

And secretly part of her was excited at spending an evening with Jack. Even if it was in the company of half a dozen parents and their offspring.

It would be lovely to have him there, even though nothing was going to happen.

Reminding herself that Jack was not the man she was dating, she sat down in her chair and waited for the patient to arrive.

CHAPTER FOUR

THE NIGHT of the bonfire party was freezing cold and Bryony pulled on her jeans and thickest jumper and wore her long black coat.

Lizzie was wearing a bright pink hat, pink tights and a pink fleece, and Jack blinked when he arrived to pick them up.

'How are my girls?' He picked Lizzie up and planted a kiss on her cheek. 'You're looking very pink, angel.' He spoke in that lazy drawl that sent butterflies flitting through Bryony's stomach. 'Do you have any pink gloves to go with that outfit, sweetheart?'

'Somewhere.'

Jack smiled and put her back down. 'Find them for me, there's a good girl.' He looked at Bryony and she smiled, determined to have a nice evening.

'Is my dress decent enough for you, Jack?'

For a moment he didn't react and then he laughed. 'Exactly the way I like it. None of you showing.'

Bryony rolled her eyes and tried not to be offended that he didn't actually want to see any of her body. Obviously she was lacking in something, or he would have pounced on her long ago.

Lizzie came back into the hall, holding her gloves, and Jack nodded.

'Good girl.' He opened the front door and led them towards his car. 'Now, Lizzie, tonight when the fireworks start, I want you to stay by me. The whole time. OK?'

'But what if I want to play with my friends?'

'You can play with them before and after,' he said firmly, strapping her into her seat. 'But during the fireworks, you stay with me.'

Lizzie's eyes were huge and solemn. 'Are you very afraid of them, Jack? Will I need to hold your hand?'

Bryony smothered a giggle but Jack's expression didn't flicker. 'I'm terrified of them, angel. And I'm relying on you to be beside me.'

'I'll be there the whole time,' Lizzie assured him, and Bryony rolled her eyes as she slid into the passenger seat, knowing that Jack had got his own way.

Lizzie's friend Anne lived in a house with a huge garden and they arrived to find that the trees had been decorated with fairy lights and everyone was gathered round, laughing and waiting for sausages to cook.

It felt wintry and cold, and delicious smells wafted through the freezing air.

'Hello, Lizzie.' Anne's mother greeted them warmly and drew them into the garden, introducing them to people they didn't know.

'Where have you stored the fireworks?' was Jack's first question, and Bryony put a hand on his arm and smiled at Anne's mother.

'Jack is a consultant in A and E,' she explained hastily, 'and we doctors are always a bit nervous of fireworks. Take no notice.'

'Anne's father has it all under control,' the woman assured them, waving a hand towards the bottom of the garden. 'The children won't be allowed near them. Apart from the sparklers, of course.'

Bryony saw Jack's mouth open and quickly spoke before he did. 'That's great,' she said cheerfully, her fingers biting into his arm like a vice. 'Those sausages smell fantastic.'

'Well, we're just about ready to eat.' Anne's mother led them to a table loaded with food. 'Grab yourself a roll and some ketchup and tuck in!'

She walked away and Jack scowled at Bryony. 'You just made holes in my arm.'

'I was trying to stop you embarrassing Lizzie,' she hissed, smiling sweetly at one of the mothers who passed. 'Now, eat something and relax. Try and remember that you only see the disasters in A and E. You don't see the normal, happy bonfire parties that everyone enjoys.'

There was a long silence and then, to her surprise, Jack sucked in a breath and gave her a lopsided smile. 'You're right,' he said dryly, running a hand through his cropped dark hair. 'I'm being an idiot. It's just that I love Lizzie so much.'

Bryony's face softened. 'I know you do.' On impulse she stood on tiptoe and kissed his cheek, feeling the roughness of stubble against her lips and smelling the sexy male smell that was Jack.

He looked startled. 'What was that for?'

'For being you.' Deciding that, for a girl who was supposed to be forgetting about Jack, she wasn't actually doing that well, Bryony left him by the bread rolls and went and found Lizzie.

'You kissed Jack.' Lizzie was looking at her curiously and Bryony felt herself blush.

'Just on the cheek,' she said hastily, and Lizzie tipped her head on one side.

'Jack would make a cool dad.'

Pretending that she hadn't heard that remark, Bryony turned to chat to one of the mothers that she knew vaguely, trying not to look at Jack who was now deep in conversation with one of the prettiest mothers in the school. He looked broad-shouldered and powerful with his back to her, and her stomach twisted as she saw the woman laughing up at him flirtatiously.

Reminding herself that she was supposed to be getting a life and forgetting about Jack, Bryony joined in with the others, handing food to the children, topping up drinks and wiping ketchup from faces.

Anne's father lit the bonfire and the flames licked towards the dark sky, suddenly illuminating the massive garden.

'You kids stay here,' he ordered cheerfully. 'I'm going to start the show.'

'Mummy, can I have another drink?' Lizzie tugged at her sleeve, her cheeks pink from the cold, and Bryony took her hand and led her over to the table.

'What do you want?' She picked up some empty cartons and then found a full one. 'Apple juice OK?'

'Great.' Lizzie took the cup and looked around her happily. 'Isn't this great, Mummy? You, me and Jack together.'

Bryony swallowed. 'Well, er, we're not exactly…' Then she smiled weakly. 'Yes, sweetheart, it's great.'

There were shrieks of excitement from the other children as they played closer to the fire and Bryony felt a stab of unease.

They were too close…

Opening her mouth to caution them, she noticed

the other parents laughing, totally relaxed, and closed her mouth again. She really must try and act like a normal parent and not like a doctor, seeing accidents everywhere.

'Can I go and play, Mummy?' Lizzie put her drink down and moved towards the other children, but Bryony grabbed her arm, struck by a premonition so powerful that it made her gasp. 'No, Lizzie. I think—'

Before she could even finish her sentence there was a series of horrific screams from Annie, and Bryony saw flames engulfing her little body with frightening speed.

'Oh, my God—*Jack*!' Bryony screamed his name at the top of her voice and ran forward, dragging off her coat as she ran.

Jack was there before her, knocking the girl to the ground and covering her with his jacket. 'Cold water—get me cold water *now*!' His voice was harsh and everyone ran to do as he said while Bryony stood there, so shocked she could hardly move.

All Jack's attention was on the injured girl. 'It's going to be all right, sweetheart. You're going to be fine.' Jack lifted his head and looked straight at one of the fathers. 'Call the paramedics and get me a hosepipe and cling film. Blondie, I need your help with her clothes.'

Bryony still didn't move.

'Dr Hunter.' His voice was sharp. 'I need your help here.'

His sharp reminder of her profession brought her back to reality. She nodded and breathed deeply, try-ing to forget that it was Annie lying on the ground.

Her daughter's friend.

Annie's mother was screaming hysterically and clinging to the other mothers while two of the fathers had fortunately listened to Jack's orders and rolled out a hosepipe.

'OK, sweetheart, you're going to be fine.' Jack carried on talking to Annie, his voice gentle and reassuring as he removed his jacket from the injured girl and took the end of the hosepipe.

Bryony dropped on her knees beside him. 'What do you want me to do?'

She felt physically sick but as usual Jack was rock-solid and totally calm.

'Her clothes are smouldering. If they're not actually stuck to her body, I want them off.'

He turned the hose onto Annie's body, the cold water taking the heat away from the burn as Bryony struggled to remove the clothing.

'Get me scissors.'

Someone quickly produced a pair and she cut the clothing away as gently as she could, careful not to disturb any that actually adhered to the burn.

'It's all below her waist,' Jack said softly, his eyes assessing the area of the burn. 'It's the skirt area. Her skirt caught fire. Has someone called the ambulance?'

'I did, Jack,' Lizzie said in a shaky voice from right beside them. 'They said they'd be here in two minutes.'

'Good girl.' Jack gave her a nod of approval. 'Sweetheart, I need some clingfilm. The stuff you wrap round food in the kitchen. The women over there are too upset to help and the men seem to have forgotten. Can you find it for me, angel?'

Lizzie nodded and shot down the garden towards the house, legs and arms pumping. She was back in less than a minute with a long, thin box.

'That's my girl. Now open it up for me,' Jack ordered, and Lizzie fished it out awkwardly and struggled to find the end.

'How much do you want?'

'I'll do it, Lizzie.' Bryony took it from her, worried about her daughter seeing her friend so badly injured. 'You can go into the house with the other children.'

'I want to help.'

They heard the sound of an ambulance approaching and Jack looked at Lizzie. 'Go and meet them. Tell them I want oxygen, two large-bore cannulae, IV fluids and morphine. Have you got that?'

Lizzie nodded and Bryony glanced at him.

'She won't remember that, Jack, she's only seven.'

'She'll remember,' Jack said firmly, his eyes fixed on Lizzie. 'Oxygen, two large-bore cannulae, IV fluids and morphine. Go, angel.'

Lizzie sped back down the garden to meet the ambulance, leaving Jack and Bryony to wrap the exposed burns.

'Can you get us clean sheets?' Bryony addressed one of the fathers who was hovering by helplessly.

'And someone put that bonfire out,' Jack added, checking Annie's pulse and breathing.

She'd stopped screaming and was lying shivering, sobbing quietly, her father by her side.

Annie's mother was still hysterical at the far side of the garden.

Seconds later the paramedics arrived with Lizzie,

complete with all the equipment that Jack had asked for.

As Bryony grabbed the oxygen and fitted the mask gently to Annie's face, Jack smiled at Lizzie, his blue eyes showering her with approval and warmth.

'Good girl.'

Despite the stress of the situation Lizzie returned the smile bravely and Jack gave a nod.

'All right, I'm going to need your help here, Lizzie. Annie needs some fluid and we're going to put a line in and give her fluid through her arm. Then we're going to take her to hospital. I want you to hold this for me.'

Bryony looked at him uncertainly, still not sure that her young daughter should be exposed to the harsh realities of immediate care, but Jack seemed determined to involve her and Lizzie was frowning with concentration as she listened carefully to Jack's instructions and did as he asked.

Too worried about little Annie to argue, Bryony turned her attention back to the little girl, following Jack's instructions to the letter.

'Shall I give her morphine?'

'We're going to give it IV.' Jack murmured, picking up a cannula and searching for a vein. 'Can you squeeze for me?'

Bryony took Annie's little arm and squeezed, praying that Jack would find a vein first time.

He did, of course, and she breathed a sigh of relief.

'Give her the morphine and cyclizine in there and then we'll put a line in the other arm, too,' Jack said, holding out a hand for the syringe that the paramedic was holding ready. 'OK, sweetheart.' He looked down at Annie, his eyes gentle. 'This is going to make you feel better, I promise. And then we're going to take you to hospital. You're doing fine. You're brilliant.'

He gave the morphine and then put a cannula into the other arm and looked at Bryony. 'OK, let's get some fluid into her and get her covered or she'll get hypothermia from the cold water.'

He and Bryony worked together, each anticipating the other's needs, until finally the little girl was stabilised and in the ambulance.

'I'll go with her,' Jack said. 'Meet me at the hospital when you've dropped Lizzie at your mother's.'

'I want to come, too,' Lizzie said firmly, and Bryony shook her head.

'Sweetheart, no.'

'Bring her,' Jack said firmly. 'I'll run her home later. She can wait in the staffroom.'

He dug in his pocket and produced his car keys, a wry smile playing around his firm mouth. 'If you prang my car, Blondie, you're history.' Handing the keys to Lizzie, he jerked his head towards the front of the house. 'Go and wait for your mother by the car, sweetheart.'

Lizzie did as she was told and Jack took Bryony by the shoulders, forcing her to look at him. 'She's just seen her best friend horribly burned,' he said quietly. 'That is going to stay with her a long time and will be easier to bear if she knows she did something to help. Trust me on this one. She's tough, our Lizzie. She'll be fine. But do it my way.'

Bryony swallowed and nodded, knowing that whatever they did now the trauma had already happened for Lizzie. Maybe it was best for her to be involved.

Anne's parents came over, her mother clinging to her husband, her face streaked with tears.

'Can we go in the ambulance with her?'

Jack exchanged glances with one of the paramedics and then nodded. 'Of course. But try and be calm. I know it's a terrible shock but she needs you to be strong. If she sees you panicking, then she'll panic, and I don't want her any more scared than she is already.'

Bryony waited while they loaded Annie into the ambulance and then she joined Lizzie by Jack's car.

She pressed the remote to unlock the door and gave a short laugh. Now she knew it was an emergency. There was no other reason that Jack would have let her near his precious sports car—he never let anyone drive it.

She strapped Lizzie in the front seat and slid into the driver's seat, telling herself that it was only a car. Exactly like her car really, except that it was capable of ridiculous speed and cost about fifteen times as much.

She started the engine and flinched as the car gave a throaty growl. 'Boys with toys,' she muttered disparagingly, finding first gear and carefully pulling out of the driveway onto the road. She just hoped she didn't meet any other traffic on the way to hospital.

When she arrived she settled Lizzie in the staff-room, promising to come back and update her as soon as possible.

Jack was already in Resus, along with Sean

Nicholson and a full team of staff. Jack was barking out instructions as he worked to stabilise Annie.

'Can someone check her weight with her parents?'

'I've just done it.' Bryony hurried into the room and reached in her pocket for a calculator. 'I've worked out 4 mils of fluid per kilogram multiplied by the percentage of the burn. Do you have that yet?'

'Just doing it. My estimate is twenty-two per cent,' Jack said, glancing up at her. 'Are you OK?'

Bryony nodded and studied the Lund and Browder charts that helped them to assess the area of the burn according to age. 'You're about right, Jack,' she said lightly, feeding the numbers into her calculator. 'I make it twenty-two per cent.'

She worked out the volume of fluid and showed her calculation to Jack.

'Right.' He gave a nod. 'So she needs that in twenty-four hours, but we need to give her half in the first eight hours and monitor her urine output. I want her to have a combination of crystalloid and colloid.'

'Catheter is in,' Nicky said quickly, 'and I've started a chart.'

'Great. Can you test her urine? And, Bryony, we need to take some bloods before she's transferred. Cross-matching, FBC, COHb, U and Es, glucose and coagulation.'

Bryony reached for the appropriate bottles. 'You're sending her to the burns unit?'

Jack nodded. 'The helicopter is waiting to take her as soon as we give the word. I've spoken to the consultant, he's waiting for her.'

Bryony took the samples and then went to talk to

Annie. The little girl was drifting in and out of sleep, hardly aware of what was going on around her.

'I gave her some sedation,' Jack said softly, covering the last of the burns and then giving Nicky a nod. 'OK. Let's go.'

'Are you going with her?'

He nodded. 'Take Lizzie home in my car. I'll see you later.'

'How will you get home?'

'I'll get the paramedics to drop me at your place, or I'll grab a taxi.' He shrugged, totally unconcerned, and she nodded.

'Fine. I'll see you later. Do you want me to talk to Annie's parents?'

'I'll do it,' Sean said immediately. 'That way you can get home with your little girl and Jack can get loaded into the helicopter.'

Bryony was tucking Lizzie into bed when she heard the doorbell. 'That will be Jack.'

She dropped a kiss on Lizzie's forehead and went to answer the door, praying that Annie's condition hadn't worsened during the transfer.

'How is she?'

Jack strolled into her house and gave a shiver, and it was only then that she remembered that he'd used his jacket to put out the flames and that he'd been working only in a jumper. He must be freezing.

'Come and sit by the fire,' she urged, and he did as she'd suggested, stretching out his hands towards the flames.

'It's nice and warm in here.' He looked at her. 'Is my girl asleep?'

Bryony shook her head, her expression troubled. 'No. She's very upset by it all.'

'Of course she is.' His jaw tightened. 'I'll talk to her.'

They both walked towards Lizzie's bedroom and Jack strolled in and settled himself on the edge of the bed.

'Hi, there.' His voice was soft and Lizzie stared up at him, her eyes huge in her pretty face.

'Hi, Jack.' Her smile was shaky. 'Annie is very badly hurt, isn't she?'

Jack hesitated. 'She is pretty badly hurt,' he agreed, and Bryony mentally thanked him for not lying. She knew that Annie's condition was serious and if anything happened to the little girl, she didn't want Lizzie to feel that they'd been dishonest.

'Is she going to die?' Lizzie's voice trembled and Jack shook his head.

'No, sweetheart. I'm sure she isn't going to die. I've just taken her to a special hospital where they know all about burns.'

'Can I go and see her there?'

'Sure,' Jack said immediately. 'We'll go together.'

Tears suddenly welled up in Lizzie's eyes and Jack immediately leaned forward and lifted the little girl onto his lap.

'Don't cry, baby,' he said roughly, stroking her hair with his strong hand and exchanging an agonised look with Bryony. 'You were brilliant. My little star. All those grown-ups were panicking and you were cool as ice cream.'

Lizzie gave a sniff and pulled away from him, but her little hands still clutched at his jumper. 'I told the paramedics everything you wanted, just like you said.'

'I know you did.' Jack smiled down at her, pride in his eyes. 'You were unbelievable. And I was so proud of you. You really helped save Annie.'

'I helped?' Lizzie's face brightened slightly. 'Really?'

'Really.' Jack nodded, his handsome face serious. 'You see, you did all the right things. Everyone was scared and I bet you were, too, but you didn't let being scared stop you from doing what needed to be done. And that makes you a very special person.'

'It does?'

'Certainly. I don't know many grown-ups who would have been as calm as you and remembered all those things and done what you did.' Jack lifted a hand and stroked Lizzie's blonde curls away from her face. 'One day, if you wanted to, I think you could be a very important doctor.'

Bryony swallowed down a lump in her throat and Lizzie's eyes widened. 'Like you and Mummy?'

Jack grinned. 'Maybe not quite as important as me,' he said teasingly, winking at Bryony who smiled back weakly. 'But important, just the same.'

Lizzie gave a gurgle of laughter and punched him on the shoulder. 'That's boasting, Jack,' she said reprovingly, and wound her arms round his neck. 'I'm glad you and Mummy were there.'

For a brief moment Jack squeezed his eyes shut, his jaw tense, and Bryony knew exactly what was going through his mind. He'd been imagining a scene where he hadn't been there, a scene where there hadn't been a doctor on site to administer first aid, a scene where Lizzie might have been the one near the bonfire.

She gave a little shudder, imagining the same scene, and Jack's eyes opened and locked on hers for a meaningful second.

'Time for you to go to bed now, angel,' he said softly, lifting Lizzie off his lap and tucking her under the covers with her mermaid. He leaned across and switched her little pink lamp on. 'Your mum and I will just be eating some supper in the kitchen. Shout if you want anything.'

'I don't want you to go home tonight.'

'I'm not going,' Jack said immediately, sounding rock-solid, dependable and altogether too male for Bryony's piece of mind. 'Tonight I'm sleeping in your spare room.'

Lizzie gave a smile and they were just tiptoeing to the door when she spoke again.

'Jack?' Lizzie's voice was a little-girl whisper and Bryony saw Jack's face soften.

'Yes, angel.'

'Tomorrow when we wake up, will you play with me?'

Jack grinned. 'Absolutely.'

'Can we play Weddings?'

'My favourite game,' Jack said softly, walking back across the room and bending down to kiss her one more time. 'Now, get some sleep. I can't marry you with black rings under your eyes.'

Lizzie chuckled, sounding much happier. 'Mummy, will you leave the door open?'

'Of course, sweetheart. And I'll pop my head in later.'

Jack followed Bryony out of the room.

'Thank you for that,' she said quietly, walking through to the kitchen and opening the fridge. 'You said all the right things. In fact, you did all the right things, too. My instincts were to just get her out of there.'

'That would have been my instinct, too, if she hadn't already seen her friend engulfed by flames,' Jack said wearily, sinking down on one of her kitchen chairs with a groan. 'To be honest, I was mostly concentrating on Annie, but I did think that if Lizzie knew she'd helped, she might feel better.'

'Which she did.' Bryony removed a bottle of wine from the fridge and handed it to him along with a corkscrew. 'I just hope she doesn't have nightmares.'

'She's a tough kid,' Jack said, yanking the cork out and setting the bottle down on the table. 'She'll be fine. As soon as Annie is a bit better we can take Lizzie along to see her.'

We.

Listening to him talking as if they were a family, Bryony found it harder and harder to remember that she was supposed to not be thinking of Jack in *that* way any more.

Remembering how skilled he'd been with Annie brought a lump to her throat. 'You're amazing, do you know that?' She reached into the cupboard for two glasses, trying to keep her tone light. 'You never lose your cool, no matter what. I just saw Annie on fire and I froze.'

'Only for about three seconds,' Jack said easily, stretching out a hand for the glasses and filling them both to the top. 'And working in a well-equipped

A and E department is very different from immediate care, as you know. Here. Have a drink. I think we both need it.'

'I should cook some supper first.'

'Forget cooking.' Jack took a mouthful of wine and gave a groan of pleasure. 'That's good. Let's send out for pizza or something.'

Bryony giggled. 'I can't do that. Lizzie will find the boxes in the morning and she'll kill me. Pizza is her treat.'

Jack shrugged. 'All right. Indian, then. I left a menu by your phone last time I was here.'

'It would be nice not to cook,' Bryony agreed, and Jack stood up.

'That's decided, then. Indian it is. What do you want?'

Bryony shrugged. 'You choose.'

So he did and the food arrived half an hour later and was wonderful.

They were well into the bottle of wine when they heard Lizzie's screams.

Both of them sprinted to her bedroom to find her sobbing and clutching her mermaid, her face blotched with tears.

'I keep thinking of Annie.'

Bryony cuddled her close, rocking her gently. 'Well, of course you do, darling. Annie is your friend. She's going to be fine, Lizzie.'

As she said the words she prayed that she was right. If anything happened to Annie...

Eventually Lizzie calmed down and fell asleep again and the two of them tiptoed back to the kitchen.

Bryony felt totally stressed and she was seriously

worried about the effect of the accident on her daughter. As Jack had rightly said, she'd actually seen it happen. What sort of impact would that have on her in the long term?

She desperately wanted to lean on Jack but she couldn't bring herself to ask him for the hug she so badly needed.

And then he looked at her and she knew he felt the same way. 'I hate Bonfire Night.'

His voice was hoarse and for the first time Bryony caught a glimpse of the strain he must have been under.

She gave a little frown. 'We forget about you, Jack,' she said softly, stepping up to him and looking at him with concern in her eyes. 'You always seem so strong—so much the one in charge. Everyone else is panicking and flapping and you're so calm. It's easy to forget that you can be affected by things, too.'

'Hey.' He gave a sexy grin that belied the strain in his eyes. 'I'm Mr Tough.'

She smiled. 'Well, would Mr Tough like a cup of coffee?'

'As I'm not driving, I'd rather finish the wine,' he admitted ruefully, reaching for his glass. 'Do you mind me staying?'

'Of course not,' she said blithely, wondering why her heart was thumping so hard. Jack had stayed in her cottage on numerous occasions. Why did this time feel different?

'I'll get you some stuff ready,' she said formally, and he reached out and grabbed her arm.

'Don't bother. I don't wear anything in bed anyway.'

Bryony swallowed hard, trying to dispel the mental image of Jack naked in her spare room.

For a woman who was not supposed to be thinking about Jack Rothwell, she was failing dismally.

'Jack…'

'What I really need is a hug.' Without waiting for a response, he hauled her against him and she went into his arms, feeling the softness of his jumper covering the hard muscle of his chest and the strength of his arms as he held her. He gave a groan and tightened his hold, burying his face in her hair.

Bryony could hardly breathe. She felt the steady thud of his heart against her flushed cheek, felt her whole body tingle in response to the feel of his body against hers. He felt strong and safe and deliciously male.

They stood like that for a moment and she closed her eyes, wishing that it could last for ever. Wishing that it could lead to something more.

And then gradually his grip on her loosened and his hands slid slowly up her arms. His strong fingers curled into her shoulders and he looked down at her, his blue eyes suddenly intent on her face.

A warmth spread slowly through her pelvis and her whole body melted with longing.

She felt his fingers tighten, saw something flicker in his eyes and then his head lowered towards hers.

He was going to kiss her.

Finally, after so many years of dreaming about exactly that, Jack was going to kiss her.

Dizzy with excitement, Bryony stared up at him, breathless with anticipation.

And then suddenly his hands fell away from her

shoulders and he stepped back, his handsome face blank of expression.

'We should probably get some sleep, Blondie.' His tone was light and he glanced at the clock on the wall. 'It's getting late.'

Bryony tried to smile but it was a poor effort. She felt swamped with a disappointment so powerful that it was almost a physical pain. *She'd been so sure that he was going to kiss her.*

But why would Jack kiss her?

She gritted her teeth, furious with herself. She was doing it again. Fantasising about Jack.

So much for her campaign to date other men. So far she'd been on one date that had been an utter disaster and she was still noticing Jack.

She had less than two months to find Lizzie a daddy, or at least someone who looked as though he had potential. It was time she made more effort.

She needed to kiss someone and see if that helped.

She needed to stop comparing everyone with Jack.

There must be another man who looked good in jeans. There must be another man who always knew exactly what to do when everyone around them was panicking. There must be another man who would make her knees wobble every time he walked into a room.

And she was going to find him.

CHAPTER FIVE

THE rest of November flew past and Annie's condition gradually improved.

'The burns are almost all round her skirt area,' Jack told Bryony one day as they snatched a quick cup of coffee during a late shift. 'I talked to the consultant last night. She's going to need extensive skin grafts.'

'Poor mite.' Bryony pulled a face at the thought of the number of hospital stays Annie was going to have to endure. 'It's going to be so hard for her.'

Jack nodded. 'But at least she's alive. And Lizzie seems to have bounced back amazingly well.'

'Yes.' Bryony smiled. 'I was worried about that but she's doing fine. We're visiting Annie a lot, which helps, and Lizzie has made it her mission to act as the link between Annie and the school. She's been taking her all sorts of books and things to do and generally keeping her in touch with the gossip.'

'She's a great girl.' Jack drained his coffee and sat back in his chair with a yawn, long legs stretched out in front of him. 'So, Blondie. December the first to-morrow.'

Bryony stared gloomily into her coffee. 'Don't remind me. I now have less than a month to sort out Lizzie's Christmas present, and I'm fast coming to the conclusion that it's an impossible task.'

Jack looked at her quizzically, a strange light in his

eyes. 'So, is the romance with David Armstrong not working?'

Romance?

Bryony looked at him. 'We've been on two dates. The first one we barely had time to talk because you kept calling—not that it was your fault that Lizzie was demanding that night,' she added hastily, hoping that he didn't think that she was complaining, 'and the second date was disturbed because you called him back to the hospital to see a child. And that wasn't your fault either.'

Jack looked at her, his expression inscrutable. 'And he hasn't asked you out since?'

'Well, funnily enough, he rang me this morning,' Bryony confided, 'and he's taking me to dinner at The Peacock on Saturday. Neither of us is on call and Lizzie is sleeping at my mother's so this time there should be absolutely no interruptions.'

And this time she was going to kiss him.

She'd made up her mind that she was going to kiss him.

She was utterly convinced that kissing another man would cure her obsession with Jack.

David was a good-looking guy. She knew that lots of the nurses lusted after him secretly. He must know how to kiss.

And it was going to happen on Saturday. She was going to invite him in for coffee and she was going to kiss him.

The next day was incredibly busy.

'It's the roads,' Sean said wearily as they snatched a five-minute coffee-break in the middle of a long and intensive shift. 'They're so icy and people drive too fast. I predict a nasty pile-up before the end of the evening.'

His prediction proved correct.

At seven o'clock the ambulance hotline rang. Bryony answered it and when she finally put the phone down both Sean and Jack were watching her expectantly.

'Are you clairvoyant?' She looked at Sean who shrugged.

'Black ice. It was inevitable. What are the details?'

'Twenty-two-year-old female, conscious but shocked and complaining of chest pains.'

She'd barely finished repeating what Ambulance Control had told her when the doors slammed open and the paramedics hurried in with the trolley.

'Straight into Resus,' Jack ordered and they transferred the woman onto the trolley as smoothly as possible. While the rest of the team moved quickly into action he questioned the paramedics about the accident.

'It was a side impact,' the paramedic told him. 'She was driving and the other vehicle went straight into her side. Her passenger walked away virtually unharmed. He's giving her details to Reception now.'

Jack nodded and turned his attention back to the young woman, a frown on his face. 'She has a neck haematoma. I want a chest X-ray, fast,' he murmured, and looked at Bryony. 'Have you got a line in?'

She nodded. 'One.'

'Put in another one,' he ordered, 'but hold the fluid. And cross-match ten units of blood.'

Bryony's eyes widened. 'Why?'

'Just a feeling. Nicky, I want a BP from both arms,' he said, gesturing to the staff to stand back while the radiographer took the chest film.

'Her blood pressure is different in each arm,' Nicky said quickly, and Jack nodded.

'I thought it might be. She's only slightly hypotensive so I want minimal fluid replacement for now.'

Bryony looked at him, waiting for a blonde joke or one of his usual quips that would ease the tension, but this time his eyes were fixed on the patient.

'Fast-bleep the surgeons,' he ordered, 'and let's take a look at that chest X-ray.'

They walked across to look at the chest X-ray and Bryony looked at him, able to talk now that they were away from the patient. 'Why did you cross-match so much blood?'

'Because I think she's ruptured her aorta.'

Bryony's eyes widened. 'But a ruptured aorta has a 90 per cent mortality rate. She'd be dead.'

He squinted at the X-ray. 'Unless the bleed is contained by the aortic adventitia. Then she'd be alive. But at risk of haemorrhage.'

Bryony stared at the X-ray, too, and Jack lifted an eyebrow.

'OK, Blondie—impress me. What do you see?'

'The mediastinum is widened.'

'And is that significant?'

Bryony chewed her lip and delved into her brain. 'On its own, possibly not,' she said, remembering something she'd read, 'but taken with other factors...'

'Such as?'

Bryony looked again, determined not to miss anything. 'The trachea is deviated to the right. The aortic outline is blurred and the aortic knuckle is obliterated.'

'What else?'

'It's cloudy.' She peered closer at the X-ray. 'I haven't seen that before. Is it a haemothorax?'

'Full marks.' He gave her a lazy smile but his eyes glittered with admiration. 'She has a right-sided haemothorax caused by a traumatic rupture of the thoracic aorta, which is currently contained. In this case we can see it clearly on the X-ray, but not always.'

Bryony looked at him and felt her heart thud harder. The patient was lucky to be alive. 'So what happens now?'

'She needs urgent surgical repair. In the meantime, we need to give fluid cautiously, otherwise the adventitia could rupture and she'll have a fatal haemorrhage.'

'So presumably we also need to give her good pain relief so that her blood pressure doesn't go up?'

His eyes rested on her shiny blonde hair and he shook his head solemnly. 'Amazing.'

She poked her tongue out discreetly and he gave her a sexy smile that made her knees wobble.

Fortunately, at that moment the surgeons walked into the room and provided a distraction. They all conferred, agreeing to take the woman to Theatre right away for surgical repair.

'So what exactly do they do?' Bryony asked Jack after the woman had been safely handed over to the surgeons and they were left to deal with the debris in Resus.

'Depends.' He ripped off his gloves and dropped them into the bin. 'They'll attempt a surgical repair.'

'And if they can't repair it?'

'Then they'll do a vascular graft.'

Bryony helped Nicky to clean the trolley. 'But what made you suspect an aortic rupture? I always thought patients died at the scene of the accident.'

'Well, if they're alive it basically suggests a partial injury,' he told her. 'It's often hard to diagnose on X-ray. A widened mediastinum doesn't necessarily indicate an abnormality. But in her case there were other classic chest X-ray signs and she had clinical signs too. The neck haematoma, asymmetric BP and chest pain.'

'And if the X-ray hadn't been clear?'

'I would have talked to the consultant radiologist and we would have done a multi-slice CT scan. It's worth finding out as much as you can about the details of the accident. The paramedic told us her car had been hit on the driver's side. A significant number of blunt traumatic aortic ruptures are caused by side impact.'

Bryony stared at him in fascination. 'What's the pathology?'

'Basically a sudden deceleration such as a fall from a height or an RTA allows the mobile parts of the aorta to keep moving. It usually tears where the aorta is tethered to the pulmonary vein—'

'The ligamentum arteriosum,' Bryony intervened, and he rolled his eyes.

'If there's one thing I can't stand, it's a brainy blonde,' he drawled, and she clucked sympathetically.

'If I'm threatening your ego then just let me know.'

'My ego is shivering,' he assured her, his blue eyes twinkling as looked down at her. 'What do you get when you give a blonde a penny for her thoughts?'

'Change,' Bryony said immediately, tilting her head to one side. 'Why is a man like a vintage wine?'

Jack's eyes narrowed and his mouth twitched. 'Go on…'

'Because they all start out like grapes,' Bryony said cheerfully, 'and it's a woman's job to tread all over them and keep them in the dark until they mature into something you'd like to have dinner with.'

Nicky gave a snort of amusement from the corner of the room and Jack grinned.

'That's shockingly sexist, Blondie.'

'Just giving as good as I get.'

Jack's smile faded. 'And talking about having dinner, haven't you got a date tomorrow night?'

'Yes.' Bryony frowned as she remembered that she had all of three weeks to find a man who might make a good father for Lizzie. By anyone's standards it was a tall order.

But at least she had another date with David so he must be fairly keen.

And he was a really nice man. Her eyes slid to Jack's face and then away again. She wasn't going to compare him to Jack. All right, so Jack was staggeringly handsome and he was clever and he had a great sense of humour— She cut herself off before the list grew too long. Jack didn't do commitment. And Jack didn't notice her. Which ruled him out as a potential partner.

At least David noticed her.

And she was going to start noticing him, she told

herself firmly, leaving the room so that she wouldn't be tempted to continually look at Jack.

'I'm really looking forward to tonight.' Bryony slid into David's car and gave him a smile. 'The food is meant to be great and Lizzie is at my mother's so we are guaranteed no interruptions.'

David waited while she fastened her seat belt and then pulled out of her drive. 'Let's hope not.'

They walked into the restaurant ten minutes later and Bryony gave a gasp of delight as she saw the Christmas tree sparkling by the log fire. 'Oh—it's lovely.'

And romantic.

How could she and David fail to further their relationship in this atmosphere?

It was made for lovers.

She handed over her coat, feeling David's eyes slide over her.

'You look great,' he said quietly, and she smiled shyly, pleased that she'd bought the red dress she'd seen on a shopping expedition a week earlier.

'So do you.'

And he did. He was wearing a dark, well-cut suit and she saw several female heads turn towards him as they were shown to their table.

All right, so he didn't make her knees wobble but that was a good thing surely. With Jack she actually felt physically sick every time he walked into a room, which was utterly ridiculous. She couldn't concentrate and she couldn't breathe. All she was aware of was him. And that wasn't what she wanted in a stable, long-term relationship.

At least being with David didn't make her feel sick with excitement.

They ordered their food and then David picked up his glass and raised it. 'To an uninterrupted evening.'

She smiled and lifted her glass in response but before she could speak she gave a gasp of surprise. 'Oh—it's Jack!'

David's jaw tightened and he put his glass carefully down on the table. *'Jack?'*

'Jack Rothwell. He's just walked in with some blonde.'

Bryony felt a flash of jealousy as she studied Jack's companion. She was his usual type. Endless legs, silvery blonde hair and a skirt that barely covered her bottom. She wore a very low-cut top and Bryony glanced at Jack to see signs of disapproval, but he seemed perfectly relaxed, his eyes twinkling flirtatiously as he laughed at something the girl had said.

By contrast, David was glowering, his earlier good humour seemingly gone as he reached for his wine.

'Well…' Bryony made a determined effort not to look at Jack and not to mind that he didn't appear to have noticed her anyway. 'That's a coincidence.'

'Is it?' David's eyes glittered ominously and he sat back in his chair as the waiter poured more wine into his glass. 'Aren't you beginning to wonder why it is that Jack Rothwell would want to sabotage every date we have?'

'Sabotage?' Bryony looked at him in astonishment and gave a puzzled laugh. 'Jack has nothing to do with the fact that our last two dates haven't worked out that well.'

'No?'

'Well, he's certainly not sabotaging tonight,' Bryony said reasonably. 'I mean, he hasn't even noticed we're here. He's with a woman himself.'

She glanced across the restaurant again and immediately wished she hadn't. Jack was leaning forward, his attention totally focused on his beautiful companion.

Bryony looked away quickly, trying not to mind. Knowing that she had no right to mind.

And, anyway, she was with David.

But he was looking at her with an odd expression on his face. 'He knows you're here,' he said quietly, 'and no man could fail to notice you, Bryony.'

She blushed at the compliment. 'Well, that's very kind of you, but I can assure you that Jack certainly doesn't notice me in the way you're suggesting.'

In fact, he didn't seem to notice her as a woman at all. Until she wore something that he disapproved of, she thought gloomily. Goodness knew how he would have reacted had she been the one dressed like his date. He probably would have had her locked up. But evidently the girl staring into his eyes at that precise moment was allowed to dress however she pleased.

Realising that she was staring again, Bryony turned her attention back to David but the atmosphere had changed. She made a valiant attempt to keep up lively conversation but it seemed like hard work.

In the end they ate their starter in virtual silence and Bryony's gaze flickered surreptitiously to Jack yet again.

Immediately their eyes locked and she swallowed hard, aware that he must have been looking at her.

His eyes held hers and everything and everyone else in the room gradually faded into the background. For Bryony there was just Jack and he seemed as reluctant to break the contact as she was.

Her heart banged against her ribs with rhythmic force and the sick feeling started in her stomach.

And still Jack's eyes held hers.

They might have stared at each other for ever if the waiter hadn't chosen that moment to deliver their next course, walking across their line of vision.

Staring down at her plate, Bryony realised that suddenly she wasn't hungry any more. Her insides felt totally jumbled up.

Why had Jack been staring at her like that?

Did he disapprove of her seeing David? Did he think that she was dating the wrong man?

She pushed her food around her plate, miserably aware that David had finished his main course and was now watching her in silence.

Finally he spoke. 'You don't seem hungry.'

'Not very.' She put her fork down and smiled at him apologetically. 'I'm so sorry.'

'It doesn't matter.'

She bit her lip, embarrassed that the evening was going so badly. 'I'm just a bit tired—it's been a pretty busy week.'

'Do you want to go home?'

She hesitated and then nodded. 'Yes. If that's all right with you.'

'Shall we have coffee first?'

She remembered her resolution to kiss him. 'No,' she croaked. 'Let's have coffee at my house.'

He looked at her thoughtfully and seemed to relax

slightly. Then he nodded and rose to his feet. 'Good idea. Come on. I'll settle the bill while they get our coats.'

'If you've finished, I'll take her home.' Jack's deep voice came from right beside her, his eyes fixed on her face. 'It's on my way.'

The two men stared at each other with ill-disguised hostility.

'She's my date,' David said tightly, and Jack smiled.

'You've had your date,' he drawled softly, 'and now I'm taking her home.'

Realising that everyone in the restaurant was staring at them, Bryony flushed scarlet and tugged Jack's arm.

'For goodness' sake, Jack! Everyone's looking at us.'

Jack gave a dismissive shrug that indicated just how little he was bothered by other people's opinions and then he smiled as his date for the evening joined them. 'Nina, this is David. He's offered to take you home.'

Nina gave Jack a longing look that left no one in any doubt as to how she felt about him. And then she sighed and shot David a dazzling smile. 'If you're sure it's no trouble…'

Wondering why Nina was giving up so easily, Bryony watched as David's eyes dropped to the neckline of Nina's dress which revealed a hypnotic amount of female flesh.

He stared in blatant fascination and then finally cleared his throat and dragged his gaze up to Nina's.

'It's no trouble at all,' he said hoarsely and Bryony resisted the temptation to scream with frustration.

Men were just so pathetic!

Boiling with anger, she said goodnight to David and Nina and followed Jack across the car park.

He unlocked the car and opened the door for her and she slid inside and yanked at the seat belt.

As Jack settled himself in the driver's seat, she let rip.

'David was my date! You had no right to interfere.'

Jack reversed out of his parking space. 'I merely offered to take you home.'

'You didn't offer, Jack,' she said caustically, 'you insisted. David was taking me home and he was ready to argue until your Nina thrust her chest in his face.'

Jack grinned, maddeningly unperturbed by her outburst. 'Impressive, isn't she? I thought as I was taking you away from him, I ought to offer him something in compensation.'

'So I suppose she was the *booby* prize?' Bryony's voice dripped sarcasm and Jack's grin widened.

'Booby prize.' He repeated her words and chuckled with appreciation. 'I admit I hadn't thought of it in exactly those terms, but now you mention it...'

Bryony ground her teeth in frustration. 'You are so hypocritical, do you know that? You have the nerve to criticise my black dress and then you go out with a girl who has a cleavage the size of the Grand Canyon and shows it off to the entire population. I didn't notice you covering *her* up with a coat.'

Jack glanced across at her and in the semi-darkness she could see his eyes twinkling wickedly. 'It would have had to be a big coat and it seemed a shame to deprive everyone of the view,' he drawled, and she felt fury mix with a very different emotion.

Hurt.

When Nina wore a low-cut dress, Jack obviously thought she looked incredibly attractive. But when *she* wore one he thought she looked awful and tried to cover her up.

David had said that she looked nice but, thanks to Jack, David was now with Nina and was doubtless enjoying the view as much as all the other men in the restaurant.

And she was with a man who didn't find her attractive and never would.

'There are times when I hate you, Jack Rothwell,' she muttered, and he gave a soft laugh.

'I don't know what you're getting so worked up about, Blondie.'

For once his use of her nickname irritated her. 'He was my date, Jack. *My date.* And you ruined it.'

To her utter humiliation she felt a lump starting in her throat. She wasn't going to cry in front of Jack.

But fortunately Jack had his eyes fixed on the road. 'How did I ruin it?'

'You really need to ask that question?' She stared at him incredulously. 'I was spending the evening with a man and you suddenly dived in and insisted on taking me home. And I really don't understand why.'

In the moonlight she saw the muscle in his jaw flicker. 'The roads are icy. I didn't want him driving you.'

Her jaw fell open. 'You think you're the only man who can drive on ice?'

'No.' His tone was calm. 'But I've never seen David Armstrong drive on ice and until I do, he's not driving you.'

'Jack, you're being ridiculous!' She looked at him in exasperation. 'And what about Nina? You were perfectly happy for him to drive Nina.'

'Nina can look after herself.'

Bryony slumped back in her seat and gritted her teeth. 'And I can't?'

'You know nothing about men.'

'I thought we were talking about ice?'

'Amongst other things.'

'Oh, right. So we're back to the fact that I haven't dated anyone for ages. It doesn't make me stupid, Jack.'

'And it doesn't make you experienced.'

'Well, it's obvious that I'm never going to get any experience while I'm living in the same town as you!' She glared at him and he gave a shrug.

'I don't know why you're making such a fuss. You had your date. You spent the evening together. Was it good, by the way?'

She opened her mouth to tell him that, no, it had not been good because she'd been staring at him all night, but she realised in time just how much that would reveal about her feelings and stopped herself.

'It was fine,' she lied, 'but it hadn't finished. I wanted *him* to take me home.' And she'd wanted him to kiss her just to see whether it was possible for another man to take her mind off Jack.

'You wanted him to take you home?' There was a tense silence and she saw Jack's fingers tighten on the wheel. 'Why?' His voice was suddenly harsh. 'Or was that where the date was supposed to begin? Keen to make up for lost time, were you?'

His tone was frosty and she gave an exclamation of disgust. 'And so what if it was? What I do with my life is none of your business. I don't need you to look out for me, Jack.'

It was only when he stopped the car and switched off the engine that she realised that they were outside her home. The house was in darkness and suddenly she felt utterly depressed and lonely. Maybe Lizzie was right, she thought miserably. It would be great to walk into her house, knowing that someone was waiting for her. It would be great to have someone to hug her at night. She'd been without a man for almost all her life and suddenly she wanted someone special. Someone who cared whether she came home or not.

But so far her quest for a man had been a disaster.

And suddenly she just wanted to be on her own.

'Well, thanks, Jack. Thanks for ruining my evening.' She undid her seat belt and reached down to pick up her bag. 'I would invite you in for coffee but, seeing as you think that's a euphemism for sex, naturally I wouldn't dream of it. And anyway I'm sure you're dying to get back to Nina.'

'Nina is just a friend.'

'I really couldn't care less, Jack,' she lied, 'because your love life isn't any of my business, just as my love life is none of your business. A whole month has gone past since Lizzie sent her letter to Santa and so far I haven't even managed to get a man to kiss me.'

'You want a man to kiss you?' Jack's voice was a deep growl and without waiting for her answer he slid a hand round her head and brought his mouth down on hers with punishing force. His long fingers bit into her scalp and he lifted his other hand and curved it around her cheek, holding her face still for his kiss.

Utterly shocked, Bryony lifted a hand to his chest, intending to push him away, but instead her traitorous fingers curled into his shirt, then loosened a button and slid inside. Her fingers felt the roughness of his chest hair, warm skin and solid muscle and she felt his grip on her head tighten as his kiss gentled and his tongue traced the seam of her mouth, coaxing her to open for him.

And then he was really kissing her.

Kissing her in the way that she'd always known only he could.

And it felt like magic. How could one person make another feel so different unless it was magic? She was trembling and shivering, overwhelmed by an excitement so intense that she didn't know where it was leading or how it would end. She only knew that she wanted to get closer to him, to crawl all over him but the seats in the car didn't exactly encourage that type of contact. So instead she leaned into him, sliding her hand around his body and trying to draw him closer.

His tongue teased hers gently and then dipped deeper, exploring the interior of her mouth with a lazy expertise that was so erotic it set her entire body on fire. With a maddening degree of self-control, he slid the backs of his fingers over her cheek and down to her neck, trailing his fingers tantalisingly close to her aching breasts before stopping just short of his target. Bryony whimpered with frustration. Longing for his touch, she arched against him but he didn't move his hand. Instead, he continued to kiss her with increasing intensity until none of her senses were under her control.

And then finally, just when she thought her entire body would explode with frustration, he touched her. His strong hand cupped one breast through the silken fabric of her dress and then he drew his thumb over her nipple, creating an agony of sensation so powerful that she gasped against his mouth and shifted in the seat to try and relieve the nagging throb between her thighs.

'Jack...'

The moment she sobbed his name he lifted his head, his breathing unsteady as he stared down at her. Then he released her abruptly and ran a hand over his face, obviously as shaken as she was.

Her whole body screamed in protest that he'd stopped and she looked at him in dazed confusion.

'Jack?'

She saw him tense and then he turned to face her, his handsome face totally blank of expression. 'Now do you see?'

She swallowed, finding it terribly hard to concentrate, still suffering from the aftershocks of his kiss. 'Now do I see what?'

'That kisses can get out of control.' His eyes dropped to her parted lips, still swollen and damp from the ruthless demands of his mouth and then dropped further still to the outline of her breasts which pushed boldly against her dress. He dragged his gaze away and stared into the darkness. 'That's what would have happened if you'd invited David Armstrong back for coffee.'

Bryony stared at him in silence.

She felt as though the world had changed shape. As if everything should look different. It certainly felt different.

For her, their entire relationship had changed in an instant. The moment his mouth had touched hers, everything had become different.

But evidently he didn't feel the same way.

Chewing her lip, she reminded herself that this was Jack. Jack, whose parents had divorced when he was eight and who had vowed never to get married himself when he grew up. And then he'd grown up and had shown no intention of changing his mind about that one fact. Jack didn't do relationships. Judging from the few conversations she'd overheard between her brothers, Jack did sex and not much else.

But even knowing that, her whole body flooded with disappointment as she realised that obviously the kiss hadn't meant anything at all to him. He'd actually been proving a point and in doing so he'd proved something to her, too.

That she'd been right all along about Jack.

He was an amazing kisser.

And she knew that the same thing would never have happened had she invited David Armstrong back for coffee. David might have kissed her, that was true, but she knew that there wasn't another man on the planet who would make her feel what Jack had just made her feel.

But it was totally hopeless.

And the raw, sexual attraction she felt for Jack shouldn't interfere with her determination to find a father for Lizzie, she told herself firmly.

That was just lust and lust always faded anyway.

She needed a man who would be kind, good company and a caring father to Lizzie. She didn't need raw sexual attraction. In fact, raw sexual attraction was starting to turn her into a nervous wreck.

So she lifted her chin and smiled at Jack, proud of how natural it seemed. 'Well, thanks for the practice,' she said lightly, leaning forward and kissing him on the cheek, resisting the almost overwhelming temptation to trace a route to his mouth with the tip of her tongue. 'I'd forgotten how to do it, but you reminded me. Now I know I'll get it right next time I go out with David.'

And with that she opened the door, climbed out of the car and walked to her cottage without looking back.

CHAPTER SIX

DAMN. Damn. Damn.

What the hell had he done?

He'd kissed his best friend.

Jack stared after Bryony, trying to decide what shocked him most. The fact that he'd kissed her, or the fact that he hadn't wanted to stop.

He sat in the car with the engine switched off, staring into the frozen darkness feeling as though something fundamental to his existence had changed.

Where had it come from? That sudden impulse to kiss her...

Blondie was family.

As much a baby sister to him as she was to Tom and Oliver.

And until tonight he'd never thought of her in any other way.

Or had he?

Had he really never thought of her like that or was it just that he'd trained himself not to?

He sat still, watching the house, and then suddenly the lights went on. He saw her walk into her cosy sitting room and shrug off her coat, revealing that amazing red dress and an avalanche of blonde hair.

For years he hadn't seen her in a dress and suddenly she seemed to be wearing a different one every week.

He closed his eyes and breathed deeply, still able

to detect the tantalising scent of her hair and skin. The instantaneous reaction of his body was so powerful that he gritted his teeth and shifted slightly in his seat, trying to find a more comfortable position.

There wasn't one.

Suddenly, somehow, she'd invaded every part of him.

He'd made an unconscious decision never to cross that boundary but now he'd crossed it there was no going back.

Whichever way he looked at her, he didn't see a surrogate sister any more. And he didn't see his best friend. He saw a woman. A living, breathing, stunningly beautiful woman.

But he couldn't do anything about it.

Lizzie was looking for a father. Someone strong who could swing her in the garden. Someone funny who'd let her watch television before school and who wouldn't make her eat sprouts.

Well, he could do that bit with no problem. He wasn't that keen on sprouts himself so he was more than happy to collude over their exclusion from their diet. And he had no trouble swinging her in the garden, hugging her and making her laugh. In fact, he was great at all those things.

The problem came with the last bit of her letter.

I want a daddy who will hug my mummy and stay with us for ever.

Jack leaned his head back against the seat and let out a long breath. He didn't do for ever. He had trouble doing next month. The whole concept of 'for ever' frightened the life out of him.

And Bryony knew that.

She knew him better than anyone.

Which was probably why she'd looked so shocked when he'd kissed her. Hell, *he'd* been shocked! And now he was confused, too, which was a totally new experience for him. He was *never* confused about women. He knew *exactly* what he wanted from them.

Everything, as long as it wasn't permanent.

Which meant that he had absolutely nothing to offer Bryony.

He started the engine and clenched his hands on the wheel. *He had to stop noticing her as a woman.* Surely it couldn't be that hard? After all, he'd only just started noticing her that way. It couldn't be that hard to go back to seeing her as his best friend.

He'd just carry on as they always had. Dropping round to see her. Chatting in her kitchen. And seeing other women.

It would be fine.

If working with Jack had been hard before the kiss, for Bryony it became even harder afterwards.

When he walked into a room she knew instantly, even when she had her back to him.

She didn't need to see him. She *felt* him. Felt his presence with every feminine bone in her body.

And she noticed everything about him. The way the solid muscle of his shoulders moved when he reached up to yank an X-ray out of the lightbox, the way his head tilted slightly when he was concentrating on something and the way everyone always asked his opinion on everything. She noticed how good he was with anxious relatives, how strong and capable he was with terrified patients and how well he dealt with inexperienced staff. He was the cleverest doctor she'd ever worked with and he had an instinctive feel for what was wrong with a patient before he'd even examined them.

If she'd had butterflies before he'd kissed her, they seemed to have multiplied since the kiss.

Which was utterly ridiculous because obviously, for him, nothing had changed.

Their relationship followed the same pattern of blonde jokes, man jokes and evenings when he sat with his feet on her table in the kitchen, watching while she cooked, a bottle of beer snuggled in his lap.

And now they were into December and there was no sign of a man who was even remotely close to fulfilling Lizzie's criteria for a daddy.

David hadn't asked her out again and she'd resigned herself to the fact that he was probably now dating Nina.

'Are you upset about that?' she asked Jack one evening, when they were curled up in front of the fire. She was writing Christmas cards and he was staring into the flames with a distant look in his eyes.

'Upset about what?'

'Nina.' She said the other woman's name as lightly as possible. 'Someone told me that she's seeing David Armstrong.'

'Is she?' Jack suppressed a yawn and stretched long legs out in front of him. 'Well, good for him.'

'You never should have sent them home together. I'm amazed you're not upset.'

He gave her a mocking smile. 'Come on, Blondie. How long have you known me?'

She stared at him. 'You engineered it, didn't you?'

Her pen fell to the floor as she suddenly realised what had happened. 'You got rid of her.'

His gaze didn't flicker. 'I encouraged her to find someone else, yes.'

'Why?' Bryony shook her head, puzzled. 'She was nice. And she seemed crazy about you.'

Jack looked at her steadily. 'She was.'

Which was why he'd ended it.

It was Jack's usual pattern.

Bryony sighed. 'Jack, you're thirty-four,' she said softly. 'You can't run for ever.'

He gave a funny lopsided grin that made her heart turn over. 'Watch me.'

'Listen…' She put her pen down and gave up on her Christmas cards. They could wait. 'I know your parents' divorce was really difficult for you, but you can't—'

'Drop it, Blondie. I don't want to talk about it.' His eyes glittered ominously and she saw the warning in the blue depths. Taboo subject.

She sighed. 'But, Jack, you can't—'

'Why did the blonde tiptoe past the medicine cabinet?' he drawled lazily, and she rolled her eyes, exasperated by his refusal to talk about his emotions.

'I don't know.'

'Because she didn't want to wake the sleeping pills.' Jack gave a wicked smile that made her heart jump in her chest.

He was so shockingly handsome it was totally unfair, and when he smiled like that she just melted.

'How many men does it take to change a toilet roll?' She smiled sweetly. 'No one knows. It's never been done. So what did Nina do wrong?'

Jack gave a sardonic smile. 'Frankly? She said, ''I love you'',' he said dryly, and gave a mock shudder. 'Which is the same as ''goodbye'' in my language.'

Bryony rolled her eyes. 'They always say that if you want to get rid of a man, you should say ''I love you, I want to marry you and most of all I want to have your children.'' It's guaranteed to leave skid marks.'

Jack laughed. 'That's just about the size of it. Why do you think I bought a Ferrari?'

Bryony sighed. 'Poor Nina.'

'She knew the score.'

But Bryony was willing to bet that knowing the score hadn't made it any easier. On the other hand, Nina seemed to have moved on quite happily to David so she couldn't have been that broken-hearted.

'One day you'll settle down, Jack,' Bryony predicted, licking another envelope. 'You'll be such a great father.'

'That's nonsense.'

'Look how great you are with Lizzie.'

'That's because I have all the fun and none of the responsibility,' he said shortly, frowning slightly as he looked at her.

'I don't think that's true. Lizzie expects a lot from you and you always deliver. How many netball matches have you been to this year?'

Jack grinned. 'Lots. You know me. Rugby, rock-climbing, netball—my three favourite sports.'

She laughed. 'Precisely. The sight of you standing on the side of a netball court would be funny if it wasn't so touching.' She added the envelope to the ever-growing pile. 'And it is touching, Jack. You're fantastic with Lizzie.'

A muscle worked in his jaw. 'But what she really wants is a father.'

Bryony shrugged. 'And who can blame her for that?'

'She doesn't realise that fathers aren't perfect.'

'I think she probably does, actually. But she still wants someone.'

'So how is the quest going? Any suitable candidates lined up? Obviously David is now off the scene…'

Something in his tone made her glance up at him but his expression was neutral.

'Well, it's not going that well,' Bryony muttered, licking another envelope and adding it to the pile. 'Christmas is three weeks away and I don't have another date until Saturday.'

His expression was suddenly hostile. 'You have a date on Saturday? Who with?'

Bryony blushed slightly. 'Toby.'

'Toby who?' Jack was frowning and she laughed.

'You know—our Toby. Toby from the mountain rescue team.'

'You're kidding!' He glared at her. 'Toby? He's totally unsuitable.'

'Calm down, Jack,' Bryony said mildly, gathering up all the envelopes and putting them on the table. 'Toby is nice. And he's always been kind to Lizzie.'

'Toby has a terrible reputation with women,' Jack said frostily, and she shrugged.

'So do you, Jack.'

'But I'm not dating you.'

And how she wished he was. Her gaze met his and held and then he sucked in a breath and rose to his feet, powerful and athletic.

'You can't date Toby.'

'Why not?'

There was a long silence and a muscle twitched in his jaw. 'Because he isn't right for you.'

She sighed. 'Jack, you're so jaded about relationships that you're never going to think anyone is right, but trust me when I say I'm not going to choose anyone who would hurt Lizzie.'

He took several deep breaths. 'I don't want anyone to hurt you either.'

'I know that.' She smiled at him, touched that he cared at least that much. 'You don't need to be so protective. It's nice, but I can look after myself.'

'Where are you going on Saturday?'

She wondered why he was asking and then decided that it was idle curiosity. 'Actually, I don't know. Toby is keeping it a secret.' She smiled. 'Isn't it romantic?'

'Suspicious is the word I would use,' Jack muttered, grabbing his coat and car keys and making for the door. 'I'll talk to him.'

Bryony gave an exasperated sigh. 'Jack, you are not my minder.'

'Toby is definitely not to be trusted when it comes to women,' Jack growled. 'I want him to know that I'm looking out for you.'

'I should think he knows that, seeing as you spend half your life in my house,' Bryony pointed out mildly, and he nodded.

'Well, let's hope so. I won't have him messing either of my girls around.'

His girls.

Bryony swallowed and her eyes clashed with his. Something flickered in those blue depths and she knew that he was remembering their kiss. 'We're not "your girls", Jack.'

He hesitated and a strange expression crossed his handsome face as he stared down at her. Then he muttered something under his breath, jerked open the front door and left the house.

The next day the temperature dropped further still and it started to snow. Wrapped up in her MRT gear, Bryony was posting her Christmas cards when her pager went off.

Relieved that Lizzie was spending the day with her mother, she drove herself to the rescue base, which was less than five minutes' drive from her house.

'Two women out walking,' Jack told her, zipping up his jacket. 'One has cut herself and one has an ankle injury.' He exchanged looks with Bryony. 'What is it with women and ankles?'

'I don't know but at least it gives you and me an excuse to climb mountains in filthy weather,' she said happily, and he smiled.

'I suppose there is that.'

The rest of the team gathered, picking up equipment and listening while they were given a brief.

'We're not sure where they are—' Sean, leader of the MRT, tapped a point on the map '—but this was where they were aiming for when it started to snow. The path is covered now and they're totally lost.'

Bryony looked at the map. 'It's really easy to lose that path in bad weather,' she said. 'I know because I've done it myself.'

Jack rolled his eyes. 'Never let a blonde loose on a mountain,' he drawled, but his eyes gleamed wickedly and she smiled back at him.

'At least a girl will ask for directions if she's lost. Men never ask for directions.'

'That's because they don't need to. Men don't get lost,' Jack returned blithely, and Sean sighed.

'Maybe you two could argue on the way,' he suggested mildly, pointing at the map. 'Ben, you go with Toby up this path and hopefully we'll come across them. Stay in touch. And watch yourselves. The weather is awful. I'll deploy the rest of the team as they arrive.'

Toby glanced at Bryony. 'I could go with Bryony…'

'No, you couldn't.' Jack's response was instantaneous, his blue gaze hard and uncompromising. 'I go with Bryony.'

Toby's eyes narrowed slightly and then he shrugged. 'Whatever.'

Bryony followed Jack out of the rescue base and they drove a short distance and parked the four-wheel-drive in a farm near the path.

Jack hoisted the rucksack onto his back and waited while she did the same thing. 'Come on. We need to get going before we freeze to death.'

They set off at a brisk pace and she glanced at the sky. 'It's going to snow again in a minute.'

'It's Christmas,' Jack pointed out. 'It's supposed to snow.'

Bryony gave a shiver and pulled her fleece up to her chin. 'Well, it looks nice on the Christmas cards but it's not so great when you're out on the mountains. Why didn't you let me go with Toby?'

'Because he'd be so busy staring at your legs he'd let you fall down a crevice.'

Bryony gaped at him. 'Jack, I'm wearing fleece trousers. They're hardly revealing!'

'Your legs would look sexy in a bin bag.'

She stopped dead. He thought her legs were sexy? He'd never said anything like that to her before. She was staring after him in confusion, wondering why he'd said that, when he glanced back at her.

'Why have you stopped? You needed to admire me from a distance?'

She grinned, suddenly feeling light-hearted. 'Why are men like placemats?' Shifting her rucksack slightly to make it more comfortable, she caught up with him. 'Because they only show up when there's food on the table.'

He smiled and as they continued up the path it started to snow again. 'I hope they've got some form of shelter,' Jack muttered, and Bryony nodded, her expression concerned.

'I hope we find them soon. It'll be dark in a couple of hours.'

They trudged on and the snow suddenly grew thicker underfoot.

'Crampons and ice axes, I think, Blondie,' Jack muttered, pausing by a snow-covered rock and swinging his rucksack off his back.

They stopped just long enough to equip themselves

safely for the next part of the rescue and then they were off again.

Bryony stayed behind Jack, watching him place his feet firmly and confidently in the snow, the sharp points of his crampons biting into the snow.

They walked for what felt like ages and then suddenly heard shouts from above them.

'Sounds hopeful,' Jack said, increasing his pace and altering his direction slightly. 'We'll check it out and then I'll radio in to base.'

Bryony breathed a sigh of relief when they rounded the next corner and saw two women huddled together.

'Watch your footing here,' Jack said, frowning slightly as he glanced to his right. 'There's a slope there and a sheer drop at the end of it. I know because I climbed up that rockface last summer with your brothers. This snow doesn't feel very stable to me.'

'Shall we rope up?'

He shook his head. 'We're all right for now, but we'll rope up before we go down.'

They reached the two women and one of them immediately burst into tears.

'Oh, thank goodness...'

Bryony dropped onto her knees beside her, aware that Jack was already on the radio, giving their exact location to the rest of the team.

'You're going to be fine,' she said gently, slipping her arm around the woman's shoulders and giving her a hug. 'Where are you hurt?'

'I'm not hurt,' the woman said, but her teeth were chattering and she was obviously very cold. 'But my sister slipped on the snow and hurt her ankle and cut her wrist. I think she must have hit a rock when she landed. It was bleeding very badly so I pressed on it hard with a spare jumper that we had in our bag and it seemed to stop.'

'Good—you did just the right thing.' Bryony shrugged her rucksack off her back. 'I'm Bryony and I'm a doctor and a member of the local mountain rescue team. What's your name?'

'Alison Gayle.' The woman was shivering. 'And my sister's name is Pamela. I feel so guilty dragging you out in this weather. We've put everyone in danger.'

'Don't feel guilty,' Bryony said immediately, 'and you haven't put us in danger. It's our job and we love it. And we have all the right equipment for this weather.'

Which was just as well, she reflected ruefully, because the weather was getting worse by the second.

The snow started to fall heavily and Bryony brushed the soft flakes away from her face with a gloved hand and looked at the sky with a frown. The visibility was reducing rapidly. She moved over to check on Pamela and Jack joined her.

'All right, the rest of the team is on their way up.' He dropped down next to her and smiled at Alison. 'Lovely day for a stroll in the hills.'

Bryony moved over to Pamela and noticed that the woman looked extremely pale and shocked.

'You're going to be fine now, Pamela,' she said firmly. 'I'm just going to check your injuries and then we're going to get you off this mountain.'

She pulled off her gloves and carefully unwrapped the blood-soaked jumper so that she could examine the wrist injury more carefully. As soon as she released the pressure and exposed the wound, blood spurted into the air and Bryony quickly grabbed the jumper and pressed down again.

'It's an artery, Jack,' she muttered and he was by her side in an instant, the bulk of his shoulders providing a barrier between her and the elements.

He was strong and confident and, as usual, she found his presence hugely reassuring.

'I've put Alison into a casualty bag so she'll be fine for the time being.' He unwrapped the wrist himself, quickly assessed the extent of the injury and then pressed a sterile pad over the laceration and smiled at Pamela.

'That's going to be fine,' he said smoothly, elevating her arm and handing a bandage to Bryony with his free hand. 'We're going to bandage it tightly and keep it up just until we can get you off this mountain.'

The woman looked at him with frightened eyes. 'I can't walk down—my ankle hurts.'

'Don't you worry about that. That's why we bring my blonde friend here,' Jack said cheerfully, winking at Bryony. 'She's the muscles of the operation.'

While he chatted and teased, Bryony tightened the bandage and gave him a nod. 'All done.'

'Good. So now let's check the ankle. How painful is it, Pamela?'

The woman looked at him, her lips turning blue with the cold. 'Agony.'

'So we'll give you some gas and air to breathe while we check it out,' Jack said immediately, reaching into his rucksack. 'I want you to take some slow breaths. Great—perfect.' He looked at Bryony. 'Right, can you cut that boot off and let's see what we're dealing with here? And make it quick. She's cold and we need to get her into a casualty bag.'

Bryony sliced through the laces and gently removed the boot and then the sock. 'The ankle is very swollen,' she murmured, and Pamela gave a little groan and took several more breaths of the gas and air. 'Could you put any weight on it after you fell, Pamela?'

The woman shook her head. 'It was agony. I fell straight away, that's how I cut my wrist.'

'What do you reckon, Blondie?' Jack asked, his arm around Pamela as he supported her.

'She's tender over the distal fibula and the lateral malleolus,' Bryony said quickly. 'I think it's probably a fracture. She's going to need X-rays when we get her down.'

'So we splint it now, give her some more analgesia and then get her into a casualty bag until the rest of the team gets here with the Bell,' Jack said decisively, his arm still round Pamela. 'You're going to be fine, Pamela.'

Pamela groaned. 'Have I broken it? And why do you need a bell?'

'A Bell is a type of stretcher that we use, and it looks as though you might have broken your ankle,' Jack said, watching as Bryony pulled out the rest of the equipment. 'Don't you worry. We're going to make you comfortable. We have these amazing fleecy bags that are very snug. In a moment you're going to feel like toast. Did you hear about the blonde who ordered a take-away pizza? The waiter asked her if she wanted it cut into six slices or twelve—' swiftly he helped Bryony apply the splint '—and she said, "Six, please. I could never eat twelve."'

'Just ignore him, Pamela,' Bryony advised with a smile. 'He doesn't know the meaning of politically correct and frankly it's amazing he hasn't been arrested before now. If I didn't need him to carry you down this mountain, I'd push him off the cliff myself.'

But despite the pain she was obviously suffering, Pamela was smiling. 'He's making me laugh, actually.'

Bryony groaned. 'Don't tell him that or he'll tell you blonde jokes all the way down the mountain. Trust me, you'd rather be left on your own in the snow than have to listen to Jack in full flow.'

She and Jack kept up their banter, taking Pamela's mind off the situation she was in, working together with swift efficiency. They'd just got Pamela into a casualty bag when the rest of the team approached out of the snow. Bryony's brother was among them.

Jack rolled his eyes. 'The last thing we need up here is an obstetrician,' he drawled. 'Who's delivering all those babies while you're wasting your time on the mountain?'

Tom adjusted the pack on his back. 'They're all queuing up, waiting for me to come back.'

'Well, you took so long you needn't have bothered coming.' Jack stood up, tall and broad-shouldered. 'You've missed all the action. Blondie and I have sorted it out as usual. Don't know why we need such a big team really.'

'If we weren't here you wouldn't have anyone to boss around,' Tom said dryly, working with the rest

of the team to get a stretcher ready. 'We rang the RAF
to see if there was any chance of an airlift but the
weather is closing in so it looks like we're going to
have to carry them down.'

Jack walked over and conferred with Sean, the
other A and E consultant and the MRT leader, and
discussed the best way to get the two women off the
mountain while Bryony kept an eye on Pamela.
Fortunately the casualty bag had zip access, which
meant she was able to check on her patient without
exposing her to the freezing air.

Finally Pamela was safely strapped onto a stretcher.
Her sister had revived sufficiently to be able to walk
down the mountain with some assistance from two
bulky MRT members who roped her between them.

Bryony reattached her crampons and picked up her
ice axe. The snow was thick now and she knew that
one false step could have her sliding halfway down
the mountain.

The snow was falling so thickly she could barely
see and she scrubbed her face with her hand to clear
her vision.

'Rope up, Blondie,' Jack's voice said, and as she
opened her mouth to answer, the ground beneath her
suddenly shifted and she was falling.

She didn't even have time to cry out, sliding fast
down the slope towards the edge of the cliff that Jack
had described so graphically.

Immediately she braced the axe shaft across her
body, digging the pick into the snow slope and raising
her feet so that they didn't catch in the snow. She
jerked to a halt and hung there for a moment, suspended, her heart hammering against her chest, her

hands tightly locked on her ice axe, which was the only thing holding her on the slope.

She heard Jack calling her name and heard something in his tone that she hadn't heard before. Panic.

She closed her eyes briefly and took a deep breath. She didn't want Jack to panic. Jack never panicked. Ever. Jack panicking was a bad sign. Realising just how close she was to the edge of the cliff, she kept a tight hold on her ice axe and gingerly moved her feet, trying to get some traction with her crampons.

'Hang on, Bry,' Tom called cheerfully. 'Jack's just coming to get you. You won't live this one down in a hurry.'

But despite his light-hearted tone, Bryony heard the anxiety in his voice. And it was hardly surprising, she thought ruefully, risking another glance below her. Another couple of metres and she would have vanished over the edge of a sheer cliff.

And it could still happen.

'Hang on, Blondie,' Jack called, and she glanced up to see him climbing down towards her, a rope attached to his middle.

'You think I'm going to let go?' Her voice shook slightly. 'You think I'm that stupid?'

As he drew closer she could see his grin. 'Of course you're stupid. You fell, didn't you? And you have blonde hair. You must be stupid. It says so in all the books.'

Bryony tried to smile but then she felt the snow give under her ice axe and she gave a gasp of fright and jabbed her feet into the slope. *'Jack!'*

'I've got you, angel.' His voice came from right beside her and he slid an arm and leg over her, holding her against the slope while he attached a rope to her waist. 'God, you almost gave us all a heart attack.'

She turned her head to look at him and his face was so close that she could feel the warmth of his breath against her cheek and see the dark stubble shadowing his hard jaw. He looked sexy and strong and she'd never been so pleased to see anyone in her life.

Then she glanced down at the drop beneath her and thought of Lizzie. 'Oh, God, Jack,' she whispered, and she felt his grip on her tighten.

'Don't even say it,' he said harshly. 'I've got you and there's no way I'm letting you go.' He glanced up the slope and shouted something to Sean, who was holding the other end of the rope. 'They're going to take you up now, sweetheart. Try not to do anything blonde on the way up.'

She gave a weak smile and he smiled back. 'Go for it.'

And gradually, with the aid of the rope and her ice axe and crampons, she managed to climb back up the slope, aware that Jack was behind her.

Finally she reached the top and Tom rolled his eyes. 'Thanks for the adrenaline rush.'

'Any time,' Bryony said lightly, but she was shaking badly now that the danger had passed, and Jack must have known that because he pulled her into his arms and held her until his warmth and strength gradually calmed her.

He didn't speak. He just held her tightly, talking all the time to Sean and Tom as they reassessed the best way to get safely down the increasingly treacherous slope.

Bryony stood in the circle of his arms, wishing that she could stay there for ever. There was no better place in the world, she decided, closing her eyes and breathing in his tantalising male scent.

And when he finally released her she felt bereft.

She looked at him, trying to keep it light as he checked the rope at her waist. 'I didn't know you were into bondage.'

He smiled down at her as he pulled on the rope. 'There's a lot you don't know about me, Blondie,' he drawled, his blue eyes teasing her wickedly. 'There's no point in learning to do all these fancy knots if you don't put them to good use.'

She smiled and then her smile faltered. 'Thanks, Jack.' Ridiculously she felt close to tears. 'I would have done the same for you.'

He winked at her, maddeningly self-confident. 'I wouldn't have fallen, babe.'

She gasped in outrage. 'You arrogant...!' Words failed her and he smiled and flicked her cheek with a gloved finger.

'That's better. At least you've got your colour back. Let's get moving.'

He turned to Sean and she realised that his inflammatory statement had been a ploy to rouse her to anger. Which meant he must have guessed how close she'd been to tears.

She gave a reluctant laugh, acknowledging once more just how clever he was.

It was much easier to get down the mountain feeling annoyed and irritated than it was feeling scared and tearful.

In the end it took several hours to get down safely

and the two women were immediately transferred to A and E in the MRT ambulance.

Jack drove Bryony home, the swirling snow falling thickly on the windscreen. 'If this carries on we're going to be busy in A and E,' he said, his eyes searching as he glanced at her.

'I'm OK.'

He nodded. 'Thanks to your ice axe technique. You did well. That's if you overlook the fact that you fell in the first place.'

She gaped at him. 'I did not fall,' she protested. 'The mountain slipped out from beneath me.'

'It wasn't my fault I crashed the car, Officer,' Jack said, mimicking her tone. 'The road suddenly moved.'

Bryony pulled a face. 'What's it like being so damn perfect, Jack?'

'I've learned to live with it,' he said solemnly, 'but I realise it's tough on those who struggle around me.'

'You can say that again,' she muttered darkly, dragging off her hat and scraping her hair back from her face. 'One of these days I'm probably going to shoot you.'

'Is that before or after I save you from falling over a cliff?'

She groaned. 'You're never going to let me forget that, are you?'

'Probably not.' He pulled up outside her house and switched the engine off. 'So are you going to invite me to supper tomorrow night?'

There was a gleam in his eyes and she felt butterflies flicker inside her stomach. 'I have a date with Toby,' she croaked, and his eyes narrowed slightly.

'Of course you have.' He was silent for a moment and then he smiled. 'Another time, then.'

He leaned across to open the car door for her and she fought against the temptation to lean forward and hug him. He was so close—and so male...

Suddenly she wished she didn't have the date with Toby. She would rather have spent an evening with Jack.

But then she remembered Lizzie's Christmas list. She shouldn't be spending her evenings with Jack. It was a waste of time.

'Lizzie and I are going to choose our Christmas tree tomorrow,' she said, telling herself that spending time with Jack during the day didn't count. 'Do you want to come? She'd love you to join us, I know she would.'

Jack grinned. 'Will I have to play Weddings?'

'Probably, but you're getting very good at it now so I don't see the problem.'

'All right, I'd like to come.'

'Goodnight, then, Jack,' she said softly, undoing her seat belt and gathering up her stuff. 'I'll see you tomorrow.'

And she scrambled out of the car without looking back.

CHAPTER SEVEN

'I WANT the biggest tree in the forest.' Lizzie clapped her hands together and beamed at Jack, her breath clouding the freezing air. She was wearing pink fleecy trousers tucked into pink fleecy boots, a bright, stripy scarf wrapped round her neck, and she was bursting with excitement. 'The tree has to be big if Santa is going to fit my present under it.'

Bryony chewed her lip and exchanged glances with Jack. 'You know, sweetheart,' she said anxiously, 'I'm not sure we gave Santa enough notice to find a daddy. That's a pretty big present.'

'He'll manage it,' Lizzie said happily, stamping her feet to keep warm, 'because I've been extra good. Sally stole my gloves in the playground and I didn't even tell.'

Jack frowned. 'Someone stole your gloves?'

'They were new and she liked them.'

Jack looked at Bryony. 'Another child stole her gloves?'

'It's fine, Jack,' Bryony said hastily, knowing just how protective Jack could be of Lizzie. 'She'll sort it out.'

'You should speak to her teacher.'

'It's fine, Jack!' Bryony shot him a warning look. 'Now, let's go and choose this tree, shall we?'

Jack sucked in a breath and smiled. 'Good idea.' He took Lizzie's hand in his. 'We'll get you some new gloves, peanut. Any pair you want. We'll choose them together.'

They walked amongst the trees and Lizzie sprinted up to one and tilted her head back, gazing up in awe.

'I like *this* one.'

Bryony looked at it in dismay. 'Lizzie, it's the tallest tree here!'

'I know.' Lizzie stroked the branches lovingly, watching as the needles sprang back. 'I love it. It's big. Like having the whole forest in your house. And I like the way it smells.' She leaned forward and breathed in and Bryony sighed.

'It won't fit into our living room, sweetheart. How about that one over there—it's a lovely shape.'

Lizzie shook her head, her hand still locked around one branch of the tree she'd chosen as if she couldn't quite let it go. 'I love this one. I want this to be our tree.'

Bryony closed her eyes briefly. 'Lizzie—'

'It's a great tree and we can always trim the top,' Jack said firmly, and Bryony lifted an eyebrow.

'You're planning to lop six feet off the top?'

He grinned. 'If need be.' He squatted down next to Lizzie, his hair shining glossily black next to the little girl's blonde curls. 'The lady likes this one. So the lady gets this one.'

'You need to learn to say no to her, Jack.'

'Why would I want to say no?' He scooped Lizzie into his arms and grinned at her. 'So you want this tree?'

Lizzie nodded and slipped her arm round his neck. 'Can I have it?'

'Of course.' Still holding the child, Jack slipped a

hand into his pocket and removed his wallet. 'Here we are, Blondie. Merry Christmas.'

Bryony shook her head. 'I'll pay, Jack.'

'My treat.' His eyes locked on hers, his expression warm. 'Please.'

She hesitated and then smiled. 'All right. Thanks.'

Lizzie tightened her arms round Jack's neck. 'Why do you call Mummy Blondie?'

'Because she has blonde hair, of course.'

'But I have blonde hair, too.'

Jack gave a start. 'So you do! Goodness—I never noticed.'

Lizzie gave a delicious chuckle. 'Yes, you did. I know you're joking.' She hugged him tight and then looked at him thoughtfully. 'Jack…'

His eyes narrowed. 'Don't tell me, you want to go home and play Weddings?'

'No.' She lifted a small hand and touched his cheek. 'I asked Santa for a daddy for Christmas.'

Jack went still. 'I know you did.'

'Well, now I wish I'd asked him to make you my daddy,' Lizzie said wistfully. 'I love you, Jack. No one plays Weddings like you do.'

Bryony swallowed hard, the lump in her throat so big it threatened to choke her.

'Lizzie…' Jack's voice sounded strangely thick and his hard jaw was tense as he struggled to find the right words. 'I can't be your daddy, sweetheart. But I'll always be here for you.'

'Why can't you be my daddy? I know Mummy loves you.'

Bryony closed her eyes, fire in her cheeks, but Jack just gave a strange-sounding laugh.

'And I love your mummy. But not in the way that mummies and daddies are supposed to love each other.'

Bryony rubbed her booted foot in the snow and wished an avalanche would consume her. But there wasn't much chance of that in the forest. So instead she looked up and gave a bright smile.

'But Santa is going to choose you a great present,' she said brightly. 'I know he is, and in the meantime we'd better buy this super-special tree before anyone else does. It's the best one in the forest and I can see other people looking at it.'

Lizzie's eyes widened in panic. 'Hurry up, then!'

Bryony took Jack's wallet and went to pay while he opened the boot of the four-wheel-drive and manoeuvred the huge tree inside, with Lizzie jumping up and down next to him.

'Most of the needles have just landed on the inside of the vehicle,' he muttered to Bryony as they climbed into the front and strapped Lizzie in. 'I think we might be decorating twigs when we get it home.'

Bryony glanced at him, wondering if he realised that he'd called her house 'home'.

'Are you getting a tree yourself, Jack?' she asked, and he shook his head, holding the wheel firmly as he negotiated the rutted track that led out of the forest onto the main road.

'What's the point? I'm going to be working for most of it.' He glanced at Lizzie who was listening to a tape through her headphones and not paying any attention. 'And, anyway, Christmas is for children.'

Bryony gave him a searching look. 'Are you coming to Mum's this year?'

Jack concentrated on the road. 'I don't know. Sean wants to be with Ally and the kids so I've said I'll work.'

'You come every year, Jack.' Bryony frowned. 'Lizzie would be so disappointed if you weren't there. All of us would. You're part of our family. At least come for part of it.'

'Maybe.' His shrug was noncommittal and she sighed.

'I know Christmas isn't your favourite time of year.'

There was a long silence and then he sucked in a breath, his eyes still on the road. 'Christmas is for families, Blondie. I don't have one.'

Bryony bit her lip. 'Have you heard from your mother lately?'

'A postcard six months ago.' He turned the wheel to avoid a hole in the road. 'She's with her latest lover in Brazil.'

Bryony was silent and he turned to look at her, a mocking look in his eyes. 'Don't feel sorry for me. I'm thirty-four. I certainly don't expect my mother to come home and play happy families after all this time. I think that's one game we never mastered in our house. When everyone else was unwrapping presents around the tree, my parents were at different ends of the house nurturing grievances.'

'Jack—'

'And that was a good thing.' He gave a grim smile. 'If they ever met the rows were so bad I used to run and hide in the garden. Once I was out there all night and they didn't even notice. I always used to think that was why we had such a big house with so much

land. Because no one wanted to live next door to anyone who argued as much as my parents.'

His experience was such a contrast to her own
happy childhood that Bryony felt suddenly choked.

'You used to come to us.'

'Yeah.' He gave a funny smile. 'You were the perfect family.'

Bryony looked at him, suddenly wondering for the
first time whether that had made it worse for him.
'Was it hard for you, being with us?'

He shook his head. 'It wasn't hard, Blondie. You
always made me feel as though I was Santa himself
from the moment I walked through the door. How
could that be hard?'

Bryony smiled. She used to stand with her nose
pressed against the window, waiting for Jack to arrive. Longing to show him her presents.

'You were just like Lizzie.' His voice softened at
the memory. 'I remember the year you had your ballet
dress from Santa. You wore it with your Wellington
boots because you were dying to play outside in the
snow but no one could persuade you to take it off.
You were in the garden building a snowman in pink
satin and tulle. Do you remember?'

'I remember tearing it climbing a tree.' Bryony
laughed. 'I just wanted to keep up with my brothers.'

On impulse she reached out and touched his leg,
feeling the rock-hard muscle under her fingers. 'Come
for Christmas, Jack. Please?'

He gave her a funny, lopsided smile that was so
sexy she suddenly found it hard to breathe. 'Better
see what Santa produces for Lizzie first,' he said

softly, turning into the road that led to her cottage. 'I might not be welcome.'

Bryony slumped back in her seat, the reminder that she'd so far failed to solve the problem of Lizzie's Christmas present bursting her bubble of happiness.

What was she going to do about Lizzie's present?

At some point soon she was going to have to sit her little girl down and tell her that Santa couldn't deliver a daddy. Otherwise Christmas morning was going to be a disappointment.

Trying to console herself with the thought that there must be something else that Lizzie would like for Christmas, Bryony realised that Jack had stopped the car.

'Ready to unload this tree?' He glanced behind him and winced. 'I can't believe you chose a tree that big.'

Lizzie pulled the headphones off her ears and giggled. 'It wasn't Mummy, it was you, Jack.'

'Me?' He looked horrified as he jumped out of the car with athletic grace and turned to lift the little girl out. 'I chose that?'

Lizzie was laughing. 'You know you did.'

'Well, we'd better get it in your house, then.'

Laughing and grumbling, Jack dragged the tree inside the house and proceeded to secure it in a bucket with his usual calm efficiency.

Bryony gazed upwards and shook her head in disbelief. 'It's bent at the top.'

'It's perfect,' Lizzie sighed, and Jack nodded solemnly.

'Perfect.'

Bryony rolled her eyes, forced to accept that she

was outnumbered. 'OK. Well, we've got it now, so let's decorate it.'

They spent the rest of the afternoon draping the tree with lights and baubles until it sparkled festively. Lizzie produced a pink fairy to go on top of the tree and Jack lifted her so that she could position it herself.

Then Jack went into the garden and cut boughs of holly from the tree and they decorated the fireplace.

Bryony produced mince pies and they sat on the carpet, admiring their decorations and enjoying the atmosphere.

Bryony smiled as she looked around her. 'I feel Christmassy.'

'That's because of the size of the tree,' Jack told her, his handsome face serious as he bit into a mince pie. 'Any smaller and you wouldn't be feeling the way you're feeling now.'

But watching him and Lizzie fighting over the last mince pie, Bryony realised that the warm Christmassy feeling that she had in the pit of her stomach had nothing to do with the tree and everything to do with the three of them being together. They felt like a family.

But they weren't a family.

Jack didn't want to be part of a family.

Watching Lizzie climbing all over him, dropping crumbs over his trousers and the carpet, Bryony wondered if he realised that he actually *was* part of a family.

Whether he liked it or not, he was a huge part of her life. And she couldn't imagine it any other way, even if ultimately she found a daddy for Lizzie. And just thinking of how she was going to tell Lizzie that Santa hadn't managed to produce a daddy on Christmas Day filled her with overwhelming depression.

Suddenly needing to be on her own, Bryony stood up. 'I need to get ready. Toby's picking me up at seven,' she said brightly, 'and I don't want to smell like a Christmas tree.'

She half expected Jack to say something about her going out with Toby. After all, he'd been less than enthusiastic about her other attempts to date men. But he just smiled at her and carried on playing with Lizzie.

Feeling deflated and not really understanding why, Bryony ran herself a deep bath and lay in a nest of scented bubbles for half an hour, telling herself that she was going to have a really great evening with Toby.

She was going to wear the black dress again.

And it was nothing to do with Jack's comments about her having good legs, she told herself firmly as she dried herself and dressed carefully. It was just that the dress suited her and she knew that Toby was planning to take her somewhere special.

She spent time on her make-up and pinned her hair on top of her head in a style that she felt suited the dress.

Finally satisfied, she walked out of her bedroom and into the kitchen, where Jack was making Lizzie tea and playing a game of 'guess the animal'.

'You're a tiger, Jack.' Lizzie giggled, watching with delight as he prowled around the kitchen, growling. 'Do I have to eat sprouts? I hate sprouts. Can I have peas instead?'

'Never argue with a tiger,' Jack said sternly, putting two sprouts on the side of her plate. 'Eat up. They're good for you.'

Lizzie stared at them gloomily. 'I hate things that are good for me.'

'He's only given you two,' Bryony said mildly, turning to lift two mugs out of the cupboard. When she looked back the sprouts had gone. Lizzie and Jack were both concentrating hard on the plate, neither of them looking at her.

'All right.' Bryony put her hands on her hips, her eyes twinkling. 'What happened to the sprouts?'

Lizzie covered her mouth and gave a snort of laughter and Jack tried to look innocent.

'Did you know that tigers love sprouts?'

Lizzie smiled happily. 'If Jack was my daddy I'd *never* have to eat sprouts.'

Jack shot Bryony a rueful look and ran a hand over the back of his neck. 'Lizzie, angel, we've got to talk about this.'

But before he could say any more, the phone rang. Bryony picked it up, expecting it to be her mother ringing about the babysitting arrangements for that evening.

It was Toby and when she finally replaced the receiver she was silent.

'What's the matter?' Jack was feeding Lizzie the last of her fish fingers. 'Is he going to be late?'

'He isn't coming.' Bryony looked at him, thinking that Jack didn't look that surprised. He just carried on feeding Lizzie. She frowned. 'She can feed herself, Jack.'

'I know she can, but we're playing zoos,' he said

calmly, 'and at the moment I'm feeding the tigers. So why is your date off?'

'Because Sean sent him over to Penrith to pick up some equipment for the team and it's taken him ages to sort it out and he's still there.' She frowned. 'Why didn't he tell Sean that he had a date?'

Jack stabbed the last of the fish fingers, not looking at her. 'Well, I suppose it was important.'

'It sounded pretty routine to me,' Bryony muttered, facing the fact that yet another date had turned into a disaster, this time before the guy had even turned up on her doorstep. She was jinxed. Or was she?

Suddenly she looked at Jack suspiciously, remembering his attitude to Toby when they'd gone on the rescue. Had he somehow engineered this so that they couldn't go out? She knew he wasn't comfortable with the idea of her finding a daddy for Lizzie. And if she found someone, obviously that would affect his relationship because he couldn't just come and go the way he did at the moment.

Was he the reason Toby hadn't turned up?

She glanced down at herself with a sigh. 'All dressed up and nowhere to go,' she said lightly, giving a shrug. 'I suppose I may as well go and get changed.'

'Why?'

Jack stood up and suddenly all she was breathlessly aware of were those sexy blue eyes watching her.

'Well, there's no point in wearing *this*—' she gestured down to herself '—to eat baked beans.'

'Who said anything about baked beans?' he drawled softly, walking towards her with a distinct air of purpose. 'Ring your mum and cancel.'

SARAH MORGAN 143

'Cancel?'

He was so close now she could hardly breathe, and he gave her that smile that always made her insides tumble.

'Yes, cancel.' He put a hand under her chin and lifted her face to his. 'I'll cook dinner and you can wear the dress. You don't need a babysitter.'

Her heart was pumping in her chest and her whole body throbbed with a sexual awareness that was totally unfamiliar. 'You hate this dress.'

'I never said I hated the dress.'

Their eyes locked and suddenly all she could think about was that kiss. The way it had felt when his mouth had claimed hers.

She wanted him to kiss her again.

'You two are looking all funny.' Lizzie was staring at them curiously. 'Are you going to kiss?'

Bryony gasped and pulled away from Jack, her face flaming. She'd forgotten that Lizzie was still sitting at the table. *'No!'* She was suddenly flustered. 'We're not going to kiss.'

'I don't mind if you do,' Lizzie said generously, sliding off her chair and carrying her plate to the dishwasher. 'Sally says it's yucky when her parents do it, but I think it would be nice.'

'Lizzie, we're not going to kiss,' Bryony muttered, not daring to look at Jack but feeling his gaze on her. She always knew when he was looking at her and he was looking at her now.

'You blush easily, Blondie, do you know that?' His voice was a soft, teasing drawl and Lizzie clapped her hands.

'Mummy only ever goes that colour when you're here, Jack.'

Deciding that the conversation had gone far enough, Bryony glanced at her watch. 'And you should be getting ready for bed, Lizzie,' she said quickly. 'Do you want Jack to read you a story?'

'Only if he doesn't skip bits.'

Bryony risked a look at Jack. 'Is that OK with you, or do you need to get going?'

'That depends…'

'On what?'

He winked at her. 'What you're cooking me for dinner—'

She rolled her eyes. 'Don't you ever go home and cook for yourself, Jack?'

'Why would I want to when I've got you to cook for me?' He smiled and held up a hand. 'Only joking. As it happens, I'm cooking for you tonight.'

'You're cooking for *me*?'

Jack never cooked. He lounged at her table, watching while she cooked. And actually she liked it that way. She found cooking relaxing and there was nothing she enjoyed more than an evening chatting with Jack.

'I'm cooking for you. A gourmet creation right under your very nose. It's your turn to be impressed, Blondie.'

'But I was going out. How can you have the ingredients for a gourmet creation?'

He stooped to pick up Lizzie. 'I just picked up a few things on my way home, in case I was hungry later.'

'But you don't even know where the supermarket

is.' Her eyes teased him. 'Or are you telling me you finally *asked for directions*?'

'No need.' He displayed his muscles, flexing his shoulders and his biceps. 'Man is a natural hunter.'

She lifted an eyebrow. 'You went to the supermarket in your *loin cloth*?'

'Of course. But I left my spear outside.' His eyes gleamed wickedly and she felt herself blush.

It was only as he walked out of the room with Lizzie that she realised that he hadn't actually answered her question about the food. How did he come to have the ingredients for a gourmet meal in his boot?

And why did he want her to keep the dress on when the last time she'd worn it he'd covered her up?

But the last time she'd worn it she'd been going out with another man.

Bryony plopped down on the nearest kitchen chair and wondered if Jack realised that he was displaying all the signs of a jealous male.

Probably not.

She hadn't realised it herself until two seconds ago.

But to be jealous you had to care, and Jack didn't care about her. Not like that.

Or did he?

She sat in silence, her mind running over everything that had happened since the night she'd walked into the pub and announced that she was going to start dating men again.

Jack had sabotaged every date.

Had he done that because of Lizzie? Because he didn't want Lizzie to have a daddy?

Or had he done it because he hadn't been able to see her with another man?

CHAPTER EIGHT

THE week before Christmas Jack, Bryony and Sean were in the staffroom discussing the mountain rescue team Christmas party, when Nicky rushed in, looking stressed.

'I just had a call from Ambulance Control,' she said breathlessly. 'Ellie has driven her car into a ditch.'

'Our Ellie?' Jack was on his feet immediately, his expression concerned. 'She's nearly eight months pregnant. Is she OK?'

Nicky shook her head. 'I haven't got many details but they had to cut her out of the car.'

Bryony was already hurrying to the door.

'She's been poorly right the way through this pregnancy,' Sean muttered, and Bryony remembered that he was very friendly with the couple outside work. 'That's why she gave up work early. Has anyone called Ben? This is his wife we're talking about.'

Ben MacAllister was another of the A and E consultants, and Ellie had worked as a nurse in A and E before she'd become pregnant.

'He's away on that immediate care course,' Jack reminded him, and Sean swore softly.

'Well, someone get on the phone.'

They heard the ambulance siren and Jack turned to Bryony. 'Call Tom,' he said urgently. 'I don't know whether there's a problem with the baby, but we're not taking any chances and I want your brother here.'

Without questioning his decision, Bryony hurried to the phone and called her brother and then hurried to Resus where the paramedics had taken Ellie.

Jack and Sean were already examining her thoroughly.

'Is Tom coming?' Jack was giving Ellie oxygen, clearly concerned about the baby.

'He's in Theatre, doing an emergency section,' Bryony told him, trying to hide her shock at seeing Ellie on the trolley. Her face was paper white and her blonde hair was matted with blood. 'He'll be down as soon as he can.'

Jack nodded and touched Ellie on the shoulder, lifting the mask away from her face for a moment. 'You're going to be fine, Ellie,' he said softly. 'The scalp wound is quite superficial. How are you feeling?'

'Worried about the baby,' Ellie said weakly, her normal exuberance extinguished by the shock of the accident and the pain she was in. 'Has someone called Ben?'

'He's on his way,' Nicky told her quickly, and Ellie gave a groan and closed her eyes.

'He'll be so worried—I wasn't sure whether we should have called him really...'

'He'd want to know,' Sean said, his face unusually white and strained as he looked at his friend lying on the trolley. 'What the hell were you doing, driving your car into a ditch anyway?'

Bryony saw Ellie smile and she lifted the oxygen mask from her face so that she could answer.

'I swerved to avoid a sheep,' she croaked, and Sean rolled his eyes.

'Well, of course you did,' he said gruffly, and looked at Jack. 'This is your show.'

Jack nodded and Bryony knew that Sean was handing over responsibility to someone who wasn't so close to Ellie. He was obviously finding it hard to be objective.

'Nicky, I need a pad for that scalp wound. We can glue it later.' Jack smiled down at Ellie. 'You're going to be fine, but I'm going to put a couple of lines in and check the baby.'

His voice was smooth and confident and he held out a hand to Nicky who'd already anticipated everything they were going to need.

Ellie shifted slightly on the trolley. 'I'm bleeding, Jack,' she murmured, her eyes drifting shut. 'I can feel it. Oh, God, I can't believe this is happening again. I'm going to lose it, I know I'm going to lose it.'

'You're not going to lose this baby,' Jack said firmly, his swift glance towards Bryony communicating clearly that she should call her brother again.

Bryony called Theatre again, and explained the situation. In the meantime Sean had put two lines in, and Ellie was connected to various monitors and had an IV running.

'Blondie, I want BMG, coagulation screen, rhesus/antibody status and a Kleihauer test. The foetal heart rate is good,' Jack said softly, his eyes on the monitor. 'Ellie, I'm just going to feel your uterus—I want you to keep that oxygen mask on now, please. No more talking, sweetheart.'

But Ellie clutched his arm. 'If Tom can't get here, I want you to section me,' she croaked, her eyes suddenly swimming with tears. 'Don't let me lose this baby, Jack. Please, don't let me lose this baby.'

Jack's eyes locked on hers, his gaze wonderfully confident and reassuring. 'If I have to section you here, I can and I will,' he promised, 'and you are not going to lose this baby, Ellie. I swear it. Trust me, angel.' He looked at Nicky. 'Get me a pack ready just in case. And someone tell Tom Hunter that if he doesn't get himself down here in the next two minutes, he's buying the drinks for the whole of next year.'

Swallowing back a lump in her throat, Bryony took blood and arranged for it to be sent to the lab, someone delivered the portable ultrasound machine and Jack carefully scanned Ellie's abdomen, staring at the screen with total concentration as he looked for problems. He squinted closer at one area and exchanged glances with Sean who gave a discreet nod.

'The foetal heart is still 140,' Jack said, carrying on with the ultrasound until he was satisfied with what he'd seen.

Ellie tried to move the mask and Jack put a hand on hers to prevent her, anticipating her question.

'The baby is fine,' he said softly. 'I can see the heart beating and he just kicked me really hard. He's better in than out at the moment.'

Ellie gave a weak smile and closed her eyes again just as Tom strode into the room.

'Sorry, folks—tricky section upstairs. How are you doing here?'

Jack briefed him quickly and Tom listened carefully, asking the occasional question, his eyes flickering to Ellie who had her eyes closed. For once he and Jack were serious, no trace of their usual banter or humour as they conferred. Tom washed his hands and approached the trolley.

'Hi, Ellie,' he said gently, 'it's Tom. I just want to check on that baby of yours.'

Ellie's eyes opened and she looked frightened as she pulled the mask away from her face. 'I want you to deliver it, Tom,' she croaked. 'Deliver it now. Please. I've got one of my feelings. A very bad feeling...'

Tom squeezed her shoulder briefly and then slid the blanket down so that he could look at her abdomen. 'Trust me, Ellie,' he said gently. 'I'm not going to let you lose this baby.'

'I marked the top of the fundus,' Jack told him and Tom nodded as he examined Ellie thoroughly.

Five minutes later he glanced at Jack. 'She's bleeding quite a bit. I'm going to section her. Is there anything I need to know? Has she had a head injury?'

'She has a minor scalp laceration but she wasn't knocked out and her cervical spine is fine,' Jack told him. 'She's all yours.'

Tom ran a hand over the back of his neck. 'Is Ben coming?'

Ellie looked at him, her face pale. 'Just do it, Tom,' she whispered. 'Don't wait for Ben. Sean, will you stay with me?'

Sean stepped forward. 'Try getting rid of me,' he said gruffly, taking Ellie's hand in his. 'Let's get her up to the labour ward and get this baby out.'

Everything happened swiftly after that.

Sean and Jack transferred Ellie up to the labour ward while Tom phoned around and called in the assistance of the top anaesthetist and two paediatricians, and then he sprinted up to Theatre after them.

Bryony and Nicky cleared up Resus, both of them quiet and worried about Ellie. They were still talking quietly, enjoying a brief lull in the usual run of patients, when Ben strode into Resus, his face drawn with worry.

'Where is she?'

'In Theatre on the labour ward,' Bryony said immediately. 'Tom is sectioning her.'

Ben sprinted back out of the room and Nicky sighed.

'There goes a man in love. I remember when those two met. Ellie just wouldn't let the man say no. Now he can barely let her out of his sight.'

'Ellie will be fine,' Bryony said firmly. 'Tom is a brilliant obstetrician.'

She had every faith in her brother, and every faith in Jack. Surely there was no way that anything could happen to Ellie or her baby?

'To baby MacAllister, as yet unnamed, and to Jack and Tom—' Sean raised his glass '—and a job well done.'

The whole mountain rescue team was gathered in the Drunken Fox to celebrate the safe arrival of Ben and Ellie's little boy.

Despite being just over four weeks early, he was doing well and was with Ellie on the ward.

Tom slung an arm round Jack's shoulders, his expression solemn. 'Just a question of knowing how, wouldn't you agree?'

'Absolutely.' Jack nodded sagely. 'That and natural brilliance.'

Tom reached for his beer. 'And years of training.'

'And finely honed instincts.'

Bryony rolled her eyes. 'And massive egos.' She looked at Sean. 'Better book two extra places at the Christmas party just to make room.'

There was general laughter and the conversation switched to the annual Christmas bash.

Bryony slid onto a barstool. 'So it's tomorrow night?'

'The venue has changed,' Sean told everyone, and Bryony frowned when she heard where it was.

'But that's miles away.'

'Over the other side of the valley,' Sean agreed, 'and if the weather carries on like this we'll have to all go in the four-wheel-drives or we'll be stuck in snowdrifts.'

'That would make a good newspaper headline,' Tom said mildly. 'ENTIRE MOUNTAIN RESCUE TEAM RESCUED FROM SNOWDRIFT.'

'It would be too embarrassing for words,' Jack agreed with a mock shudder, 'and it isn't going to happen.'

'Think of his ego,' Bryony said seriously, her blue eyes wide. 'It might never recover from the shock of such a public humiliation. It might shrivel to nothing.'

Sean finished his drink. 'We'll meet at the rescue centre at seven and go from there.'

'Bryony and I don't finish work until seven.' Jack

reached for his jacket. 'I'll drive her there in the Ferrari.'

Sean gaped at him. 'You're taking your Ferrari out on these roads? You'll land it in a ditch.'

'I will not.' Jack looked affronted. 'I am invincible.'

'And so modest,' Bryony said mildly.

In the end they were late leaving A and E and Bryony struggled into her dress in the staff toilet, thinking longingly of scented bubble baths and hairdressers. Most people spent hours getting ready for a Christmas party. She had less than five minutes and she could already hear Jack leaning on the horn of the Ferrari.

'All right, all right, I'm here.' She fell into the seat next to him, her work clothes stuffed haphazardly into a bag, her blonde hair tumbling over her shoulders. 'I haven't even had a chance to do my hair.'

'You can do it on the way. We're already late.' Jack reversed the car out of his space and drove off in the direction of the next valley.

Bryony rummaged in her bag for her hairclips and gave a groan of frustration. 'I think I left them at work.'

'Left what at work?'

'My new hair slide.'

Jack glanced towards her and frowned. 'You look great. Leave it down.'

Bryony lifted a hand and touched her hair self-consciously. 'I look as though I've just woken up.'

'Precisely.' Jack gave her a wicked smile, his voice a lazy, masculine drawl. 'As I said—you look great.'

Was he flirting with her?

Bryony felt her stomach turn over and she looked at him, trying to read his mind, but he was concentrating on the road again. She stared at his strong profile, her gaze lingering on his mouth.

Something felt different about their relationship, but she wasn't sure what. He hadn't laid a finger on her since that one incredible kiss, but something was different. He looked at her differently.

'I can't think why Sean booked it all the way out here,' Jack grumbled as he turned the car up a narrow road and put his foot down. 'There must have been somewhere closer.'

'He wanted to just give us a grid reference and see where we all ended up,' Bryony told him, removing her gaze from his mouth with a huge effort. 'At least we managed to talk him out of that one. Do you want me to look at a map?'

'I know where I'm going.'

Bryony looked at him in surprise. 'You've been here before?'

'No.' Jack glanced across and gave her a sexy wink. 'But men have an instinctive sense of direction.'

Bryony rolled her eyes. 'Which means we're about to get lost.'

But they didn't get lost and less than twenty minutes later Jack pulled into the restaurant car park with a smug smile.

'I am invincible.'

'Unbearable, more like,' Bryony muttered, shivering as she opened the door and the cold hit her. 'It's going to snow again. It's freezing.'

'Men don't notice the cold.' Jack locked the car

and held out a hand. 'Don't want you to slip, Blondie.'

'Believe it or not, I can put one foot in front of the other quite effectively,' she said tartly. 'I've been practising hard lately and I've finally got the hang of it.'

Ignoring his outstretched hand, she stalked towards the restaurant with as much dignity as she could given the amount of ice and snow on the path. She didn't dare take his hand. She was afraid she might never want to let go.

The rest of the team was already there and they had a fantastic evening, laughing and eating and drinking. Halfway through Jack looked at Bryony.

'You seem to be on water. How do you fancy driving the Ferrari home tonight?'

Her eyes gleamed. 'You trust me to drive your Ferrari on ice?'

'I'll be beside you. What can go wrong?'

But when they finally left the restaurant, several inches of snow had fallen and Bryony looked at the road doubtfully.

'I'm not sure about driving—we could cadge a lift in one of the four-wheel-drives.'

'They're full,' Jack told her, pushing her gently towards the car. 'You'll be fine.'

Bryony drove slowly but gradually she got the feel of the car and her confidence increased. Surprised by the lack of teasing from the passenger seat, she glanced sideways at Jack and realised that he'd fallen asleep.

Turning her attention back to the road, she turned

right and followed the road for a while then gradually realised that it didn't look at all familiar.

She carried on for a while, hoping to see a sign of some sort, but there was nothing. The snow was falling heavily now and she could barely see the road in front of her so it was a relief when she saw the lights of a pub ahead. At least they'd be able to find out where they were.

She stopped the car and Jack gave a yawn.

'Are we home?'

Bryony slumped back in her seat and braced herself for some serious teasing. 'I haven't got a clue where we are.'

There was a moment's silence while Jack squinted at the pub. 'Well, if you had to get us lost, Blondie, at least you did it by a pub,' he said mildly, undoing his seat belt and opening the car door.

'Where are you going?' She stared at him. 'Are you asking for directions?'

He grinned. 'Of course I'm not asking for directions. I'm a man. But I'm going to check whether the road is open further on. My ego doesn't want to spend the night stuck in a snowdrift. It isn't well enough insulated.'

He vanished into the pub and reappeared moments later, his expression serious. 'As I thought, the road is blocked ahead and they won't be able to clear it until the morning. We can stay here for the night. Do you need to ring your mum?'

Bryony shook her head and unfastened her seat belt. 'She's got Lizzie until tomorrow night. They're going Christmas shopping together tomorrow.'

'Great. In which case, we'll stay here for the night

and they can clear the road while someone cooks me bacon, sausages and mushrooms for breakfast,' Jack said cheerfully, holding the door open and grabbing her arm so that she didn't slip.

'I haven't got anything to sleep in,' Bryony protested, and Jack shrugged, pushing open the door of the pub and hustling her into the warmth.

'You can sleep in your underwear,' he drawled, 'unless you'd rather sleep in mine.'

She shot him a withering look and the amusement in his blue eyes deepened.

'Just a suggestion.'

The landlady smiled at Jack and handed over a key. 'It's the last room. You're lucky. It's the honeymoon suite. We did it up specially because we have so many couples up here looking for somewhere to spend a romantic night.'

Bryony followed Jack up a flight of stairs, a frown on her face. 'The last room? There's only one room? And it's the honeymoon suite?'

'It'll be fine.' He unlocked the door. 'I'll sleep in the armchair.'

But there wasn't an armchair. Just an enormous bed draped in fur and satin, a small dressing room and a huge, marble bathroom.

They looked at each other and Bryony gave a snort of laughter as she saw Jack's face.

'It's the honeymoon suite, Jack,' she cooed, unable to resist teasing him and he shook his head, gazing round the room in disbelief.

'I knew there was a reason I never wanted to get married.' He peered at the bed in amazement. 'Hasn't Lizzie got a bed just like that for one of her dolls?'

'There's no chair,' Bryony said, glancing round for some alternative suggestion. 'You'll just have to sleep on the floor.'

'There's no way I'm sleeping on a fluffy carpet.' Jack ripped off his jacket and dropped it over the end of the bed. 'That's an emperor-size bed at least. There's plenty of room for two of us in that. And if we shut our eyes tightly we can probably forget about the satin and fur.'

Bryony stared at him. He was suggesting that they sleep in the same bed?

Jack took one look at her face and lifted an eyebrow in question. 'We've known each other for twenty-two years, for goodness' sake. Don't you trust me, Blondie?'

Bryony looked at the bed and swallowed. She trusted him. It was herself she didn't trust. But she could hardly protest without revealing what she felt for him.

So she'd climb into the bed, turn her back on him and try and forget it was Jack lying next to her. It wasn't as if the bed was small…

Throwing a casual smile in his direction, she walked into the enormous bathroom and closed the door firmly behind her. *Oh, help!*

She stared at herself in the mirror and wondered whether she should just sleep in her dress. It was either that or take it off, and if she took it off…

She was still standing there five minutes later when Jack banged on the door. 'Have you been sucked down the plughole or something? Hurry up!'

Bryony closed her eyes briefly and then decided that she may as well get on with it. He was obviously totally indifferent to the fact that they were about to spend a night in the same bed, so perhaps she could be, too.

She used the toiletries and then opened the bathroom door and gave him a bright smile.

'All yours. You're going to *love* the mermaid taps.'

She strolled past him, waited until she heard the door close and then wriggled out of her dress and leaped into the bed, still wearing her underwear. The bed was huge and absolutely freezing and she lay there, her whole body shivering, wondering how she was ever going to sleep.

She heard sounds of the shower running and then finally the door opened and Jack appeared, a towel wrapped around his hips.

Bryony's heart started to thud rhythmically in her chest and suddenly she didn't feel cold any more.

She'd seen his body before, of course. In the summer at the beach. In the swimming pool when they'd taken Lizzie together. But she'd never seen his body when she was lying half-naked in bed. Suddenly all she could think about was the fact that he was about to slide in between the sheets next to her.

And he wasn't wearing anything.

In the dim light of the bedroom he was breathtakingly sexy. Her eyes followed the line of his body hair, tracking down over his muscular chest, down his board-flat stomach and down further still until it disappeared under the towel.

Refusing to allow herself to even think about what was underneath the towel, Bryony forced herself to breathe before she passed out. 'Are you planning to wear a towel to bed?' she croaked, trying to keep it light but feeling anything but light. In fact, her whole body felt heavy.

Jack eyed the bed with amusement. 'This bed is huge. I'm going to need a grid reference to find you.'

'You don't have to find me,' Bryony said hastily. 'It's really late. Just go to sleep.'

And with that she rolled over and closed her eyes tightly. Not that it made any difference at all. Even with her eyes shut she could still see every inch of his incredible body. The image was embedded in her brain and when she felt the bed dip slightly and heard him switch the light off, she curled her fingers into the duvet to stop herself from reaching for him.

For a moment neither of them moved and then he cursed softly. 'I'm developing frostbite. This bed is freezing.'

'Just go to sleep, Jack.'

'I can't go to sleep, my teeth are chattering too much.'

She gave a sigh and turned towards him, telling herself that it was dark anyway so she couldn't see him and he couldn't see her.

'Well, go and put your shirt back on.'

'I'm not sleeping in my clothes.'

She chuckled. 'Put my clothes on, then.'

'Good idea. I could wear your dress as a T-shirt.' He gave a shiver. 'Alternatively, we could cuddle each other. Warm me up, woman, or I'll be found dead in the morning.'

Before she could anticipate his next move, he reached for her and pulled her firmly against him so that they were lying side by side and nose to nose.

'Jack!' She tensed and planted her hands firmly on

the centre of his chest and pushed against him, but he didn't budge.

'Just relax, will you?' His voice sounded very male in the darkness. 'You know as well as I do that bodily warmth is an important source of heat.'

A source of heat?

Being this close to him, her fingers tangled with the hairs on his chest, her palms feeling the steady thud of his heart. It wasn't heat she was producing, it was fire.

And she realised that he wasn't cold at all. His body was warm and hard and throbbing with vital masculinity and it was pressed against hers.

'Jack, I can't—'

'Shut up, Blondie.' He slid a hand round the back of her neck and found her mouth with his. His tongue traced the seam of her lips and her mouth opened under his, breathing in his groan of desire.

'Jack, this is a mistake.'

'Probably.' His mouth was warm against hers, his kiss maddeningly seductive. 'But I like making mistakes. It's the only thing that prevents me from being completely perfect.'

She chortled and thumped his shoulder. Or at least she meant to thump his shoulder, but somehow her fist uncurled itself and she slid a shaking hand over the smooth skin, feeling the powerful swell of muscle under her fingers.

'Jack…' This time her voice was a whisper and he rolled her onto her back and covered her body with his.

'Stop talking.' He brought his mouth down on hers and kissed her again and suddenly she was kissing him back. And it felt like all her dreams because darkness was where she always dreamed about Jack, and when she dreamed, this was always what he was doing.

Kissing her.

And in the darkness the rest of the world ceased to exist. There was only Jack and the seductive brush of his mouth against hers, the erotic slide of his tongue and the weight of his body holding her still.

She felt his hand slide down her body and then his fingers found her tight, aching nipple through the silky fabric of her bra. She arched into his hand and he deepened the kiss, seducing her with every stroke of his tongue and every brush of his fingers. He removed her bra with an expert flick of his fingers and then reached out and switched on the lamp by the bed.

Bryony gave a gasp and looked at him in confusion. 'What are you doing?'

'Looking at you.' The expression in his eyes was disturbingly intense. 'I'm looking at you.'

Colour seeped into her cheeks and she reached out a hand to switch off the light, but he caught her arm and pinned it above her head.

'Jack, please…'

'I want to look at you because you're beautiful, Blondie, do you know that?' His voice was hoarse and he dragged the covers back, his eyes sliding down her body with male appreciation. Then he lifted a hand and touched her hair, running his fingers through it and stroking it as if he was seeing it for the first time.

She lay beneath him, powerless to move, watching

in breathless anticipation as hunger flared in his eyes. It was the look she'd always dreamed of seeing and suddenly her breathing was shallow and every nerve ending in her body tingled.

She didn't know what had finally changed for him but she wasn't going to question it.

For a suspended moment they stared at each other, and then he brought his mouth down hard on hers.

Her hunger was every bit as intense as his and she kissed him back, sliding her arms around his neck, her heart beating frantically as she arched against him. He kissed her until she was crazy for something more and then he lifted his head fractionally, his breathing unsteady as he looked down at her. His eyes glittered strangely in the dim light and for once there was no trace of humour in his expression.

'Do you want me to stop?' His voice was husky with unfulfilled desire and her own breathing jerked in response to this blatant evidence of masculine arousal.

'No.' Her hand slid down the warm, smooth skin of his back. 'Don't stop.'

Something flared in his eyes and he slid down her body, his tongue finding a path down her sensitised skin. His mouth closed over the tip of one breast and she cried out, sensation stabbing the very heart of her. He teased her skilfully with slow flicks of his clever tongue and then, when she was writhing and sobbing beneath him, he sucked her into the heat of his mouth and she gasped and sank her fingers into his dark hair, holding him against her. She shifted restlessly, trying to relieve the throbbing ache between her thighs.

Immediately his hand slid downwards, ready to satisfy her unspoken request.

With a swift movement he removed her panties and then moved back up her body until he was staring down at her, his glittering blue eyes holding her captive as his hand rested on her most intimate place. He looked dark and dangerous and unbelievably sexy and she was burning with a sexual excitement so intense that she felt as though her whole body was on fire.

And then he bent his head and took her mouth in a slow, seductive kiss and she gasped as she felt his long fingers stroking her for the first time. He explored her with an expert touch, the maddening caress of his fingers driving her wild. And all the time his eyes held hers, stripping down all the barriers between them, his gaze every bit as intimate as his touch.

She lifted a hand and ran her fingers over his rough jaw, loving the male contrast to her own softness. And suddenly she wanted to touch him as he was touching her. Her hand trailed over his wide shoulders and down his powerful body until her fingers closed around the pulsing heat of his arousal. He felt hot and hard and excitingly male and she stroked him gently until he muttered something under his breath and reached down.

'Stop.' His voice was thickened as his hand closed over her wrist. 'You need to give me a minute.'

But she didn't want to give him a minute. She was *desperate*, her body driven to fever pitch by his skilled touch.

She curled her legs around him, consumed by a feminine need so powerful that she raked his back with her nails in desperation.

'Jack, *please…*'

Breathing heavily, he slid an arm beneath her and she felt the silken probe of his erection against her. She arched invitingly and he entered her with a hard, demanding thrust, filling her with a heat and passion that she'd only known in her dreams.

She cried out in ecstasy and he gave a groan and thrust deeper still, his eyes locking with hers, fierce with passion. And she was lost in that gaze, the connection between them so powerful that she felt part of him.

'*Bryony—*'

It was the first time she could ever remember him calling her by her name and she stared into his eyes, overwhelmed by emotion and sensation, every part of her body feeling every part of his. And then he started to move slowly and with every measured thrust he seemed to move deeper inside her, closer to her heart. She felt his strength and his power and was consumed by a rush of pleasure so agonisingly intense that she sobbed against the sleek muscle of his shoulder. She clung to him, fevered and breathless, totally out of control and not even caring. Every time her eyes drifted shut he muttered, 'Open your eyes.' And so she did, and finally she couldn't look away as he drove her higher and higher until finally she felt the world explode and her whole body convulse in an ecstasy so powerful that it pushed him over the edge and she felt the hot, hard pulse of his own climax.

It was so powerful that for several minutes neither of them spoke. They just held each other, breathing unsteadily, their gazes still locked, sharing a depth of emotion that neither of them had felt before.

And then finally he gave a small, disbelieving shake of his head and rolled onto his back, taking her with him.

Bryony lay against him and allowed her eyes to drift shut, so utterly swamped with happiness that she started to smile.

Jack loved her.

She'd seen it in his eyes when he'd stared down at her. And she'd felt it in the way he'd made love to her.

Jack *definitely* loved her.

CHAPTER NINE

SHE awoke feeling warm and safe, wrapped tightly in his arms.

Bryony's body ached in unfamiliar places and she smiled as she remembered every tiny detail of the night before. She snuggled closer to him and kissed him gently on the mouth, watching as he woke up.

'I love you, Jack.'

Finally she could say the words she'd been longing to say for almost all her life.

And she sensed his immediate withdrawal. Physically he didn't move, but she saw something flicker in his eyes and felt his lack of response with every fibre of her being. Her insides lurched.

'Listen, Blondie.' His voice cracked slightly and he cursed under his breath and released her, rolling onto his back and staring up at the ceiling. His eyes were shut and a tiny muscle worked in his rough jaw. 'About last night...'

'*Don't* call me Blondie,' she said, her voice shaking as she lifted herself on one elbow and looked at him. *She wasn't going to let him do this.* She wasn't going to let him pretend that what they'd shared hadn't been special. 'Do you realise that last night you called me Bryony for the first time in your life? That was when you were making love to me, Jack.'

His eyes stayed closed. 'I thought we agreed that last night was a mistake.'

'It wasn't a mistake for me.' She knew she was taking a huge risk but there was no turning back now. 'I love you, Jack.'

His eyes flew open and he stared at her for a moment. Then he sucked in a breath and sprang out of bed so quickly that she blinked in amazement.

'Blond— Sorry, *Bryony*,' he corrected himself quickly as he reached for his clothes. 'You do not love me, all right? You just *think* you love me because last night we had sex and women think soppy thoughts after sex.'

She watched, thinking that she'd never seen anyone dress so quickly in her whole life. Trousers, shirt, jumper—in seconds he was fully clothed, his expression desperate as he searched for his boots.

'Why are you panicking, Jack?'

'I'm not panicking.' He found his boots and dragged them on without untying the laces. 'I just think we need to get going.'

'You are panicking. You're panicking because I told you that I love you.'

He scowled at her and ran both hands through his already tousled dark hair. 'I'm not panicking about that, because I know it isn't true.'

'It *is* true.' She took a deep breath. 'And I know you love me, too.'

He went completely still, his eyes fixed on her as if she were a dangerous animal that could attack at any moment. Then he swore under his breath and gave a sigh.

'Bryony.' He said her name firmly. 'We spent the night together, sweetheart. We had good—' He broke off with a frown '—well, *amazing*, actually...' He cleared his throat. 'We had amazing sex. It doesn't mean we're in love.'

'Of course it doesn't.' She sat up in the bed, deriving considerable satisfaction from the way that his eyes lingered hungrily on her breasts before she tucked the duvet under her arms. 'But we were in love before we had sex. The sex was amazing *because* we're in love. You felt it, too, Jack. I know you did. I saw it in your eyes. I *felt* it, Jack.'

'What do you mean—we were in love before we had sex?' He licked dry lips and his eyes flicked towards the door. 'We've been friends for twenty-two years, Blondie. We love each other, of course we do, but not *like that*.'

'I love you *like that*,' Bryony said quietly, 'and I always have.'

There was a long, tense silence and then he shook his head. 'We both know that isn't true. There's Lizzie's father for a start.'

Bryony felt her heart thump heavily in her chest. She'd never talked about Lizzie's father to anyone before. Never.

'Lizzie's father was my one attempt to get you out of my system,' she said quietly, watching as his face drained of colour. 'I've loved you all my life, Jack, but I resigned myself to the fact that you were never going to marry anyone. I decided that I needed to stop dreaming about you and get on with my life.'

He was staring at her. 'That isn't true.'

'It's true. I met Lizzie's father at a party. He was good-looking and fun to be with—'

Jack's mouth tightened. 'Spare me the details.'

'I thought you wanted the details.'

'I *don't* want to know that you found him attractive,' he grated, and Bryony stared at him in exasperation, wondering if he realised just how contradictory he was being. One minute he was saying that he didn't love her and the next he was showing all the signs of extreme jealousy.

'We spent the night together,' she said finally. 'I was determined to forget about you.'

'And it worked, yes?' His eyes glittered strangely. 'I mean, you've never given even the slightest hint that you cared about me, so it must have worked.'

She sighed. 'I didn't give the slightest hint that I cared about you because you would have done what you're doing now. Panic. And, no, it didn't work. At least, not in the sense that you mean. It taught me that I'm a one-man woman, and that man is you, Jack.'

'But you slept with him.'

She blushed and gave a wry smile. 'Just the once.'

'And then you slept with other men—yes?'

She shook her head. 'No other men. There didn't seem any point when none of them were you.'

He ran a hand over the back of his neck, visibly shaken by her admission. 'You're saying that last night was only the second time you've had sex in your life?'

She nodded. 'That's right, Jack. Why? Did I disappoint?'

There was a faint sheen of sweat on his brow. 'You know you didn't disappoint.' He let out a long breath and closed his eyes briefly. 'Blond—Bryony, I don't know what to say.'

'Say that you love me, too,' she croaked, 'because I know you do, Jack. I saw it in your eyes last night.'

He shook his head, his expression bleak as he looked at her. 'I can't say that.' His voice was hoarse. 'I wish I could, but I can't. You know I don't do commitment, Bryony.'

'Yes, you do.' She tipped her head on one side and watched him. 'You have been there for me for every second of the last twenty-two years, Jack, and since Lizzie was born you've been there for her, too. If that isn't commitment, then I don't know what is. I *know* you love me, Jack.'

She knew she was pushing him and her heart was thudding in her chest as she anticipated his reaction. Maybe it was the wrong thing to do, but what did she have to lose?

He shook his head. 'I can't be what you want me to be. I'd let you down. I'd let Lizzie down.'

'I don't believe that,' she said softly. 'I know that you had a terrible childhood. I know that your parents had a terrible marriage, but they never loved each other. That was so obvious. We do. We *really* love each other. We were always meant to be together.'

'Is that why you slept with me last night?' His eyes burned into hers. 'Because you thought I'd say—I'd say those three words?'

Which he couldn't even bring himself to say as part of a conversation, Bryony observed sadly.

'I slept with you because it felt right and because I love you,' she said quietly. 'I'm not trying to trap you, Jack. You're my best friend. It's just that I know you love me, too.'

'That's not true.'

'Jack.' Her tone was patient. 'Since November I've been dating other men. Or, at least, I've been trying to. It hasn't been going that well and lately I've been asking myself why.'

He looked at her warily. 'And what has that got to do with me?'

'Everything.' She stared at him and sighed. 'Jack, that first night I went out with David. You hated my dress. You said it was indecent.'

'It was indecent.'

'But the other night you wanted me to wear it for you. You didn't find it indecent then.'

Hot colour touched his cheekbones and he breathed in sharply. 'That's different.'

'You wouldn't let me invite him in for coffee, you wouldn't let him drive me home...' She listed the various incidents and he grew steadily more tense.

'I never said I didn't care about you,' he said stiffly, 'but just because I don't want you to marry the wrong man doesn't mean I love you. You're reading too much into it, which is a typically female pastime.'

'Is it?' She looked at him calmly. 'Where do you spend most of your free time, Jack? Do you go home?'

'I have an active social life.'

'Which basically means that you have sex with different women,' she said gently, 'but you don't spend time with those women, do you, Jack? You have a massive house but you never go there. You spend time with me. In *my* house. Sitting in my kitchen. Chatting about everything. Being part of my life. And Lizzie's life.'

'You're my friend.'

She nodded. 'And that's the best thing about a good marriage. I know because I saw it in my parents' marriage. In a good marriage you are friends as well as lovers.'

He backed away and stared at her incredulously. 'You're proposing to me?'

'No.' She held her breath. 'I'm waiting for you to propose to me, Jack. And then we can spend the rest of our lives having fantastic sex and enjoying the special friendship we've always had. And Lizzie gets the daddy she's always dreamed of.'

He stared at her for a suspended moment and then he grabbed his jacket. 'No.' He thrust his arms into the jacket and zipped it up firmly, his jaw set in a hard line. 'I think you've gone mad. For me it was just sex, Blondie—great sex, but just sex.'

'Jack—'

His eyes blazed into hers. 'We won't talk about it again.'

'Jack!'

'I'll go and warm the engine up.'

'Why are men like mascara?' Bryony murmured to herself, watching him go with tears in her eyes. 'Because they run at the first sign of emotion.'

'I bet Lizzie is excited about Christmas.' Nicky handed Bryony a syringe and she slowly injected the antibiotic into the patient's vein.

'Of course.' Bryony didn't look at her. 'It's Christmas Eve tomorrow.'

'What have you bought her?'

'Oh, you know, all the usual girly things. Stuff for

her hair, lots of stuff for her dolls, a new doll that she likes.'

Everything under the sun except the one thing she wanted.

A daddy.

And she still hadn't confessed to Lizzie that Santa wasn't going to manage to deliver her the present she wanted this year.

'Are you all right?' As they moved away from the patient, Nicky touched her arm. 'You're so quiet and you look really pale.'

'I'm fine, really.' Bryony gave her a wan smile. 'Just tired and looking forward to the Christmas break.'

Nicky was frowning. 'Well, you've certainly been working long hours for the past few days, thanks to Jack doing a vanishing act. Do you know where he's gone?'

Bryony shook her head. After their night in the honeymoon suite, he'd driven her home in brooding silence, dropped her off without saying a word and then disappeared from her life. Even Sean didn't know where he was, although he did confess that Jack had called him and told him that he needed time off.

Bryony sighed. So not only had she frightened Jack off a relationship, she'd frightened him out of her life altogether.

She'd thrown herself into her work and had seen a steady stream of fractures and bruises as people had slipped on the ice, and she'd dealt with quite a few road accidents as people stupidly decided to drive home after Christmas parties.

And that night when she tucked Lizzie in she felt a huge lump in her throat.

'Lizzie…' She settled herself on the edge of the bed and took a deep breath. 'We need to talk, sweetheart.'

'Mmm?' Lizzie snuggled down, her beautiful round cheeks pink from excitement.

Bryony couldn't bear the thought that she was about to dim that excitement, but she knew that she had to say something. She couldn't let Lizzie carry on believing that Santa was going to deliver a daddy for Christmas.

'Sweetheart, you remember your letter to Santa?'

Lizzie nodded. 'I wrote it ages ago.'

'I know you did.' Bryony swallowed. 'But you also said you did it in November because you wanted to give Santa time, because you knew it was a pretty hard present for him to find.'

'That's right.' Lizzie smiled. 'And he's had *ages*.'

'It isn't a time thing, Lizzie,' Bryony said softly, reached out and brushing her daughter's face with her finger. 'And a daddy isn't really something that Santa can bring you.' Tears spilled down her cheeks and she scrubbed them away quickly, not wanting her daughter to see her cry. 'It's up to me to find you a daddy, and so far I haven't managed it.' She broke off, totally choked by emotion and afraid to say anything else in case she started to sob.

Lizzie sat up and curled her little arms round her neck. 'Don't be sad. You don't have to find a daddy for me. That's why I asked Santa. So that you don't have to worry about it.'

Bryony shook her head, tears clogging her lashes. 'Lizzie, no, he can't—'

'I've been good,' Lizzie said firmly, climbing onto Bryony's lap. 'I've been so good sometimes I've almost burst. And once I've got my daddy I'm never speaking to Sally again because she's just *horrid*.'

Bryony smiled through her tears and stroked her daughter's hair. 'I know you've been good, angel, but it doesn't make any difference. Santa can't get you a daddy. I should have told you that before. He can get you toys and things like that, but not a daddy.'

'Just wait and see.' Lizzie gave her a smug smile and nestled down in her bed. 'Night-night.'

Bryony closed her eyes. 'Night-night.'

What was she supposed to do? She'd just have to wait until Christmas morning and hope that all the other presents that she'd chosen would compensate in some small way for not being able to produce a daddy.

But she knew that her daughter was heading for a crushing disappointment.

Bryony worked the morning of Christmas Eve and there was still no sign of Jack.

'I think he's at home,' Sean said when she tentatively asked if he knew where Jack was.

Bryony frowned, knowing that it was very unlikely that Jack would be at home. He hardly spent any time at home, especially not at Christmas. He either stayed at her house or camped out with Tom or Oliver or stayed in his room at the hospital.

'Are you spending Christmas with your mother?'

Sean pulled on his coat and reached for his mobile phone.

'Lizzie and I are staying in our house tonight,' Bryony told him, 'and then we're all going to Mum's for lunch tomorrow. Tom and Oliver will be there, too, patients permitting.'

Sean lifted an eyebrow. 'And Jack?'

She shrugged. 'I don't know. He usually comes but this year…' She broke off and flashed a smile at Sean, suddenly needing to get away. 'Are you off to see Ellie and the baby?'

Sean nodded. 'They're being discharged this afternoon, all being well.'

'Give her my love.'

They went in different directions and Bryony drove to her mother's, picked up Lizzie and headed for home.

Lizzie was so excited she was bouncing in her seat like a kangaroo and Bryony felt something tug at her heart.

'It would be great if Santa brought you that nice new doll you saw,' she said, but Lizzie shook her head.

'I don't want to be greedy. A daddy is enough.'

And after that Bryony fell silent, totally unable to find a way of persuading her daughter that her dream might not come true.

She cooked tea with a cheerful smile, hung the stocking on the end of Lizzie's bed and left a mince pie and a glass of whisky by the fire for Santa.

'Do you think he'd like more than one mince pie?' Lizzie asked, and Bryony shook her head.

'He's going to eat a mince pie in every house. That's rather a lot, don't you think?'

'Can we leave carrots for the reindeer?'

'Sure.' Bryony smiled and fished in the vegetable basket, hoping that Santa's reindeer weren't too fussy. Her carrots had definitely seen better days.

Lizzie bounced and fussed and squashed some of her other presents but finally she was bathed and in her pyjamas.

'This is going to be the best Christmas ever.' She hugged Bryony and snuggled down, her eyes squeezed tightly shut. 'Santa won't come while I'm awake so I'm going straight to sleep.'

Bryony bit her lip and then bent to kiss her daughter. 'Goodnight, sweetheart. Sleep tight.'

And with a last wistful look at the blonde curls spread over the pink pillow she switched on the tiny lamp and left the room.

CHAPTER TEN

'MUMMY, Mummy, *he's been.*'

Bryony struggled upright in bed, watching as Lizzie dragged her stocking into the bedroom.

She looked for signs of disappointment but Lizzie's eyes were shining with excitement.

'This stocking is *so* lumpy. Can I eat chocolate for breakfast?' She giggled deliciously as she poked and prodded and Bryony smiled.

'I suppose so. Come into bed and we'll open it together.'

'In a minute.' Lizzie dropped the stocking and sprinted out of the room. 'I've got to find my daddy first.'

Bryony sank back against the pillows and gave a groan. 'Lizzie, I've already tried to tell you, there won't be a daddy.'

'Well, not in my stocking,' Lizzie called back, 'because no daddy would fit in there, silly. I'm going to look under the tree.'

Bryony closed her eyes, listening to the patter of feet as her child raced downstairs, and she braced herself for Lizzie's disappointment. It was perfectly obvious that all the dolls in the world weren't going to make up for not having a daddy on Christmas day.

She should have tried harder.

She should have used a dating agency or gone speed-dating.

She should have tried *anything*.

Deciding that she'd better go downstairs and comfort Lizzie, she swung her legs out of bed and then heard a delighted squeal from the sitting room.

Bryony froze. What could Lizzie have possibly found underneath the tree that excited her so much?

Maybe the doll was a hit after all.

And then she heard a laugh. A deep, male laugh that she would have recognised anywhere.

Jack?

Hardly able to breathe, she tiptoed to the top of the stairs and peeped down, a frown touching her brows as she saw Jack sprawled on the carpet under her Christmas tree, talking softly to Lizzie who was sitting on him, giggling with excitement.

'Jack?' Bryony walked down the stairs, holding the bannister tightly. 'What are you doing here? Why are you lying under my Christmas tree?'

He sat up, his blue gaze curiously intent as he looked at her.

'Because that's where Christmas presents are supposed to be.' His voice was husky and he gave her a lopsided smile. 'And I'm Lizzie's Christmas present.'

Bryony felt a thrill of hope deep inside her and then she buried it quickly. Lizzie's Christmas present. Of course. He was doing this because he couldn't bear to see Lizzie disappointed. But that wasn't going to work, was it? Sooner or later he'd have to confess to Lizzie that it wasn't real.

'Jack.' Her tone was urgent but he simply smiled at her and then sat up, still holding Lizzie on his lap. He reached under the tree and handed the little girl a beautifully wrapped box.

'And because I couldn't exactly wrap myself up, I wrapped this up instead.'

Lizzie fell on it with a squeal of delight. 'It's for me?'

'Certainly it's for you.' His gaze slid back to Bryony, who was standing on the bottom step, unable to move. She wanted to know what was going on.

Lizzie tore the paper off the present and then gave a gasp of delight, holding up a silk dress in a beautiful shade of pink. 'Oh, and matching shoes. And a new tiara.'

Jack's eyes were on Bryony. 'Someone once told me that a little girl could never have too many tiaras,' he said softly, a strange light in his eyes. 'And that's the sort of thing you need to know if you're going to be a decent daddy.'

Bryony gave a faltering smile and looked at the dress her daughter was holding.

It looked like…

'It's a lovely dress, Jack,' Lizzie said wistfully, stroking it with her hand. 'Can I wear it now?'

Jack shook his head. 'But you can wear it soon. Or at least I hope you can. Do you know what sort of dress this is, Lizzie?'

Lizzie shook her head but Bryony's heart was thumping like a drum and she sat down hard on the bottom stair as her knees gave way.

'It's a bridesmaid's dress,' Jack said quietly, his eyes still fixed on Bryony. 'And I want you to wear it when I marry your mummy.'

'You're going to marry Mummy?' Lizzie gave a gasp of delight. 'You're going to play Weddings?'

Jack gently tipped Lizzie onto the floor and rose to

his feet. 'I'm not playing Weddings,' he said quietly, walking across the room towards Bryony, his eyes locked on hers. 'I'm doing it for real.'

He reached into his pocket and pulled out a tiny box beautifully wrapped in silver paper. It caught the light and glittered like the decorations on the tree, and Lizzie gasped.

'It's so pretty.'

Bryony was looking at Jack and he smiled.

'Are you going to stand up?'

She took his hand and allowed him to pull her to her feet. 'Jack—'

'Bryony Hunter.' His voice was sexy and seductive and a tiny smile played around his firm mouth. 'Will you marry me?'

Her stomach turned over and she stared at him, not daring to believe that this was real. Then she looked at her daughter who was leaping up and down in undisguised delight.

Bryony took a deep breath and looked at the box. 'Jack—you don't want to get married. You were never going to get married,' she began, and he pressed the box into her hand.

'Sometimes I make mistakes, remember?' He winked at her and she rolled her eyes.

'I know, I know. Mistakes stop you from being perfect.'

'Precisely.' His voice was a velvet drawl. 'Open it, Blondie.'

'Yes, open it, Mummy!' Lizzie danced next to them and Bryony pulled the paper off with shaking fingers and stared down at the blue velvet box.

'It *can't* be a tiara,' Lizzie breathed and Bryony smiled.

'You think not?' Her eyes slid to Jack's and then back to the box again and she took a deep breath and flipped it open.

'Oh, Mummy!' Lizzie gasped in awe as the enormous diamond twinkled, reflecting the lights from the Christmas tree. 'That's *beautiful*.'

'It is beautiful.' She swallowed hard and looked at Jack. 'How—? Why—?'

Jack's gaze lingered on hers for her moment and then he turned to Lizzie. 'On second thought, why don't you go up to your bedroom and try the dress on?' he suggested. 'Then we can check if it fits.'

Without questioning him, Lizzie darted up the stairs and Bryony was left alone with Jack.

Her heart was racing and she felt strange inside but she still didn't dare believe that this was real.

'You've made her Christmas, Jack.' She looked after her daughter, her heart in her mouth, not knowing what to make of the situation. 'But you can't get married just for a child.'

'I didn't do it for Lizzie, Bryony,' he said softly, taking her face in his hands and forcing her to look at him. 'I did it for me. And for you.'

She tried not to look at his incredibly sexy mouth. 'You don't want commitment,' she croaked. 'You don't do for ever.'

'I didn't think I did, but I was wrong.'

She shook her head, forcing herself to say what needed to be said, despite the temptation just to take what she'd been given without question. 'There's only one reason to get married, Jack, and it isn't to please a child.'

'I know there's only one reason to get married,' he said hoarsely, stroking her blonde hair back from her face with a gentle hand. 'In fact, I know that better than anyone because I saw my parents together for all the wrong reasons.'

She looked at him, her mouth dry. 'So what's the reason, Jack?'

He bent his head and his mouth hovered close to hers. 'I'm marrying you because I love you,' he said softly. 'And why it's taken me so long to work that out I really don't know.'

She stood still, unable to believe that he'd actually said those words. And then a warm glow began inside her. 'You love me.'

He gave her that lopsided smile that always made her insides go funny. 'You know I love you. You were the one who told me that I love you.'

'And I seem to remember that you ran away from me so fast you left skid marks in the snow.'

He grinned. 'I know. And I'm sorry about that.'

'Where did you go?'

'I went back to my house.'

She looked at him in surprise. 'Your house? But you hardly ever go there.'

'I know that.' He pulled a face. 'Which is ridiculous really because it's a beautiful house with lots of land and a great view.'

'But it's never been a home for you, has it?' she said quietly, and he shook his head.

'No, it hasn't. And you're one of the few people that understand that.' He looked deep into her eyes. 'I went home and I sat in that house and I thought about all the years that I'd been miserable there. And

I suddenly realised that home for me is nothing to do with beautiful houses and land. It's to do with people. Home for me is where you are, Bryony, and it always has been.'

She swallowed hard. 'Jack—'

'I was scared of commitment, of having a marriage that was like my parents', but we are nothing like my parents.' He pulled her into his arms. 'The other night, when you said you'd loved me for ever, was it true?'

She nodded. 'Completely true.'

He let out a breath. 'And I've loved you for ever, too. But I associated marriage with disaster so I didn't want to take that risk with our relationship.'

'There's no risk, Jack.' She smiled up at him. 'Lizzie and I will always be here for you.'

'And I for you.' He released her and took the box out of her hand. 'This says that you're mine. For ever. No more dating. No more looking for a man to take your mind off me. From now on I want your mind well and truly *on* me. All the time.'

She gave a shaky smile, watching as he slid the beautiful ring onto her finger. 'It's huge. I've just put on half a stone and I haven't eaten any turkey yet.'

His eyes dropped to her mouth. 'I love you, sweetheart.'

There was a noise from the stairs. 'This time Jack is *really* going to kiss you, Mummy, I can tell by the way he's looking at you. Sort of funny.'

Bryony rolled her eyes and pulled a face. 'Nothing is ever private,' she muttered, and Jack grinned.

'Oh, believe me, later on we're going to be very private.' He pulled her against him and kissed her gently, but it was a fairly chaste kiss, given that Lizzie was watching avidly, and Bryony was touched by that. He always did the right thing around her daughter.

She reached out a hand to Lizzie.

'So, angel, did Santa do well?'

Lizzie smiled, her whole face alight with happiness. 'I knew he'd do it if I gave him enough time. And just to make sure that I get what I want next year, I've just written my letter for next Christmas.'

Bryony looked at her in disbelief. 'Sweetheart, you haven't even eaten your turkey yet! You can't already be thinking about next Christmas.'

'I can.' Lizzie looked at them stubbornly and waved the letter under their noses. 'I know exactly what I want. And I know that if I'm *really* good Santa will give it to me. But he's going to need a lot of time to get ready for this one because it's *very* special.'

Bryony exchanged looks with Jack who swept Lizzie into his arms and gave her a hug, laughter in his eyes.

'Go on, then. What is it that you want from Santa next year?'

Lizzie smiled. 'Well...' she said, smiling into Jack's face and wrapping her little arms round his neck. 'For Christmas next year, I really *really* want a baby sister. And I *know* that Santa is going to bring me one.'

LET'S TALK
Romance

For exclusive extracts, competitions
and special offers, find us online:

- facebook.com/millsandboon
- @MillsandBoon
- @MillsandBoonUK

Get in touch on 01413 063232

For all the latest titles coming soon, visit
millsandboon.co.uk/nextmonth

MILLS & BOON

THE HEART OF ROMANCE

A ROMANCE FOR EVERY KIND OF READER

MODERN

Prepare to be swept off your feet by sophisticated, sexy and seductive heroes, in some of the world's most glamourous and romantic locations, where power and passion collide.
8 stories per month.

HISTORICAL

Escape with historical heroes from time gone by. Whether you passion is for wicked Regency Rakes, muscled Vikings or rugg Highlanders, awaken the romance of the past.
6 stories per month.

MEDICAL

Set your pulse racing with dedicated, delectable doctors in th high-pressure world of medicine, where emotions run high a passion, comfort and love are the best medicine.
6 stories per month.

True Love

Celebrate true love with tender stories of heartfelt romance, the rush of falling in love to the joy a new baby can bring, and focus on the emotional heart of a relationship.
8 stories per month.

Desire

Indulge in secrets and scandal, intense drama and plenty of s hot action with powerful and passionate heroes who have it a wealth, status, good looks…everything but the right woman.
6 stories per month.

HEROES

Experience all the excitement of a gripping thriller, with an ir romance at its heart. Resourceful, true-to-life women and stro fearless men face danger and desire - a killer combination!
8 stories per month.

DARE

Sensual love stories featuring smart, sassy heroines you'd want best friend, and compelling intense heroes who are worthy of
4 stories per month.

To see which titles are coming soon, please visit

millsandboon.co.uk/nextmonth